D1208458

# Naomi and Ruth: Loyalty Among Women

Best Wishes, Readers
and Thank you.
Boyd County Library,
Christine St. Clair

# Naomi and Ruth: Loyalty Among Women

Although this novel is a work of fiction, it aims to be as historically accurate as possible. I researched extensively and had editorial input from one of my friends who is Jewish and helped clarify facts. The copyediting was done by my husband, Philip, professor emeritus and former editor who is painstaking and precise.

It was a joy to write with many inspired moments that I hope will enthuse and encourage many women.

The study guide at the end of the book was developed by Dr. Rev. Roberta Mosier-Peterson.

Copyright © 2020 Christina St Clair
Cover: SelfPubBookCovers.com/RLSather

Naomi and Ruth:
Loyalty Among Women

Dedication:

For
mothers and daughters
especially
Lily Martin
daughter of Rose Anna
Randall,
granddaughter of unnamed
ancestresses,
mother of three,
cashier in a shop
superb knitter,
full of love—
my sunny mother

# Naomi and Ruth:
# Loyalty Among Women
## Acknowledgement

A special thanks is due Karen Moore who helped me craft the book: I wrote a chapter and sent it to her, and she read it through the lens of Judaic thought to clarify Jewish issues. She often gave me editorial suggestions. Without her help, I don't know if I would have completed this novel. Karen is a star! Editor and writer, Amanda Armstrong, read the manuscript and encouraged me to continue. My husband, a former editor, took the time to copy-edit the manuscript carefully and painstakingly.

One of the many books about Ruth that I consulted was especially important: *Reading Ruth, Contemporary Women Reclaim a Sacred Story*, edited by Judith A. Kates and Gail Twersky Reimer. These Jewish scholars and writers helped me understand the power of a woman's point of view for interpretation of scripture. Their work gave me permission to expand and create the story of Naomi and Ruth.

# Contents

# New Horizon

## One: Every Loyal Step

My name is Naomi. Much will be said
about me in the scriptures.
I did not want to leave Bethlehem,
but I had little choice.

    I could not possibly go without one final goodbye to my best friend, Leah.

    I slipped on my robe, the one that I'd woven for myself when I'd first been married. The wool was frayed now, and the color had faded from purple to lilac. Still it felt warm and comfortable over the thin inner garment that I'd once thought so pretty, but now as I gazed up at the chilly sky, I realized was impractical. What good were fine clothes and gold coins these days? Would we ever share bread and wine at festivals? Would we ever put on our best clothes and dance together to the sound of flutes and tambourines?

    The moon shone so brightly it blocked out the stars, but its silver light gleamed on the stone stairs so that I didn't need to bring an oil lamp with me. I soon tiptoed past the room where the Moabite trader was staying. I could hear his unfamiliar snores amongst the grunts and restless movements of my kin in the other rooms. I hurried past the donkeys, dozing behind the gate. They'd soon be readied for our departure. I prayed that the one with the hairy tufts in her floppy ears, the one that my boys fed with fig treats, did not begin braying and wake the whole household.

Outside in the cobbled alley, I stopped and ran my hand over the hard mud and straw brick in the walls, remembering the hired workers laying them so that my house would stand for years and years. I little knew that the time would come when I would have no choice but to leave. My shoulders drooped at the thought of having to let go of such a home, bigger than many, with three rooms downstairs, stalls for the livestock, and a cistern in the courtyard. It made it easy to get clean water in times of rain and plenty, but not now. Our buckets only yielded a few inches of muddy liquid hardly suitable for drinking.

I picked up a pebble from the ground and rubbed the grit and dirt off with my veil. To try to lessen the sick feeling that I couldn't seem to escape I put the stone in my mouth and sucked on it, but my empty stomach cramped. I doubled over until the pain eased. Oh, I did not want to go! But I so wanted to give Leah something to remember me by and thought perhaps I could give her the ankle bracelet that she'd always loved. Except it was packed in a pot at the bottom of the cart. What good was jewelry, anyway, in days like these?

I went back into the courtyard and grabbed a small sack of grain and slung it over my shoulder. The straps cut into my flesh, but I dragged myself outside and crept silently down the alley to Leah's home. I could not make out the color of the coarse bricks in the walls to her house. This depressed me as if all pigment were draining from my life—this might well be the last time I'd ever share with my friend. How often we'd clapped our hands together and danced in her central courtyard, surrounded by her family, enjoying their warmth, their salty breads full of pistachios, and their finest ceramic mugs filled with cool clean water.

Leah and I had raised our children together. We'd hoped my sons would someday marry her daughters, but although I wanted the best for my boys, I realized many young men would compete for them. We no longer had much money to offer as bridal dowries either. It wouldn't matter that Leah's girls and my boys were all such good friends and loved one another. Girls had little say in the matter of husbands. If only I'd had the chance to choose, what might my life have been like? But Emilelech, the husband selected for me, was a good man in so many ways and I'd come to care for him. Besides life was what it was and I loved my young sons. Truly, though, I hoped my next baby might be a girl. I patted my belly. Since the boys were not expected to do the work of women, a girl would help with the household chores. But my longing for a daughter was much more than a need for help. I yearned for the same kind of fun Leah had with her daughters. I looked forward to sharing cooking, teaching her to dress, to sing, to dance. I imagined the joy I would feel getting a daughter ready for her wedding.

This rocky passageway, even in the dark of early morning, was so familiar to me that I could have walked it with my eyes closed. Everything smelled dusty and I had to pull my veil around my nose and mouth as I made my way to Leah's house. We'd always been able to read one another's thoughts and so it did not surprise me to see a lantern glowing within her peaceful courtyard. She set the light down on the ground and rushed over to me, drawing my veil away from my face and looking deeply into my eyes. At last, she threw her arms around me and we held onto each other tightly. "I knew you'd come," she whispered.

As we moved away from one another, the tears glistening on her cheeks almost made me break down too, but I spat out the stone and held my tongue between my teeth, willing myself to be strong. The pebble rolled between her feet.

"What was that?" she cried. "Are you spitting rocks at me!"

She always could catch me off-guard with her quick wit. "No!" I cried. But in the dim light her sorrowful eyes made me want to kiss her beautiful rosy cheeks. Instead, I stroked strands of her shaggy hair off her forehead, wondering if the next time I saw her, it would be streaked with gray. Mine already was. Neither one of us had any words to convey our misery. We clutched one another's hands. But soon we were both sobbing as if we'd never stop, but of course we did. We became so silent that we could hear someone snoring from inside a nearby house.

Normally Leah would have some sharp remark about heavy breathing that would make us grin, but when she spoke, her usually deep voice was hoarse, "Now I truly live up to my name." She'd always hated her namesake, Leah, the unloved wife of our ancestor Jacob.

I patted her back just as I always did whenever she'd bemoan her name except I knew her agony now was not about her name, but about her loss. Of me. She alone was my confidante who knew my heart as I knew hers. She alone understood how I'd sorrowed about not getting to marry Boaz, the boy I'd admired and loved. It simply wasn't possible for girls to choose. We both understood our options were few but I'd always been the one, when we were girls, to tell Leah how strong she was and how her life would *not* be bitter like her namesake but full of joy. I'd tell her she would have a husband who would be a prophet who understood women. He'd be so good to her that she would live in luxury with servants doing all the chores. Often, we'd grab hands and swing one another in circles until we got dizzy and fell giggling to the ground. I told her every day how much I loved her. I did. I do. I always will.

Leah reached into the pockets of her robe and took out a pair of leather sandals, thrusting them into my hands. "For you," she said.

I stared at the shoes, knowing she'd sewn these specially. I held them up and stroked the leather straps. I held them to my heart.

"You need sturdy footwear for the trail you will be taking. I've heard the road across the mountains of Moab on the other side of the Salt Sea is steep and rocky." She patted my belly. "Take care, Naomi. Come back as soon as you can. Send me word once you're settled."

"I'll try," I managed to murmur. We stared into one another's eyes. Her eyes were swimming in mist. *How will I manage without her*, I thought, but didn't say because it would only make us cry again.

"Be brave," she said at last. "This drought cannot last forever and then you'll be able to come home."

Suddenly I remembered the grain. The straps from the sack on my shoulder hurt, but I had forgotten they were even there. I clutched my sandals and managed to put the sack into her hands. "Remember me," I said, "when you are baking barley loaves." Her eyes filled with tears but before she could refuse the grain, I turned and went back to fetch my sons and begin the wretched journey away from all that I held dear.

I walked slowly home, dragging my feet as if I could put a stop to what I knew was coming. All too soon, whether I liked it or not, the two donkeys would be laden with our blankets, grain and whatever we could put in their saddlebags. My household goods with our clothes wrapped around my most precious breakables were already loaded in a cart to be pulled by our one remaining ox. We'd sold the others long ago. This beast was getting old but at least it could be relied upon to obey our wishes, unlike the unbearably hot and dry weather. The parched ground, crisscrossed with fissures, looked as if it would crack open and devour us all. It certainly would not grow crops anytime soon. The now-barren fields reminded me of that other time before my sons were born when the wispy white clouds that floated across the sky never yielded rain. Some said it was punishment from the god whose name we were not allowed to speak, except to call him Hashem. All I knew was that my dear mother did her best to help others and lived in obedience to the law of Moses, but still she got weak from hunger and perished.

I could not bear it if the wedding platter she gave me were to get broken. She'd died too soon after my marriage. She'd never even gotten to see her grandsons. Oh, how I'd wailed and mourned for her, and I'd been grateful for the other women who'd mourned with me. I now felt her loss even more strongly and was overwhelmed by dread as if I were going to my grave. I felt myself as fractured as a broken water pot, but I needed to be strong. At least we had sacks of barley piled near the cistern to take with us.

I went upstairs to our living area and looked around slowly. It was dark now, but I wanted to remember this room where we took our meals. Every afternoon, we would gather and we would be so noisy, eating and talking. There had been squabbles too but now those times, even when we'd had to squint because of the sunlight radiating through the open beams of the roof, now those times seemed sacred.

What might we face in Moab? What sort of housing could we hope to find? We knew from past encounters that once as our thirsty people escaped from Egypt, the Moabites had denied them water. We were at peace with them now but could they be trusted? Yet this trader who'd come to Bethlehem seemed kind and welcoming. Clearly, he'd appreciated our hospitality and wanted to help us. But I couldn't imagine with whom I would bake bread, or with whom I would sew, or how I'd get water from a central well rather than my own cistern in my own courtyard. It was my one remaining luxury. And though the Moabites spoke Hebrew, the trader didn't sound the same as us. I'd pretend to understand him and nod my head while I served him bread and chickpeas, but really I often didn't know what he was saying. I worried too that I'd not given this big husky man enough to eat, but I was scared our meager supply of food would soon run out—perhaps even before we left—and then we'd have nothing to eat on the journey.

It did no good to stand around feeling sorry for myself. I must wake my sons.

Mahlon and Chilion lay on the roof, their backs against the low brick wall I'd insisted we build when they were little. I did not want them to roll over accidentally and fall onto the stone tile below. I pulled the fur blanket-given to me by Emilelech as a wedding present—away from Mahlon's shoulders. He did not stir. Chilion, too, still fast asleep with his arms above his head, was breathing softly. "It is time to go," I whispered. I almost added that their father was waiting in Jerusalem, but I clenched my teeth unable to say the words. Everyone was angry with my husband. Until now, I'd *not* admitted how hurt I felt that he'd left me and the boys and slipped away early. I not only didn't want to answer for him or try to make things right with other people, but I also suddenly had a desire to punish him. Let him get on with life by himself! See how he liked having to prepare meals, tend to goats, make clothes for our sons from scraps of cloth, not to mention weave blankets to sell for a few shekels. Yet, people would certainly feel little sympathy for me if I were to complain or refuse to go.

"Wake up, boys," I said half-heartedly. I wished I could somehow summon a sense of adventure, especially for my sons. But I couldn't. All I could do as I stood looking down at them was worry. They took after their father, already too thin. I could not bear to think of any of them dying because we ran out of food. I hated this famine that had already taken the lives of a few of our aged ones. My eyes filled, remembering old Sarah with her frail little wrists lying on a blanket, her blank eyes no longer seeing. She'd been my granny-woman, the midwife who'd birthed most of our babies in the village. Oh, how could our village still be called Bethlehem, "a house of bread!" At least, by leaving, my family might survive. Am I a coward for following my husband? Am I a traitor to my people? Or is it that I, like all women, have to meekly obey? How can I help but seek life for my family? I must go, but I am shriveling inside. I don't know how I will manage but somehow I will.

"Wake up!" I gently shook Mahlon's shoulder. He opened his eyes and stared at me.

"Come on," I said. "You too, Chilion. It's time to go! The Moabite fellow is going to take us to Jerusalem where your father is waiting."

Chilion groaned but soon both boys were following me down the stairs.

While we waited for the man to get ready, Mahlon and Chilion relentlessly questioned me. "How far is Moab? Will there be enough for us to eat? Where will we live?"

My own questions loomed large: *Why couldn't Emilelech just go by himself or take his kinsmen with him? Why did I have to move there?* Oh, I knew the answers and it wasn't only his fault or this wretched drought. I'd complained about needing to eat more for our next baby and I'd been overwrought after burying old Sarah. I'd been so emotional. My ups and downs, my tears and worries, gave him permission to take us away. "Everything will be all right," I said, biting the edge of my lip, watching the trader tying saddlebags on the donkeys. "There is plenty to eat in Moab," I muttered.

"There is," the trader said, nodding at me. "Your husband is a good man. He wants to protect you."

I said nothing.

"Boys," he said to my sons. "You are to follow behind the cart with the donkeys."

My sons grabbed the lead ropes and led the beasts outside, where they waited for me.

I stared around the gray courtyard but I could not focus. I crouched down and ripped off my old sandals. It was unlike me to waste anything, but I felt so desolate that I tossed them into the cistern and waited for the splash—that did not come. Standing barefoot, I felt as if what had once been holy ground was now tainted.

"Ma," I heard Chilion calling. "Come on!"

"Just a moment," I whispered. I slipped my new sandals onto my bare feet. The insoles fit snugly, but the backstraps cut into my heels. I knew that if I did not break them in slowly, they would give me blisters, but what could sore feet matter? These were a gift from my best friend who'd labored over them and even made them pretty. The wheat pattern she'd embroidered into the straps were for good luck. I felt wretched, but as I left my precious house so full of memories, I forced myself to keep moving. With every slap of the leather heel and with every pinch of the ankle straps, it was as if my painful steps would somehow keep me tethered to my beloved friend and all that I held dear.

# Two: Vision

*Ruth did not expect to have a book*
*in the Bible named after her.*
*But even as a young girl,*
*she had the heart of a lioness*
*and the soul of a saint.*

Ruth tossed her sheepskin blanket off her legs onto the tiled floor. She tried not to look over at the empty bedding next to her mat as she crawled to the opening and swept aside the heavy woolen curtain that served as a privacy screen. She didn't want to face her mother in the kitchen and she definitely didn't want to help prepare the dough for today's bread. She wanted to run away and be with her friend, Orpah. She got to her feet, tugged her sleeping robe down over her knees and threw on an outer garment before creeping into the kitchen. It seemed unusually silent and empty. Ruth looked around as if her mother—not that she cared—might be in a corner, but she was nowhere to be seen. Ruth's eyes grew big and startled. Where was her mother? She was always here! Surely the priests had not taken a grown woman for their ceremonies. Surely not!

Ruth rushed outside into the courtyard where other women were already at work baking, weaving, and chatting with one another. "Have you seen my mother?" she cried to one of her aunts who looked over sheepishly.

Ruth's hand flew over her heart. "Where is she?"

"She went off by herself. She refused to let any of us come with her. Don't worry, she will be back soon. She probably needs time by herself."

Ruth stared from one to the other of the women. Her favorite aunt dropped the spindle and yarn that she was spinning. She hurried to Ruth, her arms open, but Ruth did not want any of their false sympathy and turned her back. She'd heard them laughing and seen them talking as if nothing had happened. Her mother had allowed the priests to take Anna, but none of these women had made any attempt to stop them.

Ruth wanted to spit on every one of them. She almost wished her mother dead too.

When she heard the goats bleating for their morning meal, she stomped towards their pen. When the animals saw her coming, they milled around the gate. The white one with the black head sounded as miserable as Ruth felt. Her udder was full and she desperately needed to be milked. Ruth scooped grain from the barrel outside the fence and scattered it in the pen so that they all had a chance to feed and were occupied while she milked them.

Nothing seemed normal. But she fetched her milking pail and knelt beneath each goat, starting with the distressed one. As she steadfastly pulled on the goat's teats, letting down the fresh milk, the familiar musky odor wafted around, but it was not comforting. The goat, though, stopped fussing. After Ruth finished milking, she took the pails outside, and filled the smaller jugs that the women would later use to prepare their cheeses and butter. Her stomach gurgled, but how could she possibly eat when her little sister, Anna, would never again be giggling with her or slathering honey onto day-old bread? Yet the rich smell of the milk, in spite of herself, made her mouth water. She went back to the kitchen.

Her mother was there, sitting at their bread-making table, staring into space. Ruth wanted to strike her, but her mother's empty eyes stopped her. "I'm hungry," Ruth cried, but her need was not only for food. She yearned for her mother to hug her but she hated her too.

Her mother got up and fetched a jar of dried dates. "Eat these," she muttered. "Then go milk the goats."

"I already did."

"Then go again!" Her mother, normally so strong and determined, sank onto the floor, her robes falling immodestly open.

Ruth, heat rising in her face, stared at her usually proper mother. She slammed the jar of dates onto the floor, shattering the earthenware. She ran from the house, tore between the women in the courtyard, and was soon racing as fast as she could toward the village. On the main street not far from her friend Orpah's house, her breathing ragged, Ruth slowed down. It was a wonder she'd not collapsed on the way, but her need to escape her feelings and to escape her mother's scolding about breaking a jar kept her going. Soon though, to catch her breath, she stopped next to an abandoned courtyard full of weeds. This house always fascinated her and made her want to go inside, but now it seemed small, rundown, and unwelcoming.

After a few moments, no longer winded, she made her way to Orpah's where she stood at the opening to her friend's kitchen watching Orpah's mother cutting cheese.

"Hello, Ruth, you're here early." Orpah's mother put down the knife and bustled over to Ruth, threw her arms around her and hugged her. Ruth almost burst into tears, but Orpah ran into the room and looked at her curiously. Behind her came her two brothers and her father from the upstairs chamber. None of the men spoke which was not unusual but Ruth felt as if they could not meet her eyes. Orpah's mother released Ruth and patted her back. "It will be all right," she said softly. "Orpah, hurry and serve the men." Orpah smiled and poured milk into copper cups and began taking them outside. She came back to fetch the cheese and olives her mother had set on a platter next to a stack of flatbreads. "Take these out too," her mother directed, and handed her a bowl of ripe pomegranates, cut neatly into halves.

Orpah, with a mischievous glance at Ruth, snuck a handful of the black seeds from the ripe fruit and popped them into her mouth.

"Those are for the men!" Orpah's mother cried. "I have fresh figs. For you too, Ruth."

Before long, Orpah skipped back into the kitchen and plopped onto the floor and with sticky fingers tugged Ruth down next to her. Orpah's mother fussed over them, insisting they must eat cheese and bread and drink some milk. At last, satisfied that the girls were as well fed as the men, she shooed them out. "Go and play now!"

Ruth was sure her friend's mother knew what had happened, but it wasn't something she wanted to talk about. She stood up and grabbed Orpah's hand, dragging her to her feet. "Let's go to the river." She hurried Orpah to their favorite hiding spot—far away from the temple where the priests must have taken Anna to be offered to Chemosh.

The girls stood, shoulder to shoulder, on a flat boulder overlooking the flowing water far below. Usually, the whooshing sound of the ripples foaming over the rocks pleased Ruth, but not now. The walk here in the humid air had made her skin clammy. Ruth wanted to climb down and throw herself into the cold river as if it might wash away not only her sweat but also her anguish. But when she'd led Orpah down the rocky slope once before, her friend had only managed to scramble about ten feet before her foot had slipped, dislodging a big stone. She'd gotten so scared that she'd froze and couldn't go any further. Ruth had to help her inch her way back up to the top of the cliff.

A nearby scrubby acacia tree gave them a little shade. Its dangling green pods, already ripening, hung too far above their heads for them to reach. Ruth stared at the silver-white thorns. She'd gotten scratched when earlier in the year she'd gathered fragrant flowers for her little sister, but the delight on Anna's face as she'd sniffed the blossoms had been worth the pain as well as the scolding she'd gotten from her mother.

"They took my little sister away last night and she hasn't come back," Ruth cried.

"I know." Orpah flopped onto her back, grabbed Ruth's hand and drew her down onto the ground. She sighed. "It is an honor to be chosen by Chemosh. You know that."

This is not what Ruth wanted to hear. She turned a fierce look on her friend. In her mind's eye she could still see Anna gagged and bound by the priests. She would *never* forget. "My mother tried to stop them from taking her," she muttered, remembering that her mother's protests seemed only weak cries, easily ignored. Ruth wished her father, Haran, had been home. He would not have allowed anything bad to happen. But she knew it had. "My mother told me Anna will be in heaven feasting on grapes and will be dressed in fine linen. She will be a princess."

"Of course she will," Orpah readily agreed. "We must thank Chemosh for the plentiful harvest we will have this year. And Anna will make it even better."

Ruth drew away from Orpah and flopped onto her back and stared at the hot sky. Her mind raced with memories. She'd once had to prevent Anna from scooting on her bottom down the cliff. At the time, she'd been angry that she and Orpah were told to bring the toddler with them, but now she'd give anything to have Anna along. And the thought of Anna snatching her hand out of hers to race ahead of their mother to the waterhole brought tears to her eyes. She'd always let her sister rush into the shallow pond first. Sometimes, while their mother chatted to neighbors, they'd splash one another from the gushing spring that fed the pond. She always let Anna fill their water jug too, and together they'd lug it home.

"Your parents will be richly rewarded," Orpah remarked, using her foot to scrape dry leaves into a pile, unaware of Ruth shrinking away from her.

Ruth knew now what she'd always feared: Chemosh was hateful. But with Orpah so readily on the god's side, she had no one to tell what she now understood. She'd be all alone because to speak up might make her the next victim. And children with no rights could easily become a tribute for the gods. She'd always been suspicious of them, especially Chemosh, the main one. He was cruel just like his priests. *She* wouldn't give Chemosh a chance to slay her for his satisfaction. Just like her dad once said, slaughtering little children as if they were goats wouldn't make any difference to the weather or to the crops. Her dad, who was a trader, said good crops came from good soil, hard work, and plentiful rain. The wide blue expanse over her head seemed more trustworthy than any of the gods, and so she made a covenant to the sky and a silent vow to herself. She would never marry and have babies. Never!

Suddenly, Orpah's chatter faded into the background, and Ruth fell into a strange fugue state where she was both awake and yet not fully conscious. She saw herself as a grown girl at Anna's wedding to a handsome man whom her father had brought home from his travels. She felt a little indignant that Anna was getting married first. After all, in the dream Anna was only thirteen, and she was already seventeen. There was to be no procession from their house to the bridegroom's because his home was far away in Egypt. Ruth felt a moment of melancholy that Anna would be leaving before the moon arose like a silver coin. In her dream she smoothed out the special wedding garment that her mother promised would later be adorned with shining sequins for her own wedding to a man she did not recognize. Somehow she felt warmth towards this stranger even though he was not one of the princes whom she and Orpah often invented when they played their marriage game.

Anna's pretty face as she was escorted under the wedding canopy appeared in her mind's eye. Flower garlands draped the ceiling and scented the air. The women combed Anna's hair and fastened onto her head a crown wreath woven from olive leaves. After they'd perfumed her neck with a tincture of pomegranate and lilies of the valley, they gently wrapped a lacy wedding veil around her face, covering her blushing cheeks, readying her to wait for her husband to arrive and gaze into her deep brown eyes.

Ruth, happy for her sister, could smell the sweetness of the lilies, but suddenly something took her out of her trance. Somebody was grabbing her shoulder. She tried to shrug off the interruption but the person persisted, shaking her awake. At last, she opened her eyes to see Orpah kneeling over her, looking worried. "Ruth! Ruth!" she cried. "Are you all right?"

She sat up and clapped her hands. "Oh!" She grinned at Orpah who now looked startled.

"Are you all right?"

"Oh yes. I dreamed of a wedding. It was so beautiful. Anna is alive, you know. She is so pretty and her husband is gorgeous. A foreigner."

"What are you talking about?"

"Anna is alive. She is going to get married and be happy."

"Of course," Orpah said, looking dubious. "She is probably dancing and being fed ripe figs. I wonder if Chemosh chose her husband for her."

Reality once again filled Ruth with horror.

Orpah picked up a leaf and began to fan her. "You and I are going to get married and we'll have a double wedding," she said with a smile. They'd often shared silly dreams about how they'd both be married on the same day. They'd never included Anna. Ruth pushed Orpah's leaf-fan away. Like Orpah's awareness, it was far too small to cause even a slight breeze. Ruth knew her friend did not realize how troubled she felt. She tightened her fists and gritted her teeth. It would not do to tell Orpah that she would *never* wed. *Never!* Yet the sky seemed to shine especially bright and she felt as if her secret vow was no stronger than the cool morning mist that arose from the river and quickly dissipated.

# Three: Secret

*Boaz, always a faithful man*
*who protected and looked after his family,*
*little knew he would become a hero in God's plan.*

Boaz, trying to sleep, rolled over onto his side and listened to the soft thuds of animal hooves in the street below his rooftop. He almost hoped that the sounds were from marauding hyenas which had gotten bolder since game was scarce, but so far no hunting packs ever came into the village. The steady sounds of mules, donkeys, an ox harness creaking, and cartwheels turning could not be mistaken for wild animals. It was the sound of a departing caravan. He pushed himself up from the well-worn goatskins that he used for his bed and peered into the alley.

In the dim early morning light, beneath him in the street he could make out the Moabite trader in his bright purple and yellow robes leading an ox-drawn cart laden with household goods, including Naomi's upright loom, one he'd help build. The trader's mules were tethered to the back of the cart. Following them, he could see Naomi clutching her stomach as if to protect herself. She was no doubt overwhelmed. He sighed heavily. He would have spared her from such a journey. He would have kept her safe at home. He, unlike Emilelech, would find a way even in this time of famine to feed his wives and children and servants. No matter what, *he* would fulfill his duty. Even though he was too young to be an elder, he believed in *chesed* and would go out of his way to take care of those in need.

Anger filled him towards Emilelech. How could he leave at a time like this? What sort of man ran out on his people? The elders would no doubt convene to discuss Emilelech and the land he'd left behind. Since his kin still remained in Bethlehem and Boaz was one of them, someone would probably be given rights to the deserted acreage. Surely it must eventually rain and the fields would become useful again, but the idea of getting land because of someone else's desertion offended him. Boaz squinted at the procession passing beneath him. No one looked up and saw him watching them. He began to calm down. He couldn't blame them for leaving, especially upon watching those frail boys, Mahlon and Chilion, plodding along next to the donkeys,. They were so thin that a strong wind could blow them away.

Boaz glanced at his two fine sons sleeping nearby. They made him proud. He loved his three daughters too. All of his children were strong and good-natured. He was so fortunate in so many ways. How could he remain angry and, yes, jealous about Naomi? He'd done his best to bury his desire for her but in the ten years since she'd wed Emilelech, he still felt a twang of regret that he was not her husband. He thought he was over her. How he pitied her to have such delicate boys always coughing and sniffling. And he felt sorry for Emilelech, too. The man was kind and good to Naomi, but sadly unable to manage the harvesting of his own crops. Perhaps that was why it was easy for Emilelech to leave his fields behind, something unthinkable to most farmers who revered and tended their soil as a most precious gift from Hashem.

Boaz flexed his muscles and stretched his legs. He threw on a robe and decided the least he could do was follow Naomi's pitiful caravan to make sure they got safely through Bethlehem's gate to begin the trek to Jerusalem, where he'd heard Emilelech would be waiting. He would go no further than Rachel's tomb and then he would say a prayer for Naomi's safety and her reunion with her husband.

Boaz wished them peace and prosperity and knew that they were in the hands of Hashem, but it comforted him to make sure Naomi was being treated properly by the Moabite trader. The man seemed decent, but who knew what these Moabites might really be like when no one was watching. After all, they might be peaceful one day and yet full of deceit the next. There had been a time when they were detestable, the time when they'd refused to offer hospitality to his people escaping from Egypt. That was bad enough, but then there were the evil years following their conquest of Israel. One of the judges said it was Hashem's will, Hashem's justice for Israelite disobedience. But Boaz thought it was more likely about power and greed. The Moabite king who'd ruled over them was a fat tyrant who'd thought nothing of slaying anyone he thought untrustworthy. He'd killed the people who did not pander to his overwhelming need for constant admiration.

Boaz, in spite of the sorrow in his heart and mind, stared in wonder at the night sky. Hashem, who'd created the stars and the earth and all the people and animals, was indeed wonderful. Surely he would soon end this drought.

Boaz' eldest son stirred and sat up. "Where are you going, Pa?"

Boaz went over and stroked the boy's face. "You go back to sleep. I have something I must do. I will be back soon enough, probably in time for breakfast."

The boy obediently lay on his back, his dark eyes gleaming.

Boaz tucked the blankets around him, checked his other son who was snoring slightly. He quietly made his way to the stone stairwell that led to the downstairs rooms. The love he felt for these children almost buckled his knees. He thought of turning back, not wanting to be away from them for even an hour. His job as their father was to protect them but this was a time of peace, not war. No Moabite tyrant threatened them now. The danger came from bad weather. Boaz wished Hashem would use him to put an end to this famine as surely as Ehud once put an end to the tyranny of the Moabite king.

It wasn't that Boaz sought to be a hero like Ehud who'd managed to conceal a double-edged dagger beneath his robes. This very clever and brave patriot had pretended to have a secret that only he could deliver to the king when no one else was present. The king had readily dismissed all his attendants. Fool! Once alone in the king's chamber, Ehud thrust the dagger into the man's belly and it completely disappeared beneath his rolls of flesh. Ehud easily escaped and soon returned, leading a small army that overthrew ten thousand Moabite warriors.

Although *he'd* gladly lay his life down for his family, Boaz was no warrior. Neither did he pretend to be a clever man. He did not understand the reason for this lasting time without rain, this time when the land was dry and no seeds could sprout. Surely it was not a sin to want plenty of food and drink for everyone? He could not imagine what wrongs the people had committed except sometimes they did not worship as they ought, and sometimes arguments broke out that had to be mediated by the elders. Once, there had even been a murder, but that was years ago over a woman. She'd been innocent but the man who'd killed her husband, in order to make love to her, was stoned and thrown over a cliff. Could they still be held accountable for having strayed from Hashem's commandment: *thou shall not commit murder*? What other commandments had they disobeyed? Was he, Boaz, culpable because of his yearning for Naomi?

Yet he doubted he alone could be the cause of drought. It was not so unusual in these parts. After all, even their patriarch Abram left during a time of famine and went to Egypt, where he made quite a few mistakes, some unspeakable, especially with regard to his beautiful wife, yet Hashem who could use anyone and anything for his purpose eventually redeemed him. That redemption surely included Emilelech. The man deserved pity rather than anger, and perhaps he was leading his family into a better life while Boaz and his family might perish.

Emilelech must surely feel ashamed to have to make pots to earn a living. Boaz knew he himself would hate such a life confined to a courtyard rather than out in the fields. Poor Emilelech. The soil had not been good to him or for him. How would he manage in a Moabite town without a kiln of his own or even the potting bench that he'd obviously had to leave behind?

But what of Naomi? She deserved so much better and though he knew she always smiled pleasantly, never complaining about her husband, she must surely lament being married to such a weak man. She'd had no choice, of course, promised as she was to Emilelech when she was a little girl. Yet she'd made eyes at him, Boaz. He knew she had, and he'd longed to reciprocate. He'd even asked his father who was an elder to offer a good bridal dowry for Naomi, enough to appease Emilelech's people, but his father was a righteous man and refused.

As he ducked beneath the low beam to the outer door, Boaz told himself that he was dutifully making sure that his kinsman's wife was safe, and that he would also take time to search in the surrounding fields for the spring he'd once found when he was a boy. Perhaps, if it were not dry, he could build canals like they had in Jerusalem to carry the water to the fields. It was too late for this year's crop, but he had plenty of grain stored in a large storage pit he'd dug a few years back. His three wives, too, good hard-working women, had put by jars of dried chickpeas and other vegetables, and even made sure there were flagons of beer and leather sacks of wine to keep them strong. He'd be able to provide for his family and help neighbors for a while. With luck the rain they desperately needed would soon soak the ground and restore the fertility of their fields. He might yet be able to raise a decent crop of late wheat and millet.

Boaz picked up the shepherd's crook he usually carried when he herded his livestock out to the pasture. He would not need it now, of course, but he wished his journey might be one to somehow reclaim Emilelech's family who he considered lost sheep. He expected the town elders would be pleased if he brought them back, but they were in Hashem's hands, not his. He crept stealthily through the courtyard, skirting around the ovens and the looms and stepping carefully over a row of ollas his wives used to fetch water. Fortunately, none of the women were up and about this early. They would certainly scold him if they knew what he was doing. And if they questioned him, he would not like to lie about where he was going. But he certainly could not tell them about his affection for Naomi.

Jealous women could be difficult to deal with as he well knew especially since he'd married his latest wife, who was prettier and younger than the other two. He should have known. He need only remember how their ancestor Sarah, Abraham's wife reacted to Hagar, her servant girl, who she gave as a concubine to her husband, Abraham, to bear him an heir. This seemingly generous gesture backfired: Sarah was so jealous that she threw Hagar and the son she bore out of the camp only to have Abraham bring them back. Boaz hoped he would never succumb to such mean-spiritedness. But he would never agree to take a servant girl into his bed. Women would resort to any means in order to protect their own children. Sarah, after she gave birth to her own son, still felt no love for Hagar and felt threatened by the rights Hagar's boy held. Abraham, going along with his wife, allowed her to cast them into the desert. They would surely have perished if it hadn't been for Hashem.

Fortunately, he already had sons and daughters. And his senior wives eventually started being kind to the youngest one, especially after she gave birth to a baby girl. Thank goodness they were fulfilled as mothers. He did not want to create more strife in his household and rarely made conjugal visits to any of them even though he knew the youngest wife wanted more children.

*Hashem*, Boaz cried in his mind, his eyes searching the sky. *Quench our thirsting. Keep Naomi and Emilelech and their sons safe. Give strength and health to them. Bring them home to us and help us forgive them for leaving. Also, I implore you to help me find the spring and fill it to overflowing as surely as you once did for Moses and his thirsty people in the desert.*

# Four: Pillar of Salt

Naomi

Before we set out, the Moabite trader offered to seat me in the back of the cart, but I wanted my loom more than I wanted to ride, and my body would take up too much of the precious space in the wagon. Somehow the trader, with Chilion and Mahlon helping, managed to lay the wooden frame on top of other household goods, gently lowering each warp weight so they wouldn't break any of my pots. I held my breath, but I simply had to bring my loom with me. I'd woven a lot of cloth with silver threads for robes and I'd even made a few blankets from goat-hair and wool, not to mention the sackcloth we'd sold to tentmakers. I also loved my loom because it was beautiful. The cross beam and uprights were of the strongest oak. I still remember the twinkle in Boaz's eyes when the carpenters set it up for me. Boaz was so talented, so strong, a shepherd, a carpenter, a good man in every way imaginable. But enough of that. I am on my way to meet Emilelech. I wish I felt as my sons did that this was a grand adventure.

The trader checked the saddle bags and told the boys to lead our two donkeys. He tied his mules to the rear of the cart. He nodded to me, tugged on the lead rope of the ox, and off we went with dawn barely beginning to light our way. I was glad of the darkness, not wanting anyone to see me scuffling over the cobbles, not wanting anyone challenging our departure. No one showed their faces, but I sensed them behind their windows and closed doors. I knew they must resent us for leaving. I bit my lip to try to stop myself from crying as we passed through the main courtyard leading to the city gate. How many times had I and my friends gathered here and chatted and listened to the elders speak of the harvest or of threats of war, or of warriors' heroic deeds? I'd learned about births too and always gone out of my way to take the new mother a jar of olive oil and fresh-baked bread. But now as we fled through the gate leading out of Bethlehem, I felt numb.

We had not gone far before my feet began to ache and I wished I had chosen to ride in the cart, but it was too late now. I was wearing Leah's sandals and although they were strong, they were not broken in, and the straps were cutting into my heels. When I saw the mazzebah, the memorial pillar Jacob had built, rising above Rachel's grave, I was reminded of a pillar of salt. I wanted the trader to stop. I had never used his name before but now I did. "Haran," I cried. "Please slow down. I must rest for a while."

He nodded to me and tugged the lead rope on the ox. It lumbered to a halt, and I walked a little further, aware of Haran patting the beast's shoulder. Haran bowed his head, and I knew he understood how sacred this gravesite was. I wondered if his Moabite people ever honored our matriarch Rachel who must surely be a distant relative to them. His name Haran hadn't meant anything to me except I knew it referred to a village, but Leah told me that Haran was the name of the father of Lot who was an ancestor of the Moabites. It was Lot who'd fled from Sodom and Gomorrah. It was he who'd fathered children in an unholy way with his daughters. His wife was turned into a pillar of salt for looking back. I felt myself tremble and yet I too looked back towards my beloved town, Bethlehem. A lump formed in my throat to see the cluster of buildings perched on the hillside. I almost wished for Hashem's wrath upon me. When nothing happened, I managed a tiny *thank you, Hashem* even though I felt anything but gratitude.

The mazzebah might be erected from well-placed flat stones, but to me I saw salt blocks rising towards the sky, uneven and buckling under the weight of each successive layer. Oh, how Jacob must have ached for his beloved wife after she died. I could not help but feel as if I too must surely die in childbirth as she did, being taken so far from my home as she was from her home to a foreign land. She too was pregnant, much further along than me, when she got here. Perhaps it was *not* the birth of Benjamin that killed her but the journey into the unknown. I wondered if she'd loved Jacob as he'd loved her. I knew my regret about Boaz was partly due to my resentment towards Emilelech. I'd encouraged our departure because I wanted my boys to thrive. I wanted my new baby to have a chance at a good life. Bethlehem, my hometown, no longer offered me the promise of continued prosperity. Comfort and wealth mattered only a little. With Emilelech's failing health we were never going to be rich again, but my friends and family meant everything. I felt my stomach clench in grief.

I didn't much care if I lived or died except for this baby I was carrying, who I secretly hoped would be a girl. I wanted to live for her. I wanted to massage her in health-giving salt and swaddle her gently as all our babies usually were, but I did not want any of the bitterness for her that had befallen Lot's wife. In the stories we heard about her, she remained nameless and was often considered wicked as if she'd been the one to offer her daughters to the hateful men outside her husband's house. She would surely have protected her young daughters. Not *her*, but her husband, Lot, who ought to have been turned into a pillar of salt. What good was he? He did not protect his family. He also fled from his town because it was evil, but hadn't he been complicit in the wrongdoing of Sodom?

In the past, I had never felt such deep resentment towards men with power over me, but as I stared at Rachel's tomb, I wondered if somehow she was conveying new wisdom into my mind. Her life was difficult, what with the rivalry between her and her sister, Leah, and she'd not had children until late in life. Although the second birth ended her life, at least she'd known the love of her life, Jacob. I felt sure Emilelech would not build a monument to me if I died before him. But I would not build one for him either. Still, there is something to be said for duty and for having an amicable marriage. I knew women whose husbands beat them and they had no way out, no recourse, since the elders always sided with their husbands.

Unable to crouch let alone kneel, I sank onto a flat rock that provided me with a sturdy seat. My boys were standing some distance away, gripping the ropes of the donkeys, watching me—probably worried to see me so obviously weary. They did not know I was pregnant, or at least I had not told them even though they were old enough to understand. They must know, though, and most probably had heard my talk with Emilelech about the need for nourishing food.

Rachel named her baby boy, her second son, Ben-Oni meaning *son of my sorrow*. She surely knew she was bleeding and could not survive this birth. I wondered if the birth of her first son Joseph was terrible too. She'd been quite old to have babies. I felt old too. And the birth of my sons had been difficult because they came early. It was I who'd named them, calling my oldest Mahlon who'd been so little and helpless it seemed appropriate to call him *Man of Weakness*. What was I thinking to be so heartless? In truth it was Emilelech I was cross with, and I'd sought Hashem's forgiveness many times. But when Chilion was born, I did it again, naming my tiny baby with his fragile arms and floppy legs *Wasting Away*. Oh I wish Emilelech had corrected those names the way Jacob did by calling his son, the one who caused Rachel to die, Benjamin for *son of his hand*. Benjamin became strong but my boys seemed always ill with coughs. I would that this journey might toughen them up.

I glanced towards them, Mahlon leaning against a donkey, and Chilion picking up pebbles, his donkey's lead rope dangling. I hoped the creature wouldn't decide to bolt but it looked on passively. Chilion threw a pebble at Mahlon, who deflected it with his hand and picked up a rock to throw back. I sighed heavily but I simply didn't have the energy to tell the boys to stop. The trader, Haran, frowned at them and told them to keep hold of the lead ropes to the donkeys. They looked rebellious, but they obeyed. I closed my eyes. "Rachel," I whispered, "Help me to be obedient to Hashem's will in my life. Keep us safe on our travels and bless Bethlehem with rain and a good harvest. Bring me the help I need and fill my heart with love and gratitude."

There are people who seem to love to travel and I believe Haran, the trader, was one of them, but this walk, although not terribly far, was enough of dirt and brown terrain to last me forever. I almost took off my pretty sandals to walk barefoot, but the path was full of jagged rocks and might well make my feet hurt more than the straps strangling my toes and cutting into my heels. Somehow, I kept going.

We stopped near a dry wadi to eat the breakfast I'd brought with us—pita bread and hummus and cheese wrapped in cloth. The shade of the acacia trees cooled us. Even the beasts seemed relieved to get out of the overbearing sun. I wiped the perspiration out of my eyes with my head scarf. I was starved. We all were. It made me happy to watch my boys eating ravenously. Haran, too, had a hearty appetite. I was afraid I'd not brought enough bread and was going to give them my share of the food, but I needed to keep up my strength for the baby. Alas, the first bite of hummus and garlic made me nauseous. I managed to eat but it was no good. I had to go behind a tree where I threw up everything.

They must have heard me but no one said anything and I was glad no one came to my aid. After I wiped my face with the palm of my hand and rubbed sand into it to remove any residue of the food, I covered my face and went back to the men and gathered up the cheesecloth and tucked it into the cart. I felt faint and had to lean against the wheel for a moment or two before we set out again. I lagged behind, and the trail of dust from the caravan engulfed me. Somehow I managed not to cough, pulling my scarf tight around my face. *Hashem*, I whispered silently, *have mercy upon me. Give me the strength to continue. May Jerusalem be a place of rejoicing and comfort.*

# Five: Search

## Boaz

Boaz tugged thoughtfully on his beard, watching the donkeys kicking up dust as the small caravan disappeared into the distance. He'd hoped Naomi would look back and notice him and make them return, but the boys leading the donkeys tramped steadily along after the cart as it bounced across the ruts behind the plodding ox. Boaz caught only a glimpse of Naomi walking slowly next to the trader. She looked as if she were limping, but he knew she'd not complain. As a good woman ought, she would make her way to her husband even if it killed her.

Boaz lowered himself onto the rock that was where Naomi had sat. He adjusted his robe around his knees and stared at the pillar of stones rising towards heaven. Some things lasted, like this monument to Rachel, but why did Hashem take her, why did she have to die? He'd intended to pray for Rachel to protect Naomi and all the people in Bethlehem, but he felt as if a void were opening in his life. It seemed ridiculous for him to feel so dejected, and he couldn't fully understand why he should feel left behind. He knew the trader was taking care of Emilelech's family and they would soon be reunited. Now there was no need for him to keep close watch upon them. It wasn't as if he had any intention of leaving Bethlehem.

He sat there for a long time until the sun rose. He'd forgotten to cover his head, but no matter. He rested his hands in his lap and stared at the now empty dirt path. He felt so lonesome but he had too much on his mind to let himself remain morose. He must do his best to help his villagers during this time of drought and suffering. He retrieved the staff that he'd leaned against a nearby rock and looked up at the blazing blue sky. Heat arose in wavy lines from nearby rocks. He began to perspire and wished he'd brought a flask of water with him. What had he been thinking to chase after Naomi? She didn't need or want him. He had his own family and children to take care of. They were the ones he needed to protect. Now if he only could find that spring from long ago.

He'd been with a group of boys who'd come to the tomb on a pilgrimage to learn about their heritage. He and another boy wandered off and came across water dripping from a crack in a large boulder that overlooked a ravine. It was a time of rain, and the water formed a continuous stream trickling over rocks down a steep hill. The two of them found a deep puddle and began a splashing war, calling for the others to join them. The elder who'd brought them told them they were standing on holy ground and ought not to be disrespectful. Boaz, in retrospect, didn't think they'd insulted anything or anyone but simply been energetic boys like his sons who couldn't help but be a little mischievous. He smiled at the realization that being a father had given him greater understanding and perspective. He'd always believed that all things worked for good with Hashem but having sons and daughters opened his heart in unfathomable ways. Perhaps Hashem always intended for him to know where the spring was. Perhaps Hashem was preparing him for a moment like this.

He set off with determined steps down an animal trail. Rounded boulders as high as his shoulders shaded him somewhat but might also be hideouts for wild animals. He only hoped he would not encounter any lions. A pair once attacked his goats, but he'd managed to chase the beasts away by yelling and waving his staff, but with this drought they might be more aggressive, hungrier for meat, and he didn't want to become their meal. Nevertheless, he must try to find the source of water. *May Hashem go with me!* he thought. Perhaps he could strike a rock with his staff as Moses once did and fresh water would flow in torrents. After all, he too, like Moses, wanted to take care of others. But he was no Moses who'd been raised by a princess and freed the nation from the tyranny of the Egyptians. Boaz knew he was in fact a simple man who loved his home and his family and neighbors. Yet surely, even if he were a nobody, Hashem would hear him and help him. Did not Hashem favor the righteous?

As he made his way over the rough terrain, he continued to remember the history of his people. When their story was told in the temple on feast days, it seemed distant and not connected to anyone he knew, but now the thought of the wilderness they once endured without shelter for over forty years distressed him. He could not imagine being without fields to harvest or livestock to tend, nor could he envision being like Moses without women to take care of him. What would life be without family and friends and good harvests?

He stayed on the trail and searched with his eyes the nearby terrain, but no matter how hard he looked, he saw nothing resembling the place where he'd found the spring during his boyhood. Had it been a dream? Or a vision? He sniffed the air hoping he might detect the odor of water but all he could smell was dust. How could the ravine have disappeared? Perhaps the bristly shrubs growing between the rocks were hiding it. As a boy and in the company of others, he'd been fearless, but now he gingerly stepped off the trail to continue his search within the wild shrubbery. He prodded rocks with his staff to make sure no snakes surprised him, and he tried to skirt around the thorny bushes, but the longer he searched, the wearier he felt. Disheartened, he struck a large rock with his staff and shouted out loud, "How have I offended you? What have any of us done to make you withhold rain?" He angrily shook his staff at the hot sun glowing red in the sky.

Immediately, he regretted his anger. What if snakes poisoned him just as they had the disobedient people in the wilderness who'd spoken against Hashem? Who would take care of his family? Even Moses' prayers did not save the people from Hashem's vengeance. Boaz still felt angry and rebellious but he could not vanquish the bitterness arising in his heart. He fell upon his knees onto a mound of dried grass and begged Hashem to help him and to forgive him. His mind whirled as if it contained an uncontrollable dust-storm. Why did the people have to suffer drought and famine? The people of Bethlehem were faithful, worshipped regularly, took care of widows and orphans, and obeyed the commandments that Moses brought down from Mount Sinai. Why did old Sarah the midwife who'd brought his children into the world become so weak and die so rapidly? He began to weep, his salty tears reminding him of the desperate need to find a source of water. Where *was* that spring?

Slowly he got to his feet and elbowed his way through the low-growing thornbushes, not caring if his clothing got torn, not caring if his arms bled. When his sleeve caught on a branch, he wrenched his arm away, managing to rip the cloth. He stopped moving and stared at his flesh through the hole in his best robe. He ought to have worn his usual shepherd's flaxen garment not this one. He felt ridiculous at the sudden realization that he'd wanted to look his best for Naomi. What a fool he was, but as he leaned against the twisted bark of a juniper, he could not help himself. He began to laugh. If punishment came to him it would not be a lightning strike from Hashem. Vengeance would come from his wives, furious with him for ruining their beautifully sewn coat meant to keep him cool and wrapped in their love.

Quietly, he made his way back to Bethlehem. He often spent time alone and it was in those solitary times with his sheep and goat in grassy pastures when he most felt the presence of Hashem and gained insight and wisdom. But as he walked silently along and his laughter ended, he felt abandoned.

The sun was already at its zenith when he entered Bethlehem. He nodded politely at people he knew in the streets, but hurried along to his house, sweat dripping from his forehead. He'd intended on going immediately to his chamber and taking off his torn coat, but his youngest wife met him in the doorway. "Boaz!" she cried. "Are you all right?" She took an end of her veil and tried to wipe his sweaty face. He pushed her hand away, a little annoyed to have been caught. He felt guilty, too, not only for rebuffing her, but also because he'd been pursuing another woman, even if it had been with the intent of protection and nothing more.

His youngest wife, always emotional, stared at his ragged sleeve. His oldest wife soon hurried out of the kitchen, and quickly spotted the ripped garment. "Where have you been? What happened to your robe?"

As head of the household, he did not need to give them any explanation, but he knew if he wanted to keep the peace, he must explain himself. He was a truthful man but sometimes it was best to keep quiet—especially about his innermost feelings. "I remembered a spring from when I was a boy and went in search of it out by Rachel's tomb. It was so overgrown I couldn't find it. In my haste, I ripped my coat."

The youngest wife looked sympathetic and stroked his arm with her fingers. The middle wife rushed out from an inner chamber. In her hands she held a bundle of wool she'd been carding. She exchanged a glance with the oldest woman and looked at him shrewdly but quickly looked down and said quietly. "We heard that Naomi has gone off with that Moabite."

Boaz felt his face burning and was not sure if it was embarrassment or indignation. His women loved to gossip and he usually avoided their chatter, but now they were all quietly staring at the tile floor. Should he tell them off or tell them the truth? He tugged on his beard before answering them. "It was my duty to make sure the Moabite was taking care of

Naomi. I went after them to see them on their way. But certainly I did search for water."

"And did you find what you were looking for?" First wife spoke a little shrilly.

He knew she'd always felt second best, perhaps in the same way Rachel's older sister Leah always felt unloved. He did not know how to comfort her. He had married her to solidify the relationship between his family and her wealthy one. He respected her. He respected all three of these women and he loved the children they'd given him. But at this moment, they felt like a burden he wished he did not have. He did not want a confrontation. Not now. There was too much else to worry about. Still, he was dutiful and a good husband. He had done nothing wrong. He had never revealed his desire for Naomi to them or to anyone. In fact, he'd not even recognized how strongly he felt. "I am sorry I tore the sleeve. It is my best coat and I have always been proud of it. Do you think it might be repaired?"

"Cloth can be mended," wife number one said, about to burst into tears.

Her despair humbled him. He did not want to hurt anyone. No amount of jewelry or kind words could possibly satisfy her need or her desire. She'd greatly resented him getting a second wife but at least those two had formed an alliance, often sharing recipes and baking bread and giggling together. Third wife, though, was younger and prettier and they resented her. He tried to change the subject to what mattered the most, but his next words seemed to inflame his oldest woman all the more. "Did you go to the well with the other women? Was there enough water?"

"It was horrible! Everyone is upset and everyone knows Emilelech slipped away and left Naomi to manage by herself. What kind of man is he!" All of the women looked indignant.

Boaz felt his anger at Emilelech rising too but it would do no good to encourage their outrage. "She is all right. No doubt Emilelech had his reasons to go early. Perhaps he intended to get them lodging."

"Please!" His first wife turned on her heels and stormed into an inner room with second wife following close behind her. Soon they heard the clicks of a loom rapidly spinning.

His youngest wife smiled shyly, obviously hoping to make him feel better. "I will mend your coat." She lifted the sleeve and began to examine it carefully. "It isn't so bad. By the time I am done, it will look brand new."

Boaz patted her back. Suddenly he desired her but he knew his need was because he wanted to fill his emptiness and try to forget the troubles that lay ahead of them. The last thing he wanted was to beget another child. "I will give the robe to you later." He turned away, aware of her wide-eyed look of hurt. This house seemed too small to contain all these women and all the children and he needed to think and to pray. He headed outside into the bright sunlight and stood for a while looking around the yard. At last, he made his way to his mother's cottage.

Her dear face, lined from age and hard work, radiated wisdom. She'd never stopped mourning for his father yet after his death she had managed well and raised him to become a strong man. She'd urged him to marry and although she'd been the only wife to his father, the man she'd clearly adored, she'd never criticized his choices. Indeed, when he'd tried to convince his righteous father to negotiate with Emilelech's people to free Naomi from her promise in order to marry him, his mother was sympathetic, but of course in the end she'd sided with his father and suggested he take another bride. He'd been dutiful, choosing the girls who'd align them with wealthy families. "Mother," he said, as he stepped into the inner room where she was lounging on a couch covered in sheepskin. "I sometimes wish I'd only taken one woman and not three."

She eyed him shrewdly. "Your wives giving you trouble?"

His statement had been rash, seeking sympathy and encouragement, but Boaz didn't really want to talk about his women with his mother and yet he said, "You and my father seemed so happy."

"We were." She sighed. "But you have many more children to enjoy and to care for you in your old age."

Boaz hoped he would live for a long time, but he wondered how many of them would survive if the drought did not soon end. He lowered himself onto a nearby bench. "I fear I have not been a good husband like my father was to you."

"You have provided well for your wives, given them children, and you are kind. What more can any woman want?"

"I wish I knew." But Boaz felt sure the affection he and his wives shared did not compensate for his longing for a woman he could never have. He knew too that he was and always had been jealous of Emilelech, even though he'd also pitied him. He'd never acted out his jealousy the way their ancestors,

Joseph's half-brothers did. He'd spent his life dutifully seeking peace, helping others, and working hard, but now he felt raw and out of sorts. Nevertheless, he smiled at his mother. She'd known difficult times too. Did not all people face challenges and struggles, sometimes of their own making, and sometimes not?

His mother reached out her age-spotted hand and took his. "Your father used to comfort me when I'd feel depressed. He would tell me I was as beautiful and as comely as the Egyptian woman that Joseph married, a lady so much better born than I, the daughter of a high priest. I never felt worthy, but your father would remind me that all people have value in the eyes of Hashem, and that all people do and say things that hurt others. Don't worry, son, everything will be fine in the end. You are a good man. You always do what is right. Surely, Hashem will bring you the contentment you deserve."

# Six: Answered Prayer

Naomi

When I saw the walls of Jerusalem in the distance rising above the terraced fields, my sore feet picked up the pace and I hobbled past the donkeys and mules and tried to catch up with Haran. He looked over his shoulder and slowed down to wait for me. I liked him for being so considerate, knowing how anxious he must be to get off the road, shake the dust from his clothes, and have a decent meal.

Haran nodded to me. "On my way to Bethlehem, I stopped in Jerusalem, and the Gihon spring was still flowing." Haran wiggled his bushy eyebrows. "Let's hope it hasn't dried up."

"Oh dear." My face must have fallen considerably and my voice sounded weak. I'd foolishly hoped for plenty of fresh water and the very idea of no water at all exhausted me almost as much as the road we'd travelled.

Haran shrugged. "Their cisterns are probably full. And if not, we'll keep on going until we get to Jericho. There is not much there now, but the spring was still running when I came this way to Bethlehem. I've never known it to run dry."

Jericho was a city destroyed by Joshua and it was far from home. Boaz's mother, Rahab, was one of the few people along with her family who'd been spared. I remembered her well from my days as a girl and had always loved her. She was fierce and a little guarded but there was something majestic about her. She never spoke about what had happened to her in

Jericho but she'd married Salmon who was from our tribe. She'd immersed herself in the culture of my people. Indeed she obeyed our laws better than anyone. She was also a very good cook and I loved her lentil soup, but right now, I wondered if I'd be able to hold any food down.

Chilion began chattering about how he'd be as strong as Joshua who'd conquered Jericho, and how he'd be able to overcome anything and anyone. "I am going to learn to shoot a bow. You wait. I will become an expert."

When I looked over my shoulder, the donkey had its ears back. It was probably as worn out and as fed up as I.

Chilion let go of his donkey's lead rope and held his arms up as if he were an archer. "Pow," he said, startling the donkey, causing it to kick. My son, upon seeing me glare at him, grabbed the rope and grinned at his brother and the two of them prattled on about their future escapades.

I wished they'd shut up. Their young voices usually pleased me but I did not trust in the future. I was angry too. What sort of god visited starvation and suffering on his people? I immediately regretted my rebelliousness. Perhaps such disloyalty was why Hashem punished his people. Did he not know that I was simply tired and wished I could rest my feet? Then I'd surely feel better about everything.

The entrance into Jerusalem was surprisingly quiet, unguarded by the archers who Mahlon and Chilion hoped to imitate. Emilelech always encouraged their rough-housing and their dreams of becoming warriors. I wondered at times if it was because he'd never be able to strap on a sword to fight anyone. He was not strong enough, and war simply was not in his nature. I hoped my boys would be gentle too and become farmers or even potters such as Emilelech had become. But you cannot control the will of Hashem or the ways of boys and men.

As we clattered into the courtyard, a man got up from the wide wooden platform in the center where strangers were allowed to bed down. "Naomi," he cried. "Naomi!"

I had not recognized him at first but there was no mistaking the voice of my husband. It had never sounded sweeter. I almost ran into his arms except my feet could not go fast. He reached me in no time and hugged me. As weary as I felt, my heart sank at how frail he seemed. Yet he managed to grab Chilion and lift him briefly off his feet. He nodded at Mahlon and at the trader.

"Come," Emilelech said, wrapping his arm around Mahlon's shoulder. They looked so much alike it made me smile. "Let's put the animals in the paddock with the others. There is water in the trough. And plenty of fodder for them."

I stared at a camel in the pen that looked as if it were grinning. It towered over a few scraggly goats and the donkey that Emilelech had ridden here. It looked healthy but Emilelech himself looked scruffy. His eyes might have lit up to see us but I felt my own eyes clouding. "Is there water for us too?" I cried.

"Some," he said. "Not enough to waste on washing our feet, but enough to for a good drink."

Three women, their heads covered, approached. As they walked, the fabric of their mitpachaths that were draped over their shoulders blew gently in the breeze. Their beautiful lacy veils made me horribly aware of my ragged one now dangling down my back. I wished I could freshen up. Their robes too, cinched around their waists with colorful sashes, made me wish I'd worn my best robe. I knew I must look dirty and disheveled. As the women stepped daintily towards us, I hung my head, listening to their ankle bracelets tinkling. "Welcome," cried the first lady to arrive, an older woman who must be the matriarch. She smiled at the trader. "Hello, Haran."

He grinned, tugging on the halter of the ox. "I have brought you guests!"

"How wonderful," said the lady and threw Haran an amused glance. She smiled at me and went over to my sons who stood next to their father, Emilelech, with his arms at his sides as rigid as bamboo planks. His robe looked dirty and embarrassed me, and the sour look on his face was not helping. I wondered why he'd chosen to sleep out in the entrance court. Surely, such lovely women must have invited him to their houses.

"These must be your sons. They resemble you," one of the younger women said to him.

My sons looked sheepish while the women fussed over them, asking them how old they were, and what was their favorite food, and did they help with the plowing, and on and on. As soon as they could get away, the boys took their donkeys towards the animal pen.

Haran bowed to the women and led his mules after the boys and freed the beasts of their saddlebags, putting them on the sleeping platform that sat about a foot above the tiled courtyard. Emilelech excused himself, unhitched the ox, and left the cart near us.

Once our animals were released into the enclosure, they gathered around one another. The donkey that Emilelech had brought with him, the one with the ear tufts, trotted over and nuzzled our donkeys. I felt a pang of sadness but at least these friends were together. Haran's mules dipped their heads into the water trough and began slurping a long drink, and the ox started seizing hay between his strong jaws.

The women gathered around me. Their perfume helped cover the smell of the animal dung steaming in the pen. One of the ladies grabbed my hand. "Come with us," she said. "We have something for you."

I looked over at Emilelech to seek his permission, but Haran spoke first. "Don't worry, Emilelech. They will not steal your wife and add her to their harem." He roared with laughter.

"Do not tease, Haran!" one of the women scolded. "He is a welcome guest in our house and so of course are you."

I once again wondered why Emilelech had not stayed with them but decided to ask him later.

We were soon swept along one of the cobbled streets up a hill to a house much bigger than many. Clearly these were wealthy people.

Inside their entryway, we all began taking off our sandals. It was such a relief to remove the straps. The oldest of the women noticed my blistered feet. Her mouth fell open. "You poor thing. Wait just a moment. Sit, please." She brought a stool over for me. I sank gratefully onto it while she briefly disappeared and came back with a jar of ointment. She kneeled before me and very gently rubbed the salve into my sore feet. I was so grateful that I wanted to kiss the top of her head. No one had treated me with such care for many years. But these gracious women seemed to understand my plight. Very soon they ushered us up wide stone stairs into the main living area. Children of all ages peeked at us from behind various doorways. Haran grinned with pleasure and grabbed the hands of a little girl and drew her into the main room. "This is Adina," he said. I could see how much he loved children and knew he was missing his daughters.

"Hello, Adina." I wanted to hug this shy little girl with her big brown eyes, but another little one dashed out.

"Ayala," the woman who must be her mother yelled. "You behave yourself. Girls, come down to the kitchen and help us to prepare dinner."

A flurry of children and everyone else except the matriarch disappeared into the lower chamber. The older woman graciously invited us to rest around a central mat where a bowl of pomegranates and figs sat. "Please help yourself," she said with a courteous nod towards my hungry sons. As I lowered myself and sat cross-legged on the floor, I wondered where all the menfolk were. We hadn't seen anyone in the terraced fields on the way up to the gate, but they might be in fields on the other side of town. I hoped they might have a barley harvest of some sort but didn't want to ask.

"I must go and help my daughters," the matriarch said.

"I'll come with you." I felt uncomfortable sitting with the menfolk, but she would have none of it. "You stay here and rest. And have some beer. This was a particularly good brew." She got out a container and filled our cups, even giving Mahlon and Chilion a drop.

Emilelech examined the cup, obviously taking in the quality of the pottery. He took a sip and nodded with appreciation.

The trader took a long drink. "Refreshing," he said through the frothy residue sticking to his mustache. "Where is Baruch, your husband?"

"All the men and boys are at the temple," she answered. "They are sacrificing a sheep and a goat to please Hashem and the priests. But we are fine for now." She patted my shoulder.

What a wonderful kind and generous lady this was, I thought, but found the smell of the beer making me a little sick. I didn't want to offend her, but I pushed my drink away.

"Ah," she said, looking at me knowingly, and gave the mug to Haran. "You look like you are ready for more." She paid no attention to his grin and turned back to me. "I will get you something soothing." She fluttered away, her purple veil trailing behind her. Before long, she came back. As if I were her daughter, she sat a dainty cup of sweet broom tea in front of me. It tasted wonderful. I felt renewed and my appetite picked up.

I could smell the earthy odor of stewed goat and lentils rising up the staircase. I very much wanted to go down to the kitchen and be with the other women and the children. It was not seemly for me to dine with the men and I could hear their men coming into the house, their loud voices full of energy. Soon they would come storming up here. I so preferred the company of women. Slowly and quietly I managed to get up and made my way down the stairs into a hallway, following the aromas of the cooking.

When I came face to face with a rugged older man, I drew back in surprise. As I looked up at his face, the breath went out of me. For a moment I thought it was Boaz. He took my shoulders and gently moved me to one side so that he could go to the upper room. I knew he must be the patriarch of the household. I think the trader called him Baruch. The fleeting thought entered my mind that Baruch must surely be a blessing like his name, just as Boaz was like his name, a pillar of strength. *Stop it,* I told myself and hurried towards the sounds of women chattering as they cooked. The wonderful rich fragrance of bread baking in a clay oven filled the air.

The women greeted me with smiles and sat me on a seat out of their way. Little children glanced at me curiously but soon went back to their games. One little girl, hiding behind her mother's skirt, peeked out at me. The older girls showed off, proudly helping with the cooking. Their easy togetherness as they stirred the stew and prepared a dessert from dates and almonds made me smile. I would so love to stay right here in this cheerful warm house but Emilelech would never agree. He wanted to leave Judah for Moab. I knew the main reason. The dried fields of Bethlehem along with my plea for nutritious food for the new baby were only part of the story. My ailing husband wanted to take us where there was plenty, but he also hoped to find healers through Haran's connection to Egypt. We'd never mentioned this hope to anyone because if our elders found out about his desire for physicians with their incantations and magical spells, he would likely be stoned or at the very least chastised and shamed before the community. We'd tried to cling to prayer and I'd heard Emilelech whisper for Hashem's mercy, but instead of strength, he'd gotten weaker.

It must have been because these women had helped me to feel better and that they were so hospitable and friendly that I overcame my shyness and did not hesitate to speak up to the matriarch. "Blessed be Hashem," I whispered. "And you too."

She came over to me and patted my hand. "You also, daughter."

"May I ask you something?"

"Of course." Her eyes welcomed my inquisitiveness.

My words burst forth. "My husband, Emilelech, is a good man. He has done nothing wrong. But he has been unwell for a long time. I don't know what to do for him. Good food is not enough. Nor have been the priestly prayers in Bethlehem. I fear that he might not survive our journey to Moab."

The other ladies were all listening, their faces full of concern. A young woman with ebony hair down to her waist wrapped her arms around me almost making me cry. "Hashem is good. He will take care of you," she said. She was so young.

"Yes of course." I appreciated her kindness and managed to regain my composure, but doubted she had any idea about the hardships we'd been through or the ones we now faced. Everything seemed uncertain. Everything seemed hopeless. I knew I needed to put my trust in Hashem but when your feet are sore, and you've been forced to leave your home, it is hard to keep your faith in YHWH's providence. "I hoped there was someone amongst your holy men who has the gift of healing?" I glanced at the matriarch. "Your tea has done me so much good. Don't you have teas for strength?" I'd almost said potions but knew that would be frowned upon.

"We will give you meat broth to take on your journey," the matriarch said. She smiled sadly and I knew she could not, or would not, invite us to stay indefinitely.

"You are too kind," I murmured and tried to look as if I was thankful, but really inside I felt my spirit sag. Yet as I looked around the room at this gathering of women, I knew I could be strong and I would be, and I knew that although they might not be able to let us stay here, their loving prayers would sustain me as surely as their good will and good food and loving kindness had already given me comfort.

# Seven: Refuge

Ruth

Ruth overslept and could hardly get out of bed. It was a wonder her mother didn't wake her. She automatically reached for her little sister's hand, but the unoccupied sleeping rug immediately shocked her into remembering that Anna was never coming back. She managed to get up and steal outside into their walled courtyard. Women were already soaking grape leaves in brine to later be stuffed with lamb; they were busy grinding barley with their stone mortars; they were washing clothes in basins of water. Golden dust from the grain and the smell of damp linens scented the air.

Expected to help with the chores, Ruth usually enjoyed being with the grownup women, but she could not stand to be near her mother who was kneading bread dough as if nothing horrible had happened. The girl crept behind a stand of vines full of clusters of white flowers. Their sweet fragrance pleased her but also made her want Anna here to pick a flower and hold it against her nose. She crept past a donkey drinking from the trough in the center of their courtyard. He took a long sip before raising his head, water dripping from his muzzle. Ordinarily Ruth would take time to stroke the stripe on his back but today she looked down, her eyes to the ground, as she quickly escaped through the wooden gate her uncles had constructed before she was born.

Once outside, she wanted to run from her sorrow. She wanted to go to her friend Orpah, but she felt rage at the whole world and could not stand to be with anyone. She made her way to the threshing ground where she and Orpah once found a little cave between two of the big boulders that encircled the floor. No one would be there and it was close to home, set outside the village next to some fields. No sheaves of grain would be brought until harvest season, a time when she and Orpah loved to watch the oxen going around and around, treading down the long stems to separate the chaff from the seeds. Such wonderful moments seemed long ago.

On the flattened smooth floor, she stood still while a gentle breeze blew stalks of hay into a corner. She went over and with her foot scraped a pile of the dried grass into a heap to make a bed. She sank down and lay on her back and stared aimlessly at the blue sky before flopping over onto her stomach. She wanted to curl up and sleep but who would protect her, who would keep her safe? Her own mother could not be trusted, let alone the priests who worshipped Chemosh.

Rough stalks of straw stuck into her arms and legs and felt scratchy against her face. She sat up and shaded her eyes from the rising sun that shone on the compacted dirt of the threshing ground, making her hot and uncomfortable. Droplets of perspiration formed on her forehead and ran down her cheeks. With the sleeve of her robe she brushed them away. Suddenly she started to shudder, wondering if Chemosh punished those who did not like him. Certainly, she did not like him any more than she did one tiny grain of sand. Why had they chosen Anna? Perhaps she, Ruth, was the one who ought to have been selected. Ruth beat the ground with her fists.

The thought of little Anna who'd been so innocent but was now in heaven offered no comfort. Unable to stay still, Ruth jumped to her feet and ran outside to walk around the wall of boulders and find the little cave she and Orpah often went inside. It would be cool with plenty of room. No one would be able to find her in there.

Most of the rocks that once rose above her head were now at shoulder level. The two big rocks she sought were an odd shape—they did not fit smoothly together and formed a narrow gap. They should be easy to locate, she thought, but as her eyes darted up and down the craggy rocks she couldn't find them. Tears began to fill her eyes. Was everything and everyone she loved going to disappear? Was she a very bad girl to not go along with what all the adults seemed to believe? Except her father. The thought of him reassured her. He did not agree with much of what was commonly said and stayed away from rituals and celebrations. Her mother, though, once brought her to this very place because she wanted another baby. She wanted a son. Ruth did not remember much except the crowds of excited people gathering inside and then spilling out of the entranceway. They'd been moaning and praying and giving thanks. She'd seen a frenzied man and a woman lying together in the way her daddy laid with her mommy.

When they got home, Daddy laughed when her mother told him about the ritual, and then he led her to a private room. Nine months later, Anna came into the world. Anna was the sweetness in Ruth's life, a baby for her to look after much better than the rag dolls she played with. She often pretended, even though the years between them were few, that Anna was *her* baby. Ruth, at the terrible realization of her loss, began to wail the way she'd heard older women cry when they grieved the deaths of their loved ones. Her cries rose towards the sky and did nothing to ease her pain.

At last, her cries became sobs. She continued to walk around the threshing floor, kicking at the cold stones. As she shambled along, feeling so helpless and alone, she heard something moaning. She froze, chills running up and down her spine. If Chemosh wanted to kill her, then let him, she thought defiantly. But nothing happened. Instead the sounds became more desperate and seemed to draw her towards them. Suddenly, she spotted the fissure leading into the little cave. Perhaps a wild animal was using it for its den. She'd heard the howls of wolves not too long ago, and though they never bothered people, she drew back. They were no bigger than small goats, but if a female had young, she would likely be ferocious in her protection of them.

Ruth stood very still, suddenly curious. She would like to see the pups. As she waited, the noise from inside the cave began to sound like the wails of a child. It *was* a child. She clutched her chest. And then she heard words, "I want my mama." Oh, she knew demons might tempt a person into danger but hope was greater, and she could not stop herself from rushing toward the gap in the rocks. She could see the bottom of little feet. "Anna!" she cried. "Is it you?"

A ragged little girl scuttled out of the hole on her bottom and held out her arms. It *was* Anna! Ruth fell to her knees and enfolded her little sister in an embrace, tears raining onto the little girl's messy hair.

Neither of them could stop sniffling, but at last Ruth released the grip she had on Anna and pulled herself away and looked deeply into Anna's misty eyes. Could Anna really be alive?

"Are you a princess now?" Ruth asked, thinking perhaps Anna had somehow returned from the afterlife. Yet, the grubby dress all scrunched up and full of strands of hay could not possibly be the garment of someone royal, but how could Anna have survived? Ruth could almost smell the acrid odor of burned flesh. She'd seen her mother, at least at first, hysterical. She'd watched the priests bind and gag the little girl and carry her away.

Anna's eyes became as big and round as the pebbles used to decorate the outside of the fence around their house. "An angel let me go," she said. She grabbed Ruth's hand and held on. "She used a golden knife to cut away the twine around my ankles and wrists. She told me I must not yell or cry and then she unwound the rag around my mouth. She told me to run and hide."

Ruth was thinking fast. The priests must have killed a goat. What if they got hold of Anna again? She did not think her mother could be trusted. If only her father were here, but he wasn't. "You must be hungry."

Anna nodded solemnly.

Ruth wished she'd brought some raisins with her, but the folds of her skirt were empty. She'd not even brought a skin of water because she'd left in such a hurry. Somehow, she must find somewhere to keep Anna safe until her father got back. "You must stay here in the cave while I go for food and water."

Anna shook her head and clutched Ruth's hand. "I want to go home," she wailed.

"It isn't safe. You have to stay here. Just for a little while." Ruth pushed Anna to the entrance of the cave. "Go inside where it is cool. I will come right back for you. I promise."

Anna bravely crawled inside the hole and turned around and peered out at Ruth.

"I am going to run the whole way to Orpah's house. Her mother will give me some sweets and bread for you and I'll bring water." With that, Ruth, unable to bear the dread in Anna's eyes, turned and began to run. She didn't get far before she looked back. Anna was already scrambling outside.

Ruth could not leave Anna alone here. It was not right, and Anna would probably try to follow her anyway. What if the priests caught her? She trotted back to her little sister and helped her to her feet. "Come on. But if we see anyone, you have to hide and you cannot cry or say anything to anyone. Understand?"

Anna nodded and held a hand over her mouth, but her eyes were looking more hopeful.

"Don't worry. I will keep you safe." Ruth only hoped she could. She led her little sister along a narrow trail that she and Orpah often used as a shortcut. It was narrow, lined by scrubby acacia trees that led past a creek where they liked to dip their feet. Very rarely did they ever meet anyone but today they heard a group of women chatting in the distance. Although this creek led past the well, it was unlikely women would be drawing water so late in the morning. Ruth almost turned back but Anna was trembling. She needed food and water soon. Ruth put her finger to her mouth to hush Anna as they crept closer.

Four women were gathering reeds and tall grasses, no doubt for basket-making. Ruth quickly drew Anna off the path and the two hid behind some trees. One woman, sitting on the ground, looked over. She must have seen them, but she did not say anything, too busy plaiting dried reeds. Ruth didn't know any of them and thought it best to wait for them to leave. Surely they would not take too long to finish gathering the sedges growing near the water and whatever else they needed. Surely they wouldn't try to make baskets right here and right now. Suddenly it occurred to her that these women might head for the threshing floor to gather the dried straw and hay. If they did, there would be no way to avoid them.

Anna tugged on her sleeve. "I'm thirsty, Ruth." She licked her chapped lips and looked longingly at the clear water trickling over the rocks.

"Come on, then," Ruth said, praying as she led Anna to the banks of the creek that these women would pay no attention to them. She pretended to be playing a game, saying in a loud voice, "You are a very thirsty deer, aren't you?"

Anna fell to her knees and dipped her face into a pool formed between some rocks and took a long drink.

"Good girl." Ruth patted her sister's head. "Is that enough?" She didn't wait for Anna to reply but grabbed her hand and led her quickly past the women.

One of them waved and smiled. Another narrowed her eyes. "Aren't you Haran's and Hannah's daughters?"

Anna began to nod but Ruth nudged her and answered in a firm voice. "No ma'am. Our mother is expecting us though." She broke into a run, dragging Anna away as fast as Anna could go. They came upon the water-well where Anna drank more water. Ruth did too, suddenly realizing her mouth felt very dry and her lips were cracked. Soon, they approached the city gate but did not go in. Ruth led Anna under the shade of a tree. The sun, now high in the sky, was approaching its high point, the hottest time of the day. Everyone would be finding cool places to rest until later. If they waited a little while all the streets would be deserted and no one would see them. She suddenly knew exactly where she was going to take Anna to hide her. The abandoned house.

She'd always wanted to explore it. She'd often tried to convince Orpah to go inside the empty courtyard, but her friend had always refused, afraid they'd get into trouble. Ruth had no such qualms and never had. She waited as long as she was able to sit still and then drew Anna through the city gate. As she'd expected, they saw no one, but as they darted along the cobbled lanes between the houses, they heard the booming laughter of men from inside one of the dwellings. Ruth froze, fearing they might be seen, fearing these men might be priests.

They had no choice but to keep going, and though it seemed further than she'd remembered, Ruth quickly dragged Anna through the low arched entrance into the deserted square of the empty house. They crouched against a wall and waited until all they heard were their own fast-beating hearts. After their breathing calmed, Ruth, stepping over the weeds sprouting from cracks between the cobblestones, headed toward the mud-brick house at the back of the yard. They passed a bone-dry earthen water trough that must have once been used for livestock. Only a few shriveled donkey droppings remained. Ruth took Anna over to the small, deserted house and they climbed up a ladder to the roof where they found a few old blankets and some broken pots.

"I want to go home!" Anna wailed.

"You must wait here," Ruth told Anna sternly, "until daddy gets home. You will be safe in the village, but you can't go out. I am going to Orpah's to get you something to eat. Do you promise to stay right here?"

Anna nodded but her eyes narrowed in a frown.

Ruth hugged her little sister and forced herself to leave, climbing carefully down the wooden rungs of the ladder, hoping Anna wouldn't follow her again. She jumped the last few feet, landing with a thud. When she looked up, there was no sign of Anna. "Stay there," she whispered. "I won't be long." She crept out of the yard, peeking out of the entrance, looking up and down the street to make sure no one saw her leave. She ran all the way to Orpah's house which was nearby. Her friend might be stupid enough to believe in Chemosh, but she'd be loyal, and her big jolly mother was sure to give her sweets and a flask of juice. She found Orpah outside tossing pebbles towards a ring.

Upon seeing her, Orpah grinned, jumped up, and hugged her. "You look all hot and sweaty," she said. "Where have you been?"

"Nowhere much," Ruth replied, unable to meet her friend's eyes. "Is your mother here?"

Orpah looked puzzled. "Why? She's inside."

Ruth did not want to try to explain anything and rushed into the kitchen where Orpah's mother was busy grinding dried corn. "Do you have any fig bars?"

Orpah's mother looked up. "Are you two going on a picnic?" she asked in her merry voice.

Ruth nodded, all the while trying to figure out how to prevent Orpah from coming with her.

Orpah's mother wiped her hands clean on her apron and found a few fig bars and dates and wrapped them in a kerchief. "You will need something to drink." She smiled. "Here." She poured water into a small ceramic flask decorated with green birds.

When the girls were outside, Ruth looked seriously at Orpah. "You can't come!"

Orpah's mouth quivered as if she might cry.

"I will explain to you later. There is a boy waiting for me."

Orpah gasped. "Ruth!" she cried.

"It's not what you imagine. I will explain everything later."

# Eight: Figurine

Naomi

Since we left Jerusalem later than planned, after a wonderful breakfast that included meat—not that I could eat much except bread and sour pickles—we ended up camping overnight near Jericho. I slept under a canopy and the men laid on their mats under the stars.

Just as the morning light was coming up, I sat on a boulder that had rolled a few feet away from the crumbled walls of the city ruins. The light of dawn made everything look gray. It hardly seemed possible our ancestor Joshua could have defeated people within such a massive fortification, but of course it was not him nor his army or even the trumpets that they blew when they marched around the city—it was Hashem. Joshua and his army were obedient to Hashem, who destroyed the city and their enemies, mainly people who worshipped idols and did unholy acts that flaunted the laws of Moses.

I wondered how obedient *we* were being by leaving Bethlehem. In spite of feeling a little sick, I stroked my belly, filled with joy at the hopes of this baby coming into a land of plenty. I prayed Moab would be a prosperous and safe country. Haran, the trader, was such a good man, a family man, who'd helped me have a lot more confidence about this move. He'd even put up this canopy for me to sleep under so I would not be in the open. I was so grateful to have the moon blocked out. I loved the moon, but right now it made me remember my last moments with Leah. I missed her so much but I did not want to go on crying. I had to get on with life and make the best of things and help my family to adjust.

It was early, and I was the first one to be up and about. Well, not about. I'd only got as far as a rock next to the ruins where I was sitting and thinking and remembering those wonderful women in Jerusalem who'd been so kind to us and had even given us food for the journey. I was going to drink some of the sweet tea they'd supplied to settle my tummy, and I planned on serving the men dried figs and thick slices of bread slathered with the dabaš that I'd preserved from pomegranates and grapes. My mouth watered and I hoped I could hold food down, but it felt good to have this quiet time and I was glad the boys and men still slept, strewn about on their sheepskins. I'd noticed the trader's bedding was yellowed from age and the wool was flattened from how often he must have used it. I found myself wondering what his wife was like and whether or not we'd like one another. I could hear Emilelech's labored breathing, but I knew he was fast asleep, no doubt worn out. Why hadn't he immediately accepted the hospitality of the gracious people in Jerusalem? It disturbed me to think of him all alone at night sleeping on a cold wooden platform.

When the sun, a fiery red circle casting a rosy glow on the ruins, began to rise in the Eastern sky, I noticed something glowing in the rubble, and I pushed myself off the rock and went over to look. I knelt down and scraped away pebbles to discover a small statue. At first I thought it must be a doll, but this figurine was so obviously fat-bellied with big swollen breasts that I knew she was a pregnant woman, probably a statue used in fertility rites. I'd heard whispers about these rituals from other women when we'd been sequestered in our tent during our monthly time of blood. We'd giggle at the idea of men and women having sex as if that would result in a good harvest. It seemed silly to us to imagine sex would produce anything more than a new baby, but certainly babies were the best harvest of all. I patted my belly.

I managed to raise the figurine out of the rocks. Her little arms held up her swollen breasts and her face was serene. I wondered if I shone with the new life in my womb. My breasts were not yet full of milk but they ached more than normal. Such an ache was not a burden but a blessing. I smiled to myself but I felt sad for the temple prostitutes who the statue probably represented and I wondered if they were ill-used. I wondered too about, Rahab, the mother of Boaz. What must her life have been like before she was married and escaped from Jericho? I remembered her from when I was a girl, always smiling and friendly. Was it possible that she'd been a prostitute? I had no idea and did not like to think of her as having to please any gods or any men in this way. She was a gracious and kind woman and had been such a good mother. I could not imagine her son Boaz ever being cruel or abusive. How fortunate I have been. Men have always treated me kindly. My husband Emilelech might not be a warrior or even a farmer, but he is kind and gentle. Almost always.

The base of the figurine was chipped and pitted but in the main she was whole. She seemed precious to me and quite beautiful. I did not know how my husband and sons would react to her, but I wanted to keep her. I was sure she'd bring us good luck and I hoped Hashem would understand. I mean I was not actually worshipping her but revering her, appreciating her, and protecting her as surely as I hoped she might protect my pregnancy. I quietly took her to the cart and dug out a robe and wrapped her in the folds of the cloth. I kissed her swollen belly. I managed to tuck her under one of the struts to the loom at the bottom of the cart next to my basket full of jars of spices.

While I rummaged in the cart, my son Mahlon awoke.

"Morning, Mama." He pushed aside the blanket I'd covered him with and rubbed his eyes sleepily. "What's for breakfast?"

"Something tasty," I said with a smile and got busy getting out the bread and the olive oil I'd brought with me as well as the figs and honey.

Soon, all the men got up, stretching and groaning and very hungry. I stood by watching, as they began passing around the bread, ripping off big chunks, slathering it with dabaš or dipping it in the olive oil I'd poured into a plate fashioned by Emilelech. It was quite beautiful, a little larger than my hand, a deep turquoise-color, etched with pictures of wheat. I treasured it because it was one of the first dishes Emilelech ever made and although he did not act pridefully about it, it was much prettier than the usual dipping dishes decorated with scribbles. I'd not been sure about putting it out, but I felt as if we needed beauty as well as food on this hard trek. It fed my soul. After the men were satisfied, I carefully picked up the dish and dipped my bread into the oil, sopping up all the dregs, grateful I was not yet queasy. I wrapped the plate in one of my older veils and put it with the other provisions I'd brought for the journey.

Soon enough, the men fetched the livestock that they'd hobbled and left grazing on a patch of thin grass near a trickling spring. The animals stood quietly as saddlebags were slung across their backs, ready for the next part of our trip. It was not far to the Jordan River where they'd get to drink their fill and hopefully find more pasture to sustain them until the following day when we would reach Haran's village in Moab.

I must admit to feeling curious about the village, and I also felt a surge of excitement to get to see the Jordan River. Many years ago the Ark of the Covenant was carried across it by the priests as they approached the promised land. When their feet touched the water, the river grew dry and all the people were able to cross safely. The river, it was said, was very high at the time, the water lapping over its banks. Yet it wasn't only this miracle that I was thinking about but also my aching feet and my swollen ankles. I couldn't wait to dip my feet in cool river water. I longed to wash my hands too as we normally did before and after our meals. My hands felt sticky from the olive oil and I knew that the men's hands must be worse. Not that they cared. Men!

The mules picked up their pace and even the old ox lumbered along a little faster, his head up, his nose sniffing. I couldn't smell anything other than heat and dust, but Haran said we were getting close to the river and the animals could already sense the water. I wished I could skip along like a girl but could only manage to hobble slowly next to my husband behind the boys and the donkeys. We'd been travelling only a short time but I was already fatigued. The sun stood about halfway up in the sky, scorching us with its unrelenting heat. Emilelech seemed to be striding along without effort which surprised me. I thought he'd be the one ready to collapse not me. He put his arm around my shoulder and gave me a hug. His arm felt heavy and I wanted to push him away, but I appreciated him staying in the back of our caravan with me. "Husband," I said. "Why did you not accept any hospitality in Jerusalem until I got there with Haran and the boys?" I suspected he'd slept outside because he felt ashamed, but his reply shouldn't have surprised me. He is a man who enjoys solitude.

"They are generous people, I know. And good cooks too, those women. But I needed to be alone to think and to pray. I wasn't sure and I am still uncertain that we are doing the right thing by leaving." He looked sideways at me and I could see sorrow and regret in his eyes.

I felt like slapping him but what good what that do? We were on our way and we could only hope our stay in Moab would be for a brief time. "Once I have the baby, perhaps we can come back."

"I hope so," he said and dropped his arm away from my shoulder and stared ahead.

The donkeys, hot under the sun, were beginning to smell. I had no doubt that they were as weary as I felt but I hoped that they would not get stubborn and refuse to go on. One raised his tail and dropped a stream of pellets. Chilion giggled as Mahlon dodged the steaming poop, but he grabbed a pellet and threw it at his brother's head.

Emilelech hurried forward, looking as if he might cuff the pair of them. "Do you not know this is holy ground?" he yelled. "The Ark once passed this way!"

"So where is it now?" Chilion sounded sullen.

"You know where it is." Emilelech rarely lost his temper but I could see the tips of his ears turning red the way they did when he got angry.

I rushed forward and grabbed his elbow. "Isn't it in Bethel?" I knew it was because Leah's husband and a group of elders once went there to see it. She said her husband had talked about how beautiful the Ark was in real life and how the golden cherubim sitting on the lid above the box seemed to glow, and how they had felt the presence of Moses, and how they had fallen to their knees in reverence. Personally, while I respected Hashem's covenant and the ten commandments, the idea of carrying those two heavy stone tablets inside the Ark along with all the weighty gold in the lid made me feel sorry for the twelve priests having to lift the poles that were threaded through the rings on either side of the Ark. Those priests clearly obeyed Hashem, but even with their strong arms and backs, it must have been difficult, especially since it was said that the tablets were weightier than normal stone because they were inscribed with the laws of Moses. Perhaps obedience to Hashem's laws gave the men extra strength and helped them to persevere on their arduous journey, but somehow the little figurine that was hidden in the cart signified something more important to me than all their strict rules, necessary though they might be. The little icon was a woman like me, a person I could relate to and understand. She knew about carrying babies and the strength and the commitment it took to birth and raise children.

"Look!" Haran cried.

Ahead of us we could see the twelve standing-stones taken from the river to memorialize where the priests' feet once stood while forty thousand warriors crossed. I once again remembered Rahab, the mother of Boaz, who'd been from Jericho. Suddenly I felt akin to her, doing what she must to save her family. I shivered at the thought of all those fierce men in their leathers with their spears and bows and knives.

We stopped and made camp near the standing-stones monument. Before long all the animals were watered in the Jordan. It turned out to be nothing but a muddy trickle rather than the gushing torrent I'd dreamed about. After the animals were turned loose, unable to wander far, but seemingly content to stay near the river, flicking insects off each other's backs with their tails, I was glad to find a rock to sit upon and remove my sandals and dip my feet. I didn't care if the warm gritty water discolored my feet as red as the nearby clay. Emilelech wanted time to pray and insisted the boys must do the same. I could tell they'd much rather explore the river and look for fish. But first things first. There would be all evening for them to have fun.

Later, after we'd eaten and I'd rinsed and put away our dishes, I quietly took out my little figurine, hid her in my robe, and hurried under the canopy that Haran had once again put up for me. Emilelech had helped him this time. I appreciated his effort yet couldn't help but notice how thin he was becoming, how often he needed to stop and catch his breath. It grieved me and I wished the tent could shield me from the sorrow I felt for this man. He'd done his best to provide for us. He still did in his way.

Under the flimsy covering, I lowered myself onto the blanket that I'd laid on the ground. As the sun sank, turning the horizon purple, streaked with gold, I closely examined the statue. She was not much bigger than my hand and seemed to be missing her feet. I had to fold the blanket around her so she wouldn't fall over. I felt almost as if I were wrapping her in warmth as surely as I wanted to be held by a strong man. I'd thought her carved from stone, but on closer examination I could see that her body was made from red clay, pitted and blotchy with age. Probably when she was freshly baked and taken out of the kiln, she was smooth, and yet the very antiquity of her weathered exterior pleased me. She seemed to represent all of us women and all of our struggles with birth. And with life. Her belly sticking out beneath her swollen breasts looked heavy, making her feel tired and hardly able to manage her household chores. She looked as if she were ready to have her baby at any moment. I imagined that she couldn't wait, but my stomach filled with acid remembering the births of my sons. I longed for my new baby but I was also afraid of the labor pangs. I wished I might be as stoic as this icon depicted, but she was only a statue who felt no pain. I ran my hands over her voluminous breasts. I almost expected her nipples to harden ready to be suckled. I remembered nursing my boys and the pleasure it gave me. It had caused me to lose all interest I'd ever had in making love with Emilelech.

I'd been surprised when he came to my bed a few months ago and we'd shared intimacy. I'd known that he felt needy and wanted to somehow assert himself, to make himself feel better, and certainly he intended to give me pleasure. His body no longer pleased me but I didn't let him know and pretended to enjoy his attention. I did enjoy the contact in a way, but I hoped he wouldn't make a habit of visiting me too often. When I did not get my period, I was shocked. I thought my days of having babies were over. This must surely be a blessing from Hashem. We were both so happy.

I stroked the figurine's face. She was featureless perhaps to typify all women. Maybe it was the change in scenery, or my being overly emotional from my pregnancy, or my having time alone without the usual chores and chatter of others to occupy me, but my mind seemed to dive deeply within myself and I felt sad. Was being pregnant what defined me? Was I not more than Naomi, mother of two sons? Could I not be more than a wife whose sole purpose was as a helper to a man? Would I ever once again be the pleasant lady who enjoyed fine clothes and kept a lovely house? Did that even matter? Oh, I loved being a mother and I did not think it a small thing to raise children but it all seemed so limited. My life suddenly felt as unimportant as a tattered robe.

I sat for a long time feeling lost, wondering who I might yet become? Was I to simply be a mother and a follower of my husband? Would I have to manipulate and scheme to get what I needed? And what on earth *did* I need? Certainly, I hoped to regain prosperity, have a roof over my head, and cook good meals for my family. But something was missing. As I stared at the statue, I felt as faceless as her, and though I might relish being a mother, it was not enough. Was there not something more I might become? Was I merely a vessel to satisfy my husband?

Emilelech poked his head under the canopy. I'd not heard him coming. My first thought was to try to hide the figurine but it was too late. I saw his look turn from curiosity to outrage as he realized that at my feet rested a pagan idol. I'd known of course what she was and that she was forbidden, but I'd been too lost in my own musings to consider that she might actually be dangerous for me to keep. Now, even though I knew women were stoned for possessing such an object, anger arose in me, and it wasn't only directed at my husband. My rage felt as if it might annihilate the whole world. It was anger at my powerlessness and anger at myself for never having seen until now how dependent I was upon a man, how defined I was by his needs, how little had been my opportunity to choose anything for myself.

I picked up the statue and hugged her to my breast. "I am not giving her up," I shouted. "I found her in the ruins." It was an odd justification but I felt as if I too were broken rubble of no value. Yet, I hoped that somehow just like this figurine, I would endure any and all hardships. I hoped my sore feet would get better and that I would walk firmly and strongly and perhaps even defiantly. I did not know exactly what that might mean. Emilelech did not argue with me. Perhaps he feared my feelings and my determination. Perhaps he would wait until later to chastise me and throw away the statue. In any case, he backed out of my tent without a word.

# Nine: Concern

Naomi

I wanted to go out of our way down to the Salt Sea because I'd heard the water could heal anything and everything. I wanted it for Emilelech. He'd not said another word about my figurine but his energy had slumped. Now, he seemed so tired all the time that I felt guilty as if my disagreement with him had caused his weakness. Was it wrong for a woman to want to be more than just a wife and a mother of sons? But maybe Emilelech merely felt depressed to be leaving our home. I wanted to make him feel better and I kept up a spirit of enthusiasm, especially for the boys, by telling them stories about our people. They were ready to get to our destination and constantly asked Haran how much farther. So I told them how Jacob had to be patient and work hard before he got to marry Rachel, the most beautiful girl in the world. I knew they'd prefer tales of battles, but although I respected our warriors, I did not want my sons to take up spears. Further, my oldest boy was getting to the age when we must get a wife for him. But who could we possibly find? He'd rebuffed the girls we'd lined up for him when he was a young boy, and we'd decided to wait until he was older before selecting someone. The idea of a Moabite girl seemed impossible. Even if one were suitable, we wouldn't be able to afford a bridal dowry.

After we crossed the shallow Jordan river, the trail climbed higher and higher. It was so steep and littered with rocks and ruts that I thought the cart might tip over. But it wasn't our wagon that collapsed—it was Emilelech. Suddenly he slumped onto the ground next to me, and I cried out, and stood there helplessly, unsure what to do.

Haran quickly halted the ox, and the boys dropped the lead ropes to their donkeys. They all rushed back to us and together we managed to help Emilelech sit up. He leaned against my leg. Haran looked down at him, his eyes full of concern. "This trail is enough to try anyone's strength," he said with a half-smile. "Rest a while." He gave Emilelech a swig of water. It dripped down my husband's chin.

I felt disheartened. I doubted my husband had the ability to go on. He was not a man who'd ever valued strength. He'd never done much hard labor and he preferred his studies and his pottery. Clearly, we could not leave him alone in this rough terrain while we went for help. I stared at the cart and knew we would have to get him into it so that he could ride the rest of the way, but my fine loom was taking up much of the space. "Haran," I asked and almost choked on my words. "Can we unload the loom to make room for Emilelech? Surely we can come back for it later." I seized my tongue between my teeth to stop myself from crying.

"No!" Emilelech said weakly. "I will ride on one of the donkeys."

Haran looked at him doubtfully. "How will you be able to keep your balance and what will we do with the gear loaded onto their backs?" He shook his head. "I will back the cart up and we will make room for you." He avoided my eyes.

I could hardly bear to watch as Haran took the wooden frame and the warp weights and cast them to the side of the trail. This Moabite man was strong and he made my handsome loom that I'd woven tapestries and blankets upon look flimsy. I tried to tell myself that my husband's well-being was much more important but I knew my loom could never be replaced. I doubted if we would ever be able to send someone back from Haran's village to retrieve it before it fell to pieces.

Haran told the boys to untie the mules from the back of the cart and bring them and the donkeys forward. The beasts kicked at one another, but the boys tugged hard on their lead ropes and settled them down. Haran patted the neck of the ox, firmly gripped the yoke with one hand, and put his other hand beneath the creature's chin. "Hai," he cried and pushed, yelling *back, back, back*. The faithful animal obeyed. Slowly, the cart's wheels bounced over the rocky debris on the trail back towards Emilelech. "Whoa," Haran commanded, and the wagon rolled to a stop.

"Wait," I said. "Let me move my cookware out of the way and put a blanket down for my husband."

It took Haran with Mahlon's help to lift Emilelech and get him situated in the wagon. He dragged himself as far into it as he could manage. I feared he would find my figurine and blame it for his weakness, but he flopped onto his side, leaning upon an elbow. His feet stuck out from the back of the cart. He did not look comfortable, but I'd done my best to pad the wooden base where he was resting.

Before long, our dreary procession made it up to the King's Highway. "Naomi," Haran said, with a glance back at Emilelech who was still slumped in the back of the cart with his eyes shut. "I will take your husband to Egypt when next I go. There are healing temples, and they have much understanding about bringing vitality back to people who are sick. They fix broken bones and cure fevers. They understand what dreams mean."

Could it be possible for Hashem to work through Egyptians? Why, the very road we were on was the same route Moses used to escape from their tyranny. They'd enslaved our people and treated them cruelly, forcing them to make bricks until they dropped from exhaustion. They'd killed our boy babies too. How often when we'd hear the stories told about our exodus, I'd be amazed at how Hashem intervened. Everyone was sure it was Hashem who'd made certain that baby Moses was saved by the Egyptian princess. Of course, I'd only learned this story from the women who'd heard it from their husbands. Sometimes I wondered if Hashem was as pleased with women as he was with men, but I'd been happy with my boys and being a housewife. I loved to add spices and herbs to cereals and see my family smacking their lips in appreciation. I loved to exchange recipes and try out new meals too. I did not understand my present discontent but expected things would get better. Did not Hashem always redeem us even when we had been disobedient or had forgotten all about him? Could he also redeem Egypt? After all, Moab was now a country we no longer despised.

Suddenly, I remembered those wonderful women in Jerusalem who'd been so kind, and I realized that they were the hands of Hashem. Why, surely the princess who took in baby Moses understood that he was a Hebrew but nevertheless she'd hired Moses' own mother to be his wet nurse. She must have known! She must have heartily disliked the idea of killing babies, even those of slaves. I wondered, as I felt a spasm in my belly, if she'd ever had her own children. I wished it might have been so. She must surely have been a good person, so perhaps I could trust Emilelech in the hands of those Egyptian healers. And come to think of it, until I'd met Haran, I'd had no use for Moabites, but Haran was opening my mind in so many ways. Or perhaps it was Hashem broadening my understanding.

Eventually the main route became smoother and wider than the rough track we'd been on, but our animals were worn out. Their heads were hanging, and they needed to be pressed forward with the whip. Only our old ox, without urging, plodded steadily along. We rested the animals for a while near a flowing spring. The water was sweet-tasting, and everyone felt better and soon were ready to get going again. Surprisingly, even my sore feet felt a little stronger, and Emilelech looked more alert too. He insisted he could walk, and I was glad to see him standing on his own two feet, but I felt resentment at having left my only source of income and my most treasured possession in the dust.

"We will reach my village before nightfall," Haran promised.

The boys whooped and Emilelech smiled weakly. I too felt a surge of gratitude, but it didn't last long before doubt filled my mind. How would we be received? Where would we live? How could we possibly earn a living, especially now? Without my loom I could not make blankets or cloth for the market and Emilelech had no potter's wheel. Oh, I wanted to trust that Hashem was much more powerful than us. He sent plagues on the cruel pharaohs and rescued the people from slavery, but what of the famine in Bethlehem? Did it not mean Hashem was displeased? I shrugged off my worries. I must trust. I must believe. I wanted to. I really did. I felt awfully small, though, small and helpless.

As we trudged along with Emilelech and I following along in the rear, I stared at the rocky terrain on one side of the road. It seemed a dead and hopeless place where nothing could survive. Way below us in the distance we caught bright blue glimpses of the Dead Sea. It hardly seemed possible something bluer than the sky could be undrinkable. I'd expected it to be as white as the salt it yielded for burials. On the side of the road away from the sea, sands stretched out into a vast undulating world that looked forbidding. It amazed me to come across springs trickling into rocky basins within green oases. Hashem truly must be able to bring something out of nothing. Yet, it wasn't until evening when we began to notice scrubby shrubs sprouting in the poor soil that I began to have real hope. When we came across fields of wheat almost ready to be harvested, my heart soared. In the ebbing sunlight, the spikes of grain shone like polished gold.

Haran left the ox plodding along and came back to us. "About another hour and we will arrive," he announced. "My compound is on this side of the village. You will all be staying with me of course."

I wanted to hug Haran, but I adjusted my veil to hide my eyes because I didn't want Emilelech to notice my pleasure. I mean I'd hoped and expected that Haran would give us lodging until we could find our own house, but until the offer was made, I had no idea if we'd be sleeping out under the stars again.

Emilelech, who was hobbling along with one hand on my shoulder, nodded. "You are a good man, Haran. We thank you."

Haran bowed his head and hurried back to the ox to stop it from veering off the trail into the fields.

The light was ebbing, dusk upon us, when we turned off the King's Highway and wound down a lane to stop at the entrance into Haran's courtyard. I could make out many small rocks in a decorative wall that circled around the compound. Haran got a wooden key out from one of the mule's saddlebags. It was longer than the ones we used at home, as long as a child's forearm. He thrust it through a hole in a small door and ducked inside. Soon, he reappeared swinging open a much wider wooden gate. We crowded through the opening with the cart and the donkeys and mules clattering behind. In the fading light I could see four square houses with flat roofs much like the ones back home.

We had hardly gotten the gate shut behind us before men rushed out of their houses and gathered around, eyeing us curiously. Haran hooted with laughter and slapped one man on his back. No women came out, but I could see faces peeking from their doorways. "Come." Haran threw his arm around Emilelech's shoulder. "Come into my house. Let these others who are young and fresh take care of the livestock."

The boys and I followed Haran and Emilelech towards a house. Within, I could see an oil lamp glowing from a downstairs room. Two women who were waiting for us did not even get a chance to say hello when a little girl with wild black hair raced out and threw her arms around Haran's waist. "Daddy," she cried. "You're home at last!" She paid no attention to the rest of us.

She was about the same age as Mahlon so I knew she must be his oldest daughter, Ruth. Her wild hair looked almost as untamable as her spirit. She looked so much stronger than my boys, and I noticed Mahlon eying her curiously. She seemed intent on ignoring us, and when she noticed my sons, she scowled. The lady whom I assumed must be her mother, Haran's wife, took her arm and pulled her away from her husband. She told the girl in a stern voice to go back to bed. The girl reluctantly disappeared into a nearby chamber, casting a furious look in my direction.

Haran threw his arms around his wife and hugged her. She looked embarrassed and drew away, but Haran did not notice her hesitation. "I must go in to kiss my beautiful Anna," he said.

"No!" his wife cried and stared at the floor.

Haran turned around and walked over to her and gently lifted her chin. "But I must say hello to her and even if she is asleep, I must give her a kiss."

"She is a princess now," Haran's wife said, still staring down, her voice shaking. "The priests took her for Chemosh."

I'd heard this god, Chemosh, demanded child sacrifices. I'd thought it must be an ugly rumor. There again, we women talked about how Abraham in what he thought obedience to Hashem once prepared to sacrifice his son Isaac. We of course could not openly disagree with our men, who rarely discussed religion with us except to tell us how to behave. But we thought it was an abomination and that Hashem would never ask such a thing of a mother. We thought such submission went beyond common sense. We did not understand how obedience to Hashem could ever result in the death of a son or a daughter. In fact, we thought the angel who set Isaac free must have been a woman who was flesh and blood, not some spiritual being as wispy as a cloud.

I have never seen a man go from joyous reunion to such irrepressible anger the way Haran did. Emilelech looked stricken and he went over to Haran but what comfort could anyone give to a father who has just learned that his beloved daughter is dead? Haran shrugged him away. Emilelech's eyes met mine, and he looked so frightened that I immediately worried about our children and our unborn child. What had we done by coming to this place where the god they worshipped required humans as offerings? I wanted to grab my family and head right back to Bethlehem. At least in our hometown only the weather was threatening.

Haran looked as if he might explode and strike his wife. Perhaps because I knew he was a gentleman in every sense of the word and an immensely kind man, I found courage that I did not know I had. I stepped between him and his wife who was now cowering with her hands over her head. He moved me out of the way and stood very still, glowering like a storm cloud about to burst with hail.

Ruth came dashing out of her room and wrapped her arms around him. "It's all right, Daddy," she said. "I know where she is."

Haran did not seem to hear.

I gently took Ruth's hand and tried to lead her away, but she would have none of me, and snatched her hand away. She was clearly a very strong-willed girl.

"Daddy," she shouted. "I know where she is!"

"Not now!" Her mother who'd regained control of herself forcibly rushed Ruth into the nearby chamber and drew a heavy drape across the opening. "Stay there!" she shouted. Her eyes locked with mine as she took in my swollen belly and my swollen ankles. "You look worn out. You must need rest. But first we will fetch food." She clapped her hands and directed the other woman, clearly a servant, to prepare a meal.

The thought of anything to eat right at this moment, even bread and honey, made me feel like retching. "Just water, please."

Haran's wife stared after her husband as he stormed up some stone steps to the second floor. She told her maidservant to fetch me my water, and to also get cereal and fresh milk for the boys and Emilelech. "Please," she looked at me imploringly. "Would you mind going in with Ruth? She is so upset. Perhaps you can comfort her. I need to talk to Haran." She rushed up the stairs after her husband.

I was grateful to not have to climb those steep steps, and after I had accepted a drink of water, I gladly went into the room where I found Ruth sitting in a corner on a sheepskin rug. It was very dark, but I could she was hugging her knees. We could hear the angry voice of her father from upstairs and the softer murmurings of her mother. I had no idea what to say but tried to reassure the little girl. "Everything will be all right," I murmured. I knew how much her father loved her and her sister Anna. I could not understand for one moment how awful it would be to lose a child, but I knew how bad I felt about leaving my friend Leah, and she was still alive. I lowered myself next to the little girl and leaned my back against the wall. Though I was tempted to stroke her hair, I knew better than to try to touch her.

"Anna is alive!" she whispered. "Why won't anyone listen to me!"

# Ten: New Friend

Ruth

Ruth heard her father's footsteps storm upstairs and thought she would creep up to him during the night, but her mother sent in the Hebrew woman, Naomi. The young girl sat hugging her knees, more angry at her mother than ever for separating her from her father. She could hear them arguing but could not make out what they were saying. She knew her father would listen to her if she were only given a chance, but her mother obviously would stand no disobedience. What if she, Ruth, were given to Chemosh too? Not only did she feel something like thunder rising in her chest, but she also worried that if something happened to her no one would be able to help Anna. She thought perhaps she ought to fetch Anna right now and they could run away. But where would they go?

Ruth knew this foreign lady meant to be kind, but it seemed that all the grownups thought she was a silly girl making things up. She was imaginative, that was true, but she'd always tried to be kind and helpful. As the foreign woman sank down next to her, she felt the warmth of her body and felt strangely comforted. Perhaps she could take Anna to this lady's hometown. Father often brought a friend or two from Egypt but never anyone from Judah. Still, these people would no doubt finish their business and go back where they'd come from. Maybe she and Anna could go with them. Her father, though, would make sure everything would be all right again. He always did. He might never forgive her mother though. She certainly would not!

Ruth flopped onto her side and pretended to be asleep. Her father's heavy footsteps clumped down the stairs, and he went out into the night. Ruth lay there in the dark, terrified her father was going to seek out the priests. They would outnumber him and what would happen then? She could not bear the idea of losing him. Maybe she could sneak out later when everyone was snoring but what could she, a mere girl, do? She squirmed and tossed and turned for hours. It was a wonder she did not wake Naomi. She could hear the lady's deep exhausted breathing. Ruth listened intently to the sounds of the night, hoping to hear her father return. At last she heard his footsteps and managed to fall asleep.

Her dreams were full of strange colors and staring faces. It was a great relief to wake up and feel Naomi's arm slung across her waist, but she gently moved the arm to one side and quietly crawled past the sleeping woman. As she peered beyond the drape into the room glowing golden from an oil lamp, she longed to go to upstairs to her father, but she didn't want to have to climb over her mother and the servant who slept at the foot of the stairs. She crept past the two sleeping women and went out into the courtyard.

She stood for a while just outside their house and took a deep breath of the fragrant air, listening to the hum of insects while she gazed up at the sky. The bright shining stars filled her with wonder. The moon looked like the silver blade of a scythe.

"Is it not beautiful?" A voice startled her.

It was the older of the Hebrew brothers, the one who'd stared at her. She felt uncomfortable but refused to show it or run back into the house. He had no business being outside anyway. He ought to be up on the roof with his father and brother. It was where guests were supposed to stay.

He began to talk again, and she found herself listening intently so that she could understand him. He was speaking Hebrew but he sounded different than anyone she knew. "Did you know the moon is in charge of the night?" he asked.

She did not know what he was talking about, and she hated how easily she was being distracted, yet she could not seem to help her curiosity. "The moon is so pretty but how can it be in charge of anything? Is it a man?"

His voice sounded gentle and full of good humor. "Oh no. Not a man. But from Hashem who put the lights in the sky to mark our sacred times. Hashem made the sun and the moon too. The sun rules over the day and the moon rules over the night."

No one had ever talked of such things with Ruth before. She found in spite of his strange accent that she wanted to learn more, but she felt awkward in this boy's presence and she had important and urgent business. "When my father was out here, did you talk to him?"

He hesitated. "No. He did not see me. He was punching the wall and shouting at the sky."

Ruth frowned. "He is very angry," she muttered.

"I know. He might not have appreciated me wandering around his house. I hid in the kitchen until he came back inside and went back up to the roof. Then I crept outside. Do you think I was being cowardly?"

Ruth stared at the boy's face, pale in the gray light. "Are you? A coward?"

"Sometimes I think my whole family are deserters," he confessed. "There is a famine in our land. My parents were afraid we would starve. We left as the morning dawned and it has been a wretched time. We left all of our friends and family. I want to go back and make things right, but how can I?"

Ruth understood his helplessness. It did not seem as if being a boy gave *this* boy, at least, any say in his future. "It seems to me," she said quietly, "that you and I don't have any choice."

"I know."

"What did you do to make this god of yours so angry that he would starve you to death?"

"I don't know but it is said that punishment is what happens when the people do not obey Hashem's laws. There are consequences we cannot change."

Ruth stamped her foot. "Your Hashem is no better than Chemosh!" She felt so furious that she had to do something, and she did not want to reveal to this boy, even though she was beginning to like him, that she knew where Anna was. What if he tried to follow her? "I have to feed the goats." She quickly rushed to the goat pen and threw in handfuls of dried grain. One of the baby goats bounced up and down as it waited for its oats. She always counted them just as she'd been taught to make sure they were all safe. In the dark, even with so many shining stars and the sliver of moonlight, it was hard to tell as they crowded one another if they were all there.

She glanced towards the small pedestrian gate. Its bronze hinges reflected the moonlight but its wooden uprights looked dark and impenetrable. Her teeth clenched at the thought of leaving the safety of the courtyard to go out alone into the dark. She wished she were like one of the black-horned goats that butted others and showed no fear.

The boy was still outside as she made her way back towards the house. She felt strangely protected by him, and almost asked him to help her raid the kitchen for food to take to Anna. Could he be trusted? She hurried past him, saying nothing.

In the kitchen she quietly filled a basket with dried fruits and flatbreads. She found a jar of honey and a flask of olive oil that she sat upright so it would not spill. She took a string of dried dates and even considered taking a string of garlic but she'd have no means to cook anything. She found an empty water-skin, deciding to go to the well to fill it before anyone else got there. The basket of food didn't feel heavy enough and she wished she could find more scraps but this would have to do. Ruth took the basket over to a corner in the kitchen and threw a cloth over it to hide it, planning to get it in the morning.

Soon, she quietly lowered herself next to Naomi, deciding that the very moment she heard her mother getting the morning meal ready and knew that the sun was rising, she would sneak out and try to talk to her father. The trouble was that she fell fast asleep and did not wake until she heard a mule braying. She rushed outside in the early light in time to see her father riding away. He didn't even close the gate behind him.

She wanted to run after him, but her mother came outside and tried to put an arm around her shoulder. "He is furious," her mother said, her voice trembling. "He won't listen to me."

Ruth felt like yelling at her mother but she bit her tongue and stepped away, hiding her clenched fists behind her back. Her mother sighed wearily and went over to the open gate, dust from the mule's hooves still whirling into the air. While her mother stared vacantly down the road, Ruth did not hesitate. She quickly retrieved the basket of food and slipped out of the house, hoping her mother would not turn around and see her hiding it under a pile of hay outside the goat pen. Several animals trotted over to her, hopeful for more grain, but she'd already fed them. It wouldn't do to give them too much grain that might cause colic. A little hay would not hurt them, though, and it would quiet their bleating, so she tossed in an armful of the dried grass.

Once, years ago, one of her favorite nanny goats had been swollen with colic, striking at her belly with her rear legs. The poor goat had been moaning and uttering pitiful bleats. At the same time, she had heard her mother in the women's tent also crying out during the pangs of childbirth. Ruth thought the goat must be having a baby too and was terrified that the goat and her mother were both going to die. Fortunately, her father knew what to do for the sick goat and she'd survived, and her mother later brought Anna into the world. Ruth loved her dark-haired sister immediately. Everyone did. Everyone petted her and spoiled her. Ruth couldn't understand how her mother who'd cradled and nursed Anna could have so easily let the priests take her.

She watched her mother close the gate and go back to the house, her head drooping, her hand over her heart. "Ruth," her mother called. "I need you to help me in the kitchen." She sounded so defeated that Ruth felt a pang of sorrow.

As she approached their house, Mahlon came out into the yard, yawning, obviously tired. He smiled and half-waved to Ruth. His eyes looked red and watery. Ruth wondered if he'd gotten any sleep or if he'd stayed out all night under the stars. She had more important matters on her mind than to worry about him, though. Somehow she had to get away from her mother and go to Anna. Her sweet little sister must be famished and probably more frightened than ever. And what if the little girl left the safety of the abandoned house and the priests found her?

Ruth went over to the boy. "Hello, boy, " she said and wondered once again if he could be trusted.

Mahlon smiled and rubbed his eyes. He looked at her kindly.

"I need you to do something for me. It's very important and you cannot tell anyone."

"What's that?" He eyed her curiously.

Ruth heard her mother calling again. She was tempted to grab the basket and dash out of the courtyard, but her mother might well come after her. "Please," she said, "hidden in the hay next to the goat pen there is a basket of food. I need you to fetch it and take it outside and put it under the thorn tree near the gate. The tree is old and twisted. You cannot miss it but be careful not to get scratched." It was not only that she didn't want him to hurt himself; if he came back bleeding, surely his mother would be upset and demand to know where he'd been. She grabbed his hand. "You must do this. I will explain everything later, I promise."

"I will," he said, gently squeezing her fingers.

Ruth snatched her hand away and rushed over to the house, passing the boy's mother, who'd just come out and was smiling gently. "What were you and Mahlon whispering about?" she remarked.

Ruth thought fast. "Food," she said. "We were talking about how hungry we are."

The lady smiled and called out to her son. "Mahlon, come in. Hannah has prepared us a meal."

Mahlon nodded. "I'll be right there, mother."

Naomi took Ruth's hand. "Come on, let's get something to eat." She led Ruth inside, not paying attention to Mahlon who was strolling towards the goat pen.

Inside, everyone sat around a low table in a small alcove next to the kitchen. The maid brought earthenware cups for everyone and put them on the table. "Pour the spiced juice," Ruth's mother told her as she put down a bowl of fruit and two flatbreads. "I hope you like this," she said, her voice cracking as if she might cry.

Ruth felt a hint of sympathy. She picked up the carafe of juice, inhaling the fragrance of the pomegranates, and made her way around the table, serving the men first before helping the maid fetch bowls steaming with hot stew. Her mother was standing at the window-opening staring outside and did not make any attempt to help.

They'd all begun eating before Mahlon reappeared and took his place next to his father. He nodded at Ruth and she knew he'd done as she'd asked, but she could not stop fidgeting and hardly ate anything. As Ruth's mother continued to stare out the window, Ruth slowly got to her feet and backed away from the table. Without a word to anyone, she darted out of the house, ran to the small gate and rushed outside. Mahlon had put the food basket under the tree and partially covered it with leaves. She grabbed the handle of the basket, lifting it carefully so as not to break any of the jars. "Anna, I am coming," she whispered.

To her surprise, Mahlon suddenly ducked through the door and came running out to her. "What's going on?" he asked.

Ruth looked his kind face up and down. "My little sister is waiting. An angel cut her free. I found her and have hidden her away from my mother who gave her to the priests."

"Is she all alone?" The boy sounded alarmed. "We must go to her immediately! She must be terrified."

Ruth thrust the empty water skin into his hands. "You take this and fill it. There is a waterhole on the way." Without another word she began to run towards the village. Mahlon raced after her. Ruth stopped only long enough to gesture down the path leading to the well. "Once you have filled it come directly into the village," she murmured to the boy, who stood doubled over, catching his breath. "You will pass a big house, bigger than all the others, and a little farther along on the other side of the street, you will see an empty house where I will be waiting."

He nodded and soon made his way down the path, passing two women who were balancing earthenware pitchers on their heads. They looked at him in surprise and then at one another but soon continued towards Ruth. She did not recognize either of them and was relieved when they stopped and shifted their water jugs onto the nearby poles used for resting the heavy containers.

It did not take Ruth long to reach the vacant house. No one in the lane paid any attention to her. In her head she prayed, *help Anna, help Anna.* She did not know to whom she addressed her plea, certainly not Chemosh, and definitely not those priests, and as for her mother, she did not even want to think about her. As soon as her father came back, she would bring him to Anna.

She ran through the messy courtyard of the abandoned house, trampling the weeds that sprouted in between the stones. At the base of the ladder, she looked up and called, "Anna, I'm here." There was no reply. Ruth's heart, already beating fast, seemed to form into a hard knot. She put down the basket of food and climbed hand over hand up to the loft. Anna lay crumpled in a corner on the dirty blanket. She looked sound asleep. Ruth rushed to her side and kneeled next to her. At first she thought Anna was dead, but at last she noticed her chest moving up and down ever so slightly. "Anna," she whispered and stroked hair away from her little sister's forehead. The girl was hot and clammy. Ruth called her name again, "Anna." The child stirred slightly but did not open her eyes. Ruth hugged her knees and rocked back and forth. She did not know what to do. Anna had a fever, and only too often those who took ill did not survive.

As she sat there, trying not to cry, she'd forgotten all about Mahlon, but his gentle voice from below startled her. "Ruth, are you up there?" How glad she was to hear him. She scooted to the edge of the loft and looked down. "Anna is sick," she cried. "What are we to do?"

Mahlon soon joined her and brought the skin of water with him. He took one look at Anna, and his eyes clouded. He dribbled a little water into her mouth and ripped a fragment off the blanket, soaked it, and laid it on the girl's hot brow. "You stay here with her. I will fetch your mother."

"No!" Ruth stared into space. "My mother will give her back to the priests. We need to bring my father. Fetch him."

"What if he's not back? Is there not someone else who could help? I will bring *my* mother. She will know what to do." Mahlon patted Ruth's shoulder and whispered, "Hashem, you who did not allow harm to our little ones and led us into freedom, help this little girl, Anna."

Ruth was strangely comforted by Mahlon's prayer, perhaps because he had called upon a father and fathers like hers could be trusted.

They sat for a while watching the sleeping child.

At last Mahlon started down the ladder, but he quickly climbed back up and thrust the basket of food onto the roof. "Someone is coming," he said. "I'll slip out once the way is clear."

Ruth lay on her belly, her face propped up on her hands as she stared across the shabby courtyard. She could hear sandals slapping along on the cobblestone path. Orpah's mother, carrying loaves of bread in her arms, strolled past the house.

"It's my friend's mother! She must be visiting someone." Ruth quickly backed away from the edge. When she'd gone to Orpah's house yesterday for food, she hadn't explained to Orpah that she was hiding Anna in this sorry little house. Orpah would not understand the need to keep Anna away from the priests of Chemosh. "Mahlon," she whispered. "We'll have to move Anna somewhere else."

"Surely your friend's mother will help!" Mahlon searched Ruth's eyes, but she shook her head, remembering how Orpah, and probably her family too, were devout followers of Chemosh. It would not do for them to discover Anna alive. "We must take Anna back to the threshing floor. There is a cave no one knows about."

Mahlon nodded but when they tried to lift Anna, they soon realized there was no way to gently lower her down the ladder to the ground.

"I will fetch my parents," Mahlon said. "Don't worry. They will help Anna." He scooted down the ladder and raced away.

As Mahlon's footsteps grew more and more distant, Ruth clutched Anna's damp hands and began to sing softly hoping her gentle words would make the little girl feel better, but beads of perspiration ran down Anna's cheeks and then she began to shiver. Ruth wiped her face and lay down next to her, wanting to cradle and rock her the way she had seen women comforting their babies.

# Eleven: Strength

Naomi

I could hardly believe it when Ruth dashed out of the house. Upset by the girl's sudden departure, we'd all gawked at one another. Then Mahlon went after her. I'd hoped my son was going to bring her back but he disappeared too. Hannah stared into space and said nothing. She went into the kitchen and did not come back out. I'd wondered how I might help this family but didn't think there was any way I could ease their grief. I only hoped it would not tear them apart. I had seen that happen to friends in Bethlehem whose children had eaten some poisonous berries. Before anyone could fetch the priest-healers, they'd convulsed and died. Two of them. It was agonizing. The parents blamed one another for allowing the youngsters to wander away from them while they were working in the field. But who, when they have to work, can watch little ones constantly?

I was hungry, but the stew Hannah had served smelled strong to me and I wished I had more of the sweet tea given to me by the women in Jerusalem. At last, Hannah returned and stood next to the table. She half-smiled but the dull look in her eyes gave away her depression and her anguish. Emilelech, with an apologetic glance at Hannah, said a quick blessing. She stared blindly at him, surely overwrought about her husband's anger. I vaguely remembered hearing their raised voices from the upstairs chamber, but I'd been so tired that I'd almost immediately fallen asleep. Clearly they had argued and no wonder: their little girl was dead. It hardly bore thinking about. But where on earth had Haran gone when his wife needed him?

I tried to help with clean up but Hannah wouldn't let me, and I realized it made her feel better to have something to do. I wanted my own house too and my own kitchen. Who knows where we would make our home? I hoped we would not have to stay in this unhappy household for long. I felt selfish to be only thinking of myself, but I disliked being idle, and being around people in such pain seemed to rub off on me and made me feel even more sad and lost.

I wandered outside, wondering how long Mahlon would be gone, worried about him in this strange new place. The smell of the crushed barley that two women were pulverizing in a stone bowl smelled sweet and pungent. Another lady was busy threading thick strands of flax into her loom. It looked none too stable for a heavy rug, but no doubt she had successfully woven many pieces before. I thought about going over and taking a look and talking to her, but I didn't much feel like being sociable. It hurt me to remember my loom laying in the dirt on that dusty road. Built as it was from the finest oak, it was surely sturdier than her unsteady one.

Our goods were still loaded on the cart, but the mules and donkeys had been unpacked, and the saddlebags were piled near an outer wall. I found the basket filled with my cooking implements and took it out of the wagon and soon found the flint knife given to me by my mother. I had always intended when the time came to pass it on to Mahlon's wife. It was an heirloom of little value, but I loved it and used it to cut meat.

Back inside the house, I quietly handed the knife to Hannah. "This belonged to my grandmother, but I would be honored for you to accept it." I hoped it would somehow raise her spirits. Hannah took the knife and ran her finger along the edge, a pensive look on her face. She nodded and tried to smile but her eyes were clouded. "This will come in handy. I will cherish it," she said in a monotone.

I wanted to cry for her and for Haran too. He was understandably angry, but he ought not blame his wife. She had no doubt been helpless to stop the priests who had all the power. I had tried to tell Ruth in the night that her mother was in mourning, but the girl had shrugged and turned away and lay on her side and pretended to be asleep. "Mahlon will bring Ruth back," I murmured to Hannah.

"She is unlikely to listen to him. Especially now. She only wants her father." She suddenly flung the cloth she'd been using to wipe out the bowls onto the floor. She tossed me such a look of agony that I thought she might be about to keel over. "I must find my husband!" She flew out of the door, her robe whirling behind her, the knife gripped firmly in her hand.

We'd been upset by Ruth's sudden departure, but she was a girl, and an unpredictable one who was deeply troubled. Hannah's shocking departure left us even more stunned. Even the servant stood with her mouth open. No one knew what to do. But what could we do? What on earth was in store for us in this Moabite town? I looked at Chilion's thin face. He looked so much like his father. I felt such a surge of love that it almost made me swoon, but it was accompanied by an alarming thought. What if this

Chemosh, the god of these Moabites required more children? I shuddered. Although Chilion was a few years older than Anna, who had been only about four, and Mahlon was older too, who knew what a pagan god and his priests might demand? And what about my unborn child? We were foreigners and what or who was to protect us?

My stomach began to fill with acid. I managed to get outside into the fresh air and stumbled over to the goat pen, fell to my knees, and threw up in the hay. I reached through the fence and dipped water from the animal trough and rinsed out my mouth. My husband and Chilion quickly came after me and helped me to stand. "Emilelech," I whispered. "We cannot stay here!"

The women who'd been outside went over to Hannah's maid and were staring at the gate and looking alarmed, talking in high-pitched voices, arguing about what to do. A tall lady in a flowing red robe wanted to send their husbands out to find Haran and also to find and fetch Hannah back. But another lady shook her head. "We don't want to get into any trouble with the priests," she said. "Haran has always been too impulsive. Even when he was a boy."

"What about Hannah?" a younger woman interrupted and put her arms protectively around her young child. "Hannah needs us!"

Emilelech stared at our ox in with the goats. It was steadfastly chewing on a few strands of hay. Emilelech and Chilion, one on either side of me, led me away, scattering a few chickens that were pecking around in the dirt. I stopped in front of our saddle bags and tore myself free from the men and tried to pick up one of the bulky bags, but it was too heavy for me to lift, let alone put in the cart. I needed help, but one look at Emilelech's thin arms, and I knew he'd not be able to do much. There seemed no way for us to pack our belongings and leave. I felt terrible for Hannah, but I had no intention of allowing my family to remain where we might be in danger.

"Emilelech," I cried. "You must go and fetch Mahlon."

"He will be all right," Emilelech said in a calm voice, one he always used with me when he thought I was emotional. Well I was! And with good reason! "Go and get him!" I demanded, amazed at how stubborn I felt and how defiant.

"I'll go, Ma," Chilion offered, but I grabbed his arm before he had a chance to make a move. "No! Your father needs to take care of us!" The words were hardly out of my mouth when I realized how insensitive I was being, but I did not care. I felt frightened and would have marched out the gate, found Mahlon, and taken both of my sons to the King's Highway and right back to Bethlehem, but Emilelech wrapped his arms around me. His face was so close to mine that I almost began to cry to see how sad he looked, how broken. I leaned into him. At last we let one another go. No one seemed to be paying any attention to us, having returned to their chores, but I knew they were listening to our every word and watching our every gesture.

Emilelech patted my back. "Come back inside and rest a while. We are all upset. Let us take some time to seek Hashem's help. Prayer will steady us and no doubt lead us in the right direction—as it always does."

Inside the house, Emilelech took Chilion up to the roof. I wanted to go too, and I wondered for a fleeting moment why men were separated from women when it came to matters of religion and matters of the heart? I went into the kitchen where the servant was busily cleaning up the breakfast pots and doing her best to avoid me. I could not blame her. She was probably embarrassed. I would be. But I had never been anyone's servant. I flopped onto a bench and willed myself to not feel nauseous again. Oh for some of that tea! I sat there so exhausted I had no words for anyone not even Hashem. I was glad when the servant girl, without looking at me, scurried outside to be with the other women. A strong sense of loneliness overwhelmed me. I felt disconnected from everything and everyone. Somehow I rallied and managed to get up and find a pitcher of water. I took it upstairs to Emilelech and Chilion.

As I had expected, they were sitting on a rug, their heads down, their hands over their hearts. Neither one looked up. I quietly put the pitcher and the cups down and, refusing to allow myself another moment of self-pity, went down the stairs into the sleeping quarters. I lay down and tried to sleep. I must have eventually dosed but for how long I did not know before I was awoken by Mahlon's voice. Relief flooded me.

"Mother, mother, wake up!"

I rapidly scrambled to my feet. "Mahlon, you're here! Are you all right?"

"I am fine, Ma," he said, hearing the alarm in my voice. "But Ruth and Anna need our help."

"Anna is gone, Mahlon," I said gently.

"No!" Mahlon raised his voice. "She is alive but she is ill. Her face is red and her forehead feels hot. Ruth is with her in a deserted house in the village but she is afraid that her mother will give Anna back to the priests. Has her father, Haran, returned yet?"

Emilelech and Chilion burst into the room. They must have heard Mahlon's raised voice. "We must pray that no one else will become sick too," Emilelech said.

It scared me badly to realize that Mahlon might also become ill just from having been near this sick child. It so often happened that fever spread and no one knew why. Still, sometimes children whose bodies felt as if they were on fire got better all at once. Some were bled but most were cooled with water-saturated rags. I did not really want to go but some inner voice told me that I could not let a child suffer without offering help. "Poor little Anna. She has been through terrible torment. I am going to her." I stared at my husband, daring him to object.

Emilelech nodded. "Very well," he said. "We will all come and we will do our best for the child."

As we followed Mahlon, I noticed the maidservant watching us. I hoped Hannah or Haran or both would return, and that she might tell them that we'd gone into the village. I did not think for one moment that Hannah would intentionally give her child a second time to the pagan god. No, I'd seen Hannah's grief and I'd seen Haran's rage. I threw the servant a pleading look but said nothing as we exited the compound.

Haran's house seemed isolated and far from the town. I was glad to pass a grove of leafy olive trees that looked well-watered and would bear abundant fruit. I took a deep breath and inhaled the earthy fragrance from nearby fields of green barley. The grain was not yet ripe enough for harvest but stood as tall as Chilion. At home, our crop, if there had been one, would already have been cut and raked into bundles to offer to the priests in honor of Hashem. We would be looking forward to a feast to celebrate. My sigh brought a glance from Mahlon who slowed down and squeezed my hand. "It's not much farther."

Although I was badly worried and my feet, in spite of my old comfy sandals, were already throbbing, the village itself pleased me because it was like Bethlehem with narrow cobbled lanes leading between flat-roofed houses. Smells of cooking wafted into the air. I also got whiffs of many goats, always a pungent odor I didn't much like, and yet it also reminded me of home. People here seemed much the same as my people, who kept their livestock in pens in their yards, people who wanted peaceful lives. Perhaps we could find a way to belong. Still I really wished we could go home. I was more than willing to endure the journey again just to be with Leah. Dear Leah. It would be such a comfort to share with her all I'd seen and experienced in the short time since we'd parted. She would be horrified to learn about little Anna. I wondered how the girl had escaped but it was of no concern at this moment. I felt fearful and trapped. It was one thing to give grain and goats to Hashem, but another to give up one's child. I surely would not. I would fight to the death to keep my boys safe. Haran's wife gave in too easily, I thought, my sympathy for her fading.

Mahlon led us into the courtyard of an empty house. He quickly scaled the ladder to the upper quarters. I dreaded putting even one foot on the moss-stained rungs. They looked old and rotten, but Ruth was peering down and yelling for me. "Lady," she cried. "Please help my little sister."

"I will go." Emilelech stared up at the girl, his eyes narrowed.

Ruth glared down. "No! She needs the lady."

"I'm coming," I said and gripped the upright and put my foot on a rung. Chilion was right behind me steadying my feet.

As I climbed slowly and painfully, Emilelech began to pray out loud, seeking health for the child. His words seemed to burn into my brain and somehow I made it to the top where Mahlon and Ruth grabbed my wrists and helped me onto the roof.

The little girl, like a sweet angel who'd lost her wings, lay crumpled on top of a dirty old blanket. I lowered myself onto my knees and stroked her hot face. "Anna," I whispered. "You are safe now." I could hear Emilelech continuing his prayers and I was grateful for his faith. I had no idea what to do for this child other than try to cool her down. I glanced over my shoulder at Mahlon and Ruth whose eyes looked big and frightened. "We need cold water," I said. Mahlon handed me a half-full skin. It was not that cold but it was better than nothing. I tore the blanket and used a rag to soak up some water. I wiped the girl's arms and hands before laying it on her forehead

"Who are you?" I heard a deep male voice say from below in the courtyard. "What are you doing in here?"

I peeked over the edge of the roof to see a tall man dressed in a short red robe with a wide blue silk belt around his waist. I could see the top of his turban and knew he must be a priest. Ruth had seen him too and looked horrified. I quietly put my hand over her mouth and indicated for her and for my boys to hush. As I held my breath, Emilelech bowed slightly to this priest. "Shalom," he murmured. "We are newly arrived from Bethlehem where there is a famine. We brought our sons and our little daughter who is now hot with fever. That is why we came to this empty house where she will not spread her sickness." Sometimes my husband was so wise, but I hoped his lie was not obvious. He continued speaking quietly, "We beg your indulgence to allow us to stay. We can afford little, but what few shekels we have, we will gladly pay to make this our home."

The priest took a step backwards away from Emilelech. "Why have you brought this sickness to us?"

"Sir," Emilelech said gently. "Our daughter only got sick after we arrived at Haran's house. It was he who suggested we must isolate her. No one else is ailing. But perhaps you could come up and take a look. We would welcome your sacred presence."

The priest hesitated. I doubted that he would help a sick child even if he could. And certainly he would do nothing for a sick foreigner. "You may stay here," he muttered, "but you are not to mix with anyone in the village unless the child recovers. If she dies, we will arrange to burn her corpse, and then you must leave. I live opposite in the large house with the orange tiles." With that he turned and walked rapidly away.

We went back to Anna who began moaning.

Ruth gently put her fingers on her sister's lips. "Shush," she murmured, and began to stroke the little girl's cheek.

I was worried the child was getting worse but all at once she opened her eyes and cried out, "I want my mommy!"

My eyes met Ruth's and we both sighed with relief.

# Broken Road

## One: Vision

### Boaz

Boaz kicked at the parched ground in Emilelech's field. The brown dirt was as hard as rock, crisscrossed by deep cracks. A warm wind swept across the ground and particles of dust swirled into the air. He'd worn a cloth over his mouth and nose, but still the grit stung his forehead and made his eyes water. Everyone's fields were in the same sad condition but looking at this wasteland in front of his eyes, now a desert that had once been a fertile field, he wanted to cry. He was glad Emilelech had taken Naomi and their boys away. Those lads were not strong and neither was their father. More than likely if they had stayed they'd be among the first to die.

Later, Boaz led a group of men out beyond the city walls to a nearby wadi, and even though it looked dry, they dug and dug, slinging aside sand and rocky sediment, hoping to get deep enough to find water, but there was not a drop, not even anything damp. After their final attempt, they stood around, their digging axes in their sore hands, sweat dripping from their brows, staring hopelessly at one another. "We might as well go home and save our strength," Boaz told them. One man nodded, using his sleeve to wipe the perspiration out of his eyes. Another shrugged, turned away and with shoulders drooping left. Boaz waited until they'd all gone. He stood by himself staring at a tall thorny cactus, acutely aware that the sap of this plant was not fit to drink and was known to make people sick, but those bright yellow flowers looked inviting. Boaz feared that if they did not get rain soon, people would likely rip open the prickly plants with their bare hands.

His mind once again went back to Emilelech and Naomi and their boys. He wished he too could take his family and leave. He knew Jerusalem had many cisterns and wondered if they were full and if there was a way they could go and fill their jugs and buckets and bring back water to Bethlehem. Would the people of Jerusalem, who were of the same tribe, help thirsty people from another town? Perhaps Emilelech might help by sending back grain, but they did not lack food. Their storehouses were full of enough barley and bundles of wheat to keep them going for a few more months, but without water, it wouldn't matter.

Boaz, as he trudged back to his house, stared at his feet in the sturdy sandals his wives had sewn for him. He could hardly bear to face their disappointment and instead went to Emilelech's house, entering the courtyard where a group of women stood near the goat pen, talking. As he approached, they adjusted their veils to cover their hair, and were silent. He suspected that they'd been complaining about the town elders and their lack of action. Who could blame them, and who could explain that there was nothing they could do, that their attempts to find water had been fruitless? He did not want to take their hope away. "Ladies," he said and bowed slightly. "Do you have any water left in your cistern?"

A woman Boaz scarcely knew answered, her voice bitter. "We drew a little muddy muck out yesterday but today there was not even enough to fill the palms of our hands. It is hardly fit for the livestock. We might as well turn the beasts loose to take their chances in the desert."

"It is the same for everyone." Boaz groaned. "Might I climb down into your cistern to inspect its condition? Sometimes cracks form and the water leaks away."

"What good will that do? We have no rain to replenish the tank."

"But at least we can be ready for when it rains."

"Do what you like!" one of them cried. The women watched him light an oil lamp, put it in a bucket and lower it into the cistern. Next, he secured a strong rope around a column and wrapped the free end around his waist and lowered himself into the hole. Below him he could see a few inches of water, so at least it was not entirely dry, but it was too shallow to fill any container. As he got to the bottom, his feet sank into the thick, muddy sediment. His wives would not be pleased with him for ruining their sandals. It almost made him smile. It also made him despair. Although he could see no cracks in the walls that needed to be sealed, there was nothing he could do down here. In the dark hole, though, it felt pleasantly cool and he was glad to be out of the hot sun. He leaned against a wall, wondering if the pit where Joseph was once abandoned had been a cistern.

Boaz remembered from the teachings that were passed down to the young men of the village how Joseph had survived the treachery of his half-brothers. Their anger was partly the boy's own fault for lording it over them. He should have kept silent about his dream where he'd seen them gathering bundles of grain into sheaves and then bowing down to him, implying that these brothers were nothing but piles of straw. He also might have kept quiet about the sun representing his father and the moon symbolizing his mother and tiny stars signifying his brothers. Surely he did not believe that all of them must bow to him. Surely he was not *that* arrogant. Yet it was as if he were chosen by Hashem for great things that no one could prevent. Who could have known this was prophetic? No wonder those jealous brothers had decided to get rid of him. No wonder he had ended up in a pit and eventually became a slave in a foreign land, yet Joseph never did blame Hashem and he never gave up hope.

Boaz waved his fist in the air. He knew *his* strength and *his* life were from Hashem just as surely as Joseph's was and that everyone lived through Hashem's grace--but surely they were not all to die of thirst? He wanted nothing for himself now except that his people might be glowing with health, not reduced to skeletons with bloated stomachs and dull eyes.

He could hear the voices of the women above him and looked up to see one of them peeking down. "Are you all right?" she asked.

He knew she had meant was his body all right, and he *was* healthy and still strong, yet he felt forsaken. He tried to make his voice sound optimistic to reassure her. "Yes, I am fine. Please pull up the bucket with the lamp." With his thumb and forefinger, he pinched the wick, dousing the flame, and she hauled it to the surface. It was not far and he soon climbed up, his face emerging into the room where the women were waiting. Hands grabbed his elbows and heaved him into the chamber. "There is a little muddy water at the very bottom, but it would be possible to take jugs down to scoop it up. You will have to send your husbands."

"We know," one of the women said shrilly. Another woman dropped to her knees and began wiping off his feet with a cloth. After she was done, he uttered words he wanted to believe. "Everything will be all right. We can trust Hashem."

Back at his house he could not bear to reveal how unsuccessful he and the other men had been in their attempts to dig a well, and he managed to get up to the roof without anyone seeing him. He could hear his children playing and was happy that they had no idea of the troubles that they faced. He took off his robe and lay on his back, staring at the hot cloudless sky. It was a relief to be alone. "Hashem, what must I do?" he prayed, aware of his helplessness.

Exhausted in every way, Boaz fell asleep and found himself in a deep and silent place. He was no prophet and did not feel as if he were much of a leader, surely not someone favored by Hashem in any way. Yet, he began to dream and somehow he knew this was a message. In his mind's eye he saw the elders gathered by the gate bowing their heads. In his dream, he effortlessly lifted large jugs above them and poured water until they were all soaking wet. It was as if they were being washed clean of sin. They were laughing and singing. A voice in his head told him he must recite the mighty deeds recorded in the Torah to the people. He awoke to find himself drenched in his own sweat, but there was still no sign of rain. What was he thinking to lay up on this hot roof? He got to his feet and threw his robe around his shoulders and hurried down to find shade.

He could not shake the dream. How was he, an ordinary family man and a farmer, to recite the history of the people? That was a job for the priests or for a scholar like Emilelech. As he sat brooding, he felt as bad as Joseph's brothers. He should never have followed Naomi when she left, but surely that could be excused as a desire for her good. He had acted out of love even if it were tainted with desire. Joseph's brothers, it seemed, acted entirely out of their hatred. How could they have betrayed their younger brother, planning to murder him the way they did? They were disobedient to the sixth commandment: thou shalt not kill. Why were they not punished? Joseph was the one who had suffered. He had lost his family and his home. Could Hashem have been strengthening him even while he was behind bars?

Boaz hung his head, remembering Joseph's vision about a coming famine that was to last for seven years. Seven years! Could this dream of his, his dream of water, and the command to regale the people with the stories of Hashem's great acts be important? The Egyptian king had listened to Joseph and they had put by enough grain to feed the people. But, unlike here in Bethlehem, these Egyptians also had plenty of water from their rivers and streams. Their problem was not as dire as that of *his* people. Boaz wondered why *did* Hashem help Joseph and also the people of Egypt and why did he *not* help the people of Bethlehem?

That evening after they gave thanks, they ate their barley cakes and dried fruit. His women and children sipped beer and got a little tipsy and could not stop giggling. Boaz felt his cheeks swell with laughter too. The love he felt for them went far beyond duty. He cried silently to Hashem for help. If he were being called to be a leader, somehow he would know what to do and what to say.

In the morning, Boaz trudged from elder to elder asking them to assemble everyone after the sun went down when it would be cooler. He told them he had a message given to him in a dream. The priests demanded to know what it was, but he told them he would only reveal it to the gathered people. At sundown, the long horns blown by two of the priests summoned everyone. Boaz thought of how such sounds once brought down the walls of Jericho.

As the people began to gather, Boaz wiped the perspiration from his head and greeted them. He felt shaky to have to address everyone and did not know exactly what he would say. The elders sat facing the crowd with legs crossed and arms folded over their chests. The priests stood nearby. After he climbed up onto the raised platform, he was glad he could not see anyone's eyes. He feared he had made a terrible mistake. Why had Hashem laid this task upon him? He took in a deep breath, gathered his thoughts, and managed to begin. At first his voice shook but he soon began to sound stronger. He spoke of how Joseph was innocent and yet suffered for many years. He reminded everyone of the seven-year famine and how even Joseph's deceitful brothers were given food and their lives were saved. Boaz told the people that they too, like Joseph, were innocent and were not being punished by the famine. One of the priests gasped out loud, but Boaz was caught up in a whirlwind greater than human power. Rapt faces stared at him as he reminded them how at first the people prospered under Egyptian rule, but after a new pharaoh gained power, they were enslaved and mistreated. They had done nothing to deserve their fate any more than the people of Bethlehem deserved to go thirsty.

All his fears forgotten, Boaz continued to recite many of the great deeds and miracles. He mentioned how the waters of the Red Sea parted for them, and how those very same waters drowned the bloodthirsty soldiers pursuing them. He spoke of how Hashem answered their cries in the desert providing them with quail and water. He spoke too of how Moses only became a wise and a strong leader through perseverance. "Moses said *yes* to Hashem even though he had a lot of doubts and was afraid. We too must say *yes* to Hashem and trust him. We are not perfect and often we make mistakes, but does not Hashem still take care of us?"

No one responded. There was not a whisper from anyone, not even from the elders. Glancing back at the priests, Boaz knew they were furious, and he realized that they considered him a threat to their power. He knew that they had emphasized sin over love because they wanted to frighten people so that they would be able to control them. "Hashem is in charge!" he said as much to himself as to everyone else.

At last out of the silence a voice spoke. It was Emilelech's cousin. "We need to show that we are obedient. We need to show our faithfulness."

Another man spoke up. "Let us fast, all the people, the children too, no food or drink."

Boaz jumped to his feet glad he was not alone as his fellows began to speak. "We must persevere for three days and allow the spirit to fill us."

People gathered every evening to encourage one another, and no one, not a child nor a woman, broke the fast. It was easy enough to give up bread since they had already been on such slim rations but giving up the remaining beer that had kept them alive seemed almost impossible, especially at first. Yet by the third day, tired and pale, they were resigned to their fate. They comforted one another and hugged and kissed each other and gave thanks. Boaz knew they struggled, but at last the fast came to an end.

On the final night when they assembled, it was so dark that no one could see the sky, but Boaz hoped against hope that at any moment they would hear thunder and be drenched with rain. People milled around, talking quietly. Everyone was waiting for him to tell them what to do next. When not a drop fell, he felt foolish, but he knew too that sometimes you had to wait on Hashem. "Be patient," he told everyone. "Climb down into your cisterns and fetch every last drop of water you can get. Bring it here. We will share it amongst ourselves so that no one goes away thirsty."

Water was siphoned and dredged out of all the cisterns and brought to the assembly. People poured the murky drops from jugs and buckets into animal troughs. There hardly seemed enough for twenty people, let alone the two hundred or so who crowded the courtyard.

The elders began passing out scoops full of water. There surely was not enough and yet the water never ran out. Everyone drank until they were satisfied. It was a miracle.

"Sing to Hashem for he is good and his mercy lasts forever," someone cried.

Then suddenly, just as in the olden times when Miriam and all the women rejoiced, the thumping of canvas tambourines and the tinkling of their bells filled the dark night.

# Two: Daughter

Naomi

As children often do, Anna soon recovered and began to long to return home. I so wanted to tell Hannah that her daughter would soon be back with her, but Ruth was adamant we wait until we were sure Anna was no longer in danger from the priests. There was no way to be certain of what the priests might do, and there was no way we could keep Anna hidden much longer. So I did not argue with her. Besides, Emilelech disapproved of us for not telling Hannah the truth. Mahlon, too, wanted to shout it to everyone. I suspected that, although he was glad for little Anna to be sitting up and able to eat, his main motivation was to impress Ruth. The boy kept silent though. Haran, alas, had been so crazed with grief that he had challenged the priests who had threatened him, forcing him to flee from town. Hannah had no idea where her husband had gone.

We were worried about Hannah who was depressed and barely coping, and after a few days, decided to risk bringing Anna home. One morning, just as the light was coming up, Ruth and I went to the abandoned house. Ruth quickly scrambled up the ladder, but I waited below, keeping watch. Once I heard Anna's happy voice, I too climbed that wobbly ladder. I was getting used to it, but did not like it, always afraid I'd fall and harm my unborn child.

"Are you taking me home today? You promised!" Anna cried.

"Yes," Ruth said, and her face lit up with a smile as big as a crescent moon.

The little girls hugged.

I made my way down the ladder first, afraid the whole time I would slip, but I made it to the ground and was soon helping Anna onto the cobbles in the yard. The two sisters held hands as we crept past the priest's big house. I hurried the girls along, terrified one of his household would see us and alert him. But somehow we made it safely to Haran's compound.

I woke Hannah who rarely got up early these days. We'd told her we'd been getting the abandoned house ready for Emilelech and my family to live. "Hannah," I whispered, gently shaking her shoulder. " Come into the kitchen. I have someone you'll want to see."

She looked at me from bleary eyes and crawled out from under her blanket. I wanted to hug her and shout that her daughter Anna was here, alive and well, but I did not want to alert her maidservant who was resting nearby. Although, I must admit, I had no idea if the woman could be trusted or not. Obviously, she and everyone else in the compound would soon know that Anna was back.

In the kitchen, Ruth had lit the oil lamps, making everything look warm and peaceful. She stood quietly, a slight smile on her lips, her arm draped around Anna's shoulder.

"Mommy," Anna cried, rushing over and hugging her mother around her waist.

I will never forget the look of astonishment on Hannah's face, but in one heartbeat her expression became filled with the sunshine of joy. She cried and laughed and held Anna at arm's length, feeling her arms, her legs, her waist, her hips, and her shoulders, and eventually holding her little girl's face in her hands and gazing into her eyes.

Ruth silently watched, but her tiny smile got bigger with every passing moment. I knew that she was afraid because she still had doubts about her mother, but clearly she was pleased at their reunion. I, though, was worried about what that priest who'd questioned us when we'd first been in the abandoned house would do if he learned Anna was not *my* child but Haran and Hannah's, the child intended for Chemosh.

When the maidservant came into the room, I once again worried about whether or not she could be trusted. What would happen if she, or anyone else, told the priests that Anna was alive? But her smile upon seeing Anna lit up her eyes and I felt better about her.

"Are you hungry, Anna?" Hannah kissed Anna's head, and smiled at Ruth. She got out flour and began mixing it with water, adding figs and nuts and honey to the batter. She shaped the dough into balls and flattened them with the palm of her hand. "While we bake these, we will bathe you and get you fresh clothes." She instructed their servant to put the pastries in the outdoor oven. "And once you have the fire going, please fetch water for Anna's bath."

"I'll get the water while the oven is heating," the woman said.

In Bethlehem, washing our bodies and garments was usually a ritual that we rarely wasted water for, but I must admit even though it upset me to remember the scarcity at home, I was glad Hannah was making a fuss over her daughter. She even fetched a pretty silk robe from an inner room. "I was so worried about you!" she whispered.

Anna smiled sweetly, obviously enjoying the attention.

Suddenly I *knew* who the angel was *who'd* freed Anna. I so wanted to tell Ruth that her *own* mother was the one who'd saved her sister, but I began to get abdominal cramps. It was way too early for my baby to come. Every ounce of my body clenched in terror. Only Ruth noticed and asked me what was wrong, but the pain became so intense that I dropped to my knees. A rivulet of blood ran down my leg and spread across the kitchen tile.

"Oh no!" Hannah cried and rushed to me, ordering Ruth into the yard to fetch the other women. "Wake them!" she cried.

By the time several ladies hurried into the kitchen, I'd collapsed onto the floor. They managed to get me onto my feet and half-carried and half-led me into a small tent at the very edge of the courtyard. I knew it was where they went during their monthly time of blood. They settled me onto a multi-colored blanket. It's odd how I noticed such cloth but I did. I had no time to cry but I wanted to scream every time I had a contraction. It hurt much more than when I'd had my sons and it was too soon. Oh, how I wanted Leah with me. Oh, how I wanted old Sarah, my granny woman. I was almost too overwhelmed with cramps to remember that she had died. Something was terribly wrong and there was nothing I nor anyone could do to prevent this baby from coming. It took hours and hours before at last my infant was born.

She was too small to survive.

After the birth, the women coddled me and cleaned me and hugged me, but nothing helped my wailing and crying or the weight I felt in my chest. I wanted to be with my own people in my own home with my best friend to comfort me. I knew the boys and Emilelech must be outside somewhere waiting to hear what had happened to the baby. My baby girl. This was worse than anything in the world, worse than leaving my home, worse than losing my life.

The women were going to take the baby away to dispose of her body, but I demanded she be left with me and that I wanted to be alone. They whispered together and after checking to make sure I was not still hemorrhaging, they left. I cradled the silent girlchild in my arms and sang to her as if she were alive. Rivers of tears blinded my eyes. At last, when I was calm enough to see again, I realized that young Ruth was alone with me in the tent. "I am so sorry," she said and stroked the baby's head, hardly bigger than the palm of her small hand.

"Oh darling Ruth!" I wanted to mend the rift between her and Hannah. I could not bear to think of her hating her mother. "Your mother is the one who substituted a goat for your little sister. I just know it. No mother would willingly allow her child to die." I stared at the limp infant in my arms and began to cry again.

Ruth wrapped her arms around me and the baby until I managed to stop sobbing.

"I want to swaddle her," I said. "Could you find me some white linen?"

She nodded and left.

While she was gone I began to lament. "Oh my little daughter, oh my little daughter..." I would not stop until she was entombed but I had no idea where I might bury her, and I knew there would be no feast and no others to mourn with me, not even my husband. He probably would not care since this baby was a mere girl. I understood only too well. When we were first married, I'd also only wanted sons.

Ruth returned with white cloth. I could smell goat on her and knew she must have checked the goat pen. "Were any missing?" I asked.

"Yes. One."

I did not need to say anymore. Ruth was very bright. She now knew it must have been her mother who had freed Anna. It comforted me to have helped *this* daughter, even though there was no hope for mine. Not in this world.

I wrapped my precious little girl tightly with strands of white cloth just as any healthy newborn child would be swaddled. After her little arms were tightly held against her sides and her little legs were also protected, I held her for a while, rocking her in my arms. She could not move and never would, but nevertheless I imagined her little body would soon warm up. It grieved me that this little infant would never become a happy child and experience the joy of raindrops on her tongue or playful leaps into puddles to splash everyone around her. At last, with a scrap of cloth, I managed to cover her delicate face, my mouth twisting in agony that she would never see sunlight or dance or have her own babies.

"I know a place where we can bury her," Ruth whispered. "It is near the sacred ground of the threshing floor."

I tried to stand but was too weak and collapsed back onto the quilt. I held the baby out to Ruth. "Take her," I said. "Be sure no wild animals can get at her. Can you do that?"

She looked stricken. Was I asking too much of a child? I thought so. "Fetch Mahlon, my son."

"In here?" she looked doubtful but quickly poked her head out of the canopy. "Mahlon, your mother needs you."

My oldest boy, defying tradition, entered the tent and rushed to my side. He did what I told him and with a sling from the remaining linen tied the baby against my chest. He helped me to stand. With one arm across his shoulder, I managed to stumble out of what, for me, was not a haven where women could be free from chores but a death shroud.

A group of men and women stood huddled together near one of the houses. The usual business of the courtyard was stilled. No weaving, no grinding, no pot-making, nothing was going on while they tried to decide what to do with me next. I had never felt so alone.

"Get away!" I yelled at Emilelech who approached with such a look of concern I knew I ought to be ashamed, but at that moment I hated him. I suppose I needed someone to blame and he became my scapegoat. I allowed only Mahlon and Ruth to help me. But I knew a crowd of people were following.

It is a wonder I did not start bleeding again, but I suppose Hashem in some strange way was with me in this horrible suffering. I had no prayers though. I felt too weak and too empty.

Ruth took us to an opening in the stone wall around the threshing floor. I stared at the crevice. "It's bigger inside," Ruth said. She put her hands under the baby, while Mahlon untied her from my chest. I wanted to close my eyes and discover this was a nightmare. Yet I was only too wide awake. Ruth gently laid the silent bundle back in my outstretched arms. She felt lighter than the feather of a dove. I felt so low that I wished I might die, but somehow I managed to hand the baby to Mahlon. "This is your sister," I whispered. Mahlon cradled the bundle gently, holding her head in the palm of his hand as he got down on his knees and crawled inside the tiny cave.

"Oh my little daughter...oh my little daughter..." I moaned.

Mahlon, after only a minute of two, backed out empty-handed and averted his eyes from mine. Together he and Ruth began gathering rocks to pile at the entrance of her resting place until the opening to my child's grave was sealed, forever.

I was spent both physically and emotionally and wanted to lay down, but Mahlon and Ruth, one on either side of me, supported me on the way back to Haran's house where I collapsed in a heap in the portico.

"Oh my little daughter...oh my little daughter..." I wailed, and to my surprise as tears sprang from my eyes, other women joined in my lament. "Oh, our daughter," they cried over and over again.

My voice grew hoarse before I rasped one final cry. Emilelech came to me then and lifted me up from the ground. In his eyes I saw both agony and gentleness. I wondered if he could ever forgive me for letting him down, for hating him so much, and I wondered if I could ever forgive myself or Hashem, who now seemed distant and cold.

What is worse than losing a child? I had known plenty of women who'd lost their babies during childbirth, and some of those women died. It was only now as I stood in the maw of death that I understood how much they had suffered. I'd been taught how after death the righteous and the unrighteous went into Sheol, a place of stillness and gloom. To think of my baby in a place of unending darkness distressed me beyond belief. Why could there not be sunlight and life and tambourines for innocent children? I felt as if I might as well die too and I did not care if I were cut off from Hashem. He had abandoned me. And why did he judge my people so harshly? Why had he caused me so much pain to give birth to a lifeless child? I was not Eve, disobedient, eating of the forbidden fruit. But I had no answers.

Emilelech held me gently, and for a moment I accepted the comfort he was trying to offer. In spite of my resentment and my anger, he still needed me, and my sons did too. For the first few days after the loss of my baby, they helped me go to the tomb where they stood around awkwardly while I mourned and cried. Tears formed in Emilelech's eyes too but I felt numb towards him. I could not pray but I felt sure the spirit of my baby lingered. I talked to her telling her how much I loved her, and how sad I was that I had not been able to carry her full term.

Once our belongings were moved to the abandoned house, my sons and Emilelech along with

Haran's kin helped set up our household. The women scrubbed the rooms until they smelled fresh. I felt dull and listless, unable to do much. Everyone reassured me, telling me to rest. How kind they were. At long last, after my house was empty of strangers, and my sons and Mahlon lay sleeping on the roof, I searched for my statue. I found her laying on one side next to some bowls. I gently picked her up and stared at her swollen breasts, aware that my breasts ached. I stared too at her swollen belly, aware that I would never again carry a child. I wanted to hate this lump of clay, this woman-statue, but to hate her would be like hating myself.

When we had left Bethlehem, I'd looked back and I'd remembered Lot's wife being turned into salt for her disobedience. I thought of Lot's wife now and felt a deep sense of injustice. Why, I cried, shaking the statue, was Lot's wife never named as surely as my infant girl will never be named? Part of me wanted to blame this piece of earthenware for my despair and my loss but I knew it would do no good. I had never worshipped this idol either, so surely I had not disobeyed Hashem's second commandment to have no other gods except him.

I sank to the floor clutching the statue and I found myself rocking back and forth, thinking of my baby. Suddenly, I cried out, "Misho, your name is Misho." And so it would be forever. I planned to tell no one, not even my sons or my husband, for fear of being ridiculed. Misho--short for Michael--was a name for a boy. It was also the name of the archangel who watched over the people.

# Three: Hope

Naomi

While I was recovering, Hannah cooked soups and stews for me and brought me bread soaked in honey, not allowing me to do a thing. I'd wanted to take on some of the household chores, but even though I did not like being any trouble, I came to understand that sometimes we must accept help. I'd watch her brooming out the kitchen and cleaning up the dishes, and when I'd thank her, she'd shrug. "You'd do it for me!" I was not so sure I would but when we'd made the move to the shabby abandoned house, I'd only been able to carry a pot and a ceramic pitcher, and even that small amount of labor caused me to bleed. I told no one. I didn't really care but I was beginning to feel alive again. This place needed many repairs but the ladder had been reinforced and a hole in the roof had been patched. At least it was a shelter from the weather and a place to begin our lives. I was glad too that it was in the village and not as remote as Haran's place. It was a far cry from my spacious place in Bethlehem but it would have to do.

The moon shone its silvery light onto the roof of my new home. I crept up the ladder and looked in at my boys. They were fast asleep near their father who was tossing and turning. He had kicked the blanket off his legs, and I could hear his labored breathing and an occasional snort. My sons were almost grown, their skinny bodies now stretched out in the middle of the floor near Emilelech's feet. How innocent they looked as they slept, Chilion curled up against Mahlon's arm, his face boyish, and Mahlon almost a man, with a few hairs of a beginning mustache on his upper lip. I wished I could keep them young forever, but I knew I had to help them become men.

Emilelech groaned in his sleep. Was he in pain? I hated that I could do so little to ease his physical suffering. It saddened me too that I would never lie with my husband again not because it was pleasurable but because I would never have any more babies. Yet, the truth was I did not want any. Not now. I was getting too old to deal with toddlers and all the work it took to keep them safe. Emilelech groaned again. It was a wonder the boys did not wake, but even as babies they had always been good sleepers. There was no wall encircling this flat roof like at home and I worried one of them might roll off. I had suggested the need for a barrier but my sons told me they were not children and to stop fussing over them. They were right, but they would always be my little ones, and I knew I'd never stop trying to protect them.

I eased down the ladder, being careful to feel the rungs solidly under my bare feet, grateful that they were now sturdy and safe. Once in the courtyard I took a deep breath, appreciating the coolness of the air. Swallows raced through the sky, twittering. How fast they flew. How sure they seemed. I wandered over to Emilelech's new potter's wheel, the one he had traded for our ox. It sat off to one side of our little yard in front of a wooden bench given to us by Hannah. She was a wonderful woman and I was glad we were becoming friends, but I desperately missed Leah. It hardly seemed possible that this full moon, as big as the one I had last seen in Jerusalem, had already risen twice. So much had happened. I had seen the Jordan River and the twelve standing stones to honor the priests who'd carried the Ark of the Covenant. I had met people from Moab and discovered I liked most of them. I had found a pagan doll and realized the people of Jericho appreciated women. And of course I had also endured the loss of my baby. That sorrow would never be gone.

It saddened me to think of Haran far away, not knowing his beautiful little girl was alive and happy. He must be mourning. I wished I could climb on a mule and go and find the man. But what could I, a woman, do? I had never even ridden a goat! I wished Emilelech might go after him but he had shown no such inclination. It was difficult enough for him to sell off our ox and donkeys and arrange for our living quarters. I wished he might have more energy if that's what it had been when he'd ridden our donkey out of Bethlehem. I knew though that he had been anxious about my health as well as his, and I knew too he wanted to keep us all safe.

How I wish I'd been as brave as Hannah. I was certain she had substituted the goat for her daughter without regard for her own safety. How had she managed it, I wondered? No doubt there had been lots of people and probably many animals assembled for the sacrificial ceremony. When I suggested to Hannah that I thought it was she who had rescued Anna, she shook her head and quickly denied it, but her hands trembled. She must have been, and might still be, full of fear. It seemed best to say no more. It was a wonder to me that with Haran gone, this Moabite family went about their daily tasks as if nothing unpleasant had happened. Me, I could not help but worry that the priest might realize Anna was not my child, especially since we had moved into the house so close to his and she was not with us.

How I had fretted over where we would live and how we would fit in, but so far I'd liked everyone we'd met. But it was not the same. The people here all had their families and their lives, and though we had been welcomed with warmth, no one invited us to their houses or even to their sacred rites. For that I was grateful. I had no intention of following their religion. We had our own ways, and even though I was full of doubts about Hashem, I meant to keep our religious practices.

Often in the past when Ruth came to help me, we would be doing our chores downstairs, while Emilelech was upstairs teaching our sons. I had to stop Ruth from climbing to the upper story to sit with the boys. She loved to learn. I knew much of our past but could not answer her insatiable need for knowledge. She wanted to not only know *what* happened but *why* it happened. It astonished me at times to remember how young she was. Something about her seemed wise beyond her years. "Why," she once asked me, "did Hashem create people at all?" She was too deep for me so I'd divert her attention and send her to the well for extra water. She was most determined to do things her way but she always eventually went along with me. Many might find such a strong-willed girl disturbing, but I, who had always been a follower, admired her. It did not please me to realize that I almost always did what everyone else wanted.

Even with the sweetness of the birds beginning to tweet and dart about in the sky, I often still felt miserable. At first, after the loss of my baby girl, grief used to overwhelm me, but somehow those dark moods had eased. Yet I wished that I had never encouraged Emilelech to take us away from Bethlehem. I was not lonely there. I spent hours with Leah gossiping and sharing recipes. I would still have had my loom, but now it lay rotting on the side of a lonely road. And we needed more money. If I still had my loom, I could make beautiful blankets to sell.

I went over and stoked the embers in the oven, piling in twigs from the ancient olive tree growing in the center of the courtyard, and I managed to get a small fire lit. I needed to sprinkle thyme and sesame seeds on the flatbread that I had started last night. It would taste good with the apricot preserves my family loved. I was about to flatten the dough with the palm of my hand, but our nanny goat began bleating pitifully. She wanted her feed and no doubt she needed to be milked. I went over to the pen, filled her bucket with grain, and pulled up a three-legged stool. After I put the feed in front of her and she began to crunch the oats, I sat down behind her, my knees apart. I leaned forward and massaged her udder so that her milk would more easily come down. She seemed relaxed, and I gently squeezed her leathery teats with my thumb and forefinger, one at a time. The milk streamed into the pail. The earthy smell of the oats she was chewing and the moist fragrance of her warm milk reassured me.

I heard footsteps coming down the lane towards my house, but I did not stop milking. It was unusual for anyone to be about so early, and I could not smell any lamp oil either which surprised me. These passageways were quite dark even when the sun came up, and I got a little anxious. Suddenly, Ruth burst into my court and quickly found me in the goat pen. "Morning, Naomi!" As she unlatched the gate, I could hear excitement in her voice. She came skipping inside and wrapped her arms around my shoulders. I laughed. "Let me go, Ruth. I have to finish the milking!" I quickly got done and wiped the goat's teats with a cloth and pushed the milk towards her. She grabbed it and waited for me to get up. I smiled at her. "You are here bright and early."

"I know! I know! I could not wait to tell you. My father is home. He is home! And he is thrilled to find Anna safe. He wants to thank you and he is holding a feast that he wants you to attend."

"What! I do not deserve any special attention. He should honor you, Ruth. You are the one who hid Anna until you knew she would be safe. And your mother too. Without her, well, it doesn't bear thinking about."

"My father was angry with me for not telling him about Anna. He should have listened! He is still annoyed with my mother. But soon he will forgive her and everything will be all right again."

Although Ruth seemed wise at times, she was still a child. She did not understand how difficult it would be for her mother and her father to reconcile. I said nothing to dash her hopes. I took the bucket of milk from her before she spilled any. My young friend secured the gate behind me. "Ruth, I need you to filter the milk for me." She had done it before and I felt it would be good for her to have something to do to settle her down.

We went over to the table Emilelech had managed to cobble together. It stood next to the twisted trunk of the olive tree. Its two gnarled branches were topped with crowns of green leaves. I hoped this tree might eventually produce some olives, but for now it provided shade, and the many cracks and crevices in its trunk provided handy places for my spoons and knives. While I began kneading the dough I had already prepared from flour and water, Ruth fetched a clean cloth and a clean pitcher. She began to slowly pour the milk through the fabric. She became pensive and I began to wonder if there was something upsetting her. I assumed it had something to do with Haran and wanted to reassure her. "Your father loves you very much, Ruth."

"I know that! It is just that he's brought back a man with him from Egypt. His father is a well-to-do physician."

So that was the real reason for the feast. I was relieved it was not me to be honored. I much preferred to stay in the shadows. But my hopes soared. Could this Egyptian be a healer who could help Emilelech? I got lost in my thoughts for my husband. Perhaps Hashem sent us here so Emilelech could regain his strength and then we could go home. The sun began to rise behind the house casting everything in a pink and orange glow, lighting up beginning clouds that promised rain. Such clouds gave me hope for Bethlehem. Maybe even today it was raining there.

Ruth finished filtering the milk, wrung out the cloth and set aside the pitcher. "I have to go!"

"Ruth, wait. Stay for breakfast."

She smiled at me and waved a little flutter of her hand. "I will see you at the dinner later. My father especially wants you to come. She glanced up at the roof. I noticed Mahlon peering down at us. Well, at Ruth! "And them too! I am to invite Orpah and her family as well."

The day passed slowly. I could not stop thinking about this Egyptian who might be a healer. At last we set off for the dinner. I noticed how often Emilelech had to rest, and I prayed silently for his health. As we approached Haran's compound. The gate was wide open, and I could hear people strumming lyres and harps. The rhythmic thudding of cymbals along with their tinkling bells made me smile. It brought back memories of my wedding to Emilelech. What a joyous week of festivities we had shared. I so missed everyone, but my mouth watered at the aroma of roasting goat. I planned to enjoy this meal and hoped I might make new friends.

In the courtyard I could see Anna being twirled in a circle by Ruth. Her friend Orpah soon joined in, the three of them full of life. I was about to go over to say hello to Orpah's mother, but Haran rushed over and grabbed Emilelech's hands. "Peace be with you!" He quickly let my husband go, smiled at me, and clapped his hands to summon the servants. Two men rushed over with basins for washing our feet. Even I got to sit on a bench and have my sandals removed and my feet immersed in warm water. I had never experienced such hospitality except in Jerusalem. At home I was the one to take care of everyone. I had not expected such welcome here in Moab but there again Haran's wife, Hannah, had been more than kind to me.

Mahlon and Chilion looked pleased to be treated as adults. Once again I noticed how mature they were becoming, especially Mahlon. I would need to find him a wife soon. I glanced around for Hannah. She was over at a table arranging the bowls of food. I would gladly have helped her, but I must admit much as I love to cook for my family, I was looking forward to enjoying a meal I did not have to prepare. Another table, fashioned from long planks, sat next to benches where a few guests were sitting and enjoying their wine. At one end of the table sat a handsome young man. His dark skin and his deep brown eyes looked foreign. He must surely be the Egyptian. "Emilelech," I whispered. "That's him!"

My husband, obviously embarrassed, glared at me. I had shared my hopes with him that this fellow might know about healing, and even though Emilelech acted as if he wasn't worried about his failing strength, I knew he was. My poor man could hardly spin his potting wheel these days. He had never been broad-shouldered, but now he looked thin and frail. I wanted--no needed--this Egyptian to give us a tonic for good health. I knew that back home I was supposed to stay away from strangers with magic potions, but this was Moab. My husband, after my boys, was my main priority, and being there for him helped me to overcome my usual shyness. "Haran." I smiled at him. "Will you introduce us to your guest?"

"Of course. Come." He led us to the table and seated us near the guest of honor. "Pentu," he nodded towards the handsome young man. "These are my good friends from Bethlehem."

Pentu half arose and bowed slightly to me. He pressed his index finger under each of his eyes in the foreign manner and he smiled benevolently towards Emilelech.

"Shalom," Emilelech responded. Mahlon and Chilion smiled and dipped their heads respectfully.

Haran called over a servant. "Bring a fresh skin of wine." He grinned at us. "The wine is very good this year, sweet and strong."

I felt uncomfortable, and I wanted to run over to Hannah and help her rather than be at this table, but she did not need my help. Emilelech did. The grim look on his face, though, made me shudder, wondering if he was recalling the days of the Exodus. Maybe he did not want to be helped by an Egyptian. Maybe he resented their past cruelty to our people. After a few sips of wine, I almost babbled that in those ancient days this young man was not even born, and he could no more be blamed for the atrocities of the ancestors than our sons.

"Pentu," I managed. "Are you married?" Since I did not have any daughters I did not think I was being rude. It was not as if I was playing at matchmaker, but his answer surprised me.

"Not yet." He smiled towards Ruth who seemed intent on dancing with her friend and her little sister. "I hope to soon choose my first wife. Someone pretty and strong who will make a good mother. I hope to have ten children at least."

Did he mean Ruth? I could only imagine *her* response, quite possibly stamping her foot on the ground in front of him and walking away with her head held high. She certainly would not want his attention. He *was* handsome though, but she was probably too young to notice.

Haran slapped Pentu on his back. "I have two daughters who would both be pleased if you chose one of them."

I almost choked on my wine. These men! They had no understanding of women. Anna was far too young, and as for Ruth, well I had expected Haran to be more considerate about his daughter, but I should have known. All men seemed insensitive to women's wishes. I could not imagine anyone taking my children to a faraway land, and clearly that is what must happen if Ruth were promised to the Egyptian. It could not happen for at least a couple of years though, and Ruth must agree, and Hannah too. That is if they had the same customs as we had. This was no time for me to worry about the future of Ruth, though I must admit the very idea of her being promised to Pentu offended me. I suddenly realized that I had a secret hope that she might one day become *my* daughter-in-law.

"Pentu," I said, but I could not meet his look. I glanced at Emilelech. His eyes narrowed at what I knew he thought was my disrespect. Women were expected to be silent. But although I trembled at my forwardness, I was determined to do what was best for my husband whether he approved or not. "I have heard in your land there are healing temples and many rites and herbs to bring back vitality."

"Yes." Pentu frowned slightly. "My father is a well-respected physician. He has helped many people. Alas, I am not so gifted. I take after my grandfather and make my living as a scribe."

I tried to hide the disappointment that I knew must surely be turning my face distant. Pentu might well prepare papyrus for the Pharaoh, but it would not help Emilelech. I smiled as pleasantly as I could, ignoring my husband who had his arms crossed in front of his chest. "Excuse me, please." I arose to my feet, adjusted my scarf and straightened my skirt. "I must go to help Hannah." I put my wine bowl down and hurried over to the other table now laden with delicious foods.

"Hannah, what can I do? I feel so silly being served as if I am royalty."

She smiled and shook her head. "Everything is ready. You enjoy. Go and sit back down."

I knew she would not let me do anything. Indeed, she was as stubborn as Ruth and certainly as strong-willed and determined. "Might I have a private word with you?" I asked.

She looked puzzled but followed me into the women's tent. We left the flap open so it was not too dark. No one was in there except us. It smelled of spices and woman-blood. Oh, it brought back those memories that I would rather bury. Yet here I stood, feeling a little tipsy, my cheeks flushed. "Ruth was so kind to me when I miscarried," I began. "She is such a lovely girl. I have noticed my son, my eldest, Mahlon, watching her, and they seem to be friends. Am I too presumptuous to have any tiny hope that you and Haran might consider Mahlon as a suitor for your daughter? We have not much to offer as a bridal dowry but Ruth would be more than welcome in our house."

Hannah drew her face so close to mine I could smell honey on her breath. "Haran is eager to marry off our girls. He is hoping Pentu will offer a sizable wedding gift! He was so angry at what happened to Anna that he wanted to take us all away from Moab. I don't think he much cared where, but no doubt he has softened since his little Anna, the child of his heart, is safe."

My mood sank. I did not want to lose Hannah or her family. "It is very hard," I muttered, "to leave your people and to have to begin again." At the frown on her face, I hastily added, "if it were not for you and Haran, I don't know how we would have managed. In time I expect I will make other friends. But if you have to leave Moab, at least Pentu is well-connected, and Haran will no doubt take care of you."

Hannah shrugged. "My husband is as stubborn as a goat in heat. Ruth is very much like him—impulsive and determined to have her way. I can only tell you if Ruth likes Pentu, she will go gladly, and no doubt we will follow. But if she likes your Mahlon, she will move into your house and be a great help to you."

I had no idea if Hannah approved of the notion of Ruth coming to live in my humble little house, but the idea delighted me. My good spirits returned. "I don't think I have ever thanked you properly for all you've done for me," I began in all sincerity.

Hannah, not wanting to hear any more, flapped her hands in my face as if to push me away. "No, no, no!" she cried, but her mouth twitched in a tiny smile. She grabbed my hand. "Come let us enjoy the banquet."

# Four: Resistance

Ruth

After everyone finished cleaning their hands in the washbowls brought around by servants, the meal began. Ruth, sitting between Anna and Orpah at the children's table, took a piece of bread dipped in olive oil. She had been taught to nibble delicately but she was hungry and tore into it, ripping off a big piece with her teeth. Her mother saw her and frowned slightly and shook her head, but Ruth knew her mother was far too busy to come over and scold her.

Haran walked around the adult tables offering everyone platters of roasted goat. He started with the guest of honor, Pentu, who smacked his lips in appreciation, grabbing a meaty bone. Servants, hired for the occasion, ladled out big helpings of parched grain onto everyone's plates. Delicious buttermilk cheese wrapped in cloth that everyone loved was soon being passed back and forth on the tables. People murmured their appreciation as they dipped into containers of dried grapes and nuts. Conversation lulled briefly but soon everyone was chatting again.

Ruth handed Anna a dried grape, and her little sister plopped it into her mouth. "Pentu is smiling at me!" she said.

"He is smiling because he is enjoying his food," Ruth declared, sure that Pentu was in fact looking at her.

Anna pouted, pushed away her bowl and rushed into the kitchen to find her mother.

Ruth shrugged and gnawed the last shreds of goatmeat from a bone and began to lick her sticky fingers. She could still feel Pentu watching her and did her best to ignore him, glad she did not have to sit near him. The fact she had overheard her parents' discussion with him a day earlier about the need for a man to take a wife made her uncomfortable. Yet, the idea of going to Egypt excited her. She would love to see faraway lands, but she had no intention of getting married. Not to anyone.

While people were still eating and talking and drinking, Ruth nudged Orpah to get up. Her friend seemed a little reluctant, obviously relishing all the special food and the promise of desserts to come. But Ruth, more aware than ever of Pentu's gaze in her direction, could not bear to stay seated. She swung her legs off the bench and tugged at Orpah's arm. "Come on," she whispered.

Orpah gave a little frown. She, much like her mother, loved to eat, but she meekly followed Ruth, who took a half-empty skin of wine with them up the stone stairwell at the side of the house. On the roof, they sat on a fleece with their backs against a column. Ruth sipped some wine, a daily beverage that usually got watered down for the children. This was full-strength and warmed her throat. She giggled as she handed the skin to Orpah, who squeezed the dregs into her mouth before scrambling over to the side of the roof and peeking down at the people.

Ruth crawled after her and also peered over the low wall, ready to duck out of sight if anyone looked up and saw them. Her eyes found the handsome Egyptian. His beard, unlike Mahlon's few wispy whiskers, looked full. He did not join in with the boys who'd gathered in a group to examine a bow. Orpah's two brawny brothers looked as if they would love to go to war, but Mahlon seemed far too frail. Even though she had no interest in any boys, she found herself wanting to protect him. It was only a matter of time when she would be promised to someone whether she liked it or not. She knew that she could not run away, but if she were a man she would. She would take Anna with her too. Her small sister who had been so full of joy was now a changed little girl. She no longer wanted to leave their compound even when their mother went to the well where they had had such fun together. She would get tearful and tremble and hang onto her mother's skirt and beg to go home.

Ruth watched her mother fussing over some of the women seated at a table by themselves. She looked tired. Ruth searched the courtyard, suddenly wishing she had brought Anna up here with them. She inched away from the wall and whispered, "I have to find my sister."

Orpah got up too and they headed back to the gathering. Ruth almost expected to find Anna hiding under a table, but she was not anywhere to be seen. No priests had been invited to their house and never would be, but the image of Anna bound and gagged flashed into Ruth's mind. "Let's look in the house! Hurry!"

Anna was not in the kitchen nor was she in any of the downstairs rooms. They eventually found her crouching in a corner of the upstairs chamber where the men usually gathered to talk about important matters. She gazed up at Ruth and Orpah, her eyes big and startled.

"What happened?" Ruth crouched next to her ready to take the little girl into her arms. Orpah stood nearby, her eyes brimming with concern.

For a while Anna said nothing but at last words squeaked out. "I am promised to Pentu. I don't want to go to Egypt!"

Ruth almost drew away. Surely not! As the eldest daughter, she ought to be the first to be promised and married, not her little sister. Unless--her father intended to give them both away. "Don't worry," she stroked Anna's face. "I won't let anything happen to you." She felt a storm arising that fueled her legs. She jumped to her feet. "Stay with her, Orpah," she commanded in a fierce voice. Then in a gentle tone she addressed Anna. "I am going to talk to our father. It must be a mistake."

Anna nodded.

As Ruth rushed out of the house to confront Haran, she knew he would dismiss her just as surely as he had not listened to her when she'd tried to tell him Anna was safe. She stood for a while staring at all the people laughing and talking. Neither of her parents, it seemed to her, could be trusted. She decided to ignore them and found Naomi, grabbing her hand, and pulling her over to the goat pen. One of the animals bleated loudly in hopes of grain and one squatted and relieved itself.

Ruth sank to her knees and held her palms together as if in prayer, except she certainly would not seek help from Chemosh.

Naomi adjusted her veil, looking puzzled. "What's wrong? Are you ill?"

"My father has gone and promised Anna to the Egyptian."

Naomi glanced towards the table where the men still sat talking and drinking. "Has he promised you also?"

"I don't care! He cannot send Anna away. She is too young and she is too afraid."

"A promise isn't the same as a betrothal, Ruth, but I understand your fears for Anna. Where is she?"

"With Orpah in the house. I will not let that Egyptian take her away! I will not!"

Naomi became thoughtful. She took Ruth's hands and raised her to her feet. "Did your mother tell you this?"

"No. Anna did. She is terrified."

"She is just a little girl. Perhaps she misunderstood. Come, Ruth, we will go and talk with your mother. She will straighten matters out."

Most people had finished dining and the revelry was even livelier with women dancing to the high notes of the flute, their veils drifting like angel wings around their shoulders and the hems of their dresses swirling across the ground. Ruth froze as they made their way through the dusty yard. In the entranceway stood the priest who lived near Naomi. He stared at her and suddenly turned away and disappeared. "Did you see him?" she whispered to Naomi. "He wasn't invited."

Naomi's face turned pale. She put an arm around Ruth's shoulder. "Don't worry," she said. "The priest thinks Anna is my daughter. He has no reason to suspect otherwise."

Even as Naomi uttered these words, Ruth could see her mother with Anna, quickly leading her into the house. She was sure the priest must have seen them too. In the kitchen they found Anna sitting on

Hannah's lap. A flurry of relatives were gathered nearby and were sipping on jasmine tea.

"Hannah," Naomi said quietly. "Ruth thinks your husband has promised Anna to Pentu. Surely it is not so?"

"It is!" Hannah stared at the ground. "He had too much to drink! He will change his mind when he sobers up. He will betroth you too, Ruth. I cannot imagine why he did not already do so but let us hope he forgets."

"Mother!" Ruth looked imploringly into Hannah's eyes. "You have to stop him. Why would he promise Anna, anyway?"

"He is afraid the priests may come for her again. He may be right. He knows if he sends her to Egypt that she will be safe."

Ruth hung her head. "A priest was already here watching us."

Hannah hugged Anna closer and whispered to her, "Don't worry, if we have to send you to Egypt, I will go with you. It is a beautiful country I have heard." Her voice sounded high and nervous and did not inspire confidence.

"If she goes, I will go too." Ruth said quietly.

Hannah shook her head. "It is not your place, Ruth, to protect your little sister. It is mine."

"You! You couldn't even stop the priests from taking Anna!" With these defiant words, Ruth stormed away running directly over to her father. Her mother handed Anna who had begun to cry to one of her aunts, and chased after Ruth, trying to drag her away from Haran who was laughing with Pentu.

Ruth dug in her heels and could not be moved, all the while frowning at Pentu. "You cannot take my little sister away. I will not allow it!"

Pentu anxiously moistened his lips and looked to Haran for help.

"Pentu will marry you first," Haran slurred, looking pleased with himself, but Hannah looked as if she had swallowed poison.

Pentu smiled at Ruth and gazed into her eyes. Before he could say one word, Ruth shouted, "I would rather die than marry you!" She spat on the ground.

Pentu gasped and averted his eyes.

Ruth scowled at him but upon seeing Mahlon nearby had an idea. "I am already promised to Mahlon!" she said gleefully.

Haran stared at her. "You willful girl," he shouted. He looked apologetically at Pentu. "I am going to take a whip to that girl. It's time she learned the meaning of obedience."

Pentu shook his head. "No. Please."

Hannah grabbed Ruth's arm and dragged her to the house. Haran ripped a twig from a tree to use as a switch and went after them.

Outside everyone hushed to hear Ruth's cries and the sound of the lashing. It never seemed to end, but at last there was only the noise of Ruth's sobs. It did not last long. Ruth suddenly shouted at the top of her voice, "I hate you both!"

The stunned guests began to disperse, most without a word, but tongues would be wagging later. Naomi and a few other women began gathering the dishes, scraping off the leftovers into the goat pen, rinsing the plates in a bucket of water.

Emilelech and the boys looked on, obviously not knowing what to say to Pentu, who sat rigidly on a bench.

When Haran stumbled back out, he went over to Pentu. "I am sorry about my daughter," he said. "She will do as she is told. Meanwhile let the women clean up and let us go upstairs and have some more wine." He motioned for Emilelech to join them but Emilelech politely refused, and hurried his sons away, throwing a sideways glance of despair towards Naomi.

Naomi went into the kitchen, hoping to offer comfort and be a help, but mainly she wanted to reassure Ruth, who was huddled in a corner.

Hannah turned a cold gaze upon her. "You!" she shouted. "How dare you give Ruth such ideas! How dare you!"

Naomi drew back. "I suggested to *you* that Ruth would make Mahlon a good wife, but I did not try to influence your daughter. I never said one word to her about future marriage. What I told you was in private and just between the two of us."

Ruth stared at Naomi and wrapped her arms around herself and rocked slightly. "I would rather die than go to Egypt with anyone." She looked up at Naomi for support, but disrespect of fathers and mothers was something Naomi would not abide and would not encourage. Nevertheless, she spoke up. "Please, Hannah, don't be too hard on Ruth. She is only a girl who wants her own way, what she considers the best."

Clearly, Hannah was still furious. She glared at Naomi. "My daughter is none of your concern."

# Five: Field of Flowers

Boaz

Amongst the rocks and clay in the dry and desolate field, a field that ought to be a meadow of fresh green wheat, Boaz could hardly believe his eyes. The white petals in a blanket of delicate flowers seemed to shine at him like manna from heaven. A gentle breeze ruffled the slender blooms. He could not tell if the pretty buds were going to turn into new leaves or become more flowers, but they were moist with droplets of dew. His mouth watered.

After their three-day-fast when Hashem had miraculously slaked their thirst, there still had been no rain. People were surviving but only barely. Alas, one family, a man and his two wives and three children, ate some poisonous berries that they had scavenged from who knows where. They had died with other women rocking them and sobbing and moaning. The sound of those funereal wails still haunted him. He had spent every night since then unable to sleep, in constant prayer, begging for mercy from Hashem.

Seeing these flowers though, Boaz looked up at the blue dome of the sky and felt as if the hot sun was smiling. He did not hesitate but quickly scooped up a handful of the beautiful wild plants and put the thick leaves in his mouth and chewed. The taste was refreshing and the moisture from the succulent vegetation replenished him. He ate his fill and sat for a while in the midst of this unexpected plenty.

He had no doubt that these flowers were a gift from Hashem but he decided it would be prudent to make sure he did not get a stomachache or worse before telling the people about them. He lay for a while and fell asleep, waking to see the setting sun winking behind the horizon. "Hashem!" he cried. "You are merciful!" He gathered up as much of the succulent plants as he could carry to give to his wives and children. He hurried back to the village filled with energy and filled with hope.

Since most people were staying in their houses, trying to conserve their strength, no one was about. A few skinny goats milled around in the pen near the city gate and bleated pitifully. He was tempted to give them some of the succulent vegetation, but they would have to wait. He strode down the road to his complex where he could see the oil lamps glowing inside his house. He marched in with a big smile on his face.

"Where have you been?" His mother, holding his youngest child, a babe in arms, frowned at him.

"Yes," came the shrill cry from his middle wife. "We saved you dinner but it is cold."

He looked into the large stewing pot near the window. All that was in it were onions and garlic in a sparing amount of liquid. It smelled strong and rich but would hardly keep anyone alive.

"The rest is for you," said his oldest wife.

He stared at their concerned and angry faces, wondering if they had eaten. He suspected they had given their share to the children. "Look!" he held up the bountiful and fragrant foliage.

"What! Are we supposed to eat weeds?" cried his mother.

Boaz threw the plants onto the rug and smiled benevolently. His youngest wife hung her head demurely. He knew she expected him to father more children with her, but with two girls by the eldest wife, two boys from the middle one, and her baby, he did not want any more. "This is going to keep us alive until Hashem sends the rain. It is delicious. Try it!" He held out a bunch of plants.

"Are you trying to poison us?" one of the women cried, crossing her arms across her chest, and the others nodded in agreement, their eyes frightened.

"Of course not. I ate my fill and it has done me no harm. I feel renewed."

The oldest wife took some leaves and nibbled. She frowned slightly. "It is sweet and fresh."

The others, including his mother who was usually quite pushy, continued to look doubtful but each of them took a handful and held it to the noses, smelling the fragrance.

"Go ahead!" Boaz urged. "Hashem must surely have sent this manna from heaven until he opens the sky and gives us rain."

"It had better be soon," middle wife grumbled, but put a leaf in her mouth. "Oh! It is tasty!"

"Where *are* the children?" Boaz asked.

"They were so restless and irritating that we sent them to play at Leah's. We told them to get back here before it got too dark. They should be home soon."

Boaz smiled to himself, feeling more content than he had in the months since Emilelech and Naomi left. In the morning he planned to lead everyone to the field of flowers but of course once the women decided this was indeed food from Hashem, there would be no waiting.

His wives and mother exchanged meaningful glances. Middle wife gathered up the remaining wilting flowers. "Let's get the children," she said and rushed out the door with the other wives following. Boaz' mother remained with the baby until Boaz took the child into his arms and sank down onto a bench. "It is too late for us to return to the field now. We will wait until morning. Mother, go ahead and finish off the soup. I am not hungry."

She was still eating when the children came racing in behind their mothers. It was not much longer when other people started arriving, wanting some of this miraculous food that reminded them of how Hashem once provided manna for their ancestors in the wilderness. Soon Boaz' house and courtyard were overflowing with noisy, excited people.

Boaz looked around at their faces, so well-known to him and so dear, but he felt as if they were about to turn into a pack of thirsty hyenas. He doubted that any of them would wait until morning for him to lead them to the field of flowers. He understood their anguish and their desire, but he also realized that there was a greater thirst than mere physical thirst that needed to be satiated. But what good would it do to tell them to acknowledge Hashem first? Their physical need outweighed any spiritual understanding. Yet he must try. He had no idea why Hashem was thrusting him into the forefront, but he called a few of the men to accompany him to the upper room. They stood in a circle while Boaz gave thanks for the succulent flowers that he hoped would not dry out during the night.

The women downstairs heard him "We will go now!" cried a high-pitched voice and others chimed in. "Come on, Boaz, which field is it?"

Boaz knew it would be futile to resist. "It is Emilelech's deserted field."

A few people muttered. Many still resented Emilelech for sneaking away, and it did not seem possible anything good could come from any land that belonged to him.

Soon, though, a throng of people lit torches and marched out of the village heading west towards the fields. Boaz wearily trailed behind hoping they would not be disappointed, scared too that there would not be enough for everyone. He regretted his lack of trust in Hashem's providence, and he feared that his very doubt might cause the abundance of thirst-quenching plants to die before they got there. He need not have worried. People began to run towards the terraced field that was glowing and luminescent. It seemed to be lighting the way. Everyone threw themselves headfirst onto the ground and gorged on the succulent plants.

Boaz watched as more and more of the people of Bethlehem arrived. Clearly word had gotten out, and the whole field soon swarmed with people like ants upon honey. Children could be heard crying and laughing, but not one prayer was said out loud, not one word. Boaz groaned, remembering how their ancestors were not satisfied with manna and demanded of Moses that they needed meat.

Boaz sat down. What could he do? He was no Moses.

People began to wander back to the village, leaving only a few stragglers and a handful of people lying in the field, their bellies full. Even his wives and children departed without a word to him. The next day he watched the sun rise and in the yellow light, he could see how badly the field had been trodden. He doubted any of the plants had survived. There would be no more manna from this source.

He walked across the flattened earth, feeling more wretched with every step. How must Hashem feel about the hungry mob who had taken and eaten and had not expressed any thanks? But perhaps he was wrong to blame the needy people. Perhaps Hashem bore some responsibility. After all, had he not withheld the rain so that their crops failed? Boaz held his head in his hands and groaned. There was nothing left of the plants, so if others came from the village now, they would go home hungry and thirsty. It was the law to leave at least some small amount for people to glean, usually orphans and widows. Now, it seemed, they were all too desperate and had no thought for anyone but themselves.

Boaz made a silent vow that if he ever once again experienced plentiful barley or abundant wheat or overflowing grapevines, he would make sure the poor would always be welcome in his fields and vineyards, and everyone would be treated with kindness and respect by his reapers. No one ought to suffer hunger when there was plenty. He only hoped this greedy gorging on the plants would not result in Hashem's wrath for not sharing with those in need. But since everyone *was* in dire need, perhaps this very harvest was in some way the gleanings Hashem had provided. After all, did not Hashem understand their needs and want them to experience grace and love rather than starvation and thirst?

Boaz walked slowly back to the village, lost in thought. Did Hashem really punish people? If so, Boaz worried about what might come next. Yet did not everyone seek health and life? He sighed deeply as he remembered the family who had eaten the poisonous berries. He experienced, too, a surge of love for his family, especially his children. How could he protect them?

As the days passed, Boaz constantly told everyone it was Hashem, not he, who had provided, but he knew they did not believe him. He did not want their worship. He was an ordinary man but now the people constantly sought him out for help. They still did not know when the drought might end, and the unexpected herbal bounty served only to feed them for one night and sustain them for one day. They had trampled the rest of the flowers like a pack of wild beasts. He had searched hoping to find a few live plants or some seeds to begin another crop but nothing was left.

At least, though, because of their respect for him, they listened, but he knew sooner or later they would blame him, because they thought of him as their salvation and he could never live up to their expectations. An inner voice told him they would do well to go to Jerusalem and sell some of their livestock. Only a few people refused but most, even those who grumbled, readily agreed for half of their donkeys, camels, goats and sheep to be taken to the nearby city. They supposed it would be as dry as their land, but Boaz had this strange feeling of expectation. He insisted they bring carts and every imaginable vessel that would hold water. "You'll see," he told them as they set out, driving their rabble of animals. "We will trade these creatures for plentiful water."

As the great wall of Jerusalem came into sight, several of the men threw up their hands in praise at the sight of green terraced fields. They must indeed have water or their crop would not be thriving. Many wanted to rush into the city, but Boaz stopped them, insisting that they wait outside the gates and send in only a couple of men. He worried the Jerusalemites would think them an enemy out for conquest. Even if they were welcomed, it remained to be seen whether or not anyone would want their scrawny half-starved animals in exchange for water.

Three men working in the fields saw them. They stopped hoeing weeds from between the rows of grain and came to meet the strangers no doubt curious about their herd of scruffy animals. Boaz stepped forward. "Shalom Aleikhem," he said and bowed his head respectfully. He almost fell to the ground in deference to these farmers dressed in dark robes with sashes around their waists. One of them wiped his brow and adjusted his turban. "Aleikhem. Peace upon you, also. What brings you to Jerusalem?" He looked over to the others and glanced at the animals that were milling about restlessly. "Come, follow us, drive your beasts to the nearby spring. Then we will talk."

After their herd was hobbled and settled in a pasture near a flowing spring that fed a pond, Boaz took their hosts over to a wagon loaded with pots and vessels. In one large vat, he took out necklaces and hooped earrings that his wives had suggested they give to the ladies of Jerusalem. "Alas, no rain has fallen upon Bethlehem and we are in desperate need.

We bring gifts for your women. And we are hoping you will trade us water for these shabby beasts."

"We heard you were experiencing drought and we hoped by now the rains might have come. We ourselves have been blessed abundantly. But come into town and let our women prepare a meal for you. I am sure you must want to wash the dust from your sandals."

Tables were brought into the meeting square just inside the city gate. Servants brought washbowls of water for the feet of the weary Bethlehemites. They dined on goat and grapes, barley cakes, and figs. Beer was plentiful and a sense of gaiety filled everyone. But at last they settled down to business with the elders of the town.

"Our livestock is healthy but in need of fattening," one of Boaz' companions told the elders and the priests who'd gathered with them on a raised platform in the middle of the assembly yard.

"We do not need any more donkeys or even camels. And our oxen are strong and well-trained."

"Our beasts are well-trained too. They will serve you well. We ask only for the water that will fill our vats and pots."

The priests took aside the elders and they talked privately for a while, gesturing in the air, occasionally grunting. At last, they seemed to have reached some sort of agreement.

Boaz and his fellows stood nearby subdued and powerless.

The chief spokesman walked directly to Boaz and looked him squarely in his eyes. "We do not want your animals."

Boaz felt as if all the air in his lungs left his body.

But then their hosts began to laugh. "You keep your livestock. We will give you the water. We have plenty."

Boaz began to say thank you over and over as did the others in his party, but several elders gestured for them to stop. "Enough already! You would do the same for us. Now, you must rest for the night. In the morning, the women will fill your containers, and you can return to your village. And please come back for more water if you need it. As long as we have plenty, you will also have plenty."

These words brought tears to Boaz' eyes. He quickly wiped them away. It was in this moment that he came to fully understand that Hashem was not a wrathful and threatening deity out for justice and revenge. Instead his grace through the kindness and the generosity of Jerusalem's people would save the people of Bethlehem.

# Six: Doubt

Naomi

Mahlon, carrying a smoky lamp, came down to me in the middle of the night. I sat up and adjusted the blanket around my shoulders.

"Mama, I wouldn't mind being promised to Ruth. I like her and she did not deserve getting such a whipping. I will never beat her if she becomes my wife."

I could not help my smile but turned my head into the shadows so he could not see my appreciation of my gentle son. I rather doubted there would be any hope of Ruth being allowed to visit us after the uproar she had caused. I probably should not even want her as a daughter-in-law. She would be impossible to control. Yet, I admired her spirit. After all, she was only trying to take care of her sister. How terrible for sweet little Anna to have to watch her father beat Ruth! Those poor girls! I wondered just how often, behind closed doors, there were whippings in that house. I liked Haran but I detested his brutality. Hannah should have stopped him. She had been overwrought but enough was enough. As for Haran: he was understandably embarrassed, but did the girl deserve such a thrashing? It frightened me to think what he might do next. I felt helpless, but I had my own family and my own children to worry about. For once, I felt truly blessed by my husband, my Emilelech, who was such a peaceful man. "Oh, Mahlon." I sighed. "Ruth's mother is angry with me. She believes that I manipulated Ruth into declaring for you. You are old enough for us to soon find you a wife, but we do not have anything to use for a bridal dowry. Be patient, my son."

"I can work in the harvest and earn money for us."

I eyed his thin arms and felt helpless, but I did not want to discourage him. "We will all have to work together," I said. "Without my loom I don't know how I can earn much of anything. Flatbreads and baked goods won't fetch much money." I flexed my fingers. Even though my hands often ached from kneading, I wished that life could go as smoothly as preparing bread. "Go back to bed now, Mahlon, and get some sleep. In the morning everything will seem clearer."

I like to be up before everyone and it brings me joy to prepare the morning meal but as soon as I stepped into the kitchen, I realized that I had overslept. The menfolk must have crept past me and gotten their own food, but at least they had rinsed out their bowls even if they did not put them on the shelf. I could hear Emilelech's wheel squeaking out in the courtyard and smiled at his industry.

Outside, sure enough, my husband sat at his kick-wheel, pumping the lever to make it spin while he shaped lumps of clay. Several new pots were lined up on the ground, drying. I could only hope we would sell them. I did not want to have to go out in the fields to work. At home, the poor were allowed to gather the leftover grain, but I had no idea if gleaning was a custom here. I so wished a joyous harvest for Bethlehem, but gathering barley was very hard work that I'd only done once as a girl. I hoped never to become a field worker, especially not as a charity case.

"Good morning, husband." I walked over and affectionately squeezed his shoulder.

He grunted but did not stop shaping and stretching the earthen vessel he was working on. I knew he could not take his hands out of the clay, or the pot would be ruined and he'd have to start again, but I had a horrid feeling he was fuming at me about Ruth. I picked up one of the pots that was air-drying. "These are very sturdy," I said trying to placate him, but I meant it too. He ignored me again, making me sad. I wondered if he regretted the day we had left home. I could hardly bear to think about my friends and family back in Bethlehem. Of course, we never talked about much of anything. I wish we did. It seemed that I must arrange everything and pretend it is all his doing.

We had no kiln but Haran had arranged for Emilelech to use one outside of town. He was even going to lend us a cart and a mule to haul our air-dried pots there once they became leather- hard. I hoped Haran would still be our friend, but Hannah might poison him against us, especially me. How could I make her understand that I had nothing to do with Ruth's scandalous lie that she was betrothed to Mahlon? Surely Hannah realized I did not encourage Ruth's disrespect for her father. I, like everyone else, had been ashamed of the way she had spat on the ground and been so rude to Pentu. He did not deserve such treatment. Haran might be a Moabite but no doubt all men, no matter where they were from, would be ashamed if their honored guest were humiliated, especially in front of all their other guests and friends.

I decided not to wait for Emilelech to deign to speak to me. "I am going to visit Orpah's mother," I told him. I was glad at the dinner to have spoken to this large jolly woman whom I had immediately liked. I bunched my skirt into my hand so it would not drag along the ground, adjusted my veil, and hurried out to the lane. When I stepped into her courtyard, the first thing I noticed were goats running around free. I quickly latched the gate behind me as they rushed towards me. One of them began chewing on my skirt. I shooed it away and stepped through the chickens pecking about in the dust. I trod carefully to avoid the smelly animal waste and hurried past an outdoor oven. Shards of broken pottery lay in a heap near the wall of the house. "Hello!" I called through the opening that led directly into a small, cluttered room.

"Come in!" Orpah's mother greeted. "I am so glad you have come to visit. And so soon, too. Welcome! Orpah, fetch Naomi a cup of milk."

I could not refuse or I might offend her, but I hated to take anything when it was clear they must be extremely poor. Nevertheless, she led me to another room just as untidy as the kitchen but not as dirty. We both sat on a shabby rug next to a crude wooden table where she'd displayed a pretty blue bowl. I wished I could weave her a brand-new mat to show it off. I would use gold threads and make it so pretty for her, but without my loom, I was powerless. After we both settled comfortably, and Orpah went out with a basket to fetch eggs, I sipped my milk. It was strong and a little sour-tasting and I hoped it would not make me sick. I might well become as poor as she, and yet she readily shared a bowl of dried figs. She herself ate heartily. I enjoyed them too. They were sweet and nutty, possibly flavored with carob.

"It is terrible about Ruth. I hope her little legs are not too sore," I said.

Orpah's mother smacked her lips. "That girl needed a spanking years ago. She is far too bold. I ought to keep Orpah away from her before she leads her astray."

"I don't think she would do anything to hurt your daughter. Headstrong though she was yesterday, she was only trying to protect her little sister."

"I daresay, but now everyone in the village will know Anna is back at home and no one except simple-minded fools believe it was Chemosh who substituted a goat in the girl's place. The priests will not look kindly on being disobeyed. Haran had better watch out. He is already considered a rebel by the elders. It's Hannah I feel sorry for, having to put up with that husband of hers off for months at a time, barely making ends meet in spite of the fancy spices and jewelry he peddles."

I had thought Haran a rich tradesman, especially considering the fine clothes he always wore, but now I realized he might just be full of talk but little action. No wonder he had brought back the young Egyptian who sounded as if he were well-connected. No wonder he wanted to marry his daughters into a wealthy family. He must need the money.

After I took my leave, I strolled back to my house, enjoying the warmth of the sunshine and the freshness of the wind that blew my veil away from my face. I saw Mahlon and Chilion coming down the narrow alley to our house. Behind them followed

Ruth, dragging her feet. As we got close, Chilion grinned at me. "We have been hired to help with the barley harvest!" His excitement made me smile, but I wondered how long his enthusiasm would last.

"That's wonderful," I said but I was looking at Ruth whose eyes were red and swollen from crying. I could not see her legs beneath the long robe she was wearing. "Ruth, come in and let me get you a honey cake and fresh milk."

"I want some too," said Chilion, who loved sweets better than meat.

Mahlon stopped near his father at the potter's wheel, deliberately avoiding Ruth. He and his father began discussing how much water to add to clay to make it pliable.

Ruth ignored him and followed Chilion and I into the house. I wanted to help make things right between her and her parents, but perhaps Orpah's mother was right. This comeuppance might teach her wisdom. Still, I could not tolerate beatings, especially not of young girls or of women. It was all too common a practice.

I fetched some refreshments on a tray, and we all went back out into the courtyard and sat in the shade of the olive tree. I was glad when Emilelech and Mahlon joined us. When my husband politely thanked me for the tea I had served him, I felt relief. At least he was now talking to me. Ruth leaned against a wall away from my sons who were crouched down next to their father.

The sound of hurried footsteps coming along the alley made us all stop eating and look towards the entrance. Mahlon wiped breadcrumbs from his mouth.

When Hannah stormed into the yard, her veil drooping down her back, Ruth leapt to her feet.

"Ruth!" Hannah grabbed her daughter's arm. "Come with me right now!"

Ruth tugged herself free from her mother. "Why should I!"

The big sorrowful sigh and the tears in Hannah's eyes alarmed me. "Hannah, what's wrong? Please rest for a while and let me fetch you some tea."

"There is no time! Ruth, you must come with me *now*!"

"Why should I?" Ruth repeated her defiant words but this time a note of concern sounded in her angry voice.

Hannah slumped onto a stool near the planks set up on blocks to form the makeshift table where I kneaded my bread. "It is not your fault, Ruth, but Haran is demanding we all go to Egypt. He is livid with you, but he will not force you to marry Pentu. He is scared, as am I, at what will happen if we stay. Word has come that I am to appear before the elders tomorrow."

"Oh no!" I cried. I knew immediately that the priests must suspect Hannah of freeing Anna, but I had no idea what would happen to her if they found her guilty of disobeying them.

Hannah's face looked gray. "I suppose," she said, "my life for Anna's and yours, Ruth, is a fitting sacrifice to satisfy Chemosh. Haran says *that* is foolishness, and he will have none of it. But they will stone me for certain if I admit it was I who set Anna free. And if I deny it, they might take Anna again for their burnt offering."

Ruth's eyes got big with astonishment. She rushed over to her mother and wrapped her arms around her and leaned her head on her mother's head. "So it *was* you! I won't let them hurt you!"

Emilelech and Mahlon looked on in dismay. How alike they appeared. I could not help but also notice how much Ruth's unruly hair resembled her mother's. Their personalities must be similar as well. "Hannah," my husband said softly. "We will miss you and your husband, but you cannot stay where you are in danger. We will help you in any way possible." His kind eyes sought Ruth's. She was shivering so I quickly took the shawl from my shoulders and wrapped it around her. "Ruth," Emilelech said. "You must obey your parents."

"I will not marry Pentu!"

"You won't have to." Hannah slanted a look at me, and I wished we'd never had that conversation in the woman-tent. She got to her feet and with one arm around Ruth's shoulder, steered her towards Mahlon. "What if you really were promised to him?"

Emilelech's mouth turned down and I knew how inadequate he felt to be so poor. "We have no bridal dowry to offer you."

Hannah nodded. "I know. The wedding will not take place until after Ruth comes into womanhood. By then, perhaps you will have built up your business and find yourself well-to-do. If not, we will be happy to know Ruth is in a good family where she will be treated well."

"But if I am in Egypt, how will I get back here?" Ruth cried.

We will find a way," said her mother. "But first both you and Mahlon must agree to be promised to one another."

Mahlon took a deep breath. "I will come to fetch you from Egypt, Ruth, if you do agree to let me be your husband."

I did not like the idea of my son trekking to Egypt, but he needed to be his own man, and I would not object or get in his way.

Ruth stared slowly at each one of us and then she stared at the floor for many moments before she slowly raised her face and jutted out her chin. Tears glistened in her eyes, and she would not look at anyone. "All right, Mahlon. I will marry you."

Mahlon gulped but he managed a little smile.

I worried that Ruth was only going along with this promise because that was the only way to prevent betrothal to the Egyptian. I wondered if she thought she could get out of this promise to my son later on, and I worried about how that might hurt Mahlon. Still, at least Ruth was being compliant rather than the stubborn girl I had so recently come to know. The truth was I would love to have Mahlon settled, but I knew we had nothing to offer other than our welcome. And I knew there would be very few choices of brides for either of my sons.

"I have to say goodbye to Orpah," Ruth announced.

Her mother nodded slightly. "Go, but don't tarry. I will tell your father you are coming." Hannah nodded and smiled at me, but no humor shone in her dark eyes.

"We will come with you and help you pack." I remembered only too well how horrible it was to have to select only a few items to bring with me, and how I'd even had to discard my loom on that dusty trail.

Hannah shook her head. "Thank you, but Haran's sisters and brothers and children will help us."

"Oh, it is awful for you to have to leave your family!" I cried before I could hold my tongue.

Emilelech stared into space.

"Haran's friends in Egypt will no doubt be hospitable. Especially since little Anna is promised to Pentu."

*Hashem be merciful*, I thought silently, suddenly remembering how Mahlon with his thin mustache was so frail next to the full-bearded Egyptian. I could only hope as Ruth grew older that she did not change her mind. It was permissible at least within my tribe for a girl to make a different choice when she came of age. Why had I been so ready to go along with my parents' choices, I wondered? But this was no time for me to lament the past. I walked Hannah to the lane and watched Ruth head toward Orpah's, while Hannah scurried in the other direction toward the city gate.

I had a bad feeling that Ruth might become defiant again, and so I went down to Orpah's to encourage her to hurry home. I saw her go through the gate, and I waited around for her, getting increasingly anxious, until rain from a dark cloud began to pelt down and soak me through. I hurried into Orpah's house to find the father and husky sons sitting on the floor around their mat, preparing to eat lentil stew that Orpah's mother was serving.

"Where is Ruth?" I cried, hoping that the girls were in a back room.

"Who knows with those two?" Orpah's mother laughed. "They probably took off through the hole in the back wall. One of these days my husband is going to replace those bricks and put a stop to their escapades."

I was unsure if it would be wise to reveal that Haran and Hannah were fleeing from the village, and I decided to say nothing. "I am sorry to have disturbed you," I muttered, backing out and scurrying to my house where I changed out of my wet clothes. I felt so dismayed and tired that later I only managed to fetch the men bread and olive oil, a sliver of cheese and dried fruit for their dinner. I sank onto a stool and put my head into my hands, hoping Ruth had gone home. At last, I could not stand to do nothing. I put on a heavy coat and went out to search for the girl.

I had no idea where to begin and decided I must go to Haran's because Ruth might have already gone home.

Haran's sisters greeted me, their faces solemn, their eyes red. It troubled me to see that Haran's cart was packed and ready to leave.

I hardly dared ask. "Is Ruth here?"

The sisters looked at one another and were silent for a moment or two.

I searched their faces my mouth getting as dry as the thirsty fields I had left in Bethlehem.

At last, the youngest of the two spoke shrilly. "We don't know where she is, but our brother Haran was more furious than ever to learn that she had promised herself to your son again. We thought she was at your house. When you see her, tell her to come home immediately. They might well be gone, but it might be possible to catch up with them. Haran's brother has agreed to carry her on his mule if necessary. By then Haran may have calmed down."

# Seven: Stubbornness

Ruth

Ruth and Orpah got as far as the well and sat for a few minutes. Ruth could not bring herself to tell Orpah what had happened. Instead, she told Orpah that she must go home because she needed to talk to her mother alone. Orpah shrugged and they parted company. But when Ruth got to her own house, she could not bring herself to go inside. It was just as well. Unseen, behind the thorny tree where she had once hidden the basket of food for Anna, she could hear her father's thunderous voice, raging about what she had done. He stood just beyond the large gate with his brother, her uncle. She could not see their faces but she knew her father was as dark as a storm cloud, his eyes flashing fire. His younger brother's quieter voice did nothing to calm him. Because of his anger, she was afraid to go to him to try to make him understand that she did not want to marry Pentu, that she had only promised herself to Mahlon because she had felt trapped--just as she felt hopelessly trapped now. If she revealed her presence, she feared her father would beat her again.

Pentu's camels, lined up outside the gate, made Ruth pinch her nose. Donkeys smelled too but were not as offensive. In fact, Ruth liked the musky odor of donkeys. Sheep too seemed pleasant enough except when they got wet and reeked. One of the camels bellowed, perhaps objecting to the leather halter tight around its long nose. The saddle too must weigh a lot and probably hurt the animal's back. It would be a long journey to Egypt. Possibly if she went now that she was once again in the good graces with her mother, it would not be so terrible. A lot could happen before she came of age.

Just as she got up her courage ready to join her family, she heard Pentu saying something so serious that she waited and listened. "Haran," he said. "Your daughters are both lovely girls. I came with you to Moab in the hopes one of them would make me a bride. I am afraid I misled you. Anna is far too young for me, and I am not willing to wait many years to begin my family. Ruth, too, is years away from becoming a wife." He laughed. "She reminds me of a colt needing to be tamed, but I am not the man who will break her."

Ruth sank down, her hands shaking as much with fury as with fear.

Pentu went on. "I suppose I wanted an adventure before I settled down. My father and mother recommended a girl who is of age and suitable and willing. I intend to take only one wife as is our custom, but I am most glad to have come to your land. You are my friend and I want you to return with me to Egypt where you will be safe. I will help you until you can establish your own business again. Meanwhile, I have decided to marry the Egyptian girl chosen for me. She will unite her family with mine and that will make my parents happy."

Suddenly Ruth felt that she, a Moabite girl, could never be as desirable as this rich foreign girl. She wondered what would happen to her family in Egypt. She had heard Emilelech telling Mahlon and Chilion how their ancestors were turned into slaves and forced to do hard labor until Moses helped them escape. She did not want to be anyone's slave. She struck the air with her fist at the unfairness she felt and her inability to change anything. Well, she would *not* go with them!

Later, choking back tears, she silently watched as donkeys and camels exited Haran's compound, heading up the hill towards the King's Highway. On their cart, she could see her mother leaning against her father. Soon they would be traveling across the Red Sea. She wanted to run after them and tell them to wait, but if they remained and were caught by the priests, her mother might be killed. Ruth hung her head. She had never watched anyone being stoned, but she knew it had happened. She had heard people whispering about how foolish this one or that one had been. It was always the women who were punished. Ruth wanted to stamp her feet in protest but it was an impossible situation. She had to stay quiet. At the thought that she would never see her mother or her sister or her father again, she hugged herself and rocked back and forth, tears raining down her cheeks. At last her eyes dried, she sat staring into space. She crept out from behind the tree and quietly went to Naomi's house. She stood in the entranceway watching Emilelech at his bench. "I can't believe it!" Naomi ran over with a little cry and gathered Ruth into her arms. "Your uncle will take you after your family on his fastest mule."

"I want to stay with you," Ruth said quietly.

Naomi let her go and stood back, her face creased with worry.

Emilelech stood up and came over to them. "You must obey your mother and father."

"I will not!" Ruth felt rebellion swelling in her like a puff-seed about to explode. "If they take me to Egypt, I will never be able to come back. Besides, I am promised to Mahlon." She hoped this would satisfy them and make them let her stay.

"You can remain here tonight, but in the morning we must take you to your uncle," Emilelech said.

Naomi nodded. "There is no other way."

But in the morning Ruth got up before anyone else was awake. She wrapped Naomi's shawl around her as much for comfort as for warmth and crept away, going to the stream where she and Orpah always went. This time, instead of sitting above the water, she scrambled down the steep precipice, dislodging rocks, hanging onto weeds to prevent herself from slipping. At last, she made it to the water's edge. It was running fast from the recent rainstorm, but she raised her gown above her knees and waded out and sat in a deep pool, letting the water eddy around her. At first it was so cold that it stung the scratches on her legs, but after a while her legs got numb. She sat in the water until a school of minnows flashed past her feet. She stared at the little fish as they swam with the current. If only her life was as uncomplicated as theirs.

When she got up, her saturated robe felt heavy and uncomfortable. Even Naomi's shawl, wrapped around her shoulders, was soaked through. She did not care. She climbed onto a flat boulder and lay on her back and stared at the sky. The sun warmed her until she fell into a deep slumber. When she woke up, she watched birds twittering above her head, darting about and feasting on insects. A blue-headed kingfisher with a long beak and a bright orange breast sailed just above the water before diving to snatch up a silver fish. She wished she had something to eat.

When a dead fish floated up to the rock and lodged in a crevice, she managed to grab it and peel back the brown skin. She bit into the yellow flesh and almost gagged and quickly spat it out. She tried to rinse away the sour taste in her mouth with the stream water, but the rotten taste persisted. At last she splashed to the shore and climbed onto the embankment, staring up at the steep cliff she had scrambled down. It looked treacherous, and besides she did not want to return home for fear she might yet be sent to Egypt. She did not want to become a slave girl or anyone's wife. She had listened once to Emilelech telling his sons the story of Abraham who was her ancestor, too. His wife, Sarah, could not have children, and so she provided her husband with a slave girl who had given birth to his child--a boy who was to be his heir. Instead, Ruth remembered how Sarah's baby, born much later, caused her to send the slave girl and her child into the desert to die. *I might die*, she thought, *but at least I would be the one to choose my destiny.*

She rolled up the robe around her waist and went back into the stream, and began to wade upstream, away from the village. She hopped from flat stone to flat stone and found herself enjoying her adventure. At times she had to push brush aside to travel along the channel that was full of slippery rocks and getting narrower. Eventually she took off her sandals, thinking her toes would better grip the moss-covered rocks, but a stone shifted under her feet, and she lost her balance. Her shoulder broke her fall, but she lay half-submerged while blood from a scrape on her arm seeped into the water. Shivering, she managed to crawl out of the stream to squat near brambles along the bank. She felt sick to her stomach and her mouth still tasted of the tainted fish.

The dense foliage around her seemed impassable. Her legs ached, her arm was bleeding, and she was wet all through, but some deep inner voice reassured her. It was as if the buzzing insects flying around her head in the hot afternoon air could not do her any serious harm with their stings. It was as if the cold and impassable streambed could not prevent her from something important that lay ahead. It was as if a deep silence settled her rapidly beating pulse and quieted her growling tummy.

A tall bird on stilted legs stalked towards her. She held out the palm of her hand, but even though its orange beak almost touched her fingers, it waded several feet upstream. At last, it turned, and with a loud squawking and flapping of its wide wings, it took off and flew noisily above the brush. It was as if a spell had been broken. Ruth knew now that she must move on from this deep quiet and continue her journey. Aching and feeling a little sick, she yearned for the comfort of home. She followed the bird, stopping when she came to where it had flown away. She discovered a trickle of water entering the stream.

She wrapped Naomi's shawl tightly around her hurt arm and sloshed through a marshy inlet, eventually coming out on a sandy patch that led up a slope. Her feet sank into the sand, but as she made her way up the hill, at least it felt warm. It was not as steep as the cliff she had come down into the stream, but it was full of low-growing cacti with flat, thorny leaves. She carefully stepped around them and almost trod on a striped snake. It slithered away, probably as frightened of her as she was of it. Her heart racing, she began to run. One of her sandal straps ripped, yet she managed to keep going.

When she came upon a narrow trail, she sank to the ground and slipped off the torn sandal. With her thumb and forefinger she pulled out a cactus thorn that had pierced the heel of her foot. It hurt so much that her eyes watered. She held her sore foot in both hands, wondering how she would be able to walk any farther, but she had to do something. She could not stay here. What if that snake came back? What if there were others? She quickly ripped the shawl into rags and tied them around her foot, hoping this would make it easier for her to walk. She managed to hobble along and soon realized this path was a well-trampled animal trail. When she came out onto a wider road, she discovered a palm-shaded spring, probably where wild animals came to drink. She limped towards the trickle flowing from between two rocks. With her lips pressed against the stones she managed to swallow a few drops. Water dripped down her chin.

Sinking to the ground, she unwrapped her sore foot. Her heel was flaming red and hurt. But when she noticed a pile of animal scat, she forgot all about her pain. This animal waste looked like it might be from a big cat, and she knew this would not be a safe place to stay for long. She had lost her bearings and seeing the setting sun did not help. With her foot once again bound by the strips of linen from Naomi's shawl, she began to limp along, her heel throbbing. The road looked barren and foreboding in the waning light, but she walked on, resting once in a while, listening to the clicking of locusts and the rustle of creatures in the undergrowth on either side of the road.

Surely this must be the King's Highway, a road her father so often took. She yearned for his strong arms around her and wanted to forgive him for punishing her. She yearned for the coolness of the house away from this air that felt as hot as an oven. She began to perspire, salty droplets stinging her eyes and running down her cheeks. Her forehead was as hot with fever as Anna's had been. Her mouth tasted of the dead fish, and she thought she would throw up. She lay on the ground and tucked her feet inside her robe and fell into a feverish sleep.

When she awoke, she did not know where she was. Nothing looked familiar. The sun, a fiery disc, glared down without mercy. Not far distant, she heard the shrill laughter of hyenas. Rising to her feet, she began to totter along until she could go no further. On her knees, her stomach began to go into spasms. She heaved but nothing came up. She got to her feet and stood there wobbling, wishing she could escape this nightmare, but she could hardly walk. She had not come much further when in her mind's eye she saw the face of Naomi. "Help me," she managed to cry, and continued to limp along. When she came across a heap of round stones that had been tossed onto the ground, she realized they were warp weights similar to the ones she had seen her aunts using when they weaved. She sat and leaned against the wooden frame close by.

A large bird soared around in circles over her head, and then another, and another. Their majestic wings turned them gracefully in the air, but Ruth knew only too well what they were. Vultures! One landed not too far from her feet, its beady eyes staring towards her. She picked up a nearby slat of wood and waved it in the direction of the ugly bird. It shifted a few yards away, but others landed nearby. She began to shout as loud as she could "Get away from me! Get away!" The noise she managed to make caused the birds to fly farther from her, but they did not leave. They hopped about, waiting. She threw the wooden slat like a spear at the birds. One of them rose from the ground and shifted out of the way. Ruth got onto her knees and crawled behind the frame of the discarded loom, taking with her another wooden slat.

All of a sudden the vultures arose, their flapping wings sounding as loud as a hailstorm against dry palm leaves as they flew away. Ruth felt a little calmer, and she dropped the slat and examined her foot. It was still throbbing but not as much, and mercifully she no longer felt as nauseous.

When a fierce cat trotted into view, she almost wished she were seeing things. The beast stopped some feet away and stared at her through slanted eyes. For some reason, she was not terrified of this beautiful creature. She almost wanted to go and hug it like she did her favorite goat or one of the new lambs. The two watched each other for several moments. The lion yawned and sniffed the air before flopping onto its side and rolling around on its back like a big kitten. Ruth knew, in spite of its size, it was still young. After a while, the cat stood up, shook itself vigorously, and trotted away.

The rumbling wheels of a cart and the soft thuds of donkey hoofs sounded. Ruth stood up, hardly able to believe what she was hearing. She soon saw a man leading a wagon with a woman sitting on the front seat. Two loaded-down camels trotted behind. Ruth smiled and limped towards them.

# Eight: Daring

Naomi

My arms felt chilled and I realized the moment that I awoke that Ruth was no longer next to me. I silently scolded myself for not having taken the girl directly to Haran's compound and put her under the care of her uncle. What on earth did I expect? I could only hope she had made her way there on her own, but the sinking feeling in my stomach told me that Ruth, as headstrong as she was, might well have run away.

"Emilelech! Boys!" I yelled up the stairs. "Get up! Ruth is gone!"

My sons clattered down the ladder, their hair tousled from sleep, their mouths yawning. Mahlon narrowed his eyes and looked around the courtyard. He ran to the gate into the street and went outside, looking left and right before returning. "How long has she been missing?"

"I have no idea but we must go and find her." I noticed my shawl was not on the hook where I had left it and knew Ruth must have taken it. It was my best one, soft, woven from flax, stained blue, but I was glad for Ruth to have it wrapped around her as if it would somehow protect her. "Emilelech," I cried, staring up to the second floor. "I am going to Haran's to see if Ruth is there."

I did not wait for his response but hurried towards the alley with Mahlon and Chilion trailing behind me. I looked back and still saw no sign of my husband. Sometimes I wanted to slap that man, but I knew it took him a while to rouse himself. This morning I had little sympathy. "You stay here, Chilion, and tell your father where we have gone." He looked sulky but returned to the courtyard. I wished the boy knew how to milk the goat but only women performed such chores. I went over to the olive tree and took out a loaf of day-old flatbread from a basket hanging from a branch. It was already getting stale but I ripped it in two. "Here." I thrust one half toward Chilion who immediately sank his teeth into it. That boy was always starving. I stared at his slight body for a moment. "We will be back as quick as we can. There is minced chickpea and herbs in a bowl in the kitchen and also dried fruit and pomegranate seeds. Mahlon, you do not have to go with me." I handed him the rest of the bread.

"I want to come," he said, and ripped the bread into pieces and took a bite.

I was hungry too but I could wait to eat. I always did. I bustled out of the yard and hurried past the priest's house grateful that no voices called out to ask me where we were going. I was glad too that Mahlon, even though he was a gangly lad, had come with me. As a woman I was forbidden to go anywhere without asking other than for fetching water, but I refused to wait for my husband's permission. I did not like Ruth leaving the way she had, but once again I admired her courage, her refusal to simply go along with what was expected.

As we approached the village gate, we could hear women chattering and coming towards us. We stopped and waited for them. At first I wondered if these women were bringing their water jugs from the well, but it was still too early even for that. Soon enough the women from Haran's compound, Ruth's aunts and cousins, bustled up to us and gathered around us. One of them came within a hairbreadth of my face. "Have you seen Ruth?" she demanded.

I felt guilty and was taken aback by the woman's obvious anger. I leaned away and managed to stammer, "She was at my house last night and I was going to bring her over to you this morning, but when I awoke she was gone."

A couple of the other women tsked angrily.

"I hoped she was already with you," I added lamely.

"Come," said one of the others. "We must search for her!"

"She might have gone back to be with her friend Orpah," I suggested.

"I can show you where Orpah lives," Mahlon said, and one of the women rolled her eyes, probably well aware of who Orpah was and where she lived. My son paid her no attention. He turned around and headed back down the shadowy lane, not seeming to mind being the lone boy ahead of a cluster of worried women.

Orpah's mother must have heard us coming. She rushed out of her house with her head uncovered.

"Is Ruth here?" someone asked.

"Not since yesterday," the usually cheerful lady said, dismay all over her face.

"She has run off," I said. "We are worried about her."

"Orpah!" her mother called into the house. Her daughter trudged out. "Do you know where Ruth might have gone?"

Orpah stared at her feet.

"Tell us now!" her mother demanded.

Orpah raised her eyes sheepishly. "We have a secret place above the river."

"Take us there immediately," one of the aunts said.

With a big sigh, Orpah led us around her house through the hole in the back wall. We followed her through winding streets out into the rocky wilderness. Too busy trying not to trip on my long robe, I soon gathered the cloth above my knees like the other women. It was unseemly of us especially if any men saw our legs, but there were no men around except for my son, and he did not look back. I certainly did not want him to see me displaying myself, but he was clearly more interested in finding Ruth, than worry about his mother's propriety. As we approached the edge of a cliff above a trickling stream, I could see flattened grass underneath a tree.

"Ruth always wanted to go down into the water, but we never did," Orpah said.

It was a steep bluff and none of the women, even with their clothing hitched around their waists, could possibly have made it safely to the bottom. We stared down the cliff, not knowing what to do next.

No one said a word but Mahon did not hesitate. He started down the precipice, treading gingerly, almost losing his balance as small rocks were dislodged by his feet, and even if I had wanted to stop him, scared he would fall and hurt himself, I would not have succeeded. In that moment I understood something new. I had heard that strength came from Hashem, but I realized that strength did not come from an outside force but from the love within people becoming action in the world.

Eventually Mahlon went onto his hands and knees and crawled to the bottom, and stood next to the stream bank, his head turning back and forth, searching for Ruth. A flock of birds flapped out of the water, making a racket above his head. All we women seemed to be holding our breath as he walked upstream and then stood with his hands behind him. For one dreadful moment I feared Ruth had drowned, and he could see her body, but after what seemed an age, he yelled up to us. "There is no sign of her down here!"

My dear son somehow crawled back up that steep slope. His robe was ripped and I could see dirt all over his knees. He sat on the grass and took off his sandals and picked up a stick to scrape off clay and pebbles. To me he will always be my little boy, but his serious eyes told me he was becoming a man who could take charge. "Orpah, where else is Ruth likely to have gone?" he asked. His gentle voice was full of determination, and he was not to be trifled with. I felt proud of him.

"I don't know," she wailed. "This is our favorite place, but sometimes we go to the well, and sometimes we walk around the village and peek in people's houses."

"We will split up," Mahlon said. He directed a few women to search the village and told the rest of us to follow him.

It surprised me how readily everyone obeyed, but I suppose none of us had any better ideas.

We did not find Ruth at the well. Mahlon and the rest of us made our way back to Haran's compound. Someone fetched us tea. Children gathered around us but were shooed away to play. I was glad for the hot cup in my hands.

Once the others who had searched the village joined us, and did not have a word to say, we knew that Ruth was nowhere to be found. No one they had asked had seen her either.

"Very well," Mahlon announced. "I will go to the King's Highway. She must have gone up there."

"You will never be able to catch her on foot," someone remarked.

"Take our donkey. My husband did not need her this morning and she is still in her pen with the goats."

I knew Mahlon could not ride. He had never even driven a team of oxen, but I felt as if we had no choice but to try. "Do you not have a wagon we could borrow?"

"I do," a woman, with her veil now draped over her shoulders, said. "It is outside the field where our donkey is grazing. Let me fetch the yoke and harness."

One of the women frowned at me. "It is unacceptable for your son, especially since he is the cause of all the trouble, to be with Ruth alone!"

How ridiculous! I wanted to shake her. It was not Mahlon who had caused trouble but Haran's stubbornness and drunkenness and the hateful treatment of Anna. The image of my Misho-angel flashed into my mind. "I will go with my son," I announced, but my words sounded hollow in my ears, and I felt myself shrinking. I ought to ask Emilelech if it was all right for me to go with Mahlon. I hoped no one noticed my anxiety, and I trusted that that no one would challenge me for not asking permission.

Even if someone did object, I decided that I was going to find that feisty girl who was like a daughter to me. I drew myself upright and straightened my shoulders.

Before long we had made our way to a nearby field. Someone took the donkey by her fetlock, led her away from the goats, and harnessed her to a cart used for bringing in hay. The driver's seat was wide enough for two. I dragged myself onto the seat and tucked my garment securely around my knees. Mahlon hopped up next to me, stood behind the running board and picked up the reins and shook them. "Move on," he said, and the donkey dragged us away from the field up the dirt trail leading to the Kings Highway that was rutted by many iron wheels. This was the main road that we had come down when we had arrived at Haran's. Mahlon tugged on the rein to turn the donkey, but the beast planted its hooves and refused to move. It defiantly tossed its obstinate head, unwilling to obey. "Get down, Mahlon, and lead her," I said. My son looked doubtfully at me, but he handed me the reins. They felt sticky from his sweaty fingers. My pulse pounded in my neck.

Even with Mahlon tugging on her yoke, the donkey still refused to budge. He even tried wrapping his arms around her rump and pushing her, but she still refused to move. Mahlon, disgusted, sat on the back of the cart with his feet dangling. I did not realize how determined I could be, but I was not about to let a donkey get the better of me. I took the sash off my robe and, using it as a whip, I flicked at the animal. My belt was light and could not hurt, but the donkey swished her tail in my direction, before slowly dragging the cart into the middle of the highway.

Without any warning, the donkey tossed her head and brayed, and kicked at the shaft of the cart, taking off at a fast trot. I tugged hard on the reins, but I was not strong enough to stop the beast. She ran faster, her hooves pounding the rough surface of the road. I hung on afraid the cart would roll over. I glanced back at my son who had managed to get into the bed. At last the donkey, snorting and wild-eyed, slowed down to a walk. As frustrated as I was, I felt sorry for her.

Mahlon crawled up to the front and sat next to me. He grinned, obviously excited by our escapade, one I could have done without. "Ma," he said. "I can see your knees again."

I raised my eyebrows at him and frowned at his disrespect. My robe had blown to one side and my veil was hanging loose. I quickly covered up, and my heart was pounding but I felt very much alive. An idea burst into my head. "Ruth was so angry with her parents I wouldn't be surprised if she went in the very opposite direction from Egypt to spite them. I think we ought to keep going this way at least for a while."

"You may be right," Mahlon mumbled, and took the reins from me and shook them to get the donkey moving again. She ambled along, and I was once more reminded of how tired women often were from overwork. We rolled slowly until midday when the sun shone hotly down. With no sign of Ruth, I began to doubt my decision and wished we had turned around and gone towards Egypt.

At last we came across a spring seeping from between two rocks. Mahlon hopped down and led the donkey over to it. The poor creature looked as weary as I felt. I hoped she would not keel over or refuse to go another step. My son knelt at the gurgling spring, cupped his hands to fill them, and offered a drink to the donkey. Its thick pink tongue licked up every drop. He gave it several more handfuls, and when she wanted no more, he splashed water into his face before quenching his own thirst.

I got off the cart and went over to the spring and stood next to him and also took a drink while Mahlon backed the donkey away. The sweet water restored me. "Perhaps it is time for us to turn back," I said, but as I returned to the cart, I noticed a few strands of blue thread at my feet. I stooped down and picked them up and dangled the threads in front of his eyes. "Mahlon, look! these are from my shawl, but why would Ruth have torn it?" A startling thought crossed my mind that a wild creature had attacked Ruth, and that this was all that remained, but Mahlon's eyes got wide with hope. "She might be close by. Let us go," he said, and we set off again.

We had not gone far when we heard the rattle of wheels and the steady thud of hooves. As we rounded a bend we saw a caravan coming towards us. I could see a man with no turban to protect his head leading a donkey-cart followed by two camels. Soon we were near enough to see his eyes. He nodded and I nodded back, unsure of what to say, waiting for him to speak. All at once, a woman sat up from the back of their wagon and raised her hand in greeting.

I waved back. "Have you seen a girl?" I called.

"I am here," cried Ruth, and she came tumbling out of the cart and limped towards us. I had a strong desire to scold her, but Mahlon handed me the reins and leapt down and raced past the man, throwing his arms around her.

Our donkey threw its head in the air and snorted. I feared it might bolt again, but it only brayed, causing the other donkey to draw its lips back from its big yellow teeth. "Whoa," the man said and grabbed the halter of his donkey.

I dropped the reins and jumped off the cart and quickly caught up with my son and pulled him away from the girl. "Ruth," I cried, taking her face into my hands. "We were so worried about you!"

Mahlon pointed to her sore foot. "What happened?"

Ruth began to babble about a cactus thorn and a big cat and black vultures. I thought she must be feverish and felt her forehead but her skin was cool.

"She will be fine," the man said. "I wish my wife were as strong as this girl." He let go of the lead rope to his donkey so that it touched the ground. The donkey lowered its head quietly, obviously well-trained. He fetched our donkey and secured her reins on the branch of a scrubby wattle bush.

While he was busy, I noticed how thin and pale his woman seemed, peering at us from big luminous eyes. She was sitting on a straw-filled mattress crowded against piles of household goods. She said nothing and appeared to be fatigued, reminding me of how Emilelech collapsed on this very road. I felt my stomach churn. My husband was probably as concerned about *our* whereabouts as we had been about Ruth's. "You should not have run away, Ruth." I wanted to take a switch to her but quickly regretted feeling such fury! "At least you are safe!" I turned to the man. "Thank you for rescuing her. I hope she has not been any trouble to you."

He laughed. "No. Not at all. She even showed us a loom where she had been hiding. Someone must have abandoned it on the side of the road. If we had had room, we would have brought it along. Since my wife is unable to weave anymore, we could probably sell it."

My mouth opened and I gasped. "Mahlon, that must be my loom!" I wished we could fetch it but it would take too long. We needed to get Ruth home as fast as possible and relieve everyone's worries. Emilelech was probably furious with us.

The man looked me over, his eyes lingering on my breasts. I felt like a goat he planned to buy.

Flustered, I felt a need to explain and also emphasize that I had a husband. "We left the loom behind so that my husband who felt a little poorly could ride in the wagon."

"Ah," the man responded. "We are going to the Temple of Sety in Egypt where people have been known to recover their strength. I am taking my wife there. You and your family could accompany us. Where is your husband now?"

I hesitated, unwilling to reveal that we were alone, just Mahlon and I. Yet, I also felt hopeful. Perhaps we could send Ruth to Egypt with this couple.

"A lion scared off vultures," Ruth muttered, her face flushed.

I had no idea what she was talking about, but even though I was tempted to send Mahlon by himself to fetch my loom, I knew it would be unwise.

How could he lift the heavy oak crossbeam of the frame by himself? And I did not want to be alone with this man, no matter how obliging he seemed. There was something about him that made me uneasy, but perhaps I was only being silly, unaccustomed as I was to being alone in the presence of strange men. Nevertheless, I found myself acting agreeably. "We can travel together to my village," I said, feeling odd to call Moab mine. "We would welcome you to stay with us where you can rest and get more supplies for your journey." I took Ruth by the arm. "Come along, Ruth. It's time to get you home."

"Ma!" Mahlon interrupted, scowling. "First, I will go and fetch your loom. You know how much it means to you!"

"I will take your cart and fetch it," the man said. "You stay here with the women, son." He eyed me lasciviously, adding, "you need not worry about paying me a shekel." His thick accent and his implication made me blush.

His wife covered her eyes and turned away.

The way he had ogled me made me realize that he wanted a payment of the sort I would never give. What a swine! No wonder our men wanted to protect us women. I pulled my veil around my face and stepped away from him.

He grinned, then sidestepping me, leapt into the cart, gathered the reins, and sent the donkey trotting. I was unnerved, but once he was out of sight, I moved my veil to one side so that the woman, who still had not said a word, could see my eyes. I smiled at her, wondering if she even spoke our language. She too moved her veil aside and smiled back and in a clear easily understandable voice said, "I am glad you came for your daughter."

I did not correct her and tell her that Ruth was not my child. Ruth must be returned to her family in Egypt, but I did not want her to travel with them. Clearly, the presence of his frail little wife would be no protection from her husband, whom I did not trust. It occurred to me though that if I could convince Emilelech, he and I could take Ruth to Egypt, and I could encourage him to go to the healing Temple of Sety.

# Nine: Peril

## Ruth

After they had done screaming at her for running away, Ruth's uncles and aunts ignored her. Her younger cousins looked on without sympathy, nudging one another and giggling at the trouble she had gotten herself into. The foreigners who had found her were quickly seated on cushions and given ale and fussed over. A young goat was slaughtered to be roasted on a spit over an outdoor fire. Ruth was not even offered stale bread. Naomi and Mahlon who had followed everyone into the house got no thanks either. They were ignored as if they did not exist. Ruth, humiliated, rolled her eyes in embarrassment. Mahlon approached her and gently squeezed her upper arm. She managed a little smile at his comforting gesture.

"You!" Ruth's aunt glanced at Mahlon, her lips tight. "You have caused enough trouble!"

Mahlon's face flooded with color.

"You!" the aunt spat again, this time at Ruth, "You are lucky these kind strangers are willing to take you with them tomorrow! Now, get out of my sight!"

Naomi, looking alarmed, spoke up. "Please," she said. "There is no need to trouble your guests. My husband and I will take Ruth when we go to Egypt. In the meantime she can stay with us."

"Certainly not!" the aunt retorted, frowning. "We are not letting her out of our sight until we know she is definitely on her way back to her parents." She stared angrily at Naomi.

Naomi took Mahlon's arm, obviously knowing it was useless to argue, and led him out of the house.

Ruth wanted to run after them, but knew better, and limped quietly to her room. She pulled the drapery closed. She had not meant to cause trouble, but how could she explain her fears that her mother and father—and she too if she went to Egypt—were going to be turned into slaves. How could she say *anything* when everyone was furious with her and wanted nothing more than to rid themselves of her.

She managed to sleep fitfully until morning when she felt someone shaking her shoulder. She opened her eyes. "It is time to go," her aunt, the kind one, said. "Get up! You'd better eat some bread and dates while your uncle and our guest are fetching the camels and the donkeys."

Ruth stumbled into the kitchen and poured a cup of milk. When she noticed the pale little stranger sitting off to one side, she held out the pitcher to her but the woman shook her head. Ruth could not help but feel sorry for this lady who must be quite ill and obviously weak, her back bent as if she carried a great weight. Ruth wondered would her spine one day look as if she had been burdened with something unimaginable. Somehow Ruth knew it was more than a physical problem. Even though Mahlon was thin, his eyes were always clear and shining. Ruth went over and sat next to the lady and offered her bread dipped in milk. The woman once again shook her head as if food were repellent to her. Ruth shrugged, and even though she was ravenous, she too found it difficult to eat, worried about what was going to happen next, aware she had no option but to obey.

Before long she heard a camel bellowing. The thin lady slowly got to her feet, gathered her skirt off the floor in one hand and walked as if she were treading on hot coals. She seemed to be in a lot of pain. Ruth's throbbing foot already looked less red but it still hurt too. She followed the woman through the courtyard, matching her slow pace until they stood at the wide-open gate. Her uncle was standing next to the woman's husband. He greeted her and helped her up onto the front seat of their cart. He checked the ropes to the camels that were tied to the back and hopped up and sat with a thud next to her.

Ruth looked back to see some of her cousins and aunts standing nearby looking on. When a little girl waved and called out bye-bye, her mother grabbed her hand and hurried her back to their dwelling, a house similar to the one Ruth was raised in, one she had often been inside with Anna. They had all played together. Ruth felt her throat constrict with sorrow. She did not want to go, yet she did not want to stay either.

Her uncle glared at her. "Ruth," he said sternly. "Get in the back!"

Ruth wanted to throw her arms around him and hug him, but she knew she would be pushed away. She climbed over some boxes and luggage and leaned against the side of the cart. "Uncle, I am sorry," she murmured.

Her uncle made no reply but spoke to the strangers. "Safe travels," he said. "Thank you for taking this wayward girl with you. If she gives you any trouble, you have my permission to punish her."

Ruth shivered and tucked her robe around her legs to cover the scratches. The thin scabs would soon fall away and her legs would look better, but they had left a mark deep in her heart. Her father had been her champion, but now she felt as if he were a traitor and an enemy. Her only friends here in the village were Naomi and Mahlon, but they had not even come to say goodbye. Ruth felt abandoned and alone.

The man shook the reins and clicked his tongue and the small caravan rumbled up the trail to the Kings Highway.

"Uncle," Ruth shouted back. "Please don't forget to take the loom to Naomi."

The man grunted, turned his back, and walked haughtily into the compound, slamming the gate behind him.

The man reached back as if he meant to stroke her hair. "I will take good care of you, girl."

Ruth ducked out of his way wishing she were grown up enough to wear a veil and could hide from his cold, judgmental eyes. His pale little wife stared straight ahead.

They traveled many miles on the rutted road, sending clouds of dust behind them into the air. At last they arrived at a village with flat-roofed houses shaded by leafy trees. Behind, in the distance, twin peaks from a mountain rose up into the sky. They found an inn for the night, a place that also served food.

A platter of vegetables and fruits and spicy bread was set out for them. Ruth had never tasted anything like this before. The food was so hot that her mouth burned and she had to drink many cups of water. The lady hardly ate anything but kept sipping something from a small flask. Ruth thought it might be some sort of medicine, perhaps something to ease her pain. Her husband went on drinking beer until he began to slur his words. His wife, who had hardly said a word the whole way, now whispered. "Come with me to the sleeping rooms." She glanced at her husband, but he paid her no attention, too busy swilling back his drink and swapping stories with a couple of other men.

The woman took Ruth's hand and led her to a small room and settled her on a sleeping mat against the wall.

Ruth stretched out her legs.

The lady patted Ruth's shoulder.

Ruth looked into her eyes. This woman might look unhealthy, weak, and helpless, but her expression showed strength and courage. "Thank you," Ruth murmured.

The lady dragged another mat over next to Ruth where she lay down. Ruth knew her father and mother liked to go to bed together sometimes, but this lady had put a third mat against the far wall. When her husband staggered into the room, she moved closer to Ruth as if to shield her. The man fell onto his mat and was soon snoring.

In the morning, they left early, after eating more of the spicy bread dipped in garlic and olive oil. All that day, they covered more dusty ground, eventually arriving in a town built against a large expanse of water. "Ezion-Geber," the man said in his heavy accent. Ruth knew it was a port city, a place her father had often visited.

The man continued to talk, his voice so animated that Ruth had trouble making out what he was saying, but she thought he meant that this was where he had been born. He leaped off the cart and led the donkey down some narrow streets, obviously knowing where he was going. His wife wrapped a shawl around her shoulders and glanced back at Ruth, then threw her a little smile. "His sisters are very kind," she whispered.

Women rushed out of their houses that surrounded a large courtyard. They quickly made sure the livestock were watered and settled down in a pen. They fussed around the man, all talking at once, pointing at Ruth, apparently asking who she was. At last, they led him under a shady portal and settled him on a pile of cushions. One woman ran into a house and came out with a pitcher of wine. Meanwhile, Ruth stayed in the back of the cart until a lady wearing an earth-brown gown and a bright orange headscarf attended to the wife. She gestured to Ruth to follow them into a house.

As they left, Ruth could feel the man watching her. She was greatly relieved to be sent with the small children to the far end of a spacious tiled room. The man's wife sat with some other women who spoke gently to her. They rubbed her back and offered her fresh fruit. Ruth's mouth watered, but she knew that children were often the last to be served, and since she was a girl, she might have to wait even longer than the boys before being given something to eat. She smiled at one of the little girls who was about the same age as Anna. "You are very pretty," she said, touching the child's healthy cheeks.

One of the women spoke to Ruth, but she could not understand her words. She shrugged. The man's wife interpreted. "She says you are very pretty too. She asked you if you would like some honey-soaked pastries."

"Yes, please," Ruth nodded, hoping they would get to stay here for a while so that she got a chance to look at the sea that she'd heard about from her father. The pastry was thinly layered, crispy golden brown, and delightfully sweet. Ruth tried to eat delicately but honey dripped down her chin. She used her fingers to wipe it away and licked them. Her enjoyment pleased the women who clapped their hands and brought her a glass of juice. She almost forgot about the man until he loomed in the doorway and announced he was going out to see his brothers. Ruth was happy to watch him leave. She hoped he would not come back any time soon. Later, with the women busily preparing the evening meal, no one paid any attention to her. She wandered outside of the courtyard and walked into the salty wind coming off the sea. Her hair blew all over the place and she wished Orpah were with her to share this moment.

When she rounded a bend and saw the sea, she stopped and stared at the white-capped waves. The water rippled and seemed to be in constant motion. She sidled past fishing boats lined up along a dock, their nets flapping in the wind, and made it to a rocky beach. She plopped onto the ground and dipped her feet into the water, surprised at how warm the waves lapping gently across her toes felt. She leaned over and cupped some of the water into the palm of her hands and took a sip, but it was so salty she spat it out and laughed. Seagulls circled, dipping, and soaring above a boat that was sailing into the port, laden with nets full of silvery fish. Another boat, no doubt a ferry like the one her father had mentioned that he took on his way to Egypt, was rowed next to a wooden pier where it was moored. A man led a camel down a ramp onto the shore. Ruth smiled at the likelihood that she would get to go on this ferry when they continued the journey. She almost forgave her father but a loud male voice startled her.

"What do you think you are doing here?"

Ruth looked up into the eyes of the man she had been forced to travel with. She shrank back. "I wanted to see the water," she said as calmly as she could. Standing behind him were two other men with dark tanned faces who she knew must be his brothers. They smelled of fish. The man grabbed her wrist and tugged her to her feet. "How dare you come out unaccompanied. What kind of girl are you?" The other men narrowed their eyes and tightened their lips in obvious disapproval.

If she could have, Ruth would have broken her arm to free herself from his grip, but the man had a strong hold on her and dragged her towards a building with tall stone columns. His brothers sauntered alongside. As they got closer to the entranceway, Ruth thought it must be some sort of temple. Near the doorway, two men with shaved heads wearing gold breastplates thrust long spears across the opening. The man spoke to them in a language Ruth did not understand. The guards quickly lowered their weapons and allowed them into a central hall with a domed ceiling.

Several women lounged around on cushions while an almost naked young man played a flute and danced. Perfumes and incense scented the air. A woman wearing sheer clothing, revealing her bare midriff, with her breasts wrapped in jeweled cloth, got to her feet and smiled. Ruth stared at her delicate sandals that were so unlike hers, now saturated with sea water. The woman's smile did not reach her eyes.

The brothers wandered over to sit with some young women who fawned over them.

Ruth looked all about feeling confused and all too aware that she was helplessly trapped. She stared at a stone statue of a woman with her hands covering her breasts placed behind an altar similar to the one where the priests at home made sacrifices. When she heard the man say fifty-five shekels, Ruth shuddered, afraid they were arguing over how much *she* was worth. The woman moved her hands in a downward gesture clearly indicating that she would not pay as much as the man wanted, but with a salacious smile, she ran her hands up and down Ruth's body.

Ruth squirmed. The way the man and his brothers were now looking at her made her desperate to escape.

A servant was summoned and put several coins in the palm of the man's hand. With a grin, he called his brothers, and the three strode away.

The woman took Ruth's hand firmly in hers and led her to an inner room where women took off her dirty clothes, washed and perfumed her. They smiled and painted her face and dressed her in scanty clothing like theirs. Ruth, too shocked at what was happening, did not resist. Even her feet were washed and scented. These women seemed friendly, but their attention frightened her. All of a sudden she realized what these women did. She had heard about temple prostitutes and always knew that she could never face such a life. She realized that these women probably had no choice.

After they left her alone in the small chamber, she peeked out and saw one of the bald-headed guards leaning against the wall. She heard the murmurs of men and women nearby and smelled sweet wine. It was all she could do to stop herself from sobbing and begging him to let her go. Terrified, she lay hugging her knees waiting for what was about to happen.

The curtains rustled and slid partially open. Ruth could hardly believe her eyes. There stood the man's wife in front of the guard. The frail little woman could not possibly pose any threat. She smiled and offered him a mug of ale. "My husband sent you this as a token of his regards," she said.

The man took the tankard and suspiciously sniffed the liquid.

"It is freshly brewed from our best hops," said another woman, the one who had given Ruth the pastries.

Ruth pulled the curtain open a little further.

The guard was staring from one woman to the other, but finally he took a sip, and a smile flashed across his face.

"We would like to say goodbye to the girl if that is all right," the woman said.

The guard rose to his full height, dwarfing both women. His arm and leg muscles bulged beneath his clothing. He said nothing but he drew the curtain to one side and pointed inside. He stood watching as they stepped into the room. "Ruth," the woman said quietly, holding her fingers over her mouth to let Ruth know that she must be quiet. She wrapped her arms around Ruth and whispered, "We have come to get you out of here."

They heard a slump and saw the guard drop the tankard, spilling its contents as he fell to the ground. He grunted and rolled onto his back, his arms flailing across the tile.

"Put this on. Quickly!" The women produced a heavy coat. "Hurry! We managed to sneak in through a side entrance without anyone seeing us."

Ruth tugged her arm through a sleeve of the tight coat, glad to cover the flimsy material wrapped around her body.

"You should not have gone out by yourself," the sister-in-law muttered. "But you don't deserve this as a punishment."

"Never mind!" the frail woman said. "I am glad we realized what my husband had done." She patted Ruth's arm. "My husband bragged about the money he took. There is a musical troupe leaving tonight for Moab. They will take you as far as Hebron. It is not far from your home. You will be able to walk the rest of the way."

"The guard!" Ruth said in alarm. "What about him?" She was terrified he would jump to his feet at any moment.

"I have taken care of him." The woman took out her flask of liquid from an inner pocket.

Ruth's eyes grew big.

"It will not kill him. He is asleep, but he will wake up soon. Now hurry!"

Ruth tied a sash around the coat to keep it from flapping open. The wool scratched her skin and made her almost burst into tears. She was being spared from something too ugly to name, but she still felt ashamed and she wanted to drown herself in the sea.

# Ten: Shock

Naomi

As soon as Mahlon and I returned to our courtyard, after leaving Ruth and the strangers at Haran's, I noticed Orpah sitting close to Chilion on a bench, her arm around his shoulder. His head drooped and what I could see of his face looked pale. "Chilion." I rushed over. "What is wrong?"

Orpah looked up at me, her eyes red and swollen as if she had been crying.

"Where is your father?"

"He is dead," Chilion said, but did not look up.

I stared from one to the other. Orpah's eyes filled with tears.

Mahlon poked a finger into Chilion's chest and told him not to fool around. Chilion did not act furiously as he normally would when Mahlon picked a fight. He simply sat there, his arms limp at his sides. I felt cold chills down my spine. "What has happened?"

Chilion slowly raised his face. "I could not wake him after you left. I tried, but he would not get up."

Mahlon frowned and yelled for his father, but no one replied. Could my hopes of taking Emilelech to Egypt be futile? Was it too late? I felt such a surge of rage. Surely he had not left me in this foreign land, made me a widow with two young sons? It must not be so! I would not have it! But already I saw Mahlon scrambling up the ladder to find his father. I felt as if

I were in a dream when a few minutes later I saw him standing on the roof covering his eyes with his hands.

"Emilelech!" I cried and ran to the ladder. I could hear Mahlon's sobs as I gripped the uprights and began to climb. I did not want to find what I knew I was going to find. How was I to comfort Mahlon when all of a sudden I felt numb? Somehow I found myself on the roof. I kneeled next to Emilelech's body. I expected him to wake up and ask me what I thought I was doing on the floor next to him. I took his shoulders and tried to shake him, but his limp body felt as heavy as a rock. Tears began to swell and leak from my eyes. It was not merely grief. It was my overwhelming sense of helplessness. I did not even know how I would get his body off the roof. Mahlon knelt next to me and put an arm around my shoulder and a hand on his father's chest. Already, in what must have only been a few hours, his face was caving in on itself, making him scarcely recognizable. His body did not yet stink, but it would, and I had no spices or herbs to mask the odor, nor could I afford any.

I was always a practical person, always the one who took care of the household, making sure everything was orderly, making sure everyone was fed and clothed. I'd insisted Emilelech pay all the bills on time. I'd ensured all of our servants back in Bethlehem were given rest. I'd spoiled and cared for the guests we entertained. I'd always tried to do everything in a cheerful manner. Even when we had left Bethlehem, I'd gone out of my way to take that sack of grain to Leah. I had not even noticed the straps cutting into my shoulders. Such was my love, but I think I had hoped that she somehow would find a way out of my woes. I only remember her eyes swimming with tears and me turning my back and running away before I lost control. Leah had always been the strong one with definite opinions. She had always protected me. Hashem surely knew I never felt protected by Emilelech. I had made myself pretend that he was a perfect husband and I often bragged about him to Leah. But now, all of a sudden, I realized I'd not only been lying to her, but I had also been lying to myself. I had even blamed myself for having manipulated him into taking us away from our home and our friends and family. I had left my beautiful house without complaint. I looked around at the ill-swept and cracked rooftop where my dead husband now lay. I no longer wanted to pretend or make-do or say that everything would be all right. It was *not* all right. It would *never* be all right. Yet somehow my habitual practicality and sense of duty took over. "Take Chilion and Orpah away," I commanded Mahlon. "Go to her mother's. I need time alone."

Mahlon reluctantly left my side and silently slipped back down into the courtyard.

I did not really want to be near my husband's corpse, but in truth I was exhausted from the journey to find Ruth. I had no energy left. My mind flew into a hundred places. I knew Orpah's mother would feed my sons and take care of them. I wanted to run away, but I only had to think about Ruth's attempt to escape and realize she would probably have died on that dusty trail if no one had helped her. I suddenly thought about Boaz and wondered what my life would be like had I married him and not been so dutiful doing what my parents wanted. I had always done what was expected, excelled at being a nice girl, a dutiful wife, and a good mother, but now I felt as if scales were being ripped away from my eyes.

In spite of me fooling myself and feeling so comfortable and self-righteous, my carefully arranged life had not yielded me peace. As for my dreams of Boaz: was that not merely my attempt to find who would better take care of me? Why did I even need a man? Now I was left husbandless, virtually homeless, with no means of income and no friends. I felt like sobbing, but it would not be for Emilelech. It would be for myself and what I faced and did not want to face. I once again wished for another husband, a Boaz with a strong constitution, but for all I knew he too was dead.

I could not bear to look at Emilelech's body. I crawled away and stared into space. I did not know where to turn. Even if I managed to go back to Bethlehem and the drought was over and I could still have babies, who would marry me in order to produce an heir? My husband and I already had two sons. There would be no help coming from family. No one except my dear Leah would bemoan my situation and what could she do? I groaned out loud.

Back when I had lost my baby, the Moabites had helped me to mourn her and entomb her, but now I could expect no help from them. Haran was gone, and his family blamed me for not taking Ruth directly to them in order for her uncle to catch up to her family on their way to Egypt. They had repeatedly scolded Ruth, and I was glad to get away from them. Before Mahlon and I left, I managed to tell one of the young aunts not to allow Ruth to go with that man who I felt sure could not be trusted.

How was I to survive without a husband? My sons were too young to take on the role of head of the household, and yet it seemed Mahlon must grow up quickly. He would inherit Emilelech's fields, but far distant barren acres seemed of little value. And the boy would never be a farmer.

I stared mindlessly into the empty courtyard below with its simple bench and the old olive tree that was as barren as I felt. At least we had Emilelech's pottery wheel. Perhaps Mahlon could begin crafting ollas. And those strangers had promised to deliver my loom to me before they left. It was still on Haran's brother's cart. I wondered if I would have any vigor to even wind the yarn onto the posts? And without money, where would I get wool? I still had my spindle and distaff, but how could I find the strength in my arms to use these tools? The idea of threading my wooden needles to sew any clothes made me begin to weep, remembering how Emilelech always praised my needlework.

Oh Emilelech!

I crawled back to his body and stroked the creased garment covering his bony shoulders. He had been so pleased with this sleeping robe that I had sewn from the linen I myself had woven. It was a special gift to him after the birth of Mahlon. He had been so proud! Oh I wished I could lay down next to Emilelech and die with him, but my sons still needed me. Somehow I was able to summon enough energy to get up and go down the ladder. I would visit the priest who lived nearby and seek his help. Surely he would not turn me away, and surely the smell from a decaying corpse would cause him to help me dispose of my poor Emilelech. I wanted so much more than for my husband's body to be cast out in the desert for vultures and hyenas, but I had not a shekel to pay for even a simple burial in the earth.

My legs felt heavy and so tired that at the bottom of the ladder I dropped to the ground and had to lean against the wall. I needed to get up and get moving, but I found myself worrying about Ruth. At least, she had not perished in the wilderness, and no doubt her swollen foot and ankle would soon get better. I should have insisted that she come home with me so that we could take her to Egypt. But there was no *we* now. At least I still had my sons who were everything to me.

I gripped a side rail on the ladder and dragged myself to my feet. I knew I must look ragged and dirty, but this was no time for bathing myself or putting on a clean dress. As it was, I felt like ripping my clothing. But how would I replace anything since I had no man to provide money?

I forced myself to walk toward the road towards the priest's house, but when I got to the entrance of my court, I heard the voices of young men, and I hesitated.

Orpah's strapping brothers and my boys—who looked like shadows next to them--turned into the courtyard. The pitiful expressions on the faces of my sons tore at my heart.

Mahlon looked into my eyes. "Where are you going?"

"We need help to bury your father." My voice sounded raspy and I began to cry. I was ashamed at my need and display of emotion.

Chilion let out a low groan and kicked the wall, dislodging a loose brick.

One of Orpah's brothers picked it up and put it back. As he stood up, his eyes met mine. "We will take your husband's body to the cemetery where our kin are buried."

"I have no money to pay you," I quietly told him.

"We want none. We are here to help! Our father is going to borrow a cart tomorrow, but we can get him off the roof now if you like."

I could not meet his eager eyes, too embarrassed by my poverty and having to accept charity. My helplessness both humbled and enraged me, but I managed to nod my agreement. I would have preferred to leave his body where it was until it was taken away for burial, but I had no real choice.

Orpah's brothers shimmied up the ladder. With a rope tied around Emilelech's chest beneath his arms, they began lowering him down. Mahlon and Chilion waited below ready to catch their father's body that dangled like a broken tree limb. I looked away.

After the young men put Emilelech next to his pottery bench, Chilion took my hand and Mahlon put his arm around my waist. I needed their support or I would have fallen to the dirt.

I barely heard Orpah's brothers tell me that would come back tomorrow.

I do not know how I did it, but I sent Mahlon for a bucket of water, and I bathed Emilelech's body and pulled his eyelids shut. It was already dark when I lay on the ground next to him and fell into an exhausted sleep, only waking at dawn to the sound of the wheels of a cart coming down the lane. My sons' voices calling me quickly reminded me of my duty and I scrambled to my feet.

"Ma, come on. They are here."

Orpah's husband led a donkey-drawn cart up to the entrance to our courtyard. It was the same one we had used to find Ruth, and upon it sat my dismantled loom. "Where do you want this?" his sons asked as they jumped down from the running board.

It gave me a tiny surge of hope, but I was not sure that my loom would fit into this small courtyard, yet I managed to point at Emilelech's pottery wheel. "Near there, please." The thought of the last time I had seen Emilelech working the clay almost brought me to tears, but I controlled myself in front of these men whom I hardly knew. Emilelech was, or had been, a true artisan. How often I had yearned for him to be as robust as these fellow, but in this sorrowful moment, I suddenly respected my peace-loving and scholarly husband. I wished I had told him how much he had meant to me, and that I really hadn't minded him spending time with his scrolls, and time away from me teaching our sons. But it was too late now. The part of me that had thought him a coward to take us away from Bethlehem and avoid the gossip and anger of the people fell away. Now I realized he had been strong and in some ways brave. Even though it made him look weak, he had done what he thought best for his family and for me.

I watched as the wooden slats, the heavy frame, and the stone weights were laid on the ground. I hoped I would remember how to put the pieces back together. For now, I simply could not bother about something so ordinary. Yet I longed for the commonplace too: I wanted a return to the life when everything had been normal and boring, when I and my sister-in-law sat beneath the palm trees, smelling the ripening figs. Sometimes we grew irritated with one another, but I would be glad for her to be here now. Sometimes, from her tight-lipped silence, I had known that I had offended her. Once, I had patted my swelling pregnant belly, chirruping happily that I hoped to have another son. She did not have any children at the time and was jealous of me, but I hadn't meant to make her feel inadequate. Oh, suddenly I wished I could hug that woman and play with her sons and daughters who came along later. Would I never see them again? Had their cheerful faced been silenced by the drought?

Life was not always easy, but somehow sorrow had never touched me the way it did now. I felt even more abandoned by Hashem, even more wounded by the unfairness of my situation. I found myself looking upon Mahlon and Chilion as burdens that I wished I did not need to bear. Yet it would be for them that I must continue to live. Why then did I find no comfort in them now, both of them standing nearby, allowing Orpah's brothers and her father to take care of everything? Yet in my confusion, I too stood idly by, beset by anger and aware of my helplessness. I wanted to be dressed in well-cut robes; I wanted a decent burial for my husband, one that would garner respect.

After most of the parts were scattered on the ground, Orpah's brothers began talking to one another. "It's too bad about Ruth," the older one said. "I thought she would make a good wife someday."

Orpah's father frowned and dropped the last armload of wooden slats next to the frame "That girl is well on her way to Egypt," he said, "It's good thing she's gone. She always was a bad influence on your sister."

I almost cried out that this was not true: Ruth had simply been a determined girl, but when I saw Mahlon's face darken with emotion, I said nothing. He had enough loss to endure.

After my husband's body was carried over and put on the flatbed next to shovels and other digging tools, Orpah's father hopped up onto the driver's seat. Until this moment, he had said little to me, but to my surprise the man patted the bench next to him. I had expected to have to walk behind, as was our custom in Bethlehem, but I gratefully let my sons help me up. Orpah's father shook the reins and set the donkey moving. It clopped along, dragging the cart behind, its wheels clicking across the cobbles. All the young men followed.

We passed clean, orderly courtyards full of flowers and grape vines. I could hear goats bleating. Did these wealthy people also have their own cisterns as I once did and probably never would again? A few people came out and stared at our procession. A woman wrapped her veil around her eyes, and the man who had come out with her bowed in respect. For some reason, his gesture heartened me. I felt a little less alone. At home, women would *never* be acknowledged in this way.

The cemetery was a square of overgrown weeds far beyond the limits of the village, enclosed rocks that served as a wall that would do little to keep out invading hyenas. A few basic tomb-markers, little more than piles of rubble, were scattered about. Mainly the graves were dirt-covered, some forming sunken pits and others still mounded. It hurt me for Emilelech to have no priest to perform the rites and, even worse, to be buried so far from his ancestors. I said nothing to my sons about this lack of decency and I hoped they did not feel as upset as I did, not only at the loss of their father but also at the horrible manner in which he was being buried. And that was only a favor from Orpah's family. I ought to have been thankful but I felt disconnected.

Mahlon helped unload his father's body and also helped dig the grave. Chilion stood by sniffling helplessly. Since he had been the one to find Emilelech's body, I worried that in some way he blamed himself. "It's not your fault," I managed to splutter. "Of course not," he snapped, and turned away. Nothing I said could reassure him. He was clearly angry and felt as helpless as we all did in the face of death. I hoped that in time he would feel better.

After the men mounded sand and dirt over the corpse, Mahlon put one of the most beautiful of Emilelech's pots, one I used for chicken soup and stews, on top. He must have slipped it onto the cart without my noticing. Since we did not have the proper prayers or a priest to consecrate the grave, I was grateful for this small tribute. At home we respected our dead and it was against the law to even take a shortcut through a cemetery. Here though, looking around the scruffy lot, I doubted anyone much cared about their forefathers. I could only hope the pot would not be stolen.

Although I felt deserted by my husband and by Hashem, these Moabite people who hardly knew us were helping us. To bury a stranger *was* as holy a deed as giving bread to the hungry or clothing to the naked. Perhaps, regardless of their religious practices or death rites, they were not so bad. I wished I had some way of thanking them. Perhaps later, if I could muster the strength, I would bake something special for them--as long as we had flour.

After the burial, we went back to Orpah's where her mother had prepared a meal for us. I bit my tongue to stop myself from crying at this act of generosity and kindness, but I simply could not prevent myself from the tears seeping down my cheeks. Out of respect for Orpah's mother, and in an attempt to be strong for my sons, I managed to eat a few bites of bread and garlic. Alas, then I broke down again. Mahlon rushed to my side and wrapped his arms around me, while Chilion looked on coldly. How on earth were we going to manage? We faced an uncertain future as surely as did Ruth, forced to go to Egypt with that dreadful man, but perhaps I could learn something from that headstrong girl and instead of being shy and retiring become more outspoken and determined.

# Eleven: Surprise

Naomi

When we got back to my house after the funeral, I went into the kitchen, telling my sons I needed to be alone. I wanted to comfort them, but the grief and sorrow in their eyes made me feel worse. I had no strength for much of anything and there was no way to help them mourn. I knew it would take time for all of us to recover from our loss. Yet, I wanted comfort now and got my Misho statue out of the basket where I kept various odds and ends. With my fingers gripping her shoulders, I slumped onto a seat. I begged her as if she were a living angel to restore Emilelech and make me feel better. I pleaded with her to help my sons too. But as I stared at her drooping breasts, I felt as misshapen and as cold as a lump of clay. I was not at all consoled. My grief over my lost baby seemed to mingle with my loss of Emilelech, making it ten times harder. I was angry too. With my fingernail. I picked at a crack in the statue on one of the figurine's pitted feet, causing a chip to drop to the floor. I felt ill at ease, fearful that I was worshipping something forbidden, something that would cause more harm.

My poor sons were now fatherless. I was helpless, trapped in a life I had not chosen. How I wished I had not so readily gone along with tradition, but what other opportunity was there for me? I had not known of any other way to live. I had trusted ever since I was a young girl no older than Ruth that my life with Emilelech would be a good one. Certainly, it was steady and pleasant until the drought when we'd had to leave our home. How could Hashem bring such devastation down on ordinary people? Why should we deserve such wrath? I felt unsure of everything—shaken, weak, and friendless.

I clutched the statue and sat there remembering when and where I had found it. I had done my best to prevent anyone from seeing it, and not just because it was a forbidden goddess. I have never been a rebel and never wanted to go against the rules. I kept her simply because I liked the way she looked. She seemed so special, something that somehow justified my experience as a mother, and as a woman whose body was beautiful. I liked those big breasts and that swollen belly. At the time when I found her, I felt as if she were a sign of good luck. I had wanted a baby girl, and this statue encouraged me to appreciate the idea of a daughter rather than another son. Women, she seemed to say, deserved greater respect.

I warmly remembered those ladies in Jerusalem who had welcomed me and taken care of me. They didn't need to lift a finger for needy strangers who could not return their hospitality. Yet they did so freely. Women so rarely got credit for their kindness and care. Why, even Moses was saved by a princess, a foreigner at that. I wonder if anyone ever thanked her? She could so easily have let a strange baby drown, but she had seen his innocent eyes and rescued him. She did not obey her father, the Pharaoh, who had ordered all infant Hebrews to be killed. It occurred to me that Hashem always worked through women—even when we were ridiculed and used and left behind. It scared me to think of divorced women who were thrown out on the street and forced to do who knew what to stay alive. Could such an end be my fate? I tried to convince myself of my value as a woman, one who had always helped others and been part of a community. Now, I did not know what I was or who I was or what was to happen.

I wrapped my arms around my waist and rocked back and forth. Eventually, I got up and began looking around the kitchen for somewhere to put the statue out in the open. The room was dark, but I could see the shelves that Emilelech had attached to the walls. Somehow he had driven holes into the clay mortar and inserted wooden pegs on which he had laid wooden planks. I selected a shelf under a window opening and opened the shutter so I that could see better. I gently put the statue down between two earthenware bowls, leaning her against the back wall so that she would not fall over. This ancient symbol reminded me of the strength of women who endured childbirth and loss without complaint. This very figurine had survived a brutal war and been buried in the rubble of a broken-down fortress. Who knew how many women had been reminded by her that they were of value in their own right, not merely as wives and property of husbands? I had thought she would keep my baby safe and help us all to survive the journey and the new life we faced, but she had not helped. Yet, I wanted to look at her every day and remember how women so often supported one another. Perhaps she might have been owned by a woman like me who faced loss and hardship.

The idea that another woman shared my difficulties gave me a spark of hope. I suddenly remembered the bright and strange shooting stars that

Leah and I used to gaze at in a midnight sky. They were like magic when we would tell each other about our dreams. As girls we often talked about what husbands we would marry, and how many children we would have, and how pretty our wedding gowns would be. How safe we had felt, and how certain we were of the future. I so wished Leah were with me to hug me and tell me everything would be all right.

Chilion trudged into the house and I tried to smile at him, but my eyes darted toward to the statue on the shelf. I had never explained to him why I'd kept it and what it meant to me and did not intend to say anything to him now. How could he, a boy, understand how powerless I, a woman, felt? The truth was that I had only just begun to become aware of my helplessness. When I'd had no choice but to follow Emilelech out of Bethlehem, I had not valued myself. Even my obedience had not been about me but about my sons and my unborn child. I'd wanted to protect them. How could I help my son respect women as more than wives and mothers? I was not trained to be the breadwinner. I did not know how we would survive, but one look at that pitted old statue reassured me that somehow I would find the strength.

Chilion glared at me grimly and waved his fist at the statue. "Father should not have let you keep it!" he shouted, his eyes flashing. "It made Hashem angry and now father has paid!"

I hung my head feeling momentarily ashamed. "No," I said quietly. "She is not to blame. No one is to blame." Even as I uttered the words, I thought perhaps my son *was* right. It might be my fault that my husband had died. I had kept a forbidden figurine, and I had gone off without his permission, and now he was dead. I wondered, though, looking at my son's tear-streaked face if he thought he could have prevented Emilelech's death. "Your father was often sick long before we left Bethlehem," I told him. "Remember how tired he got on the journey here? It was a wonder he ever recovered his strength. At least he died peacefully."

"How do you know?" Chilion raged. "You ought to have been with him to comfort him! He was all alone and you went off with Mahlon in search of a girl who isn't even our sister."

The thought of Ruth with that horrible man almost undid me, but Chilion's anger stirred me to do what I always did for my boys: I tried to placate him with gentle words. After the loss of my baby, I had truly believed the spirit of my infant girl had lingered. I wanted to believe Emilelech was still with us. "Your father's spirit will remain with us for a while," I told him.

"Oh Ma," he said, his eyes narrowed with anger. "That is a silly superstition and will do no good!"

I tried to reach out and put my arms around him, but he stormed away. "Chilion," I called after him, "please come back! Listen to me!" But he did not return, and I had no idea where he was going. I had neither the strength nor the will to run after him.

Mahlon, who was in the courtyard, crept up to me. "Ma," he said and hugged me. I could feel how thin he was through his robes. I felt so unhappy for him to have lost the father he idolized, and yet here he was doing his best to comfort me. I began to sob. He too could not hold back tears, and the two of us cried. How I loved my oldest son. He was steadfast like his father. It seemed unthinkable that Emilelech was gone. I could hardly believe that I had seen the clumps of dirt fall upon his lifeless body. My other son, Chilion, resembled his father with serious eyes and a somber face, but he was far more flighty and moody. I was not surprised he had rushed away, but I was worried about where he would go and what he might do. I stepped back from Mahlon and sighed. "Mahlon, please go after your brother and bring him home."

I knew Mahlon would do anything to ease my fears, but he seemed to be hesitating. My two sons often competed and fought with one another as boys are prone to do, but they sometimes went off together to explore. As long as their father did not object, neither did I, but now a cold fear filled me. "Where has he gone?" I cried.

Mahlon sucked in a deep breath of air and from pursed lips blew it out in a noisy sigh. "He likes to go to a nearby stream and soak in the water."

I touched my forehead with my fingers as if I could make this information go away. I could only hope he did not undress where anyone could see him. I did not ask if it was a place where women went to bathe and wash clothes. I did not want to know. "Go!" I said. "If he is there, bring him back here, and we will decide what is to be done with him." I wondered how I was to discipline him. I doubted that he would listen to anything I told him, especially now. He blamed me for keeping the statue that he thought must surely have invoked the wrath of Hashem.

It turned out that I did not need to worry about him after all. He had gone back to Orpah's house where he felt welcome. It all seemed harmless, and though I fretted until the two boys came home later, he no longer made any attempt to remove the statue. Yet as moody and aloof as he was for days, hardly saying a word to me, I thought I might have to hide the figurine under my sleeping mat. Somehow I resisted. I decided that I was now the head of the household, not him, and not Mahlon either. I did not know what I would do if either of them challenged my authority, something I had not wanted, but I knew I would not merely bow to them. I had believed my husband and all the men I knew deserved to be in charge because of their natural superiority. I had believed I was as tainted as Eve who had misled Adam in the garden of Eden and caused all of us to suffer forever after. I no longer believed that was true. My husband should not have left me in such a plight, I thought, unskilled, with no relatives to help.

The days passed slowly as they always do when one is mourning. Somehow I kept on going. Somehow I got out of bed in the morning. Somehow I tried to encourage my boys, and they did their best to help, even Chilion. Together we managed to reconstruct my loom. It was a triumph that brought smiles to our sorrowing faces. Mahlon, like his father, began working with clay. I was glad to see his delicate fingers covered with the brown mud as he tried to shape bowls. His first attempts resulted in misshapen lumps. If we were not so desperate to sell them, these peculiar looking vessels would have made us laugh. As it was, I felt as misshapen as those pots-- a woman without a man, a widow with no prospects. I was terribly afraid, but a part of me began to feel stronger. I was no statue that would crumble over time. Misho, my ancient reminder of the power of women, gave me hope. It was as if she were watching over me, but it was *I* who would keep my family whole.

Chilion seemed too quiet and did not eat as ravenously as before. It was only young Orpah who managed to enliven him, often bringing us pastries. She always took time to smile at him and to tell him about the adventures she used to have with Ruth. Clearly she missed her friend and wanted Chilion to fill her loneliness. They were still young enough so that I did not worry about a boy and a girl playing together. I had told him that he could no longer go to the stream and bathe as if he were a baby. He had not liked being told that he was acting like a child, but I felt as if he had listened.

I began to wonder about all the laws and rules I had always followed in Bethlehem, the ones the priests insisted we must keep. Many of the same customs existed here, but at home I would have had to walk several paces behind my husband. I still could not do whatever I wanted, but now that I had no husband, I felt free to walk on my own, not behind anyone else.

I went from house to house offering to clean or bake or do chores. It was at the priest's home where I least expected alms but was received with kindness from the ladies of the house. They gathered around me and admired my clothes, stroking the fabric, exclaiming how tightly it was woven and how neatly stitched. I wore my best veil: a delicate material laced with gold and purple thread. I had been very proud of it and still was, but I offered it for sale to them. "Oh no!" said the priest's wife. "It is beautiful but it is yours. I would like you to sew something for me, a dress perhaps or a shawl." The other women nodded and said they also would like me to make them garments.

"But I have no wool or silk," I lamented.

"Don't worry," one of them said. "We will supply you."

As the days passed, I began to enjoy being on my own. I was sitting on a mat looking at the rolls of yarn I had been given, knowing I needed to get busy with my weaving. I wanted to make my lady-patrons the most beautiful cloth for their clothes. But at least for a few moments I was taking time to rest. Mahlon and Chilion were off in the fields helping plow in preparation for the barley planting that would be done later in the year. It must have been back-breaking work, but in return they were given grain from a storage barn. They usually came home exhausted, and I prepared them stews with lentils and onions, and sometimes I added goatmeat that I had bartered for my cleaning jobs. I wished our tiny courtyard were big enough to start a vegetable patch like many of the women had, but at least we were managing. Serving others and doing jobs I once thought demeaning no longer bothered me. It certainly was better than my worst fears. Every day I felt a little braver and a little more sure of myself.

One day, as I sat down to enjoy some fragrant pomegranate tea, I heard footsteps coming through the courtyard. I sighed, hoping it was not Orpah's mother. She often stopped to see me, and though I liked her and was grateful for her friendship, I did not feel like chatting about recipes. I wanted to be alone and I didn't want to talk to anyone, but I looked expectantly with a smile on my face toward the gate.

I could hardly believe my eyes. It was Ruth.

"Ruth!" I cried, almost dropping my cup. "Is it really you?" I had all but forgotten about her, thinking she must be in Egypt by now with her parents and her sister. But when I took in the girl's dirty face and the delicate fabric of her clothes sticking out from beneath a heavy woolen coat, I knew something dreadful must have happened.

"I have nowhere to go," she moaned.

"Why aren't you in Egypt? What has happened?"

"It was horrible," she cried.

"What!" I felt my body tensing. That horrible man must have hurt young Ruth. I had warned her family and even emphasized the danger to an aunt, but that had not prevented them from sending the girl with them. I had known but simply shrugged it off as a situation I could not control. I could however do something now. I quickly set my cup down and went to the girl and wrapped my arms around her. She leaned into me and hugged me back.

"The man sold me to become a slave in a temple of women but I escaped with a troupe of musicians," she said, her face grim. "But they were not much better. They wanted me to dance and sing for them."

I sat her down on a bench and crouched opposite her. "Tell me everything," I urged, worried about what she must have endured. "Who were these people?"

Ruth's eyes flashed. "The women dressed me with see-through fabric like they were wearing." She opened the coat and showed me skimpy clothing that made me blush for her.

I was relieved she did not yet have breasts, relieved her blood must not yet have started. At least she could not be pregnant. Yet I was confused. I had heard about a troupe of people who played the drums and flutes. They had come to a bigger town nearby to partake in a wedding celebration. Could they be the ones she had been with?

"You said you were lost," I prompted, and waited for her to continue.

"They made me shake a tambourine while they beat on drums and other women danced. I hated the way they laughed at me. They said I must learn to lead in the way Miriam once led her people to freedom. I did not know what they were talking about and I felt stupid. They clapped their hands and drank wine and I was afraid the men would get mean."

I thought of how Haran had acted when he was drunk, but hearing that they had called her Miriam, I could not help but smile. Ruth stared at me indignantly, her mouth open. I wanted to reassure her. "Of course you don't know anything about Miriam," I said. "But she was one of your ancestors and she was very brave. She was Moses' sister."

"Oh," Ruth said with her hands on her hips.

Miriam suddenly seemed even more important than my Misho-statue, but why could I not revere both? I grabbed Ruth's hand and sat next to her on the bench. "Miriam was a girl no older than you. She looked after her baby brother, Moses. His poor mother was trying to protect him from the Pharaoh who had made a decree for all Hebrew boys to be killed. It must have been agonizing for his mother to watch her little son float amongst the bulrushes with only a basket to keep him safe. Miriam saw an

Egyptian princess retrieve the basket. When Miriam learned that the princess needed a midwife for the infant, she fetched her mother."

Ruth considered this for a while. "She got her family back together then?"

"She did help keep her family together, but there is much more to the story. I will tell you more later. I want to hear about you."

"The musical troupe left me at a crossroads and gave me directions, but I got lost. I walked and walked. There was nothing but rocks and desert, but then I came upon a green pasture. It was so beautiful, full of sheep and goats grazing near big tents."

"Nomads!" I smiled, remembering how caring many of these wandering tribes could be and how much they loved their children. As girls, Leah and I had dreamed of running away with them, but of course that was unheard of. And when we had learned that we would be the ones to have to set up and take down their heavy canvas tents and probably carry them too, we quickly gave up that idea. It was the idea of sleeping under the stars that appealed to us.

"The men wore long beards and the women wore bright clothes and lots of beads. Their children ran around naked. We ate meat every day even for breakfast. I wanted to stay with them, but they told me that they would be moving on, and I needed to return to my own people. They took me up onto the King's Highway and sent me down the trail to the village." She put her face into her hands. Her lower lip trembled. "My aunts and uncles shouted at me and they said I have disgraced myself. They would not allow me to stay."

"You must live with me," I quickly said, troubled for her to have been so poorly received by her own kin. "First you must eat and drink, and then I will get water for you to bathe." I brought her a bowl of cold soup and a loaf that I had made the day before.

She tore off chunks of bread and dipped the thick slices into the broth and ate hungrily.

After she had drank the watered-down wine that I had given her to help her relax, she seemed calmer. I could not bring myself to question her about what had happened at that temple nor with those musicians. I had no idea how to approach such a delicate subject. But one thing I knew: single women who were no longer virgins would be barred from marriage, possibly because they might be pregnant with another man's child.

For now, though, she needed care and fresh clothes. My robes would have to be shortened to fit her, so after she had bathed, I fetched her a linen tunic that I had made for Mahlon. I wrapped a sash embroidered with pomegranates around her waist. I could see she felt relieved to have on clean clothes and be rid of the garments that reminded her of her ordeal. I did not tell her that the tunic belonged to Mahlon. I knew he would not mind. "Promise me one thing, Ruth."

She nodded, her dark brown eyes searching mine.

"You have done nothing wrong." I kissed her forehead. "Do not tell Mahlon about what happened. He is a good boy, but like all men, even if he knows it is not your fault, he might refuse to marry you."

"What!" she cried. "I know I made a promise but I am not going to marry anyone!"

"Hush, Ruth. You say that now but you might change your mind. And I would love to have you as my daughter-in-law."

# Day by Day

## One: Shabbat

Naomi

Time oozed by like mud, moment by moment, day by day—somehow we got on with life. At times I still felt so immersed in grief that I could hardly keep on moving, let alone doing any weaving or any of the other countless chores. Yet sometimes I felt pleasure to work with beautiful yarn. I greatly appreciated the priest's women who continued to supply me with raw wool that needed to be carded. Without their generosity, my family and I would probably have been homeless, and who knew how we would have survived? It was tiresome work washing and separating the fibers into pliable white threads, but even when my arms and back ached from the effort, it kept me occupied. Ruth always helped me wind it into big balls of wool. The girl was such a treasure. Mahlon scoured the surrounding areas and found purple flowers that he crushed and soaked in water to make a dye to color the yarn. Sometimes it made the wool blotchy with pink and lavender tones, but when I wove small rugs from it, the color was so unusual and so pretty that I was easily able to sell them. I had even managed to put a few shekels aside.

I had no idea how hard life would be without Emilelech. He used to occasionally help me with household chores but it seemed very little to ease my burden, but now his help would have been a great blessing. If not for Ruth, I do not know how I would have managed. But it was not only those physical chores that he had taken care of—like repairing cracks in the courtyard or building shelves and benches. It was also that I found myself missing his emotional support when we would relax after a hard day when we would sit quietly not having to speak, or when we would glance at one another over some clever moment that our sons made us proud. He had been a knowledgeable teacher too. How was *I* to instruct our sons in the Torah. Who would teach them how to be men? I often thought of returning to Bethlehem so that a relative might marry me and be a father to the boys. But men only married their brothers' widows when there were no heirs. Plus, what man wanted a woman who could not have any more babies? Clearly I could bear no more children. I did not much like Emilelech's kin, either. Thank goodness I had my two boys. Still, in Bethlehem my sons would inherit the field we had once owned but there was no guarantee we would ever be able to get it back. And anyway I had horrid visions of everyone there being dead and gone while dried grass blew through the empty streets.

Eventually, I did not think about Emilelech or Bethlehem nearly as much. And Mahlon became a potter in his own right. At first, I used to secretly watch him twisting the clay and stretching it upwards to create bowls. Often it would collapse into a sodden mess, and then he would sit there staring into space. I so wished I could wrap my arms around him the way I used to when he scraped a knee, but I managed to leave him alone. I knew any interference from me would make him feel even more inadequate. I wanted him to know that I appreciated and trusted his efforts, so I cooked special meals for him and for Chilion, who'd grown as tall and lanky as his brother. Sometimes Chilion stood nearby making snide suggestions about turning the wheel faster or slower, which Mahlon ignored. Brothers! I knew nothing about the process, but eventually Mahlon was able to carefully press a rough ball of clay down onto the wheel and form a bowl. His first successes were not quite as uniform as Emilelech's fine pots but they would, once dried and fired, hold water. He sat grinning at a row of his pots well-pleased with himself. I came out of the shadows and applauded him. These first pots were the beginning of many more of all sizes, some for water, some with wide mouths for grain, and some that he painted and glazed just to make them beautiful. I was so proud of him. And Chilion pleased me too often going with Mahlon to dig up clay and bring it home. They had fashioned a cart on crude wheels that they used to drag the hardened pots to the kiln on the other side of the village. It made me so happy to see them helping one another.

Ruth also looked on with a smile at those two. She continued to be a blessing, helping me more and more with the everyday necessities of cleaning and cooking and fetching the water. She learned how to bake flatbreads that we sold to our neighbors. The girl continued to card the raw wool and soon became far quicker and more proficient than me. We would sit on a rug opposite one another and work away. Sometimes she would ask me questions about what Judah was like. I got to the point where talking about my former life no longer made me sad. I found myself remembering many wonderful times. As we cut and sewed custom dresses for rich women, I described my betrothal and my wedding to Emilelech. "Oh," I said. "you should have seen my gown!"

I continued to smile at Ruth who in spite of her declaration that she would never marry often giggled with Mahlon. They seemed so close that I worried the two would make love, and she would get pregnant before they were married. I need not have fretted. It was Chilion and Orpah that brought me shame. I should have known. That Chilion! He always was a renegade and often disobedient. He and Oprah had become good friends after Emilelech died; I suppose because of how Orpah had cozied up to him. She was a warm and loving girl, so much like myself when I was young. I had become a lot tougher so perhaps being a single parent was a blessing, but I often wished I was not so exhausted all the time.

On the night when a sliver of moon revealed Orpah and Chilion cuddling together in the courtyard, I felt myself turn pale. "What are you doing?" I yelled and waved my oil lantern over them to reveal Orpah's bare legs wrapped around my son. I was horrified and stood there with my mouth hanging open.

Chilion rolled aside and Orpah quickly covered herself. My son adjusted his robes and jumped to his feet, offering Orpah a hand to help her get up and stand next to him. "We are going to get married," Chilion announced.

"I should think so," was all I could manage to answer, but I knew for a fact that Orpah's mother hoped for her daughter to fetch a decent bridal dowry. We had none to offer. Speechless, I stared at the crescent moon, trying to come up with a way to smooth things over, to make this breach of propriety all right. I once again yearned for my wise husband to be here with me. This mess would not have happened if he had been alive. Chilion would not have dared to behave so poorly with a girl.

In this scandalous moment, seeing my son with Orpah in such a compromising position, I realized I'd not done a thing to ensure my boys got their religious training. It had been far too long. Where was I to turn? I certainly would not ask any Moabite priest to instruct them, and my own knowledge of our religion seemed slight. Yet I was all they had, and I had often listened to Emilelech instructing the boys so perhaps, even if it was forbidden for a woman to teach, I would have to step in and begin giving them their lessons.

"You two!" I scolded. "You ought to be ashamed of yourselves."

"We aren't," Chilion boldly declared but Orpah was trembling. He put his arm around her shoulder. "Anyway, Orpah cannot get pregnant."

"What!" I cried, thinking he must have spilled his seed on the ground the way Onan was said to have done so as not to impregnate Tamar, his brother's widow. This was clearly different. Orpah was no widow like Tamar who needed to give birth to an heir. My heart sank at the thought of Onan who was punished by Hashem. By death! I wanted to question Chilion as to exactly what the two of them had done. Orpah was hardly more than a girl, and she needed to stay sexually pure until her wedding day. Was she still a virgin or not? I was too embarrassed to ask specific questions. I needed to think. "Both of you, go in the house while I decide what to do."

I groaned out loud, remembering only too well how Mahlon had been blamed for the trouble with Haran's family. He had merely tried to comfort Ruth with kind words when we'd got back with her after she'd run away. The fact she had been brought home safely did not help. Haran's family were angry and unthinking. They did not care that Mahlon was innocent of any wrongdoing. They needed to blame someone, and Mahlon became their scapegoat. People could at times be so irrational. It once again crossed my mind that Mahlon and Ruth might have been misbehaving too, except I trusted them both, especially Ruth. Now my youngest son was going to cause a rift between Orpah's family and mine. I had come to love Orpah and appreciated her robust brothers and her kind mother and her hard-working father who had helped us so much. What sort of repayment was this, to have to tell them my son had violated their daughter, and now they must by law be married? But perhaps it was not a Moabite law. And perhaps Orpah would not get pregnant and we could pretend that this had never happened. Except Chilion was not steadfast like his father. Who knew what he might do or say? He had always been defiant.

As I entered the house, I planned to tell the two of them to never let this happen again. But when I saw them sitting side by side on the bench in the kitchen with their knees touching, I knew my wishes would be ignored. They simply would have to be married. I would have to convince Orpah's mother of this without estranging her, but how on earth was I to welcome a daughter-in-law into my house? We only had a kitchen and a space partitioned off where Ruth and I slept, and the upstairs roof was where the boys spent the night. I felt helpless and wretched, but that sliver of moon glowed through the window and seemed to shine into my stunned brain. Suddenly I realized there was one thing I could do.

I would start the holy practice of Shabbat.

"If you hope to marry, you will have to abide by our laws—starting now!"

Chilion's eyes got big and Orpah looked confused. Ruth popped out from behind the partition curtain and beamed. "I would love to learn more. Mahlon has been teaching me your ways. What do we need to do? How can I help?"

Mahlon emerged from behind the curtain and would not meet my eyes. My jaws felt tight. What had happened to my sons to believe that they could spend so much time alone with girls to whom they were not yet married?

"There are many rules," I shouted, wanting to shock them into respect for me and for our customs. I knew though that it would do no good to scold them, and I was far too embarrassed to talk about sex. I did not have the authority of a man. "Do you even know what Shabbat is?" I asked, not sure I myself understood.

"Of course," Mahlon answered. "It is a time to remember how Hashem created the world and took time to rest from his labors. It is also when we give thanks for being freed from slavery."

Chilion stared sullenly into space.

"Very well," I nodded to Mahlon as if I had known. What I did remember was that we always had a special meal in the evening, but it was too late in the day for that now. "We will start by honoring Hashem. We will begin religious lessons again."

"You do know, Ma," Chilion said defiantly, "that we don't need to follow the laws of Bethlehem. Here in Moab those rules don't apply to us."

"They most certainly do," I responded, wracking my brains to remember what activities were banned. We had become careless in so many ways, but what choice had we in order to fit in? One thing I did remember was that I was not to do any weaving or baking the day after we began Shabbat at sunset. Truly it would be a welcome respite. I also remembered some of the rituals. I had no candles to light, but I did have the scissors I used for yarn and decided to clip the boys' hair. After all, hadn't Moses commanded his sons not to let their hair become unkempt because of their grief? I was not entirely sure, but Emilelech always kept his hair trimmed, and so did most of the men I remembered from Bethlehem. "You boys," I said, "will get your hair cut. Orpah, you go home and tell your mother you want to marry Chilion. You do, don't you?"

Her face colored but she nodded solemnly.

"On second thoughts say nothing to her. Tell her I will visit her the day after tomorrow. Now go!"

She threw a pitiful look to Chilion, but I crossed my arms over my chest and frowned to quell any nonsense from either of them. The girl raised the hem of her robe slightly off the floor and scurried away.

Emilelech had never initiated Shabbat here in Moab. I got a strange satisfaction out of my clumsy efforts to follow our traditions. I sat the two of my sons on the bench I had pulled out from the wall and with Ruth watching, an amused look in her eyes, I proceeded to trim their long hair until they no longer looked like shaggy sheep. This seemed to me to be obedience to Hashem whom I knew I had not been honoring, let alone obeying. That was about to change. I also sheared Mahlon's beard, not letting his obvious regret as he watched the wads of his curly hair laying all around his feet bother me. He looked tidier and more respectable. Chilion still only had a few whiskers so I let him keep his wispy mustache and scraggly beard.

Ruth stared at Mahlon and started to giggle, but he threw her a glance that would wither an olive tree. She managed to suppress her glee.

It was already dark when I decided we must ritually light two candles. Since we did not have any, I fetched two spare oil lamps. It bothered me to waste fuel, but I felt this was important. "Ruth, you are to light these, while Mahlon says a blessing."

Ruth lit a taper from an already burning lamp and quietly touched the flame to the wicks of the other two lamps that I'd placed on the floor. They flared up and glowed into the small space, making everything bright.

My son bowed his head.

Chilion finally realized I was serious and he also bowed his head.

Ruth looked to me for guidance and I motioned for her to close her eyes and hold her hands together on her lap. Mahlon said nothing for a while. I worried that he had no idea of how to proceed. Since only Emilelech had ever said a blessing for Shabbat, and that had been in Bethlehem, I had no idea what my son might say.

At last, Mahlon began to speak, his voice so deep that he sounded quite grownup. "We give thanks to the angels who keep us safe. We give thanks to our mother who bakes bread and prepares our meals and who, without a husband, has managed to keep us together. We seek your blessing, Hashem, who created heaven and earth. We thank you to guide us and lead us not only this Shabbat but all the days of our lives. Amen."

As we sat in silence for a few moments, suddenly a vision of Miriam, sister of Moses, entered my mind. I saw her compassionate face. I clearly heard her voice:

Sing to the Lord,
for he is highly exalted.
Both horse and driver
he has hurled into the sea.

I was astonished and yet in my mind's eye I saw women holding up their skirts and clutching their veils as they fled from the Egyptians. I saw their path through the sea close behind them as the waters rained down on the chariots and drowned all the pursuing soldiers. I saw Miriam dancing ahead of everyone leading them into freedom.

The vision faded but remembering how Ruth was forced to dance scantily clad in front of men, I felt suddenly sad. How fortunate I had been with gentle Emilelech who had never physically forced himself upon me. He and I were both innocent of the ways of men and women, but he had been gentle and undemanding.

I glanced at young Ruth, her eyes dutifully closed, her hands in her lap. She was strong and determined, but her spirit had been damaged by the ill treatment she had received from men, including her father, and perhaps even her mother who'd had little choice but to flee for her life. Hannah must surely have suffered greatly to leave her daughter Ruth behind. Why, even now I knew she must want her back. I pondered if there was some way I could reunite them, and I realized I did not want to! I did not! But I could not be so selfish, and surely my love for this girl was great enough to do what was best for her and not merely what I wanted, and what Mahlon wanted too. I peeked at his eyes so full of warmth toward Ruth. I questioned how on earth I could ever return Ruth to her parents, even if there was a way, when it would surely greatly cost my son.

Yet, I understood that Hashem would take care of all our troubles too and show us a path into new freedom. I knew, at least in that moment, that I did not need to worry. Something holy was happening. I felt a sense of awe. In the lantern light my children's faces seemed gentler and also more mature. I wanted to hug them all, my sons and my Ruth, but I contented myself basking in a feeling of peace such as I'd not experienced in a long time. "Now," I whispered. "We must all remain quiet and get some sleep. Tomorrow, we will do our best to continue Shabbat as your father would have done."

In the morning, the kitchen and the courtyard were filled with bright yellow wildflowers that Ruth had gone out early to gather from near the stream. How could she have known it was our tradition to adorn our house with such fragrance and beauty? She had already prepared the breads and foods so that we women—well, actually, she and I—could rest from our labors. How could she have known? There was no obvious explanation. I felt heartened and strengthened by this young woman. I could hardly wait to make her my daughter-in-law.

I looked at her hands rough from grinding grain for the wealthy women who did not want their slender fingers spoiled. I wished I could relieve her of such hard work, and I wished I was back in Bethlehem again where I had maids and friends. Yet, I knew too, this young woman, this Ruth, was all the stronger and deeper for her willingness to trust me and help me and become a part of our family. I wondered how I could help her stop rebuffing the very idea of marriage. But for now, this Shabbat seemed a beginning of better times. I felt happier than I had since before Emilelech died.

# Two: Sigh

Ruth

Ruth balanced the empty earthenware olla—the one crafted by Mahlon—on the top of her head and walked toward the well. She had become proficient at fetching the water by herself and was happy to have this time in the late morning to be alone. Yet in the past she had dreaded going because she had so often seen her aunts and cousins around the water. They invariably ignored her, making her bite her tongue rather than speak, or even worse, making her want to cry. But she never did, not in front of them. And she never explained to Naomi the reason she began fetching water later when the sun was getting hot. Certainly, Naomi would have understood. She continued to be kind, but Ruth wished Naomi would give up her notions of a marriage between herself and Mahlon. She liked him, true enough, but that was no basis for marriage. Men made her angry. How could her father have gone off and so readily left her behind? How could he have beaten and humiliated her the way he did? She knew she had been difficult and had embarrassed her father in front of everyone, but still, she had been seeking justice, wanting to keep her mother safe from the cruel priests. And the fact that their neighbor was a priest whose women now helped Naomi did nothing to soften her opinion.

She had been so much younger than she was now, perhaps not in years, but in understanding. She had been too sensitive and too self-centered and ought not to have run away. She still remembered that moment of silence in the wild when she had somehow known everything was going to be all right. She wished for such a moment again, but life went on. She was getting her period and had to go to Orpah's to sit in the woman-tent, using wads of linen to staunch the blood. Orpah, who was younger than she, started her period too. It became a time when they would get to do nothing but eat date bars that their mothers provided. They were the only two girls there and so they could gossip about all sorts of things. Orpah was worried about the rich boy who was paying attention to her. She did not like him, and even though she had told her mother that she was not interested in him she was worried that her parents would insist upon her accepting his offer. Her parents hoped for a big bridal dowry, one that Chilion could not give.

"Wouldn't it be wonderful for us to have a double wedding? You and Mahlon, and me and Chilion." Orpah said, grinning. "We could wear matching dresses."

Ruth shook her head. She felt so much older than Orpah and regretted that the time when they had been inseparable was coming to an end. Nowadays they did not seem to have much in common. No matter how often Ruth told Orpah that she was never going to get married, Orpah refused to listen. Now, the girl had gotten herself into a compromising position with Chilion. Ruth thought it probably had been on purpose with the intent of forcing her parents to let them get married. It made Orpah seem like a fool. Orpah's mother would probably be angry but eventually forgive her. Her father, though, might throw her out and there would be no marriage to anyone. She would end up living with Naomi, and they had no room for anyone else. Still, if she did marry Chilion, she would be moving in with them anyway.

Ruth, approaching the dug-out well, got so lost in her own thoughts that at first she did not pay any attention to the woman and the little girl filling up their pots from the pond. They did not look up at her, too busy getting their water. But when Ruth lifted the olla from her head to put it on the ground while she waited for her turn to fill it, her eyes widened in shock. "Ma! Anna!" she cried, but when the woman looked around, her face was that of a stranger. The little girl grabbed her mother's skirt and buried her head in the cloth. "Sorry," Ruth mumbled. "I thought you were someone else."

After they were gone, she sat for a long time so quiet at the water's edge that the frogs, unaware of her presence, began leaping about and croaking their hoarse calls to one another. She thought about her family. Where were they? Her mother, her sister, and her father? Were they happy? Had Anna gotten over being taken forcibly from their mother? The little girl had been too young to fully understand what the priests meant to do with her. Her escape brought about by their mother did nothing to relieve her fear of abandonment. She had been horribly hurt. Ruth worried that in Egypt her family would be forced to do hard labor. If only there was a way for her to find out how they were. She thought perhaps that she could wait on the King's Highway in the hope of encountering a passing caravan from Egypt, one with news, but she knew it would be unlikely.

She filled her jug and carefully balanced it on her head, but for some reason it felt heavier than usual as if her neck were getting stiff with the effort. Perhaps it was her body reacting to her sense of loss and her helplessness about her family. She missed them desperately, even her father, blame him though she did. She suspected she was not being completely fair to him. He had been away on business when Anna was taken. He was *not* the one to initiate sacrifices, not even for a good harvest. In fact, he had always decried the idea of animals given to Chemosh to try to plead for mercy. She. thought Chemosh cruel. She simply despised him and could not understand how anyone could worship a god who thought it all right to kill little children.

Sometimes nothing made any sense. She stopped and shifted the heavy jar onto the post that women used when they needed to rest. Water leaked out of the jug and soaked her hair. A memory arose of the groans of her parents. It had so alarmed her when she was a little girl that she had rushed to their chamber to find out what was going on as if she could keep them safe. Her mother was bumping up and down atop her father. They did not notice her peeking through the curtain. In spite of her father's closed eyes and tight jaw, they seemed to be absorbed in their game. Only recently did she fully understand what they had been doing.

She certainly would take no pleasure in having relations the way her parents seemed to enjoy. She had had a narrow escape from being turned into a girl that others used in such a way. The whole idea of her parents in this act, let alone of herself and a boy, made her stomach churn. If Mahlon knew she had almost been turned into such a lost girl, he would surely reject her. Perhaps she ought to tell him and put an end to his hopes. She wanted no men. Never. And no children either. Anna had survived but at what cost? No longer the outgoing sweet little girl she had once been, she had become frightened and timid. Ruth could not help but realize that Anna's personality had changed from that of a trusting child to that of a tearful one. Ruth groaned at the thought of how her sweet little sister had been so wounded as surely as she too had been harmed by forces that they could not escape.

The vast blue sky seemed to glare down and the sun's heat was unrelenting. Drips of sticky perspiration trickled down her neck. She lifted the jug from the post onto the top of her head and began the walk back to the house where Naomi would be waiting. As Ruth entered the yard, she could smell something savory wafting out of the kitchen. A soup of lentils and vegetables scented the air and made her mouth water. Naomi's eyes were running from having chopped strong onions, but upon seeing Ruth, a wide smile brightened her face. Ruth genuinely loved her and it felt good to be loved in return. She so wanted to please Naomi. Part of her wished that she could get over the hurdle of her past experiences and be willing to accept Mahlon as her husband but she did not want to hang on to such impossible ideas.

"Ruth, you must sample this!" Naomi, using a square of heavy cloth to protect her hands, took the round-bottomed pot out of their clay oven. She set it on a tripod that Mahlon had fashioned as a serving stand. The smell of the stew mixed with the earthy odor of the dried goat dung that fueled the fire in the stove was pleasing. The liquid continued to bubble while Naomi took a spoon and stirred it, before scooping out a mouthful. She blew on it to cool it and offered it to Ruth.

Ruth took a sip. "Delicious." She smacked her lips approvingly.

"Does it need anything?"

"Perhaps a little salt."

Naomi took a pinch of salt from a crock and added it to the liquid and stirred. "Could you put this back in the oven and keep the fire going? It is cooked through, but I want to keep it hot until I get back. When Chilion gets home, he will be starving, not that he deserves anything other than a whipping! I am going to visit Orpah's mother to talk to her about what has happened."

"Does she really need to know?" Ruth asked. "Her mother and father have in mind a rich boy for Orpah and they will never agree to her marrying Chilion. Her father will get angry, and then who knows what will happen?"

Naomi stared into space. "When I was a girl, I had strong feelings for a boy but my parents chose Emilelech for me. He was a good and kind man and I have my two sons to thank him for, but I wonder how different my life would have been if I had been allowed to choose and had not been hobbled by family tradition. If Chilion wants to marry Orpah, I wish I could find a way to help him. It seems clear that Orpah returns his feelings. If only we had a dowry to offer."

Ruth shrugged. They both knew they were helpless in the face of tradition and the need for money.

A little later, when Mahlon returned from taking his pots to the market, he joined them in the kitchen, and after listening quietly, the frown upon his face deepened when Ruth began to speak.

"I could offer to become Orpah's family servant!" Ruth said. "I know how to grind grain and bake all kinds of breads. I could milk their goats and get the eggs. They'd be far more likely to let Orpah marry Chilion if her mother knew she'd have me to help."

Naomi's jaw dropped open. "Ruth, you are so generous to suggest such a thing." She glanced at Mahlon. "I hoped you would marry Mahlon and become my daughter-in-law and stay with me!"

"I *want* to stay with you."

"I am the head of the household, Ruth," Mahlon said angrily. "I forbid you to consider turning yourself into a servant even if you *never* marry me."

Ruth could not meet his gaze. She liked him, and if she were to marry any boy, it would be him, but that was not what mattered in this moment. "We need to offer a dowry so that Chilion can marry Orpah."

"We will offer them our goat!" Naomi declared.

Mahlon sighed deeply. "I want Chilion to be happy," he said. "I could give Orpah's parents some of my best pottery," Mahlon added.

"I would be glad to bake them sesame loaves," Ruth murmured.

They went on talking about possible ways to provide a dowry and they did not hear Orpah's father come through the yard, but he had been listening to them. "Nothing you can offer is enough," he said angrily. "What kind of people are you to have allowed your son to have his way with my innocent daughter? I know they have already been living here as if they were married."

"I am so sorry," Naomi whispered. "I only just found out what they were up to. I was coming to talk to you. How can we make things right between your family and ours? We will do whatever you ask. But I beg you to be gentle with Orpah. She is not much more than a child and neither is Chilion. I would be delighted to have her as my daughter-in-law and would welcome her to live here with us."

Orpah's father looked around their poor little house and burst into laughter. "You have hardly enough room for another goat, let alone a married couple. As oversexed as those two obviously are, who knows how many children will soon arrive? I cannot deny that I am furious with her. I came here to whip your son, but what good will that do?"

Naomi stared at the floor. "I can't tell you how sorry I am."

"Orpah is my only daughter," the man continued, "and her mother will miss her, but as it turns out my oldest son is promised to marry the priest's girl."

"How fortunate she is," Ruth disdainfully interjected. She certainly would not say yes to his nasty son.

The man did not notice the scorn in her voice.

"In the fullness of time," he said, "*that* young lady will be coming to stay with us."

"Your wife must be very pleased," Naomi said pleasantly.

"Yes. She is. The priest and his wife do not even care what sort of dowry we offer. The girl gets whatever she wants, and she has decided she wants my son. He is a handsome boy if I do say so myself."

"He takes after you," Naomi said with a weak smile.

Ruth thought the oldest son resembled his mother rather than his father. She could not stand him.

"Please," Naomi said. "Would you fetch your wife and join us for dinner later? We have fresh barley soup. Perhaps we can agree upon a contract for your daughter Orpah and my son. It would be wonderful for us to be officially united as a family. I am so grateful to you."

The man grunted but said no more and took his leave.

After Orpah's father left, Naomi absentmindedly stirred the steaming pot of stew. "What if they want Chilion to worship Chemosh?" she whispered, seemingly into thin air.

"They are *not* very religious," Ruth told her.

"It is truly not our way to rush into a marriage," Naomi moaned. "Emilelech approached my father when I was but a girl before the contract was finalized. We waited five years after the betrothal before the marriage was consummated. Now, there is not to be a contract, and no waiting. It is unheard of!"

"I don't understand," Ruth said. "What does it matter except that they will be together and that they love each other."

Naomi sighed deeply. "How will we manage a wedding feast? And where will they sleep in this tiny house?"

Mahlon who had said not a word until now clenched his teeth. "We will build a wedding canopy in the courtyard. They will have to begin their married life out there. And surely we can expect Orpah's family to hold some sort of wedding celebration."

"How?" Naomi despaired. "They are unhappy about Orpah getting involved with Chilion. That is clear. And even if there is to be a festival, who will we invite? We have no friends here except the priest's wife and the clients who have bought our wares. We have nothing to offer as a dowry. None of it is right! None of it!"

Mahlon came over to his mother and put an arm around her shoulder and hugged her. Naomi leaned into him and looked into his eyas. "What about you and Ruth?" she asked.

"We have done nothing wrong," Mahlon said, his face coloring, and Ruth nodded, turning away, looking flustered and also red in the face.

"You must find out," Naomi cried, "if Orpah is still a virgin." She stared into space and whispered to herself. "If she does not bloody the wedding cloth, what might happen then?"

"It may not be their custom," Mahlon murmured.

"It is," Ruth muttered. "But for now we need to get a meal ready."

" I will select one of my best decorated pots to offer them," Mahlon added.

Naomi studied her son and Ruth. She loved them both so much. "You're right," she said at last. "It does no good for us to bemoan the way things used to be. We will make the best of today. Let us prepare figs and honey in our tastiest pastry."

"And bread dipped in olive oil and garlic?" Mahlon suggested.

Ruth grinned. She knew he loved the sop she often prepared.

Chilion sauntered into the room. "What's going on?" he asked, looking so innocent that Ruth wanted to slap him, the silly boy. "Tonight you are going to accept Orpah as your betrothed bride."

Chilion grinned stupidly. "I love her," he declared.

"We know," Mahlon responded. "Now, go to the neighbor's house three doors down and see if they will give us beer or wine in exchange for my pots. They have expressed interest in the one I decorated with doves. I'd hoped to sell it to them after it was glazed but they will no doubt be delighted to give us a jug of wine as payment."

Chilion bounced happily out of the room.

The three remaining, Mahlon, Ruth and Naomi, stared at one another and began to laugh. "That boy!" Naomi managed to sputter.

"It will be pleasant to have Orpah here with us," Ruth said cheerfully, but in reality she was not so sure, and the idea of babies scared her.

"Wait until he realizes what he is in for!" Mahlon shook his head. "For one thing, he will have to help me put up a wedding canopy."

"But what will we make it from?" Naomi asked.

"Chilion and I will go out into the woods and cut poles for the uprights and the frame."

"We have all that goat-hair ready to be carded. Can't we weave blankets to cover it?" Ruth suggested.

"Very well," Naomi said. "Perhaps we can have everything ready fairly fast. The sooner the better."

Ruth wondered if the reason that Naomi wanted to hurry things along was that she was worried that Orpah might already be pregnant.

Later, at the dinner with Orpah's family, who brought yams and honey cakes and two jugs of beer, everyone seemed calmer. Chilion, who had been instructed by his mother and by his brother, spoke respectfully to Orpah's dad about his longing to marry Orpah.

"Surely you don't want to marry *him*?" the father barked at Orpah.

Orpah's mother patted her husband's arm. "Now, now," she placated.

"What do you have to offer my daughter, Chilion?" he said, his scornful expression speaking words he had not voiced out loud.

Chilion began to stutter. "I will work the fields for you and make her a good home."

"You'd better!" the father said, glaring at Chilion before turning to his daughter, his look only slightly more gentle. "Well, what do you say, Orpah? You've got yourself into a right mess."

Orpah lowered her eyes. "I am ready to marry Chilion. We love one another."

# Three: Plenty.

### Boaz

Boaz, smiling at the rows of green sprouts arising like fresh whiskers out of the moist earth, raised his arms and praised Hashem. He had come every week all winter long glad of the cold that chilled his face. Now, all alone in the fields, he had prayed for hours for Hashem to provide abundance. They had coped on a bare minimum of food and water—a time as black as a starless night. Yet perhaps not all had been darkness. The help they had received from neighboring Jerusalemites surely originated with Hashem. Indeed, the people of Jerusalem were Godly, not merely in how they practiced their religion, but also in how that very religion inspired their generous and compassionate behavior. Boaz smiled to remember how strangers, their hospitality etched on their hearts, had gladly provided water and food and welcome.

In the quiet times that he spent in the fields, listening to birds, feeling the breezes ruffle his hair and his beard, he reconsidered the miracle of the succulent plants that had sustained them when they'd been the most desperate. It was a miracle as great as the manna from heaven that Hashem once gave the people as they wandered for forty days in the wilderness. They too were in a wilderness time, not geographically, although the drought certainly could turn Bethlehem and the surrounding fields into a permanent desert. No, their wilderness was not only a time of great need for food and water for their bodies, but also a time of need for nourishment of their souls. Who would have thought or understood how in such a time of distress his people would come together to help one another? They had shared what they had with one another. They had comforted one another. They had regularly attended worship in the courtyard at the city gate. Certainly there had been quarrels, but somehow they had stood together and never stopped trusting.

Boaz was astonished that Hashem seemed to have selected him as a leader. He felt small and helpless, but he tried to give people hope. He found himself no longer believing that the drought was a result of Hashem's wrath for something they had done wrong. He knew he did not understand much about eternal justice, but did not Hashem choose them and would not he take care of them? It seemed as if such difficult times reminded them that there was a greater force than themselves. True hope lay in trust of Hashem, who had freed them from slavery and brought them to this promised land. Was not Hashem always trying to free them in some way—physically, emotionally, spiritually?

He shook his head. He was no philosopher. He was a farmer. He picked up a clod of dirt and rubbed it between his fingers, letting the granules drop back to the ground. The neat rows of barley seedlings stretching to the horizon brought him joy—not only at the thought of the threshing floor overflowing with grain, but also for the sheer lush color and the sweet fragrance scenting the air.

He suddenly found himself proud of his people who, in spite of their grumbles, had chosen to rely upon Hashem. They had desperately wanted to use their scant barley seed for food, even though they knew that once the seeds were in their stomachs there would be nothing left to plant. Then they would surely perish. They had listened to Boaz's pleas to attempt one more harvest. He proudly remembered when the people dug shallow dusty trenches with their heavy shovels and he had worried that their efforts might fail, but he never let anyone know how anxious he had felt.

With a few seeds between their thumbs and fingers, they had gently sprinkled the precious grain into the furrows. People walked behind the sowers, raking a thin layer of sandy earth over the precious seed and tamping it down so that not even one grain would blow away. His people, especially his wives complained like their ancestors about their aching backs and hungry bellies, but somehow they kept going. He too kept going with a power not his own, managing to reassure everyone that all would be well. He too yearned for plentiful meals and vats filled to the brim with oil and wine. He too longed for the times when his wives would host feast days and prepare honey cakes.

Surely that day would come again when they would drink beer until they were all laughing and chatting together. Looking now at the promise of the green sprouts not yet taller than his ankles, he felt confident, for these once barren fields would mature into stalks loaded with multiple golden seeds. He took a deep breath, looking forward to the time when the honey scent of ripe barley would fill the air.

Once again, he raised his arms, intending to praise Hashem, but suddenly in his mind's eye he saw a woman covered in a white rash. Leprosy! He groaned, not wanting such a vision. What was Hashem telling him now? He remembered how Miriam was punished because she spoke against her brother Moses. Was someone going to speak against him? He was no Moses. Did he, Boaz, deserve punishment for not having complete trust in Hashem?

He certainly did not expect anyone to trust his abilities alone.

Even his own wives made him wonder. They were angry with him—especially about his youngest wife. She was entirely innocent, having so recently come from her father's household into his. He stared down proudly at the neat stitches in his new sandals recently sewn for him by her. His senior wives obeyed him, and they were dutiful, following the traditions they'd learned from their families. But they did not appreciate that he had brought this young woman into their household to unite two families and also to help with chores and child-rearing.

In the days of his youth, he thought that he had understood all there was to know—including women. How foolish he had been in his yearning for Naomi. Even though he was sure she had felt the same way, it had done neither of them any good. Those longings were over. These days he was just an ordinary husband, a steady man and a good provider. He did his best to be kind to his wives and to his children, even when they irritated him. He settled squabbles justly and played no favorites. That was enough for him, but women seemed to want more.

When the rain came in large droplets, it was both exhilarating and frightening when the deluge caused streams of water to run down the narrow streets. Everyone feared that their new seedlings would be washed away, but people could not help their joy. Children and families rushed outside and waded in the puddles, splashing one another and laughing. Oh, it was wondrous indeed to feel the rain soak his hair and drip from his beard. It made him roar with laughter to watch little children jumping up and down to see who could make the biggest splashes. Who could blame the women who cast off their veils, letting the rain wash their hair and saturate their clothes until they looked almost naked? He tried to look away from the breasts and the firm buttocks of the young women, but what man could help himself? Some of the middle-aged ladies frowned at the younger ones. Many shook their heads in disapproval, yet even the elderly women did not seem to mind their sagging breasts clearly showing through their wet robes. Before long all the women, young and old, gathered in circles and danced.

Boaz had been carefully avoiding any sexual relations with his three wives. He did not want to bring any more children into these difficult times. But now the third wife, the youngest, caught his eye. She strutted with the other women, clearly displaying her charms for him, and when she ran into their house, he did not resist, but glancing over her shoulder he quietly followed.

It did not surprise him that when spring came with its bright and cool days, third wife's belly swelled. She glowed and thrived, clearly excited at the prospect of the new child, thrilled to be the center of attention. Even his children treated her gently and with respect. Boaz let her know how pleased he was with her by privately giving her a bejeweled cymbal. He wanted her to dance and sing with joy and make music for everyone. Her gratitude brought tears to his eyes. "Boaz, my wonderful husband," she cried, clutching his arm. "I am going to give you another strong son!" He too hoped for another boy. What man did not want sons to help tend the fields? And daughters, dear hearts though they were, eventually would go into someone else's household. The thought of his girls leaving made him sad, but he knew he could not and would not prevent any of his precious daughters from betrothal and marriage. At least though there was no hurry.

One day, as usual, he went out to the fields and stood smiling at the plants now up to his knees. He plucked one from the damp soil and held it to his nose and inhaled the fresh scent. None of the plantings had been washed away. They were growing taller, firm-rooted, clearly healthy. The thought of fresh-baked barley loaves and plentiful fodder and bedding for the remaining livestock made his eyes sparkle. He felt as if Hashem had understood his heart and was pleased with him. The barley would soon grow as tall as his head. Bethlehem would once again be true to her name: a land of bread. And in time there would also be wheat harvests with bees buzzing around the blossoms. There would be honey and sweet treats. Grape vines and olive trees would provide vats full of wine and oil. Lost in wonder, he did not pay any attention to the sound of sandals slapping across the grassy path from the village towards him. "Boaz," cried wife number two. "Come! The baby is on its way. Your youngest wife is in the birthing tent and the midwives say this child is racing into the world!"

His chest swelled with enough air to sustain twenty men. Although he knew there was nothing he could do to help with his wife's birthing process, and indeed he had always been in the fields when his other children were born, yet he hurried into the village. His delight seemed to know no bounds. As soon as he would be allowed by the formidable midwives who guarded the womanly process, they would show him his new child, and he would get to hold a new baby son.

Outside the large canopy with its striped linen walls and domed roof, his other children raced all around him. Above their noisy chatter and the flapping of the tent in the wind, he could hear women murmuring encouragement. He could hear his young wife crying out and panting and groaning. It might seem a quick birth to the midwives who were used to this painful process, but to Boaz the sound of every cry from his young wife made him hold his head in his hands. He wished he could put an end to her agony.

At last the crying of a baby came to his ears. The laughter of excited women's voices praising the new mother made him grin. Suddenly, though, he heard his wife sobbing. He knew he was not allowed and would not be welcomed into the tent of women, but his concern for this young wife was so great that he defied convention. He bowed his head, pushed the tent flaps aside, and ducked into the shelter lit by oil lanterns and lined with sheepskins and colorful quilts.

Women gasped and muttered at his nerve, but he ignored them and went quickly to his wife, who lay on a pile of bloody linen cloths, rocking her skinny baby. Her eyes upon seeing him grew wide with surprise and with something else. "I'm sorry," she cried, tears spilling down her cheeks. The baby as if sensing its mother's remorse began to bawl again. Boaz stared at them. What on earth could be wrong? The child looked red-faced and healthy enough and certainly had full-bodied lungs. Then it dawned upon him: this was not another son but another daughter! He hid his disappointment and gently put his arms around his wife and baby. "Hush," he murmured. "She is beautiful like you. Listen to her strong voice!" Even as he uttered these words, he realized that he wanted his girls to always be as strong as his sons. He wanted for them the power that Miriam once sought not to overthrow anyone, but to become sure of themselves, including becoming leaders of the people.

Third wife stopped her tears and gazed tentatively into his eyes as if assessing his true response, as if doubting any man would want a daughter. He remembered now how she had prepared infant clothes for a boy. He stroked her face and kissed the newborn's head. He already had two sons, heirs to his wealth, future fathers of their own clans. This young woman sought power through men rather than through her own merit. Glancing around at the indignant women scowling at his presence in their sacred place, he could not help but realize that they had a different sort of authority than men.

Even though perfumes masked the odor of birth, it reminded him of the richness of the earth and how it could provide food and much more. Without women, without children, without the good soil, what joy could there be in living? All seemed so much a part of Hashem's plan, so much more than he could understand. Women's bodies seemed to be conduits of something greater than all of them. Yet both men and women were equally important. He had always thought up until now that men were superior to women, but now he glimpsed a greater truth.

He regarded his wife tenderly and felt a cloud of sadness arising from deep within him. This girl whom he had selected, not because he honored her, but simply because he wanted to unite his family with another prosperous family here in Bethlehem had been given no choice in the matter of her marriage. She, like Naomi, had to go along with the wishes of her parents who accepted the dowry that was paid for her. It reduced her to not much more than chattel. He had always thought of Hashem as masculine, even though everyone understood Hashem was more than male or female, but the idea of Hashem in the image of a woman seemed blasphemy to him. And yet, and yet...his feelings were soon interrupted by a strong hand on his arm, drawing him away. "Come," said a midwife. "We have not washed and swaddled the infant yet, and she will soon be needing her mother's breast."

Boaz patted his wife's shoulder, feeling like an intruder in a foreign land, and then he bowed his way out of the tent into the bright daylight. His children gathered around him. "All is well," he said. "You have a strong new sister. You will get to see her soon enough. Go on home and help your mothers." They scattered, punching one another's shoulders and laughing together. These children made him so very happy, but instead of going back to his house, he went to the city gate and stared out at the road that led to Jerusalem. If Naomi had been allowed to be his wife, how might his life have been different? He could not even guess, but perhaps he would not have wanted more than one woman. He hoped that Naomi and Emilelech and their sons were blessed with good lives in Moab, but he wished they might come home. He swore before Hashem that this new little one and his other daughters too would have some say in future husbands. He would make sure they were honored for more than their abilities to cook and clean and take care of men and children.

Boaz wanted to name his baby girl Deborah, who had been fierce and smart, after the female judge he had learned about from the teachers. Although, in the past, he had always gone along with whatever his wives chose for their baby's names, he foolishly believed this decision to name this child would please his youngest wife. He imagined her clapping her hands when she brought her baby home. He could see her dancing with her new cymbal. He looked forward to welcoming her after the ritual time she had to remain separated. As soon as the harvest was in, he would host a special feast day to celebrate. In fact, he would ask his other wives to make it extra special.

The day that they were expecting his wife to come home with her new baby, everyone was gathered downstairs. His other wives and the children had done their best to prepare a special meal to welcome the new member into their family. The last of the dried apricots glistened in their colorful bowls. Pistachios, a little dry but still edible, were sprinkled across the table. They had even baked cinnamon bread with the remnants of their wheat flour. It smelled wonderful. Boaz lipped his lips and swallowed hungrily. "Later, after the harvest and we are back to normal we will have a bigger feast, a special celebration of life!" He thought such a statement would please his women. Did they not enjoy preparing foods and inviting others to eat with them? He did not understand their response.

"Why," shouted his senior wife, the mother of his boys, "are you naming this girl Deborah!"

Boaz stumbled over his words. "She is beautiful," is all he could manage, not able to say he wanted her and his other daughters to know they were loved equally by Hashem and were as strong as men in their own way.

"And *my* daughters did not deserve your input into their names," said his second wife. "Are they not also beautiful?"

"It's not that," he cried. "All of our children are special. I love them all. The girls are as special as Miriam, Moses' sister."

"Then call *her* Miriam, if you think she is so much better than Abira and Ada!"

"I don't think she is better. They are all different. Abira is strong and sturdy and Ada is sunshine in our lives."

The women shared knowing looks while the children stood by, listening and watching.

"Please," Boaz said. "Let us not spoil the homecoming for your sister-wife and her new infant."

Senior wife shook her head. "She can play the tambourine you gave her! That should cheer us up!"

Boaz sighed. "Enough!" he said sternly. "I will get all of you cymbals just as pretty, or I can make you reed flutes and we will make music together!"

His oldest wife shrugged, turned her back, and went out to tend the fire where her lentil soup with onions was simmering. He seemed to be making matters worse.

When the new mother arrived, he felt excluded especially when all the women took turns holding the child, cooing at her and telling her that she was beautiful. Boaz stared at them wishing he thought she was as pretty as a princess but the swaddling bands of cloth made her look like the cocoon of some strange insect, protected until she was strong enough to break free and fly. Her face was no longer as red and she had wispy strands of fine hair. He wanted to kiss the new mother and the infant, but he was afraid he would cause more resentment. "Come," he said, after the baby was gently laid upon a mat, and his other two little daughters were sitting next to her, stroking her face, "Come," he cried. "Let us give thanks to Hashem for how blessed we are today. Let us look forward to the blessings of tomorrow."

# Four: Trouble

Naomi

At Shabbat, I lit the candles that I had bought specially for this sacred day, whilst my oldest son solemnly said the prayers. He always gave honor to all of us women who worked so hard keeping our household together, but the way he bowed towards Ruth was especially tender.

It saddened me that my youngest son, Chilion, got married before his older brother. I had expected it was only a matter of time before Ruth and Mahlon would announce plans for a wedding. It was plain that she and Mahlon cared for one another. They made me smile, always being so gracious to one another. Ruth acted like a good wife and even baked special bread just for Mahlon, bread that she went out of her way to brush with an egg-wash to make it shine.

Alas, my hope seemed in vain. At least I could enjoy Chilion and Orpah. The two of them were so much in love in spite of their tiny "room" that consisted of blankets suspended over the wedding canopy poles in the corner of the courtyard. Eventually, the boys built them a lean-to with a wooden roof and three walls. Orpah was so excited. She proudly decorated with dried flower arrangements that she pinned to wooden tiles that she managed to hang across one wall. On another, Mahlon put up hooks for their clothes. Orpah's mother and father, who had not been pleased at the lack of a real bridal dowry that would have made their lives easier, could not resist loving these two either. It helped that Chilion made good on his promise to work in the fields with his father-in-law. His skinny arms grew more muscular and he began to look more mature.

The two lovers were always hugging one another. It was a wonder babies did not burst forth. Yet Orpah's belly never swelled nor did the lack of children diminish their affection. They could not have hidden their joy even if they had tried. We who knew them benefitted from their contagious happiness, demonstrated by loving looks, by kind behavior, by devotion. It did not seem to matter that Orpah never got pregnant. She said little about it, but from what Ruth told me after they had been in the woman's' tent during their periods, she was always sad to see the monthly blood flowing again. She did not blame Chilion and he did not blame her. They continued merrily always smiling at one another and seeming to cherish each other.

Then something changed. Perhaps it was the lack of children. I do not know. I was at home as usual, sewing a special dress to be decorated with beads for the priest's daughter, a young and beautiful girl soon to be married to Orpah's brother. Their betrothal had lasted three years. It was a wonder to me that her father, the priest, had ever considered this young man who might be a hard worker but was penniless. I knew Orpah's family could not afford much of a bridal dowry. Perhaps the priest's wife had intervened, and since they were rich and certainly pampered their only child, their daughter got what she wanted. Most young women would have been in trouble for the liberties she took. One day Chilion told everyone that he had seen her walking to the well with her mother and aunts. He said she had smiled at him and waved. He would not stop talking about how pretty the girl was and how wonderful it was that we got to attend *her* wedding. He never mentioned that it was also the wedding of his brother-in-law.

Orpah was jealous. Of course! She was so furious with him that she made him go onto the roof to sleep with Mahlon. At first I thought it would all soon be forgotten. If only there had been something I could have done to repair their relationship, some counsel that I might have shared with them, but I did not realize how serious this rift between them was actually becoming.

One day Orpah sullenly told me that Chilion was being unfaithful. I did not believe her. In fact I scolded her and became enraged. "What do you expect when you aren't sleeping with him anymore!" I yelled.

"I've smelled her perfume on him!" She yelled back, packed her clothes and went to stay with her mother.

I questioned Chilion, but he denied everything. "Orpah is upset because she isn't having a baby yet. She blames me!"

Although I managed to convince Orpah to come home, she still refused to allow Chilion in her bed, but they were at least talking to one another. I thought everything was improving between them until a week later she came rushing into the courtyard, sobbing uncontrollably. Neither Ruth nor I could console her or get her to tell us what was wrong.

I did not imagine such a catastrophe could happen.

The priest himself marched into our yard and stood in front of me with his arms crossed over his chest, his eyes flashing, and his mouth tight. He stared for a while until at last he spat these words at me. "I knew no good would come of you foreigners staying here! Do not think that I did not know how you hid the child Anna and helped Haran leave! Do not think that I am unaware of you coddling girls who are not even your daughters! It was a disgrace when your son, Chilion, was obliged to marry Orpah, but at least I thought he would settle down." His voice rose and his chest heaved. "There is no excuse for him defiling my daughter! She is betrothed to another!" He stared at the pretty veil I was working on for his daughter's wedding.

Orpah with a cry of distress ran into her house and hid.

"It cannot be so," I said, setting aside the veil and wiping the perspiration off my forehead with the palm of my hand. "You must be mistaken. Chilion is out helping gather the crop."

"He was seen with her by two of my kin."

My heart was beating so hard in my chest that I thought it would burst. "But what was your daughter doing out there alone with the harvesters?" It was the wrong thing to say and infuriated the man even more.

"How dare you accuse my daughter. Your son lured her out there. When the others were eating their midday meal, he strolled off to a nearby thicket of trees and thought he could not be seen. Now he will pay the full price of the law. He will receive the wrath of the people at noon tomorrow."

Ruth and I stood there frozen unable to speak. We both knew that they would stone Chilion. We would not be able to prevent it. I did not want to believe Chilion had done anything wrong and yet he had not hesitated to bed Orpah when she was still a maiden. The fact that she had reciprocated and it had ended in marriage seemed to have resolved his lust. How could a son of mine be such a fool! I felt as if this punishment was so unjust. How could they stone my son when the priest's daughter must have encouraged him? I wanted to scream yet I had no recourse.

Chilion was being held prisoner in an abandoned cistern. Unlike at Bethlehem, there was no meeting place by the city gate where a rebellious son would be brought before the elders who would hear the evidence and pass judgment. Ruth and I plotted ways we might help him escape. Orpah merely cried and cried until I wanted to slap her, as if she were to blame for my son's behavior. He was caught alone with a girl, and he surely knew it was forbidden. Of all the girls for him to meet privately, this one, the daughter of the neighbor priest whose women had helped me so much, was the very worst choice. Why hadn't he realized the jeopardy he put himself in? And us!

At last, I made up my mind. I wore a somber brown robe and intentionally did not cinch it at the waist so that I looked shapeless. I covered my head and face with black cloth so that only my eyes peeked out, and I went alone to see the priest. He received me in a large inner room adorned with beautiful carpets. Even some of Mahlon's pottery was on display. "It grieves me," I began. "My son is a good boy. I cannot understand why he met your daughter alone. It is so unlike him. He knows better. Your girl is a good girl,

I know, but perhaps she went there by herself without thinking and they accidentally met. It would be like my son to want to protect a young maiden." This was a lie but I did not care. I would do anything to save my son.

The priest pointed to a stool for me to sit. I did so but he remained looming over me, intending to intimidate me. But nothing would prevent me from appealing to his better nature. I bowed my head. My modesty clearly made no difference to this stern self-righteous man. I even wondered if it would have been better for me to have sent Ruth and have her flirt with him. Yet I suppose had *my* daughter misbehaved, I might want to blame someone else too. "They were both disobedient," I muttered and pulled the veil away from my face so that the man could see the tears streaming down my cheeks. "Take pity on a widow!" I cried. "How will I manage without my son!"

He grunted. "You have another son."

I was not about to say that Mahlon was a fragile lad because Chilion, in spite of his strong arm and legs, was not exactly robust. I knew it might make matters worse to bring up the fact that my sons were not as nearly as vigorous as his future son-in-law. "Your daughter did no wrong, I am sure," I managed to say, although I doubted it. "And I am sure she is going to make a fine wife to the brother of Orpah. They will be sisters-in-law. Wouldn't it be better for them to not have such a rift come between them? Wouldn't it be better for them to get along? And how can they, if Orpah's husband, Chilion, loses his life because of an innocent moment with your daughter? It will be an everlasting thorn in your daughter's heart."

"Nonsense," the priest said through pursed lips.

"Very well," I said, my tears still flowing. I fell on my knees and clutched at his robe. "Justice must be served. Take me in place of Chilion. I am old. I am of no use to anyone. I beg you, take me!"

The priest stared at me, tugged the cloth of his robe out of my trembling fingers, and clapped his hands to summon a servant. "Show her the way out," he ordered, and turned his back on me.

I thought all was lost, but his wife scurried after me into their courtyard and quietly whispered in my ear, "I will do my best to change his mind!"

I had no idea what she could do, but nevertheless it gave me hope. Unless the daughter confessed that she had a part in this meeting and insisted it was innocent, I could not imagine how Chilion might be freed. In Bethlehem there would be little doubt about who was to blame. If no one could hear their cries for help, women were never held responsible, but I knew my son would never force himself upon a girl. I simply could not believe such a thing of him.

The more I thought about it, the more I wondered why a girl about to be married to a strong and handsome young man like Orpah's brother would look twice at scrawny Chilion. Perhaps it was because Chilion was *not* fierce. Perhaps Orpah's brother tried to force himself on the priest's daughter and frightened her! Was she trying to find a way to stop the wedding by angering her fiancé? If she were no longer a virgin, it certainly would be cause for him to dismiss her.

I was too distraught to do any sewing or much of anything. I had retired to the house and was sitting aimlessly on the bench when Orpah's mother appeared in the doorway. "Well," she said, her arms held indignantly across her chest. "This is a fine mess!"

"Chilion is innocent," I cried.

"I doubt it," she responded. "He has caused nothing but trouble. And even worse my husband is furious because the priest's daughter has changed her mind about marrying my son. Now he is heartbroken. That girl is hopelessly spoiled. She wanted her father to release Chilion and she has rejected my son."

My mouth drooped. I hardly knew what to say. "I cannot tell you how sorry I am for what has happened, but you cannot blame me for being glad if Chilion will be freed. I promise I will see to it that he is punished." I wanted to beat him but I could at least insist that he fast with only juice and water to sustain him. Then, meaning to comfort Orpah's mother, I added, "Your son is such a handsome young man. He will surely have no trouble finding another bride."

Orpah's mother stared at me as if I were as foolish as a chicken. "That girl would have allied us with a prominent family, but now my son will probably have to settle for some landless nobody. I want Ruth to wed my son! She is a good worker, and I know he likes her. We have no dowry to give you— not that you deserve one. She is not your daughter."

"But I will soon be," Ruth cried, coming out of our bedroom and looking from one to the other of us. "I cannot marry your son! I am promised to Mahlon. We will be setting our wedding date soon."

I could hardly believe her words. I knew they were not heartfelt. Chilion's misfortune and the mere suggestion she marry Orpah's brother seemed to have prompted Ruth to mention marriage between herself and Mahlon. It was the wedding I had longed for yet it made me uneasy. I narrowed my eyes towards Ruth, but she shrugged and flounced away.

Orpah's mother also bustled out of the house, her robe clinging to her sagging bottom. Orpah was getting as fat as her mother and I worried that Chilion no longer found her pretty. I had a strong desire to defend her. Why did men expect women to constantly please them? Orpah's disposition would light up the moon.

Chilion arrived home after midnight. I suppose he thought he could sneak in without us noticing, but I heard Orpah shouting at him. Both Ruth and I lit our lanterns and went outside. Mahlon came hurrying down from the roof, and the four of us gathered around Chilion. "What on earth were you thinking!" I said, almost too quietly to be heard.

Mahlon, as the older brother, drew his fist back as if he were going to strike Chilion, but I seized his arm and stopped him. "Have you any idea the trouble you have caused us?" Mahlon said through gritted teeth.

"And me," Orpah cried. "And my family!"

Chilion covered his face. At first I thought it was out of shame, but when Orpah pulled his hands away, I could see that his face was bruised and his lip was bleeding.

"Who did this to you?" I asked.

"Your brother," he moaned to Orpah. "He ambushed me after they let me out of that hole."

"You deserve it," Orpah said in a choked voice, but then she wrapped her arms around him, and held him as if he were a child. He began to weep like one, so at least he felt some remorse. "I'm sorry, Orpah," he whimpered between his sobs. "I know," she said and rocked him.

I silently thanked Hashem that Orpah appeared willing to forgive him. I could only hope she would not punish him later on as women were wont to do when they had been betrayed. "Tonight," I said, "we will give thanks that you are still alive, Chilion, but you are to go without food for at least a week. You understand! And you must ask Hashem to forgive you!"

"I will," Chilion muttered, no longer crying, his head hanging, his arms limp at his sides.

The boy managed to keep his promise of drinking only juice and water. He took no solid food for ten days. His thin body became more gaunt. Orpah treated him like a child. He went about sheepishly, unwilling to meet anyone's eyes. I feared he would take ill. I wanted to give him bread and honey, but I resisted. He needed to atone in some way for his mistake. We were all paying for his folly—a married man committing adultery. Although he denied he had done anything wrong and said the priest's daughter was the one who had set up the meeting, it did not matter. The priest had all the power. We had none. As bad as it was to be disgraced in the eyes of the community, the loss of payment for the wedding dress that I had so carefully sewn made me afraid of the future. Who would buy anything from us now? What if the priest's wife told her wealthy friends to stop buying my blankets and clothing? What if Mahlon had to reduce the price of pots to sell any of them?

I sat in the courtyard one warm day all by myself, watching dried leaves blowing across my feet and listening to the chirruping of birds. I had brought the Misho statue out with me and balanced her upon my knees. I had hoped to find comfort in that ancient stone, but I felt more wretched than ever and completely helpless. I began to relive the loss of my baby. What an awful time it had been! Yet somehow I had survived, and somehow life went on, and somehow I had gotten strong again. I needed to be resilient now and brave, but I did not feel as if I had one more drop of energy left. How was I to go on!

But as I stared at those sagging breasts resting upon the pitted swollen belly of the statue, my gratitude for the stamina of all the women who had come before me arose. We were strong. I raised my eyes to the heavens. Oh, I wanted to beg Hashem to make things right for my family, but that is not the prayer I said. In fact I had no words to express my needs, but I suddenly felt a surge of wellbeing and an inner understanding that my strength would not crumble. In my mind too I heard a gentle voice say, "Do not worry, Naomi, everything will be all right." Perhaps I was dreaming, but I felt as if the voice that I had heard was the voice of my mother. I felt instantly comforted.

# Five: Mercy

Naomi

As I sat watching Ruth carding wool, her long legs stretched out on the mat, I felt joyous that she would indeed become my daughter-in-law. A month had already passed since the scandal about Chilion and the priest's daughter had exploded. Orpah's family refused to talk to me and the priest's family ignored me too. It made me sad, but, strangely, I felt a sense of trust in Hashem. I was repeating every day the prayer Mahlon had taught me, remembering how Hashem had led the people to freedom and was compassionate with them even when they worshipped the golden calf. The idea of worshipping idols over Hashem gave me a few moments of anxiety because of the goddess statue, but I did not worship her. She was merely a reminder of the value of women. She helped me remember my baby girl who I had grieved for and had wished would have had the chance to breathe in the sultry air of a thunderstorm and feel my loving arms around her to protect her. My goddess statue certainly was *not* a golden calf. It had no monetary value whatsoever.

I had been planning to let out the bodice of the wedding dress intended for the priest's daughter so that it would fit Ruth. She was becoming more and more beautiful with deep lioness eyes that sometimes shone with fury. Right now she looked as gentle as a lamb. Her wedding to Mahlon, I decided, must be done following our Hebrew traditions. Chilion and

Orpah's rushed marriage, well, it was better now, but I wondered if they might both have avoided all the heartache if they had had to wait a while, and if they had received instructions about courtship and the expectations of married life.

Emilelech, if he had been living, would certainly have talked to Chilion, but I had not said a word to the boy, too overwhelmed by their impropriety and by my own shyness about sexual matters. That was then! This was now! I determined that I *would* talk to Mahlon. He and Ruth shared friendship, but she seemed indifferent to the fact that he was a man who needed and wanted more. I knew he loved her, and I hoped I could encourage her to find him appealing in the ways of men and women. She simply could not go on running as wild as she usually did as if she were still a carefree girl out gathering flowers. She was decidedly independent, but at least she showed an interest in learning. Everything! From how to weave beautiful cloth, to learning from Mahlon about Hashem. It was improper for a girl to seek such knowledge, but I too felt a hunger for greater understanding of Hashem's ways.

Now, I could hear the squeaking of the pottery wheel and I smelled damp clay. "I need to talk to Mahlon," I remarked to Ruth, who looked at me questioningly. I could not tell her my plan to instruct Mahlon about how to properly woo her. I said nothing, smiled, set aside my wool, and got to my feet. Outside, I stood for a while next to a bucket of mud littered with rocks and broken sticks. It needed to be filtered so that the clay would be clean enough to mold into earthenware. Mahlon, with his back to me, busily pumped away at the lever to his wheel while he carefully shaped a bowl into an upside-down bell. How talented my son had become! I was so proud of him! When he finished working the clay, he turned to me with a look of irritation. He did not like to be interrupted when he was working. "Mahlon," I said, gathering my courage and yet feeling a little weak in my knees. "I need to talk to you about something important."

"Can't you see how busy I am?" he muttered.

"Doesn't the bowl you've just finished need to dry?" I asked nervously, and before he got a chance to answer, I continued. "What I have to say is important." I glanced back at the house, realizing that I could not speak to him here because Ruth would certainly listen to every word. "Walk with me," I said in what I hoped was a commanding voice. I raised the veil draped over my shoulders to cover my hair.

Mahlon, looking even more annoyed, took his foot off the pottery lever and carefully placed the new bowl on two strips of wood. He dipped his hands in a bucket of water and wiped them clean with a rag. His mouth set in a rigid line, he followed me out of our courtyard. We had already passed the priest's quarters and were going towards Haran's compound when I began. "Your marriage needs to be done properly," I said.

"Of course," Mahlon responded. "I am not like Chilion."

"I don't mean that!" But of course I *did* want to talk to him about sex and how a boy needed to treat a girl. I prayed for help! I pulled my veil over my cheeks so he could not see how hot my face was becoming. I was not at all prepared to tell any man, let alone my son, how to please a woman. "You and

Ruth need to sign a proper betrothal contract in front of witnesses," I murmured.

"Just whom do we know here in Moab who will be our witnesses," he replied. "Especially now."

"Hashem will guide us," I said.

He threw me a sidelong glance of disgust as if he no longer trusted anyone, not even Hashem, but I did. I did! "We are going right now to talk to Ruth's relatives and get their permission for the marriage." These words popped out as if they had a life of their own, as if someone other than me had said them. "I think the wedding should take place after you wait for at least a year." I was afraid of what he would say. I took a deep breath and lowered my eyes.

His words reassured me but only slightly. "I don't mind waiting, but I doubt that you'll get much satisfaction from Haran's family. They won't acknowledge Ruth at all."

"We will make them!" I said, trying to sound confident, as we went outside the village, passing fields of wheat and barley where men were hoeing. This road, much brighter than the passageway through the houses, but far less traveled, was hard beneath my feet. I was wearing the sandals Leah had made for me. They were stretched now and more comfortable, but a sharp pebble almost pierced the soft leather sole of my left foot and I stumbled.

Mahlon caught me and helped me straighten up. "Are you all right?" His concern made me smile. He was a good son. He would listen to whatever I said, but I still could not bring myself to talk about anything sensitive.

I stared at the sandals thinking about Leah, and what she had taught me about the ways of men because she had been married before me. I had tried to tell Emilelech to take time with me if he wanted me to be more responsive. He was so embarrassed. And so was I and still was! I took Mahlon's arm. "Come on," I said. "I am fine. Let's go." As we got closer to Haran's house, I hoped all the men would be out in the fields. I felt as if the women were bound to be more sensitive to our hopes for a marriage between Mahlon and Ruth.

We opened the side gate closest to the goat pen. As usual the animals' strong musky odor wafted around us. I felt comforted at their familiar scent and their bleating. We made our way into the main courtyard where two women sat at their looms, weaving cloth that I yearned to go over to examine and touch. I hated confrontation and I wanted to talk about fabric not about Ruth, who I felt had been wronged by the people in this household. The weavers were chatting but when they glanced up to see Mahlon and I, they froze, their eyes narrowed, their mouths open. My mouth was open too but not with words. I felt intimidated and could find nothing to say, no way to be polite.

Somehow I found the courage to hustle past them as if I were expected. We hurried into Haran and Hannah's familiar quarters. I suppose I wanted to hide there, but I also had an absurd notion that Hannah would be in her kitchen and would greet us with open arms. I would do anything for my children. Surely in their heart of hearts Ruth's parents would do the same for her, and surely her aunts and uncles also loved Ruth. There were still a few old pots hanging from the kitchen walls, but the house was empty. It felt barren and in need of people to give it life. It was so much bigger than the little house I now occupied but not nearly as luxurious as my old house in Bethlehem with its indoor cistern and indoor stalls for livestock. I drew back the drape to the cubbyhole where I had first stayed with Ruth. A blanket lay atop a straw mattress where mice were nesting. Quickly, I dropped the drape and stepped away.

When we heard the voices and the footfalls of people coming, we stared at the door, waiting to see if they were willing to talk with us. One of Ruth's aunties appeared in the opening with her arms held stiffly at her side. Two other women, the ones who had been weaving, huddled behind her. From the expression on their faces, it was clear they were not here to welcome us.

"What are you doing here?" one of them demanded to know.

I felt an urge to tell them off for abandoning Ruth, but I managed to hold my tongue. I knew if I scolded them, the anger I could see in those suspicious eyes would only get worse. Although I was feeling uneasy, I managed to speak calmly and quietly, hoping to win them over. "I am so sorry to come here uninvited, but I hope we can be friends again. Everyone in your family was so kind to us, and I miss Hannah." I suddenly wished that I had brought a gift for them, but it was too late for that now.

Their faces softened slightly.

"I want to marry Ruth!" Mahlon knotted his fists. "We came for permission because we want to do things the right way!"

I was relieved he had not said *our* way.

The woman who had led them into the house shouted, "What about your brother! Are you as unreliable as he? And Ruth should have behaved herself instead of running off and doing who knows what!"

Mahlon glared at the woman. "Ruth is a wonderful girl and has done nothing wrong. If anyone is in the wrong it is you and your treatment of her. How could you turn away one of your own family who had been ill-used and in need? She was just a girl! How could you!" He strode towards the woman and stopped within a hairbreadth of her face.

I must admit I felt some satisfaction at my son's fury especially when this stubborn woman stepped back and seemed unable to meet his look. Her eyes rested on mine briefly, and I thought I noticed a tiny quiver of shame.

Mahlon's voice grew quieter. He unclenched his fists. "I am sorry. This must all have been painful for you too." The anger in his face faded, and he remained silent, staring at the woman. After a long moment he added, "Please, at least agree to let her marry me. As you know I have no dowry to offer. We have so little to give you except our gratitude."

The woman who had been so hostile at first stared at her feet. Tears formed in her eyes. "Ruth was such an active little girl. We were so upset at everything that happened. I will talk to Haran's brother. He is the head of the household now. He always loved Ruth."

I wanted to rush forward and grab the woman's hands and thank her, but she abruptly turned and led the others away. We also went outside and were soon at the side-gate when she called out to us, "Come back tomorrow after the sun goes down. We will settle everything then."

We were silent on our way home. I could not bring myself to talk about anything intimate, and Mahlon was quiet, lost in thought, I suppose. As we passed the priest's house, a servant girl came running out and pressed a heavy pouch into my hand. "Here," she said. "For the wedding gown!" She darted back inside before we could say anything more. My hands trembled as I untied the sack and looked inside to see enough gold shekels to support us for months. What could this mean? Mahlon looked confused too. I almost ran after the servant girl, but we desperately needed money, and I did not want to offend them again. Had their daughter already been betrothed to another man? Were they already planning another wedding for their daughter? I tied the money bag securely inside my robe. I would deal with this later.

Within a few minutes as we entered our courtyard, Ruth leapt to her feet to greet us. She grinned and looked gleeful and pleased. "The wedding is on again!" she cried. When we both stared at her dumbfounded, she added, "between Orpah's brother and the priest's daughter."

I was shocked and not particularly happy. Did Ruth think that since Orpah's brother was once again spoken for, she could back out of the marriage to Mahlon? I worried that my son might think the same thing. I wanted to settle matters once and for all. "What good news!" I managed to say. "They will probably be married before you and Mahlon, but we will arrange your wedding date tomorrow. When we go to your father's house, we will get the contract between you two witnessed by the aunts and uncles."

Ruth's eyes flashed angrily. "I am never going into that household again!"

Mahlon groaned. "Don't you want us to get married?"

Ruth kicked a pebble across the ground and stared down. At last she raised her eyes with tears glistening in the corners. "You don't understand," she said all too quietly. "It is not that I don't want to marry *you*. I don't *ever* want to get married."

"But why?" Mahlon cried, his face sad and heartbroken.

I felt a desire to hug Mahlon and slap Ruth. I did neither but I spoke. "Ruth, the very least you *can* and *must* do is accompany Mahlon and I to your old house. I know your kin hurt you, but sometimes you have to excuse those who are in the wrong."

The girl looked at me sadly. "I know," she said. "I want to forgive them but I can't."

"Just come with us tomorrow and make your pledge to Mahlon, please!" I heard the begging tone of my voice, and almost added that Ruth *owed* me, but I realized it would only make her more stubborn. "Your aunts miss you," I said.

"Did they say so?" she asked, a glint of hope in her eyes.

"They remembered you as a little girl and how much they loved you and how one of your uncles had a soft spot for you. I am sure he still must."

"Uncle Bebai," Ruth whispered as another tear dripped from her eye. She quickly brushed it away.

I realized that I had never seen her cry over the loss of her family. I suppose I had been too preoccupied with my own grief to understand how Ruth had felt. She surely must have been hurt and still was. I wrapped my arms around her. "You are strong," I told her. "Try to forget what happened." I did not only mean her mother and father leaving. I found myself also hoping and praying that during our visit tomorrow night—if she even agreed to come—she would approve of Mahlon.

Mahlon stood nearby with one hand on his chin. "You don't have to marry me. I have nothing to offer you."

Ruth stepped out of my arms and looked steadily at Mahlon. For a while she said nothing, but at last she began to speak in a measured tone. Once again, I realized that this girl, this Ruth, was not some silly child. She was kind and wise beyond her years. "Mahlon," she murmured softly. "You are so smart and such a good potter."

Mahlon bowed his head before looking at her. "Then you will marry me?"

"I don't know. I swore long ago that I would never marry and have babies that could be taken away from me."

"I would protect you!" Mahlon cried.

"We will go back to Bethlehem!" I said, even though I had no idea how things were in my hometown.

Ruth wrapped her arms around her chest, hugging herself. "I am not what you think, Mahlon."

I feared she was going to reveal that she was no longer a virgin, and I shook my head to stop her from saying anything further. "No one is ever what we expect in a marriage," I said hastily. "It takes time to get to truly know one's spouse, and it takes commitment to get through the good and bad times." I looked at their solemn faces and suddenly I felt like laughing. They were both so young. "Come, let us get our dinner ready, and let us plan for tomorrow. We must take your relatives gifts. Perhaps you can bake bread for them too, Ruth. And what about that green platter decorated with sunflowers, Mahlon? That would make a wonderful present."

Although Ruth still had not said she would marry my son, nor had she agreed to go with us, I knew that if she baked bread it would be her way of saying *yes*.

# Six: Uncertainty

### Ruth

Not wanting to disturb Naomi, who was on the mat next to her breathing softly, Ruth tried to be still, but she kept on tossing and turning, her mind racing with memories, especially of that lustful man who had tried to sell her into a Goddess Temple. It comforted her to recall his frail little wife hovering in the background. This woman had been brave and strong and saved her from a fate she could not even imagine. Yet after her escape, all had not been terrible: the nomads had treated her with kindness and they had taught her about helping others, but Ruth wished that she could think better of *her* people. No doubt Uncle Bebai expected her to be reunited with her parents, but how could *he*, how could *any* of her aunts and uncles, have so easily cast her aside? When she had arrived on their doorstep after the nomads brought her close to home, she was obviously upset, but her own family had not given her a chance to tell them what had happened. They had assumed that she had somehow invited the very worst to fall upon her.

Mahlon was gentle and considerate: maybe it would not be all bad to become his wife. It gave her pleasure to watch him eat the bread that she had baked especially for him. In fact, not much would change. Her future with Naomi in this kind household would be assured. She would have to go on working hard, but she enjoyed carding wool and did not mind hard labor. Eventually she hoped to make new blankets using freshly dyed wool. It would be wonderful to learn how to craft pots too. For some reason she loved the idea of dipping her hands into clay. The thought of Mahlon teaching her helped allay her fears of their potential marriage. It might turn out well. He wanted more from his wife than a good cook and the mother of his children.

In the morning everyone gathered outside in the cool morning air. Orpah prepared bowls of chickpeas in goatmilk sweetened with honey. She served the men first. The day-old bread was a little stale but would make a good sop. Mahlon hardly touched his food, but Chilion grabbed his bowl and finished it for him, smacking his lips appreciatively. He soon went out to meet with the other farm laborers, including Orpah's brother. At the mere thought of the man, Ruth shuddered. Mahlon glanced up at her as if he also felt her repulsion. He quickly wiped his mouth and he went over to his pottery wheel.

After the women finished their chores and sat down, Naomi smiled hopefully at Ruth, who knew that her eyes did not shine with her usual good humor. Orpah took her basket and headed over to her mother's house to gather the eggs she liked to barter for raisins and cinnamon. Naomi wandered back into the house, leaving Ruth outside watching Mahlon, who seemed to be pedaling the wheel faster than usual. His anxiety about the upcoming meeting made her smile, not at his discomfort, but because he cared so much. He seemed to feel her watching him and pedaled even faster.

Ruth decided she would prepare some bread to take to her relatives as a peace offering. Those heartless aunts and uncles needed to offer *her* peace though! She went to the stream and washed her hands and brought back fresh water. She set a small amount out in a bowl in the sun to warm, the way Naomi had shown her. Then she added the raw dough that she had mixed yesterday, left out in the air to capture the wild yeasts to add a sour flavor that everyone loved. She vigorously stirred the dough with a wooden spoon, gradually adding in more and more flour. When it was thick enough, she turned it onto a wooden board, one Mahlon had fashioned and sanded from oak planks. The more she used it, the more she appreciated its usefulness. With the heels of her hands, she pressed the sticky dough down, turning it repeatedly, occasionally dusting it with flour. Her hands and arms ached from the effort and a bead of perspiration rolled off her forehead, but she was glad to be working. She began to hope perhaps it *would* be all right with her aunts and uncles. Perhaps she *would* be able to share times once again with her cousins, go to their weddings, and hold their babies. The truth was that she loved children. She had adored her baby sister Anna. Perhaps she *could* one day have her own children. She wished the fear that made her stomach clench would ease. She punched the dough flat and cut it into six smaller pieces. She rolled out three long strands and plaited them together, knowing that this particular type of loaf would please Naomi. For a moment she dared wonder how it would feel to teach *her* daughters how to bake.

After putting a cloth over the moist loaves to keep them warm while they rose, Ruth went into the house to light the fire in the oven. She wanted the flat stone that she used for baking to be good and hot. Though she had successfully made dozens of golden loaves, today she worried that her bread would end up burned. As she piled the dried fuel onto the kindling, she watched Naomi out of the corner of her eye. Neither had acknowledged one another. Ruth could not find the right words, but she hoped that Naomi, seeing and smelling the aroma of the baking bread, would understand that this was her way of agreeing to go to her old house where her relatives not only waited but probably condemned her.

The wedding gown that Naomi was finishing for the priest's daughter, with silver trim and silver beads sewn into the skirt, might have been *hers*, Ruth knew. She *did* think it was pretty, more beautiful than any dress she had ever seen. A pang of sadness filled her to think about how *her* mother would have made sure that she, Ruth, would be married in such a beautiful gown.

Naomi smiled gently as she sank her needle in and out of the silken cloth. "I will make you an even prettier dress, Ruth" she whispered softly.

Ruth could not bring herself to look directly at Naomi, but she nodded and managed a little smile.

Later in the afternoon, while Ruth sat outside near the old tree, staring into space, Naomi came over. "Your bread smells delicious!" she remarked.

Ruth was pleased the loaves had turned out well. Yet she still dreaded the rapidly approaching evening when she would have to face Uncle Bebai and the rest of them. "I hope they'll like it!" she murmured.

Naomi began wringing her hands. "The wedding gown for the priest's daughter is finished, at least as much as I can do without her trying it on."

She glanced uncertainly at Ruth. "Would you come with me to her house and help me with a fitting?"

Ruth almost laughed. Did Naomi think that she would be jealous of the girl? "Of course," she answered. "I will be happy to help."

Naomi held up the bodice while Ruth walked behind, raising the skirt off the ground.

At the priest's house, they were quickly admitted into a small parlor, and they were soon surrounded by the women of the house. The future bride, upon seeing the dress, squealed with delight. Her mother murmured about how beautiful and how soft the material was. Other womenfolk stroked the cloth and admired the beading. The girl quickly disrobed and tugged the dress over her head and tried to smooth it over her waist, but it was too tight. Ruth exchanged a knowing look with Naomi, who busied herself tugging the skirt over the girl's knees. It seemed a little too high above her ankles. "I will have to let out the waist so it doesn't ride up and then it will be more comfortable. Have you decided on the date of your wedding?" she asked.

The mother could not look at Naomi but answered for her daughter. "It's next month. We hope you will attend."

"Of course we will," Naomi said, delighted. "It will be an honor."

The future bride smiled but there was little happiness in her eyes. After she had disrobed, Naomi gathered the dress with promises to have it ready in a day or two for another fitting.

On their way home, neither Ruth nor Naomi said much until they were back in their own house. "Are you thinking what I am thinking?" Ruth asked.

"No wonder they want such a rushed marriage. The girl is either eating too many sweets or she is pregnant," Naomi observed wryly. "It's a good thing that she is already betrothed to Orpah's brother." She looked suddenly alarmed. "I can only hope Chilion is not the father," she exclaimed.

"It can't be Chilion's," Ruth responded. "She looks much further along than since the time they met in the woods."

"I hope you're right," Naomi moaned. "Let us say no more about it. Meanwhile, let us get ready for our meeting tonight. I know you are worried about it, Ruth, but I am sure everything will work out for the best. Why don't you wear your pretty purple dress, the one with the wide sash around the waist? After your official engagement to Mahlon, we will wait a year as is proper before your wedding."

The idea of waiting for a year before getting married relieved Ruth. But she doubted Uncle Bebai would consent or even bother to come and meet with them.

As it turned out, Uncle Bebai was near the gate waiting for them and, to her surprise, he wrapped his arms around her. "Ruthie," he said as he hugged her. "I am so happy to see you." He stepped away from her, sizing up Mahlon who, even with his hair neatly brushed and his beard trimmed, looked boyish. His freshly laundered robe, cinched tightly around his middle, fell just below his knees so that his thin legs were showing.

Mahlon, ignoring or unaware of the scrutiny, took a colorful platter that he had brought as a gift out of a satchel. "This is for you." He thrust it towards the uncle.

The man took it and examined it. "This will please my wife. She likes bright colors. Come, let us go into the house."

Ruth choked back tears. She had imagined the very worst, that she would be disowned, but clearly this was not going to be the case. She looked over at Mahlon, who gave her a reassuring smile. Naomi grabbed her hand and gave it a little squeeze.

Bebai, much like his brother Haran, Ruth's father, was an outgoing man who loved his family. He ushered them into his house where his wife and several other aunts and uncles were waiting. They all assembled in an upper room and sat in a circle on a thick mat. Two girls, young cousins of Ruth's, served them hot jasmine tea and clove-spiced cakes.

They chatted for a while, saying not one word about the past as if nothing unfortunate had happened. Ruth realized that sometimes it was better to keep silent about old arguments rather than stir up more anger. Part of her, though, wanted to ask them how they could have treated her so badly, but another part of her was grateful for their warmth towards her now.

At last the conversation turned to the impending betrothal. Naomi glanced over at Ruth before looking candidly at the uncle. "I don't know your wedding traditions, but in ours it is appropriate to ask the future bride's mother and father for their permission. Since Ruth's parents are not able to speak for her, we have come to humbly ask for your agreement. The bride must agree too and, of course, the groom."

"I agree," Mahlon said quietly.

"And you, Ruth? Do you want to marry Mahlon?" Uncle Bebai asked.

Everyone seemed to be holding their breath. "Of course I do," Ruth said at last, and almost added *who else would have me?* In any case she knew of no one else who would suit *her*.

"About the dowry," Bebai began.

He was interrupted by Naomi who produced a pouch of money. Ruth knew it must be the payment for the wedding gown. "There will never be enough to compensate you for your loss of your niece Ruth from your household," Naomi said, "but I am more than happy that Ruth will be remaining with me. She is already like my daughter."

Bebai took the pouch and rattled the coins but did not bother to look inside. "You are a widow, Naomi," he said and gave her back the purse. "You keep this." He sought the eyes of the other members of his family. Each of them, seeming pleased, smiled back at him.

Naomi clutched the moneybag. "Mahlon and Ruth are willing to wait one year before they are finally married. Alas we do not have a proper wedding contract, but..."

One of the aunts nudged Uncle Bebai. "Tell them our plan, Bebai."

"We are happy to allow Ruth to marry Mahlon," he said. "We also agree it would be best for them to wait. But we want Ruth to live with us during the time of their engagement. Does everyone approve?"

Ruth felt a sharp stab in her stomach. "Of course," she managed to squeak, but she wanted to shout, *I don't want to live here again, not ever*. She would be lost without Naomi, who was now clenching the money bag with both hands. Mahlon managed a sheepish smile.

Bebai smiled kindly into Ruth's eyes. "It is settled then. We will send someone to fetch your things. And Naomi, this is a big house and there is plenty of room for you. We hope you will also come here to live."

At first Naomi's hope surged, but then her eyes clouded over. "You are so gracious and kind," she said. "But I must stay in my own house with Orpah and Chilion. Mahlon has his pottery wheel set up in our yard. I have my loom." She turned to Ruth. "Dearest one, I cannot imagine life without you during this year of waiting, but we won't be far away. We will visit often. And before you know it, you will come home with us. Much as it would be wonderful to live amongst a family again, especially *your* family, it is best for me to remain in my house, small though it is."

Ruth nodded weakly. She wished she too might learn to survive without a husband.

Naomi turned to Bebai. "We will return with the marriage contract after Ruth is settled back here with your family. I hope that is satisfactory."

"I have the contract," Mahlon said quietly but firmly. "I have been preparing it for a long time, hoping this day would come."

Everyone got quiet as they watched Mahlon dig into his satchel.

Bebai cleared his throat. "Although we do not want a bridal dowry, we expect Mahlon to faithfully promise to treat Ruth with respect and love." He smiled broadly, and everyone in the room nodded.

Ruth looked around at those faces now smiling at her—the same people who had cast her aside. She wanted to scold them, but the tender look from her youngest aunt and the giggles from the cousins prevented her from speaking.

Mahlon at last, fumbling, handed her an object wrapped in a swath of deep blue silk.

Ruth unwrapped the material and stared at a square platter hardly bigger than her hand. Along the base, it was exquisitely decorated with colorful flowers and pretty birds. Next to a central image of a goblet overflowing with red wine were printed words that she could not read. She ran her finger over the inscription. "What does it say?"

Mahlon's face turned red, but he began to speak. "For my wife, Ruth. I will follow the laws and the tradition that Moses taught. I will do my best to please you and cherish you. I will honor and support you always from this day forward."

Her uncle clapped his hands enthusiastically. "We must celebrate your official betrothal with a special meal. Will tomorrow be soon enough?" He grinned.

Mahlon looked into Ruth's eyes. "Do you like it?"

"Oh Mahlon," Naomi exclaimed. "This is so precious. How incredibly beautiful. My wedding contract with your father has always been special to me, but it was painted on a scroll by a scribe not by your father. This is so much more personal."

"I have nothing to give you, Mahlon," Ruth murmured, overwhelmed.

"You are everything to me," Mahlon said. "I only regret that I don't have silver and gold necklaces for you as a bridal gift."

"Such things don't matter to me." Ruth looked at him fondly. "I would love for you to teach me to make pots! I could paint them too."

"Ruth," Naomi cautioned. "You will probably be too busy with babies!"

## Seven: Birth

Naomi

At first I greatly missed Ruth, often feeling alone at night. Eventually, after a few months, I began to enjoy having the curtained area where we had slept to myself. Orpah and Chilion sometimes went up onto the roof together to enjoy the cool of evening. Perhaps they stared at the stars that seemed to me as precious as the gems created by Hashem. I hoped it would not be long before I would have a grandchild on the way.

The priest's daughter's marriage to Orpah's' brother was a weeklong festivity. The girl danced and smiled and seemed happy. Her young husband, too, beamed with pride. She managed to look thin, but I thought the dress seemed tighter around her belly than during her final fitting. Weeks later, I was at the well and saw the girl, who looked radiant as pregnant women often do, wearing a loose-fitting robe. I felt a pang of envy. I would so love for Orpah to give me a grandchild. But I was troubled with more than my envy about a new baby to the priest's daughter. I was worried that Chilion really might be the father of this child. The girl was dark-skinned and so was her husband. What if the child looked like Chilion, who was as fair as a maiden who has never removed her veil? Chilion's work in the fields might have toughened up his muscles, but it had not tanned his skin. I dreaded the birth of this baby.

I buried my fears by working harder. My finest fabrics, especially my purple, pleased me. My cloth began to be in so much demand that I could not keep up with the orders. The money that I earned began to accrue so that I began to feel quite prosperous. I even had some money left over from the wedding dress. I knew I had been paid too much, and I could not help but wonder if the priest's wife had felt guilty that Chilion was almost killed because of what I had hoped and prayed was a harmless encounter, but I remained unsure. After all, he had spent time alone with the girl, who was known to be a flirt. At least these days my son was behaving in a more mature way and seemed solicitous of Orpah, even though the days of their joyous togetherness were now tempered with work. Still, sometimes, I heard them laughing after they had retired at night. It gave me hope.

Orpah and I got along fairly well, but we were nowhere near as close as Ruth and me. In all her spare moments, Orpah went home to her mother. I might have insisted that she help more with the chores and the weaving, but I preferred to work alone. For one thing, Orpah never stopped chattering, and it was all just idle gossip that I really did not want to hear. Orpah's younger brother was courting a girl whom Orpah said was known to break off engagements and not return the bridal dowry. But it was none of my business and brought my mood down. I would much rather hear about people being kind and successful than mean-spirited and greedy. Orpah's people had not given any money as a dowry to the family of this girl. Instead, the boy was toiling for the father in his ironworks. Orpah said the family were using him for free labor. If so, I mused, at least he would be learning a trade.

Really, it made no difference to me whether the young man was being manipulated or not, but I did feel sorry for Orpah's mother. She had already been more than hurt after the priest's daughter and her oldest son defied convention and refused to come to live with her. The girl insisted upon staying with *her* mother, and so they moved into the priest's spacious house. Clearly this girl was very spoiled. Orpah's mother not only needed help—she had also looked forward to having another female companion. No wonder Orpah went home so often. I could not blame her. I doubted that the priest's daughter, who seemed sweet enough even if she were devious, would dirty her delicate hands. She preferred to preen and look pretty. I hoped that at least she might make a good mother, but the very thought of who her baby might resemble made me shudder.

One day as I looked around my tiny house, I wondered how we had ever managed when there had been five adults packed in here together. And once children came along, it would be even more crowded. I found myself yearning for my old house back in Bethlehem with more than enough rooms for everyone. Feeling restless, I went out for a walk to the well. I so hoped I would find Ruth there, but she was not allowed out of the sight of her aunts. Only when I went to visit her did I get a chance to talk to her. Although I empathized with my headstrong young friend's lack of freedom, I always encouraged her to persist, reminding her it was only a matter of a few more months when she would join Mahlon in marriage. I was still unsure of her desire to marry my son, but I knew she wanted to come and live with us.

On my way home, carrying two jugs of water in my arms, I encountered the priest's daughter and her maid. She was walking slowly, her belly as big as an oversized watermelon. The scowl on her face made me pity her. "It won't be long now," I remarked with a big smile, hoping to make her feel better, even though the very thought of who that child might belong to upset me. The girl frowned and said, "I can't wait to be done with this nuisance!" Her remark made me cringe. An expectant mother, one who had all manner of comfort, plenty of money, and a husband who doted on her, ought to be overjoyed at the thought of her first baby. She seemed angry that she must endure discomfort. I shook my head in disbelief, but if she noticed my disapproval, she ignored me and hurried out of my sight into her house.

I so longed for grandchildren racing around, playing and giggling, but now I felt envious of the priest's luxurious compound, bigger than ordinary folks could afford. It suddenly occurred to me that rather than harbor such negative feelings, I could look for a bigger house for when Ruth came home. With such a happy thought in my mind, I felt better. I went into my kitchen and put down the heavy jugs of water on the floor.

On my knees, I reached underneath a pile of linen needing to be dyed. I soon found my savings. I dumped the coins on the floor and counted them, feeling proud of myself, but I also felt quite insecure. Emilelech had always handled money matters. I had no idea how much a bigger house would cost. Since a home was far more substantial than pretty jewelry, I had not minded giving up my golden bracelets and my pretty necklaces for Emilelech to help pay for this house. I had no more jewelry, but I did not miss it. I had *no* man to look beautiful for. I did not want another husband to tell me what to do, but I would have welcomed advice on how to go about purchasing another house. I was afraid I would be cheated.

I wrapped a woolen shawl around my shoulders as much for comfort as for warmth. Since it was quite breezy, I exchanged the flimsy scarf I usually wore over my head for a more substantial woolen one. On my way through the village, the wind tore down the narrow streets. I clasped my shawl with one hand and hung onto my scarf with the other. I did not want to talk to anyone and kept my eyes down on the path. I had only been this way once before on the wagon carrying Emilelech's body. Except for the man who had bowed so graciously as we passed, I remembered little of that procession. I walked briskly to the outskirts of the village.

When I made my way out into the wilderness where the burial ground was located, my heart began to beat as hard in my chest as the wings of a trapped bird in a cave. I hated to leave the safety of the village, especially all by myself, but I needed to talk to someone. Even if my husband was dead and buried, somehow I hoped to hear his counsel. The cemetery looked forsaken, but at least there were no new burials. The beautiful pottery bowl Mahlon had laid over Emilelech's grave was still there, its bright colors dulled by dust. A gust of wind swirled my scarf off my head. I bunched it up in one hand, and then spat on it to use it to wipe the dirt off the bowl. It really needed a good scrubbing to make it shine as it once had, but I did my best. After I had rubbed and rubbed without much success, I sat the bowl back on the soil sunken over my husband's grave and rocked back and forth.

I was so used to covering myself in public that I felt exposed. Anyone would be able to see my hair and my face, but no one was here, so why should I be worried? I was doing nothing wrong, yet I quickly smoothed out my scarf, preparing to cover myself, but I did not like the idea of putting something on my head that I had used as a rag. I turned it upside down so that the grimy spot was underneath.

"Oh, Emilelech," I cried. "Is it possible for me to sell the house and buy another? I don't know if I have enough money, and I have nothing to barter except what I've woven and sewed?" Thinking of the things women without husbands were forced to do, I slapped the ground, causing a cloud of dust to rise up, causing me to cough. "You promised you would get me a bigger house!" I cried angrily. "Why did you leave me!"

Only the whistle of the wind answered. It seemed to become a shrill voice in my head, telling me to be careful, to watch out, that I was a woman alone, that I had no understanding of financial matters, that I ought to stay where I was. On and on that critical voice told me to doubt myself.

I felt foolish to have spoken out loud in this deserted graveyard, yet I also felt irritated and stubborn. All at once, I slipped off the woolen veil, allowing myself to feel the breeze on my face. I thought perhaps I would walk back home without wearing it, but what if someone questioned me? Even a frown from a stranger might dampen my resolve. Allowing my face to be exposed in public and being alone on the street was prohibited. But why should I care, except that I needed the good will of the people of this village in order to earn my living. Yet, perhaps if I were more assertive, it would make them realize that I was my own woman. I did not only produce pretty clothes, but if I were allowed I could also make my own financial decisions. I felt infuriated by my powerlessness, but I did not want anger to overcome me. I scrambled to my feet, dusted off my robe, adjusted my shawl and scarf, trying to appear modest as I traipsed back through the village.

Would it be possible for me to hire men to build me a house, I wondered, but where could I build it unless I had land? I would certainly have to seek the help of a man if I were to make any serious transactions. The only man I could think of, apart from my sons, was Haran's brother. I resolved to go immediately to talk to him to ask him if he knew of any bigger houses for sale, but what if he said no? What if he insisted I come and live with his family? There was the priest, of course, who had been cordial to me recently, but I did not trust him. Perhaps, I thought, I could seek his wife's help. She had helped me so much in the past, and perhaps she could discreetly find out about other houses and arrange a purchase. It seemed a possibility, one that I much preferred.

I had not been in their spacious courtyard since the wedding of the priest's daughter but was not surprised to see a birthing tent, as big as the tents used by nomads, set up in one corner of the yard. Its cloth walls, lavishly decorated with golden swirls and embroidered flowers, was pretty. Usually only friends and relatives would be welcomed into the tent, and since I was neither, I almost hurried away. I did not want to be reminded of my miscarriage, but when I heard moans from inside the tent, I froze. I could smell the vinegary wine used for washing the newborn. It reminded me of Leah bringing fragrant water to bathe my sons' delicate skin before they were oiled and swaddled.

At last, gathering my courage, I pushed aside the entrance flap and peered inside. Several women were gathered around the laboring girl, who sat propped up on a birthing chair. A midwife, with her hands reaching between the girl's legs, knelt in front of her. The priest's wife sponged her daughter's sweaty forehead and murmured words of encouragement. No one noticed me as I slipped inside. My heavy shawl made me feel hot and clammy in this humid area packed with women. I felt improperly dressed and worried that I might smell bad, but I crept as close as I dared.

I had suffered the loss of a daughter, but as this infant burst into the world, all of my hurt faded. It was a wondrous thing to watch a baby being born. It did not take long before the midwife sat back with the wet and scraggly infant in her hands. "It's a boy," she said, and briefly held the baby up so everyone could see him before she put him on the receiving pillow. The women clapped their hands and smiled and laughed.

Suddenly the new mother squealed and bloody afterbirth gushed out of her womb. "Shush," her mother murmured, stroking her face. "It is almost over. You will soon be holding your son!" The girl fell sobbing into her mother's arms.

Another woman held a cloth saturated with pennyroyal under the girl's nose to calm her. The mint scent was a welcome sign that the worst was over and the best yet to come. At least, that was how I had felt after the birth of my sons.

I tried to get a good look at the infant over the shoulders of the women, but I could not see much. They were busy cutting the umbilical cord and bathing the tiny thing. In no time, thick cloth strips were gently wrapped around the small torso, securing the baby's arms and legs. There was even a swath of cloth around the baby's head, making it difficult for me to see the color of his skin. As he was carried to the mother, I managed to glimpse his face, but I could not tell if he was pale or dark.

The priest's wife stopped fussing over her daughter and her first grandchild, turning to the other women to accept their hugs and congratulations. When she noticed me in the background, she came over and looked deeply into my eyes. If she suspected the child was Chilion's, she did not care. "He is beautiful," she whispered.

"Yes," I answered, but my mind was elsewhere. I knew this was the wrong time for me to broach my need for a bigger house. I felt a little ashamed to want more, when most people I knew lived in one room, crowded together like a flock of sheep. I might not be a princess, but neither was I some old ewe. I was accustomed to a better life. I wanted it for my sons and for their wives and for future grandchildren. "I cannot wait until I too have a grandchild!" I murmured.

She smiled. "May you have many!"

"When Ruth marries Mahlon in a few months, I don't know how my house will contain any more people. Do you know of any bigger places? I have been saving my money."

There was a hush as if I had committed a crime. I felt like running out of that hot tent, but a woman who, judging from how much she looked like the priest's wife, must be her sister moved behind me, blocking my escape. "I know where you can go," she said, her voice determined.

I turned to face her, frightened of what she was going to reveal, but her eyes met mine kindly and she nodded. "You could move into our mother's place. They have three houses around a big empty yard. Mother and auntie only use one of the houses, and they are getting too old to care for themselves. The other two have been unoccupied since, well, since..."

The priest's wife clapped her hands. "I will have my hands full taking care of my daughter and the baby. I won't have enough time to take mother and auntie their meals, let alone clean for them." She grasped my shoulders. "Naomi, would you consider moving there? If you would take care of my mother and my aunt, it would be a big help."

"I don't know what to say. I would be happy to help your family." The thought of how much this woman had done for me made me bow my head. "I will treat your mother as my mother and your aunt as my aunt." I almost burst into tears.

The priest's wife looked elated. "Wonderful!" she said, then turned back to the throng of eager women. "Come, ladies, let my daughter get some rest." She led us from the tent into the house where we were served fresh juice and figs. The priest did not appear, but his wife left the gathering and must surely have gone to tell him the good news.

# Eight: Confusion

Boaz

Boaz held his head in his hands and wept, hoping no one could hear him crying over the loss of his mother who had been quite old. As a farmer, he dealt with life and death all the time, but it was hard to accept that he would never again see her frail face or hold her thin little hands in his. She was already buried in the family grave next to his father, where he too would eventually be laid to rest. Even though of middle years, he was still a virile man with no interest in taking any more wives. He was, however, deeply troubled at his mother's recent words, seemingly uttered out of nowhere. She was often not lucid and her memory had slipped, so probably she meant nothing. "Boaz," she had said a few weeks before she passed, "You must take care of Naomi!" Then she had gripped his hands in hers and would not let go until he'd agreed.

Now that she was dead, he felt a more urgent need to find Naomi and Emilelech and bring them back to Bethlehem. But he did not even know what town they would be living in except it was in Moab, a large area on the other side of the Salt Sea. He wished he might go and search for them, but how could he leave his family? Who would he get to supervise his field hands? In addition, he was officially a village elder and had duties to perform. He taught the Torah to the young men of the town, something he very much enjoyed.

"It would be a fool's mission and I am a busy man," he muttered out loud, wiping his eyes with the sleeve of his robe. Only then did he notice his youngest wife standing quietly in the corner watching him. He knew she wanted to comfort him, but he wanted to be alone. "Leave me," he said.

"Your mother loved you very much," she murmured, not meeting his eyes. "But she is resting with your father now. I expect they are happy."

His chest heaved with a sigh. He waved her away, but he knew she meant to be helpful. "You treated my mother with love, and she loved you also," he said as she left. "Thank you for caring so much for her when she could no longer help herself." He grew sad remembering how vague she had become and how needy. His mother had once been quite beautiful, always taking great care of her appearance: her piercing brown eyes were her best feature. But recently, aging had ravaged her face and her mind.

Boaz' wife disappeared back down the stairs to the kitchen area, probably to tell the others that he was weeping. He just hoped that they would not all rush up here to try to make him feel better. They could not help him overcome his grief. It would take time. They too were mourning, he knew, but he had no comfort to offer them. Perhaps their wails of sorrow during the burial had given them some relief. At least they had a means of expression with nothing to hide. How could he tell them what his mother had said about Naomi? Most likely his mother had meant nothing at all. He had hardly thought about Naomi for years, and yet his heart raced at the mention of her name. It was foolish. He would *not* try to find her.

Then there was the ugly matter of what he had discovered tightly clasped in his mother's hand when he had found her lifeless body. He had been greatly disturbed to see her grasping a stone idol from Jericho. He had pried it out of her hands, deeply troubled that she had kept such an offensive relic of her past. He thought she had been devoted to his father. After her marriage, she was more devout than many of the women born in Bethlehem. She had spoken with great reverence of how Hashem could melt any opposition with his goodness. Boaz had always assumed that she had equated the defeat of her hometown, Jericho, with how Hashem had parted the Red Sea. He had thought she was more than glad that such a pagan city, even if it was her hometown, had been laid to ruins. So what could this remnant from her past mean? For years she must have kept it hidden. Surely she could not have missed her life in such an evil place. She never talked about her life in Jericho, but he knew she had helped to overthrow the city. Did she regret what she had done when she hid the Hebrew spies and helped them to escape? She had even advised them how to get safely away by telling them to hide in the woods for three days so that Jericho's soldiers could not capture them.

To Boaz his mother was a shining light, but this relic made him wonder if she had lamented the day she had seen her city in ashes. When she had married his father who had brought her to Bethlehem, her family had not come with her. What a void in her life that must have been. Perhaps, even though it was thanks to her that her family's lives were spared, they might have considered her a traitor. They might have resented her and refused to have anything more to do with her.

Boaz, who had never considered the possibility of having relatives he'd never met, now wondered if his mother had remained silent about her kin because of painful memories. He could not bear to think about the sort of life she might have led in Jericho, especially upon seeing this small statue with points upon its head to represent the rays of the moon. He knew only too well what it usually meant to those who foolishly worshipped this pagan goddess of fertility. Why did she keep it? Did she continue to secretly pray to the goddess? Clearly, she would never have been able to admit to such a thing here in Bethlehem. "Oh, mother," he whispered.

Once again he thought about Naomi in a foreign land. His mother, a good and wise woman, was sad when Naomi's parents did not recommend him to be her husband, but he had never revealed the depth of his feelings. Mothers, though, often understood more than they let anyone know. Did she realize how depressed he had become after Naomi wed Emilelech? He had pretended to be happy for the newly married couple, but he had bemoaned his loss of the girl who he'd spent nights dreaming about. That was years ago. It made no sense now for his mother to tell him to take care of Naomi. Surely his mother was simply dwelling in the past as old people often do, but he knew she had always been proud of him and wanted him to succeed and be happy. When his father died, she had grieved and might have felt lonely for her husband, but at least she had been surrounded by family, and she had adored her grandchildren.

What would happen to Naomi and her sons if Emilelech did not survive? They had no one in Moab.

Boaz could not bring himself to dispose of the statue, but he did not want his wives to find it and ask him questions that he could not answer. They kept the house clean and knew every nook and cranny—they would surely find it if he hid it anywhere in the house. There was no one he could give it to for safe keeping, no one who would not be scandalized and tell him to destroy it. At last, he decided he must bury it somewhere appropriate, and in the meantime he would keep it inside his robe next to his heart. It was as if his mother's hand rested on his chest, and he felt somehow comforted.

Boaz wanted to *do* something to honor his mother's memory Perhaps, if they had settled in Jerusalem, he could find his mother's people. Even if they had gone on somewhere else, he could seek them. They had never been included, remembered, or respected in any way, but they were *his* family too. He, like his father, was a staunch defender of their Hebrew faith and traditions, but unlike his father, who would most likely have turned them away, Boaz wanted to provide chesed, the kindness and love he considered foundational to his faith, and that included taking care of those with no money, especially relatives.

Boaz had plenty but he was hesitant at the idea of giving to poor relatives he did not even know. He needed nothing more, happy with his children, with his land, and with his money, and he did not want his peaceful household disrupted. So he did nothing for a while. At last, continuing to be plagued by thoughts about Naomi, he told his wives he was going to Jerusalem on business.

"What sort of business?" they demanded to know.

He shrugged. "It is something I need to do. I will only be gone for a few days. Do not question me."

They did not like the idea of him leaving, but they prepared food and supplies for him to take along. They personally supervised the saddlebags being secured to the camel his manservant brought into the courtyard. The three wives stood side by side, with their children around them, watching him get ready to go on his journey.

"Down," he commanded the camel which obediently lowered itself onto its front knees. He quickly threw his leg over the back of the animal and settled into the saddle. "Up!" He tapped the camel's neck with his short shepherd's hook, and the beast lumbered to its feet. He quickly set it to trotting out of the village. No doubt, he would be the subject of gossip but he did not care. Let the women talk. Let people speculate.

As he rode towards Rachel's grave, a memory of his mother cooking lentil soup for him, brought tears to his eyes. Those had been such happy times. Near the tomb, he halted the camel, dismounted, and tied the animal to a pole. Even though Rachel was an honored ancestor, he had rarely given her story much consideration, but now his mind was full of thoughts about women dying in childbirth.

The statue beneath his robe felt warm against his chest. He quietly took it out and decided that he must get rid of it once and for all. Somehow, throwing it away seemed an affront to his mother's memory. He sat on his haunches rocking back and forth, staring at the stones in the mazzebah. He remembered the story of Rachel, who had been used by her father to trick Jacob into marrying her oldest sister. Jacob had to wait seven years for Rachel, who had not conceived for a very long time. She had died here, giving birth to her second son. He had always seen her merely as the vessel of an important man, but now her story made him realize how little he understood about the significance of women. "Oh Mother," he cried. "There is so much I would like to ask you."

He stood up and walked around the pillar that marked her grave, remembering his mother. As a boy, she used to take him outside at night to gaze at the moon. How she must have loved this carved stone. Many people who revered Rachel would not appreciate him leaving a pagan statue at her grave but noticing a flat piece of rock that jutted out like a shelf, he did not care what anyone would say. He carefully stood the statue on its base and leaned it backwards so it would not fall off. *Hashem,* he prayed silently, *help me learn the truth and if it should be your will, let me find my mother's relatives.*

In the afternoon, he reached the outskirts of Jerusalem and spent a few minutes admiring the terraced fields full of green sprouts. Inside the city walls, he quickly found a man to look after his camel. With the saddlebags slung over his shoulders, he went directly to the house where he had stayed during the drought. He was heartily welcomed. They relieved him of his luggage, brushed his clothing clean of dust, and washed his feet in a basin of warm water.

The men returned from work in the evening and invited him to join them for supper. He gladly followed them upstairs to sit around a low table. After the meal was finished and the women removed the dishes, they were joined with more of the town elders who had heard that he was here. At first they exchanged small talk about the crops and farming methods. At last, he mentioned why he had come. "Sirs, you have been so kind to me in the past. Without your support and generosity, I do not believe I would be alive to return here today. Once again I must ask for your help." The men eyed him suspiciously, no doubt worried he had come to ask for money. "My mother, Rahab, recently passed away. She was from Jericho."

"That viper's pit," an aged man muttered.

"Yes, it was, but my mother became one of *us.* It was she who rescued my father and his companion so that they were able to bring back Joshua and his army. Two of the brave soldiers, one of whom was my father, made a promise to my mother to keep her and her kin safe when Joshua attacked Jericho. They escaped unscathed. I am wondering if my mother's kin came to live here in Jerusalem. She never spoke of them but I want to honor my mother's memory and find them. They are my relatives."

"Rahab was your mother's name?" the older man, who had been disgusted at the mere mention of Jericho, asked.

"Yes. She was devout and a fine mother. She always helped other people."

The man frowned. "I believe I knew her sister. I'm sorry to have to tell you that she died some time ago."

Boaz felt his heart pounding in his chest. He hoped none of these men could see how flustered he was becoming. He wished he had not come, but here he was, and who knew what he might learn. "Did she ever talk about my mother, Rahab?"

"She was my wife's servant so you'll have to speak to her." He called over a girl who was standing nearby. "Go fetch my wife."

It did not take long before the girl came back. "Your wife is coming, Sir. She will be waiting for you downstairs."

Boaz pushed himself up. "Thank you, gentlemen, for your time." He bowed to them. "Once I get home, I will try your techniques for winnowing." The men nodded and wished him well.

Downstairs he had to wait some time before an elderly lady arrived. She shuffled into the house, staring at the ground. He cleared his throat and greeted her politely. "I want to honor my mother Rahab, who recently died. I understand you employed her sister."

The old lady looked up at him and stared. She paused a few moments before she spoke. "Why, she was a slave! Her family sold her to us for a donkey and a cart. We paid them enough so that they could go north. We heard no more from them after that."

Boaz was glad his beard hid his reddening face. He did not approve of slavery. "Did she ever talk about her sister? I believe her sister might have been my mother?"

"The girl was young. She may not even have remembered what happened. She served us for many years." The old woman studied Boaz as if deciding whether to reveal anything else. "We buried her in the family plot," she added, and then was silent and thoughtful. "Wait here," she said. "I have something to show you."

Boaz waited impatiently, tapping his foot on the floor. He wondered why the old man upstairs did not bother to come down. Could he be ashamed of having purchased a young girl? Yet for her to be buried with the family must surely mean she had been treated with respect. The thought of his young daughters ending up in bondage made him shudder, although it might have been worse for his mother's sister if Jericho had remained standing.

The old woman returned. With trembling hands, she took out a strand of scarlet cloth that she had tucked inside her robe. "She brought this with her, and I recall that she said it was tied around her waist when she'd been lowered to the ground before the battle. She said the walls of Jericho shook when the soldiers repeatedly marched around the town."

Boaz took the old, fraying cord. "May I keep this?"

"Yes. I am sorry I could not be of more help. Your mother's sister, by the way, was a very pretty girl. I always thought it a pity she never expressed an interest in boys. I do believe we would have released her had she wanted to marry."

"My father doted on my mother, who was also exceptionally beautiful. Not that I as a little boy paid much attention to her looks. She cooked well, pleased my father, and ran our household superbly."

"He was a lucky man to have found such a wife," the old woman said, nodding, before shuffling away.

Boaz, feeling sorrowful and yet comforted, stayed overnight. He wished his father might have come looking for Rahab's family and freed her sister. He groaned to think what sort of life his mother had had to lead in Jericho, and he could hardly bear to think that she might have been forced to do. But suddenly he had an epiphany. Even if his mother were the most beautiful woman in Judah, his father would *never* have married a former prostitute. *Never*!

With this understanding, Boaz managed to get some sleep before rising with the sun and heading home.

# Nine: Service

Naomi

If I could have done so, I would have
remained in my little house rather than go to the
priest's wife's mother's place, but my house soon
became occupied by the priest's daughter and her
husband. Orpah had told me that her brother was
unhappy and wished that he had married someone
else. The very fact that no bridal dowry from his
mother and father was ever paid to the priest's family
must surely have made him feel inadequate. He no
longer had to work in the fields alongside his father,
but that was not such a good thing. Now he was bored
as well as humiliated. At the mercy of his father-in-
law, who apparently wanted him to become a scribe,
he seemed doomed to fail. The boy was a farmer, not
a scholar. Orpah's other brother—the younger one—
was still hoping to marry an ironworker's daughter.
He worked for free as a way to pay a dowry for the
girl. Orpah thought he was being used and that the
marriage would never happen. *At least*, I thought, *he
was learning a trade*. Orpah, though, remained upset
for her brothers. I suspected that she was also sad that
she did not yet have a child. I prayed every day that
Hashem would soon bless her with a baby.

We did not have many household goods and
could have easily carried them by ourselves to our
new residence. But the priest hired a man to help him
move our possessions. To my surprise, the priest
helped unload the wagon. He set up my loom inside a
large foyer in the house, and he made sure all of my

yarn and materials were carefully arranged on nearby shelves. I could only surmise that his wife, Anika, must have warned him to treat me with respect.

I will never forget his reaction to the old women whom I had agreed to care for. He pretended not to see them but his eyes were raging.

The oldest of the two sisters, Faige, who was sweet but had never grown up, grinned at him. "Saladin, are you here to fetch your bride?" she said, giggling. Anika had been married for years! She was a grandmother! Did Faige think Anika was a new bride about to be escorted to her wedding chamber? I glanced at the priest, hoping he would show some sign of kindness, but with a hard look in his eyes he turned his back and continued to unload my household goods.

The priest's mother-in-law, Chaviva, was standing in the open doorway to her house, watching us. "You!" she pointed imperiously towards the priest, her hand quivering. "Fetch me water for my tea."

What a sharp tongue she had! I could only hope that she would not turn it on me.

"You! Saladin!" she shouted. "Did you hear me?"

When he did not react, she shrieked at him to do as he was told. He ignored her as if she did not exist.

I was unsure as to what to do. Chaviva could hardly stand up without her knees buckling. She needed help. I did not care if the priest approved or not. "I will fetch you water," I said. She staggered towards me, almost falling. I rushed over to her with my arms outstretched, but she pushed me away with surprising strength.

"Where do you keep your water jugs?" I asked, standing back.

"What business is it of yours?" the old woman spat at me.

Had she forgotten that I was here to take care of her and her sister? I looked at the priest, hoping he would help. The expression on his face for his mother-in-law was ugly. I was shocked. In my family we treated our elders with respect. But perhaps he viewed these old women as worthless, incapable of even drawing their own water, let alone able to do anything of value.

"They have a cistern behind their house," the priest told me begrudgingly and gestured behind the old woman. "You will find their water containers back there. Go!"

I felt indignant. I was not *his* servant, nor did I like the idea that I was to be nothing but a servant to this bossy old lady. Her mother, Anika, had been so good to me that I had been happy to come here, but now I felt reluctant. Even the promise of the roomy houses and the spacious courtyard had lost its appeal. Obviously, the priest disliked his wife's kinfolk. He was wealthy with no need to take over their property, but I worried that he might decide to evict them. Then what would happen to me? I felt powerless. From that day forward I disliked the man more than ever.

Faige smiled sweetly from behind her sister as if nothing had happened, but everyone else was tense. Even the workman, helping move my things, was hurrying as if he could not wait to get his pay and go to buy a beer.

A cold wind whirled into the yard, making me shiver. I felt like leaving but it was too late to back out now. "Why don't you go into the house where it's warm," I suggested to the old sisters. "I will fetch the water and prepare some tea."

Chaviva did not acknowledge me. She backed up, grasping Faige's arm to steady herself. They both retreated behind the heavy drape that served as a door.

I busied myself getting the water, but I wished my sons were here to carry the heavy iron kettle I had to use. Chilion, though, was off working, no doubt preferring to avoid the priest who had almost had him stoned to death. Mahlon was gone too. His pottery wheel sat in a corner next to the house where he and I would soon be staying. Orpah and Chilion were to be given the house opposite the place where the two old women lived.

Somehow, we all settled in, adjusted, and formed new routines.

As the first year passed, the priest's wife, Anika, visited fairly often, and we became good friends. I learned from her how similar the Moab wedding customs were to ours in Bethlehem. I suppose this was not surprising, considering that we had the same ancestors. I found myself realizing our ethnic differences were much like quarrels between family members. What good ever came of arguments and wars? I remembered the ruins of Jericho. Were those people really so evil? Did Hashem really want them destroyed? Yet, we had often heard how Hashem favored Joshua. We had heard too what a great military strategist he had been. Such matters meant little to me. I, like most women, preferred to take care of our children and our homes.

It was a shock to me when Anika revealed that when she was a little girl, her father used to beat her. She showed me the faded scars on her thighs. I hugged her and cried, but she merely shrugged. Her mother, she said, had been too weak to protect anyone, including her simple-minded sister. Anika's admission made me wonder if Moab was a far more cruel place than I had imagined. Beating women, though, was common everywhere.

It grew increasingly difficult for me to take care of Chaviva's needs. Knowing that she had done nothing to protect Anika made me despise her. I could not imagine how any mother could stand idly by while her daughter was being ill-treated. I would die to keep my children safe. My parents, even when I disobeyed them, had been loving and kind. This woman was demanding and spiteful. Nevertheless, I took good care of her. I prepared her tasty meals. I bathed her. I washed out her chamber pot every day. All she did was complain, but since she was elderly and demented, I persisted. Faige, at least, was a joy to be around, always hugging me, and always helping me. I began to love her.

At last, as Mahlon and Ruth's wedding drew near, Anika and I were babysitting, watching the colorful poles for the bridal canopy being set up. Anika became a little teary-eyed. "I remember getting married," she said. "On our wedding night, after the moon was down, Saladin came to fetch me. Lanterns lit the way back to his household. It was such a happy time. Saladin treated me like a princess." She rocked her grandson in her arms. "Don't worry, Naomi. This home will soon be filled with the patter of your grandchildren." She kissed the top of the baby's head.

"I hope so," I said. "I can't wait for Ruth to come to live here. She is like my daughter."

Anika put her hand over her heart. "My daughter has always been special to Saladin and me." She beamed. "We've spoiled her, I know. After she got married, I tried to insist she go and live with her mother-in-law. Saladin would not hear of it, and naturally I was glad to have her stay at home. This child though," she patted the baby's hand, "is teaching my daughter in ways that I would never have expected. She is becoming less self-centered."

"Your daughter is a most beautiful girl. I understand why her father dotes on her."

"Saladin is a decent man," she said. "He has been so good to me and for me." She must have noticed my surprised expression. "He *is!*" she exclaimed.

"I don't doubt it," I said with a wry smile.

"Yes you do! He comes across as aloof and stern, but that is only on the outside." She paused for a moment. "You must promise to never reveal what I am about to tell you to anyone."

I could not imagine what she was going to say and was not sure that I wanted to know. I glanced at the infant, but I had long ago stopped worrying about his paternity. He looked nothing like Chilion. Besides, what could it matter as long as he was raised with love?

Anika's next words surprised me.

"The reason Ruth's little sister, Anna, was allowed to escape is because Saladin pretended not to notice her running away. He loves his own daughter so very much that he could not bear to see anyone's daughter, especially pretty little Anna, used to satisfy the gods. But he will never admit this to anyone."

I stared at her in shock, hardly able to take it in. I had certainly misjudged Saladin. From now on, I decided, I would try to be more respectful.

Anika began to talk of other things before leaving the baby with me for a few hours. He needed constant attention and I enjoyed him, but when Orpah came into the house, I asked her to look after him. I needed to attend to the old women. I watched her coo over him, and I knew that she would not neglect him. But it must surely have concerned her that she had not quickly gotten pregnant. I hoped that having an infant in her arms, even one not hers, would comfort her. It saddened me for both Orpah and Chilion that they were not yet parents, but they were young. There was still plenty of time.

I went over to the big house where the old women lived. I almost wished I had sent Orpah instead of me. It was far easier to keep a baby clean and fresh than bathe the feeble old lady, Chaviva, who soiled her nightclothes at least once a week. While I gathered her smelly bedding from under her, she often moaned that I was treating her poorly. Her attitude did not make it easier for me. I had to drag her soiled blankets to the stream to scrub them. While I was gone, I was in constant fear that sweet little Faige, who reminded me of a sparrow, would wander off and get lost. I would tell her she must stay with her sister. Fortunately, she was obedient. After we settled Chaviva onto fresh bedding, Faige would cuddle up next to her.

Today Chaviva looked gray and seemed weaker than usual. I tried to massage her weak legs and feet, but she scowled at me. "Leave me alone!" she groaned. I wanted to be kind but most days, and this was no exception, I dreaded having to tend to her. It hardly seemed possible a whole year had passed. There was no respite. My sons could not be expected to help. This was woman's work. I really ought to get Orpah to assist, but I was the one who had brought us here, thinking it would be wonderful to have plenty of room. Now I understood that even though this house was better than my house in Bethlehem, it was also a prison. I did not want to make Orpah hate being here too.

This was one of those days when I wished I had never met Chaviva. Truth was that I did sometimes wish she would die. It would be such a relief. Her life was miserable, and she inflicted suffering on everyone else. A month ago, the skin around Faige's eye was bruised and puffy as if she had been slapped. It could only have been Chaviva who had hurt her. I had taken Faige aside and questioned her. "What happened?" I asked. She smiled and did not seem to understand. I gently touched the bruised skin on her face, making her wince. "Hurt," she had said, and smiled gently. I had taken her hand and led her into her sister's chamber. My shoulders had stiffened the way I always get when I am upset. "Did you hit her, Chaviva?" I managed to keep my voice even.

"I don't know what you're talking about!" She glared at me.

I had such an urge to slap her. "Look at her eye," I said, sucking in a deep breath and trying to calm down.

"She fell, didn't you Faige?"

"I fell," Faige repeated.

I could not imagine how she could possibly have tumbled in such a way to cause the puffy dark circle around her eye. Clearly it would do no good to continue to confront either of them. I decided that I would mention it to Anika.

After this incident, I never did find time to discuss my suspicions with Anika. I felt ashamed to keep silent, but I was full of dread that we would be turned out. How would we find another house? I knew Anika would never countenance us being forced to leave, but what control could she exercise over her husband? I wanted to trust him, but he was the head of the house, and he had all the power.

Today, though, seeing droplets of perspiration running down Chaviva's gray face, I quickly fetched a damp rag and gently wiped away the sweat. The very fact that she meekly allowed my ministrations made me suspect the worst. I set Faige to fanning her with a palm leaf. As we tended to her, I found myself wondering if her long illness was justice from YHWH. Why did some people live past the usefulness of their bodies? Wasn't Chaviva now as helpless as a child? Was she suffering as much as Anika once suffered? But at least there was no one was beating her. In fact we were trying to keep her clean and comfortable. How sad that only her sister, Faige, loved her. Even Anika, ever since I had taken over her mother's care, rarely came to see her. I would have been overjoyed for my mother to have lived this long. I could not imagine that I would not be constantly at her side.

The old woman coughed so feebly that I thought she might expire at any moment. I felt the pulse in her neck. It was beating too fast! Her skin looked blue! I hesitated, trying to decide what to do. I dared not leave Faige alone for too long with her sister. She would not be able to understand if Chaviva died. "I am sending for Anika," I told her. "I'll be right back." I hurried into the courtyard where I could hear the clicking of the potter's wheel. "Mahlon," I cried. "Mahlon!"

My son glanced up but continued pumping the lever and molding the clay. I waited impatiently for him to finish what he was doing, my ear attuned to the noises from the house. I could still hear the swishing of the palm leaf. "Hurry Mahlon, please. I think Chaviva is dying."

He stared at me briefly, and then quietly put the pot he had just formed into a stand so that it would keep its shape. "What can I do to help?" he asked.

"Fetch Anika! Hurry!"

Without another word, he ran out of the yard.

I returned to the bedside. The old woman's eyes were now closed and her breathing was more labored.

At last Anika rushed into the room. She took one look at her mother's sunken face and fell to her knees beside the bed. She took the frail hands into hers.

Faige patted Anika's hair. "Hush, child. It will be all right. You will see."

Anika's shoulders slumped as her aunt spoke. I suspected she must have heard these words many times when she was a child.

Suddenly Chaviva's eyes flew open. She tugged her hands free and held them out as if in a greeting to someone who we could not see. She called out a name.

"That is her brother's name," Anika said. "He died after I was married."

We all stared at the empty space, seeing nothing.

Many moments passed until Chaviva's eyes at last focused on her daughter's. The lines in her forehead deepened. "I am sorry, Anika" she said, her voice not much above a whisper. "I should have protected you. Forgive me."

"Of course." Anika's voice shook and her eyes filled with tears.

We sat vigil until the sun went down, and then Chaviva passed from this life into the next.

# Ten: Ups and Downs

Ruth

Unable to trust her eyes, Ruth stared at Haran in disbelief. Could this really be her father smiling at her in the sunshine? Whenever she'd thought about her fast-approaching wedding, she'd felt sad that her parents were so far away and did not even know that she was getting married. Now she feared she must be dreaming.

"We've come home, Ruth!" There was no doubting the sound of his deep familiar voice.

Tears welled up and spilled down her cheeks. She had not realized how much she had missed him. It was as if she were a little girl again, a child who had waited for her father to get back from his travels to hug her and give her presents. She had lost all hope of every seeing any of her immediate family again, not her mother, not Anna, and certainly not Papa.

But here he was!

She dropped the stone pestle she had been using to grind grain and rushed into his outstretched arms as if she were ten years old again. When at last they stepped back from one another, they were both crying.

"I have a special gift for you," Haran said, using his fingers to wipe her tears away. "Two presents. Wait here!"

Ruth watched him, mystified, as he hurried to the small courtyard door and disappeared outside. A gathering of her aunts and cousins were all watching, all of them smiling. She hardly dared hope! But through the opening she saw her dear mother, gathering her silken robes up from the dusty ground, stepping towards her. Behind her came a beautiful young girl. Her innocent face glowed as if she were an angel. Anna!

Ruth flew to them, her feet as fast as the wings of doves. She stopped near the goat pen. "Is it really you?"

"Ruth!" her mother cried, stretching out her hands.

Ruth seized her mother's fingers, not caring that her own were covered with flour. In the past, her mother would have scolded her and told her to wash. She gazed into her mother's eyes trying to take in all the changes. Her mother's gray hair above her wrinkled face made her look older, but her eyes were the same, shining with delight.

"I knew you would be beautiful once you grew up," her mother cried.

"Oh Mama, I am so glad to see you. I can hardly believe you are really here."

"Nor I! Egypt was not a land of wonder but a land of chains. At least for us. I missed home, and you, more and more every day. They were going to make Anna marry Pentu's old uncle! I would not allow such a thing! Never!"

Ruth took in her slender young sister who smiled shyly back. After a while, her face broke into a huge grin. "You've got breasts too!" she said, giggling, her voice so much richer than the childish one Ruth remembered.

All three of them began to laugh.

Other women gathered around them and drew them into the main court, bringing them cushions, fetching them tea and pastries. Everyone was talking at once, their chatter so high and excited that no one noticed Haran leave.

"Where is Papa?" Ruth suddenly asked, peering beyond the women, her eyes darting around the courtyard.

"He's probably gone to see to the livestock," her mother, Hannah, replied.

Ruth did not want to let any of them out of her sight again for fear they would disappear, but she managed to hide her anxiety and smiled as if nothing had changed. "I am soon to be married." Her stomach filled with acid.

Hannah's eyes partially closed.

Anna chimed in. "That is wonderful. I want to hear everything!"

"Mahlon is to be my husband." Ruth wished she felt her sister's enthusiasm. "Uncle Bebai has agreed. Mahlon has given me a special marriage plaque that he painted just for me. It is beautiful. I will show it to you." She hurried into the house and retrieved the pottery tablet, taking a few moments to be grateful for the decorations of birds and flowers. She still could not read the inscription, but she remembered how Mahlon had promised to cherish her from the day of their betrothal. Such an announcement was almost as if they were properly married except nothing had yet been physically consummated.

When she came back out into the courtyard, her father and uncle had returned. They stood facing one another. The women, still lounging on blankets and pillows, looked on uneasily.

Bebai, his face within inches of Haran's, looked angry. "Mahlon's mother is a widow," he said. "She offered me a dowry but I did not take it. We were glad for Ruth, given the circumstances, to have found a man who loved and wanted her."

"No dowry!" Haran roared. "What circumstances?"

Ruth shrank into the shadows of the house.

"I forbid this marriage," Haran said. "Ruth can do better than a penniless boy."

Ruth felt as if her father viewed her as if she were a prized goat he needed to sell for the best price. Her joy at the reunion with her parents turned to sand. She marched outside and thrust herself between her father and her uncle. "You gave up all your paternal rights when you abandoned me." She glared at her father, trembling with rage. "I *am* going to marry Mahlon. The wedding canopy is already up. I am not exactly sure when Mahlon will come to fetch me, but when he does, I will be waiting!"

Some of the women tittered but Ruth silenced them with a stare. She defiantly stamped her foot.

"You haven't changed a bit, you willful girl!" Haran said a little sheepishly.

"You cannot make me do anything I don't want." Ruth turned away and rushed back into the house, with her mother and her sister following. They could hear her father's and her uncle's angry footsteps striding away. After they were gone, they could hear the voices of the women in the courtyard like the chirruping of many sparrows.

In the privacy of the house, her mother sighed deeply. "We are penniless, Ruth," she murmured, averting her eyes.

Anna wrapped her arms around her mother's shoulder. "Mama, I will fetch a good bride price. You saved me from that horrible old man. Surely we can find a suitable match for me here in Moab now that we are home."

Hannah sank onto a bench and held her head in her hands. "I want what is best for both of you." After a few moments, she lifted her face and looked up. "Do you want to marry Mahlon, Ruth? Is that what you want?"

Ruth ran a finger over the inscription in the marriage contract. Mahlon would teach her how to read and write. He would let her help with his work. She might eventually become a skilled potter. Further, she would be able to learn clothmaking. Her future seemed bright. She did not want or need a wealthy man, not that there were any men who would look twice at her. She had never spoken of what happened to anyone, not even to Naomi, too humiliated to talk about such things. It saddened her that she did not feel physical longing for Mahlon, but she did not feel that way for any man. She looked steadily into her mother's eyes. "I am glad I am to be Mahlon's wife. He is good to me, and Naomi saved my life!"

"You are not thinking clearly! You will be stuck with all of them, and they are not even Moabites like us. It will soon feel crowded in that tiny house of theirs, and you will regret your decision."

"I will not! Naomi lives in a much bigger place now. There are three separate houses and a large courtyard, bigger than this one. Mahlon and I are to have a private house next to Chilion's and Orpah's. Even if it were not spacious, I'd happily go wherever Naomi goes. She took me in when my own kin would not!"

Hannah sighed deeply. "What about Emilelech? Does he approve?"

"He died..."

"Emilelech died!" Hannah cried. "What happened?"

"I wasn't here. All I know is that he died suddenly soon after I was left with that hateful merchant. If it weren't for his wife..."

"I am so sorry, Ruth, for what you suffered. How horrible for Emilelech to have died! Poor Naomi." Hannah smiled weakly. "It's a wonder she was able to cope. It is good you are going to marry Mahlon. I'm surprised that Naomi allowed her youngest boy to get married before him, but I suppose she had no real control."

Ruth almost laughed out loud at the thought of Chilion's marriage and the trouble he'd caused, but it would do no good to speak of the matter. "Orpah and Chilion are happy. Naomi has started her own clothmaking business and she is successful. She is a generous woman. Right now, she lives with Mahlon, but she wants us to have our own house. She is moving, across the courtyard, with Faige."

Hannah frowned. "Anika's sister, Faige? Surely not! That simple-minded girl and her older sister Chaviva are nothing but trouble!"

"Chaviva is dead!"

Hannah shook her head. "No loss. Chaviva was callous. She did nothing to stop her husband's brutality. Anika was my best friend when we were growing up. She would escape to my house, and my mother would clean the wounds on her legs. I was glad for her to get away from both her parents, even if she did become the wife of that awful man, Saladin. At least he treated her with respect. You do know that he is a priest?" She slanted a look at Anna. "You do know that he is part of the council of elders? Why would you involve yourself with anyone of their selfish clan? Don't you remember what happened?"

Ruth looked awkwardly at her mother. "Chaviva and Faige needed help. Naomi agreed to look after them in exchange for living with them. Faige still needs care. I wish I had been allowed to continue to live with Naomi so I could help her, but Bebai made me come here. My aunts hardly let me breathe. They chaperone my every move. I cannot wait to leave!"

Hannah pursed her lips.

"Oh Mama!" Ruth patted her mother's hand. "If you had been here, everything would have been different."

Hannah sighed and looked away.

"Listen," Ruth said. "I have something to tell you but you must promise not to tell anyone. Not anyone!"

Hannah sighed again, but her eyes met Ruth's. "What now?"

"Do you promise to keep this to yourself?"

"Very well." Hannah's eyes glittered angrily.

"You too, Anna."

Anna nodded eagerly.

"Naomi told me something that I am not supposed to talk about," Ruth said. "But I think you need to know the truth. Mama, the reason you managed to rescue Anna was because the priest,

Saladin, let you. It is thanks to him that Anna is alive today."

Hannah's mouth fell open. Her hands flew over her eyes.

Anna took her mother's hands. "I want to forget that awful time. Let us rejoice at Ruth's upcoming wedding. Let us not ruin our homecoming with bad memories." She looked hopefully at Ruth and then at her mother. "How wonderful that we are all here together and we can help with the preparations."

Ruth smiled at the thought of her little sister here to help her. It sounded so normal, yet nothing seemed to be what she expected.

Somehow, she spent the rest of the day with her mother and sister, who talked constantly about life in Egypt and their odd customs. Anna, unlike her mother, had mastered the language, but she still had very little self-confidence. Ruth wished there were a way to help Anna trust in herself, but she didn't know how.

Pleased as Ruth was to have her family back, she suddenly felt the need to be alone, and quietly went outside, and slipped out of the compound. She had no intention of being meek and obedient. She would question and seek answers. Mahlon would teach her, but she would teach him too about how to care for others, and just what true strength meant— not conformity because of helplessness, but insight and understanding. She realized this would be a lifelong struggle, but she felt as if her life-experiences had already taught her much. For one thing, she had come to understand the need to accept and give help. She had also come to appreciate how, having forgiven her kin, she had been freed of the bitterness that used to plague her.

She had not gone far when Naomi came smiling toward her. The older woman seized her hands and swung her around in a circle. "Normally in our tradition," she said, "Emilelech would set the time and day for Mahlon to fetch you to your new home." She grinned. "But since I am Mahlon's only living parent, I choose the day he will fetch you. I am not going to tell you the hour, though."

"I hope it is soon," Ruth said. "My mother and father have returned with Anna."

Naomi's eyes grew wide with surprise. "What!" she cried.

"They are back," Ruth said. "For good."

"That's wonderful!" Naomi beamed. "They will get to attend the wedding feast and help you get ready."

Ruth frowned. "My father does not approve."

Naomi's voice faltered. "He is your father. He has a right…"

"He has none!" Ruth declared.

"Come." Naomi took Ruth's arm. "I cannot wait to see your mother and Anna."

Back inside the house, Hannah greeted Naomi. "I am so happy to see you again. Thank you for helping Ruth. We have much to talk about."

"Ruth is a daughter to me and I am more than glad that she will soon live with me again. I can only imagine how you must have missed her. We will be living close by and you must visit often. I hope Haran won't be stubborn and stand in the way."

Hannah rolled her eyes. "How soon is the wedding?" she asked. "I would like to help as much as I can."

"What about Papa?" Ruth clenched her fists.

"Haran is as stubborn as an old ox at times," Hannah said. "Don't worry about him. I will calm him down. He will go along with our plans. Your marriage will be special!"

Ruth, slightly pale, nodded. "What day is Mahlon coming for me?"

"Tomorrow!" Naomi cried. "All is ready. Your aunts know. And now, even better, your mother and sister are here for you. They will help you with your mikvah, your bath. I have explained to your aunts that is what we do back in Bethlehem. They told me that here in Moab they have a similar rite. In fact all of our wedding traditions are similar."

Hannah patted Ruth's shoulder. "We will make sure the water is good and warm before we dunk you."

Nearby, the aunts were grinning.

"I have made a special crown for you, Ruth." Naomi reached into the bag she had been carrying and took out a headdress adorned with leaves and flowers.

Ruth took it and inhaled the fragrance of lavender. "I love it. Thank you."

"You are going to look so pretty," Anna said.

The next day, Ruth was bathed by her mother and her aunts. Anna, who had learned about cosmetics in Egypt, applied kohl so that Ruth felt as if she were as wide-eyed as a gazelle. The dress she was squeezed into displayed her curves. It shone with sequins sewn into layers of silk that flowed below her knees. She could hardly breathe, but it was as much from the anxiety of having to wait until well after dark as from the tightness of the dress. When she heard the high notes of a shofar horn, announcing that the bridegroom was coming, her shoulders tensed. Her mother kissed her cheek and Anna squeezed her hand. Together they set the crown over her shining hair. The aunts tittered around her and gently arranged a delicate veil over her face.

Soon she was led out of the courtyard and seated on cushions in a velvet-covered palanquin. She tried to calm herself, but when the curtain was lifted, and when she saw Mahlon in the light of an oil lamp, she felt faint. "My love," he said. "Is it really you?" He gently lifted her veil and peeked at her face. "You are so beautiful!"

She was not allowed to say anything. Mahlon's brother and other men, including her father, who had gotten over his pique after Hannah spoke to him, quickly drew Mahlon away. Soon her palanquin bounced along the streets. She could hear laughter and singing.

Once they got to Naomi's quarters, her bridesmaids led her under the bridal canopy into the tent. She hugged Anna and her three cousins, who stood by her, fussing over her dress before leading her to the bed. Mahlon had built a wooden frame and lined it with furs covered by a white virginity cloth. The girls, all of them giggling, helped her disrobe before departing. She knew they would be waiting outside, along with her father, and everyone else to hear Mahlon's shout for joy after he entered her and could display the bloodied cloth.

She had told no one what had happened to her unable to speak of sensitive matters and stubbornly angered by the way her kin had believed the worst.

Slowly the curtains to the door parted. There stood Mahlon silhouetted in the opening to the chamber. She managed to smile warmly at her new husband. He did not care about the past. She found herself filled with love for him as he stepped inside. For a while he simply stood above her, gazing at her naked body. She almost wrapped the white sheet around herself to hide her embarrassment. At last, he too disrobed, and took her into his arms. As he raised his body above hers, he told her not to be afraid. She hardly felt any pain, and he did not cry out as he spilled his seed into her.

After a while, Mahlon gently tugged the sheet from beneath Ruth's hips, and he began to laugh. There was *not* a lot of blood but enough for everyone waiting outside to see. "It did not matter to me if you were a virgin or not, Ruth, but I am so happy to make you mine!" He rolled the cloth into a ball and tossed it outside into Naomi's hands. She unraveled it and, with a relieved smile on her face, held it up for all to see. There were whoops from the men and titters from the ladies.

The next day the feast began and there was dancing and singing for a week.

# Eleven: Endings and Beginnings

Naomi

After the feasting wound down and all the guests had left and everything was cleaned up, I felt a pang of sadness: I wished I could have shared this time of joy with Emilelech. I heard Faige singing as I prepared us jasmine tea. As we sipped our drinks, I smiled into her friendly face. Her sweet nature always cheered me up.

Life settled into pleasant routines. My cloth business, with Ruth's help, grew. Orpah did not much care for weaving, but she gladly cooked and did much of the cleaning. Chilion continued to work in the fields while Mahlon produced more and more exquisite pottery. His ceramics became popular and in demand. He often ran out of clay, but he and Chilion would go into the wilderness where they would dig from an abundant supply they had discovered near a stream. Ruth wanted to go with them, but they rarely let her. Instead, she learned how to make colorful dyes from flowers and herbs that she had gathered. The garments we sold were beautiful and much praised by our customers.

We were so happy, but one particular sorrow never went away. Month followed month and Orpah and Ruth would go into the women's tent, set up in a corner of the yard, for their time of blood. I wondered what their problem could be. I considered asking them about their sex lives. Were they even making love? After years of their childlessness, I was determined to broach the subject, but my plans came to nothing.

As usual, just as the sun rose, we had all gathered outside. Mahlon said the prayers of thanks for the bountiful meal we were about to receive. Orpah set out platters of steaming bread stuffed with olives and chickpeas. I poured us hot tea in delicate cups. "I'll fetch Faige," Ruth said. We waited, but suddenly Ruth reappeared, her face solemn in the dawn light. "There's something wrong, Naomi. I cannot wake her."

As she had aged, she had become more and more frail but I'd never worried about her health. I rushed into the tent carrying an oil lantern.

Faige lay very still on her mattress with a blanket covering her and tucked around her shoulders. I put my ear to her mouth and listened for her breath. There was none. "Oh!" I moaned and stroked her wispy hair off her forehead. Both Ruth and I began to cry. Eventually, we went outside and told the others. "Faige has passed away in her sleep."

Orpah, ever practical, tilted her head to one side and regarded us all. "Faige is peaceful now and there is nothing more we can do for her. Let us eat. We need strength."

I could not eat a thing, but the others managed to finish the meal Orpah had so lovingly served us. After we were done, Chilion left to fetch Anika so that she might help with the preparation of her aunt's body for the burial. Everything moved quickly. Saladin accompanied his wife and daughter. They brought their two grandchildren along. Their firstborn, quite an active little boy now, stood watching as we applied the spices and oil before wrapping the frail body in linen.

I suppose, because of Saladin's importance as a priest, many people accompanied the funeral procession to a tomb not far from the cemetery where we had buried Emilelech. We brought Faige's favorite dress with us, one we had given her for her birthday. It would be placed in the sepulcher near her remains. She had clapped her hands with pleasure at the color and softness of the material. She had worn it until it was faded and threadbare. For the memorial meal, Orpah supplied bread and Faige's favorite honey-cakes. Other people, too, brought offerings to go with Faige into her resting place.

The sun was rising and getting hot so it was good that we took the body as soon as we did into the coolness of the family tomb. After the rock was rolled away from the entrance, I was allowed to go inside with Anika and her family, but everyone else waited outside. The cave was not at all like the poor grave where Emilelech was buried, but it comforted me to know my husband's body was covered with soil and had not been disturbed. This cave was well protected so that no wild animals could ever get at the corpses. I could make out several skeletons lined up in the rock cavity that stretched far back into the hillside. It was somehow reassuring to me for them to all be together.

Faige's linen-wrapped body was laid on a long platform next to the remains of her sister. The food items and her clothing were put nearby on the stone floor. As Saladin said some prayers, I found myself wishing Mahlon were here to recite some of our Hebrew prayers too. I could not help but remember how Chaviva had been such a poor sister and an even worse mother. I was sad that Faige had never had the opportunity to give birth or raise children. We women valued ourselves mainly when we had sons. Was that part of Chaviva's anger? She'd had a daughter and *no* boys. Faige might have been simple and childless, yet she had brought light and kindness to all those she met, even those who treated her cruelly. Perhaps childbirth did not matter so very much. Nevertheless I wished with all my heart for grandchildren like these little ones of Anika's. Her daughter scolded the oldest one for trying to wander deeper into the cave and poking at the bones. Children did not respond to death the same way as adults. They were so innocent. They eased everyone's sorrow.

Life went on, of course, as it always does, and although I missed Faige's cheerful presence, I was too busy to let myself get depressed. It pleased me that Mahlon decided to give weekly lessons about our history to Chilion. I insisted that the girls and I must also listen. That would not have been possible in Bethlehem where only boys were educated in the faith. Both Chilion and Orpah came, of course, but mainly to please me. When Mahlon talked, it did not take long before they would begin fidgeting and whispering together in a most annoying way until I frowned at them. Mahlon never corrected them, but I felt sure that if we had remained at home, he would have become an elder. He was too young now, but in time his obvious knowledge and memory of what he had been taught by Emilelech would have made him an important man of our town. Ruth always listened intently and asked many questions, especially about the parting of the Red Sea. She would clap her hands when she heard how the Israelites escaped the

Egyptian army. If she had been a man, she would have been a warrior. She was much fiercer than her husband, fiercer than any of us.

With no religious community to share our understanding with, it was difficult to persevere. Even though I had made friends with our Moabite neighbors, and my daughters-in-law were Moabites, it was not the same. Still, I loved Anika and Hannah and even Orpah's mother, who was such a gossip—like her daughter. I smiled remembering how Leah and I used to tell each other all of our secrets. Her beautiful daughters must surely be married and have many children. Leah deserved joy and I certainly wished it for her. I had heard that prosperity had returned to Bethlehem, the famine long since ended. It made me wonder what my life might have been like if I had married Boaz instead of Emilelech, a farmer instead of a scholar.

For one thing I would not be living here, but still there were many things I liked. I had my delightful daughters-in-law. I lived in a wonderful house which I had eventually managed to purchase. I, *me*, had become an independent person, as wealthy as any man. I had only managed it with help from Ruth and Anika, but I had become a far different person from the shy, eager-to-please girl of my childhood. I had no one to obey but myself. Sometimes, though, I was lonely. How good it would be to let a strong man help me lift bolts of cloth, provide me with plentiful food, and most of all share his evenings with me while we chatted about our days.

My melancholy never lasted long. I soon enough came to my senses. Emilelech and Boaz were Hebrew men who expected their women to wait upon them. They were the masters of their households and wanted to be obeyed as if they were gods. I was trying to teach Mahlon and Chilion to respect their wives as equals and not expect them to constantly serve their every need. I encouraged Chilion do some baking, but he would never consent to that. It made me chuckle to realize Orpah did not bow to him, though. She often scolded him when he was late home; she expected him to help her far more than I ever asked of Emilelech. Ruth, too, was flourishing with Mahlon who shared so much with her, perhaps too much. Except for not letting her go with him and his brother to dig clay, they spent a lot of time together. She even learned the rudiments of pottery making.

One evening the ground began to shake—a pot fell off a shelf and broke into pieces. There were often tremors, even in Bethlehem, so I was not too worried. It surely would not be like that long-ago earthquake that flattened towns and killed many people. Nevertheless, we all paused what we were doing and looked at one another, but soon everything got quiet and still again.

Chilion and Mahlon did not get home in time for dinner. After the girls and I ate and cleared away the dirty dishes, I wanted to calm Orpah down. She was furious with Chilion for being late since she had baked the pheasant he had provided with his bow and arrow. She had scalded the bird and plucked all the feathers, keeping them to use in a quilt. The bird had not much meat on it, but there was enough, and she had baked it with rosemary and garlic until it was tender and delicious. She had served it with a side of spicy beans and feta cheese. We kept some brown meat for the men.

After it got dark, I had an uneasy feeling and slept fitfully. It must have been midnight— the air was already cool and I could hear night birds calling as Ruth came running into my house. She squatted near me and wrapped an arm around my shoulder. "I heard the cry of a big cat! I am going to go to look for them."

"It is far too dark for us to venture into the wilderness. Chilion is an expert archer and will protect them from wild animals. No harm will come to them." My words did not make me feel any better.

Orpah must have heard Ruth come across the courtyard. She soon joined us and the three of us wrapped shawls around our shoulders and went outside. We stared at the stars shining down from heaven. Suddenly I had the horrible thought that two of those stars were now the souls of my sons. I said nothing. It would do no good to further alarm the girls. I certainly did not want to send Ruth off in search of them. "Don't worry," I said. "They'll be home before you know it. Now go indoors and get some rest."

But morning came and none of us had slept well. We gathered outside to wait for the men.

As soon as it got light enough, the three of us set off in search. Ruth knew the valley where they went to dig clay. It was on the other side of town past Haran and Hannah's place. We made our way to the King's Highway and hurried along until we found an animal trail leading through the rocky terrain that eventually ended at the Dead Sea. The path got more and more uneven. Ruth stopped suddenly and gasped.

At her feet was a deep gash in the earth. "Look! Those tremors last night must have caused the earth to open up."

We all stared at the crevasse until Ruth jumped across it to the other side. Orpah gathered up the hem of her clothing and stepped after her. Ruth held her hand out to me which I gladly took. I had the feeling this ground might give way at any moment. I carefully crept next to my daughters-in-law as we continued down the trail.

"They might not have come this way," Orpah ventured. "They might already be home."

I wanted to turn back but Ruth jutted out her chin. "They dig for clay at the bottom of a cliff not far from here! They might be hurt." She threw the veil off her head, letting it dangle from her shoulder. "Mahlon!" she shouted. "Mahlon! Chilion!" There was no answer, but we could hear her the echoes from her voice bouncing off the rocks.

"Mahlon! Chilion! Where are you!" Orpah and I also shouted.

From ahead of us we heard a low rumble. I glanced at the sky. There was no lightning and no rain. My fear leapt around in my chest, filling my throat with acid. I grabbed Ruth's arm, but nothing would stop her now. She raced along and we hurried behind, catching up with her at the edge of a steep cliff. Below us we could see a pile of rocks in the valley. The three of us stood shoulder to shoulder unable to speak, terrified of who might lay beneath those heavy stones.

Orpah said quietly, "They might still be alive."

I wanted to scream that they might not be under the giant boulders that I could see strewn in the stream beneath us.

Ruth fell to her knees and began crawling and scrambling down the cliff.

"Go for help!" I yelled at Orpah. "Bring men and digging axes. Hurry." Ruth was already halfway down the rockface when I rolled up my skirt and sat down and managed to scoot along, grabbing roots to slow my descent. I do not know how I made it to into that valley. I do not know how I ended up standing next to Ruth. She was crying and frantically digging in the rocks, throwing small ones to one side. I could see part of the sleeve of a colorful coat, one she had made for Mahlon. "He always took his coat off when he got too hot," she wailed. Her hands were bleeding, but she would not stop until she had managed to drag the coat out from under the rubble. She held the torn remnants to her chest. She stared at the larger boulders we could see further down the stream. "They must have walked down there. They are under there!"

I sank to the ground. I knew, as only a mother knows, that my sons would not be recovered.

Ruth began scrambling over the rocks as if she might find a way to remove boulders bigger than houses. At last, she flung herself face-down and began screaming and beating the ground.

I could not utter one word. There was nothing we could do.

When Haran and his brothers arrived, they confirmed our worst fears. My insides shrank, and I felt as if my body was being crushed as surely as my sons were now broken and bleeding. It was more than I could stand. I could barely function, but in that moment I made my decision: since I could not take my sons or my husband home, I would return to Bethlehem so that I might be buried amongst my own people. Nothing was left for me here in Moab.

It took me but a few days to dispose of all my possessions. No one could dissuade me. It was as if even my best friends, Akita and Hannah, no longer existed. I had no grandbabies. It mattered nothing to me that Orpah and Ruth insisted that they would come with me. It was Orpah who made us bring a few things with us. Us indeed! They needed to stay with their mothers! Yet here we three were, stopping to say goodbye to Hannah and Haran and their family. When Hannah said goodbye to me, I had no tears. "I understand," she whispered. She embraced Ruth who went around and hugged everyone, even the little children who stood solemnly nearby. At last, we trudged out to our wagon. Ruth jumped onto the drivers' seat while Orpah and I climbed into the bed. None of us looked back as the donkey hauled us up to the King's Highway to begin our journey back to Bethlehem.

Orpah could not stop weeping. Ruth had her back to me and I wondered if she were crying too. "Stop the cart," I commanded.

Ruth reined in the donkey and we all climbed down. Ruth, like me, was dry-eyed, her mouth set in a firm line. I myself felt as dry as a parched field that would never again bear fruit. Both of my daughters-in-law were still young enough to have babies. Why should I drag them with me to a land where they would have no family? They would be in the same straits I had once been in here in Moab: husbandless with few prospects. They deserved to get on with their lives. "It would be best if you go home to your mothers," I told them quietly. "Your kindness to me and my sons means so much. I want you both to find new husbands whom you can love." I held each one of them by her shoulders and took a long look at their dear faces. I wiped away their tears with my veil. "Don't worry, I will manage the donkey. Orpah, I see that you have provided enough food to last me a month!" The laughter stuck in my throat and came out as a sob.

It set Orpah off again. Then Ruth began to weep. "We want to come with you," she moaned.

I felt so empty. "Go home, you lovely girls. I will never have any more sons for you to marry. I am too old. My only desire is to rest in the land of my birth." I did not say *die* because I knew they would protest. "At least you two can still make lives for yourself." I could not hide my bitterness. "There is nothing left for me now that my sons are gone. Hashem has turned against me! Go home! Go home!"

Orpah's mouth curved down in sorrow and her eyes were swollen and red from crying, but she kissed me on both of my cheeks. "There will never be a better mother-in-law than you. I will miss you." She quickly turned and began to walk away.

"Go with her, Ruth. Be with your own people."

Ruth stamped her foot, sending up a cloud of dust, causing the donkey to toss his head. She held tight to the lead reins. "I will never turn my back on you. I am going wherever you go. I want to stay wherever you stay. I feel as close to you as I did to Mahlon and my own family. You have taught me so much. I will be happy to embrace your people as my own. I choose your Hashem over Chemosh. I hope you live a long time, but when I die, I want to be buried in the same tomb. Let Hashem punish me if it is not so!"

I realized that Ruth was determined to go with me and I had no more energy to try to dissuade her.

We watched Orpah trudging away and turn down the lane into the village.

We settled ourselves into the wagon, sitting side by side on the driver's seat. Mahlon and I had once set out on this very stretch of road to find Ruth. Then, the donkey had bolted. Now, this one was docile, but I might not have had the strength to drive it all the way to Bethlehem. Not that I much cared.

Ruth took up the reins and shook them.

"Giddup," she commanded, and the donkey began dragging us towards Behtlehem.

# Return of Plenty

## One: Grief and Hope

### Ruth

Naomi sat silently staring into space while Ruth dug in the back of the wagon, planning to fetch them something to eat. Something hard wrapped in cloth got her attention. Curious she unwrapped it to discover a fertility statue. She took it out and stared at the pregnant belly and the full breasts. Where on earth could it have come from? From Orpah maybe? She knew her friend had so wanted a baby. Perhaps she had been praying to this lump of stone. Ruth walked to the front of the cart and held up the figurine. "Look what I found with all the supplies Orpah packed for our journey? Just look at her feet!" she remarked. "We'd have broken toes too if it weren't for having this donkey and cart for our journey to Bethlehem." She hoped to get Naomi to laugh but instead Naomi frowned. Nothing, it seemed, would cheer her up. Ruth too felt the sting of loss but she knew she would have to be strong for Naomi.

"It's mine," Naomi said. "Please put it back where you found it."

Ruth was surprised, but Naomi's tone of voice did not invite questions. She returned the statue to the rear of the cart and replaced it amongst a few garments that Naomi had brought with her. She had sold the loom and the pottery wheel and all of the bolts of cloth that they had produced. It saddened Ruth to realize their way of making a living was now gone. She had loved being a clothmaker, mixing dyes and sewing clothes. She had loved handling yarn and setting up the loom to create intricate designs. Their work pleased many people in Moab and they were respected there. She wondered what on earth she would find to do in Bethlehem. Naomi knew people there and would probably ease back into her old life, but she doubted there was much for *her*. Nevertheless, as surely as Naomi had stood by her, she would be there for her mother-in-law.

She rummaged around in one of the baskets Orpah had packed and found some flatbread and olives. "Orpah's baked loaves are always the best," she said, remembering how she used to bake special breads for Mahlon and never would again. She choked back the tears threatening to engulf her and offered half of the round loaf to Naomi.

Naomi pushed it away. "You eat it. I am not hungry."

"You must eat to keep up your strength," Ruth insisted.

Naomi shook her head. "What does it matter?"

"It matters to me! You must eat or I too will eat nothing and we will both starve. We will never reach your hometown. Eat it!"

Naomi reluctantly took the bread and nibbled on it, her eyes sad.

Ruth could not help herself. She *was* alive and she enjoyed the meal, even managing to feel a little excited that an adventure lay before them. They had already passed the area where she had once seen a lion and found Naomi's loom. Although it had been the beginning of difficult times for Ruth, somehow she had survived and up until now her life had only gotten better.

"What have I done to deserve this?" Naomi moaned. "Why has Hashem turned against me?"

Ruth pondered the question. She had learned that the Hebrew God did not sacrifice children. He had freed his people from slavery in Egypt. "Perhaps it is not about you. Accidents happen. People die. That is just life!"

Naomi groaned and threw the remaining half-eaten bread onto the ground. "You understand nothing!"

Ruth clenched her teeth and bit back the hurt she was feeling. She hated to see Naomi being hateful and worn down. She searched for words to ease Naomi's distress, but she was afraid that anything she said would be taken amiss.

They continued their travel, stopping to camp near the banks of the Jordan River.

While they let the donkey drink and graze on a patch of nearby grass, Ruth could not resist kicking off her sandals and wading in the water. It was fairly shallow and warm. She felt as if she were ten years old and her grief was being washed away. Glancing back, she saw Naomi hunched over, leaning against the back of the wagon. Air went out of her lungs in a big sigh. If only she could help her mother-in-law feel better, but it seemed clear that Naomi wanted to be left alone.

Enjoying a gentle breeze, Ruth wandered upstream. No one else was here now, but she could see the remains of camp sites where other people had stayed. It made her think about her father Haran's travels. She would miss him, but now she realized why he had so loved to sell spices and jewelry. It was more than a way to earn a living: it was a way to see more of the world. She looked forward to reaching Jerusalem where they would stay with friends of his. She even longed to see the ruins of Jericho, but for now she reveled in the warmth of the setting sun. Rays of light shone down on the river, making the water rippling around her turn silver.

Suddenly, she smelled burning wood. Worried, she hurried back to their campsite. To her surprise Naomi had managed to light a small fire. Ruth could not help but admire this older woman who had achieved so much in spite of the obstacles she'd had to overcome. Though she'd always said she'd been a timid girl, she had become a strong woman. She'd already rolled out their beds and heated water and was making them tea. It smelled sweet and welcoming. Naomi handed her a cup. Ruth had not realized that she was beginning to feel cold and gratefully let the cup warm her hands. "Thank you, Naomi. This is welcome."

Naomi did not look at her. "You should stay close to our camp. You are no longer a foolish girl who can wander as she pleases!"

Ruth sipped her tea. "It is beautiful here," she said.

"Is it? I hadn't noticed."

"Just look at how pretty and red the sky is becoming," Ruth remarked.

Naomi glanced, her eyes expressionless, at the horizon. "You'd better get that donkey lest he ends up fodder for hyenas."

Ruth doubted that the animal was in any danger. She certainly had not heard the cries of any wild beasts. But for Naomi's sake, she quickly finished her tea, and fetched the donkey and tethered him to the back of their cart. She got out sheepskins and the pretty woolen blankets that they had woven themselves. She laid them out on the ground. "We will be warm tonight, at least," she said.

Naomi shrugged. She tossed a blanket aside and lay down.

Ruth knelt next to her and laid the blanket over her. "You'll feel better in Bethlehem," she whispered.

After a while, she prepared her own bed and sank down next to Naomi, soon falling asleep.

Naomi, as if she were hurt, cried out in her sleep.

"Naomi, it is all right. Wake up," Ruth whispered.

Naomi groaned and flopped onto her side but did not awaken.

Ruth rolled onto her back and stared up at the hundreds of tiny sparks of light above her. Mahlon, as a boy, had told her that Hashem put the stars in the night sky to mark their sacred times. They gave her hope. She had not even known Mahlon's name then let alone that she would end up marrying him. She wanted to remember their many good times and not lament his loss, but her tears welled up. She cried silently for a while until she finally managed to close her eyes.

In the morning, they both got up with the sun. The air was chilly but would soon heat up, so they quickly harnessed the donkey and set out without breakfast. When they came by the ruins of Jericho, Ruth was awed. She knew the story of its conquest but somehow seeing these massive piles of rubble of what was once a grand city, she realized that anything was possible when YHWH was on your side. She halted the donkey near a spring so that it might get a drink, and so that they could break their fast.

Naomi stepped down and went to the back of the cart. Ruth assumed she was getting them some food. She certainly seemed to be taking her time. When she came back and stood next to the donkey, she had not brought anything to eat. In her hands she held the fertility statue. "Misho," she said. "I named my baby girl Misho because she was an angel. But I kept this pagan thing and now Hashem has forsaken me. I am going to put it back where I found it in this hateful place. It deserves to be smashed. Hashem has punished me. I deserve it!"

"You do not!" Ruth cried. She stared at the pregnant belly and swollen breasts on the stone statue. "I am so sorry I never had a grandchild for you."

"Hashem did not open your womb. It is my fault." Naomi walked slowly towards the rubble and put the statue down amongst the ruins. It blended in with all the other stones as if it were indeed a part of this fallen place.

Ruth remained in the cart watching sadly. She did not believe that Hashem had anything to do with her childlessness. But what good would come of telling Mahlon's mother that after that first night when her husband had taken her virginity, he had lost interest in sex and rarely initiated it. She knew he felt inadequate, but she had worried that *her* lack of passion was a problem. She had never felt physically attracted to him and made no attempt to encourage him. Even though part of her wanted a baby, she had not forgotten the oath she had made to herself, one that she had broken by getting married.

Naomi came back over to her. "You should have returned to your mother. She would see to it to find you another husband."

"Perhaps there is a husband for me in Bethlehem, not that I want one. I will be happy to remain with you, Naomi."

"You say that now, but you will change your mind."

Ruth refused to argue with Naomi. She understood from everything Mahlon had taught her that Hashem wanted not the worst, but the best for people. She smiled to herself remembering the discussions she and Mahlon often shared about spiritual matters. He had taught her so much. Their lack of physical intimacy simply had not mattered. Their connection ran deeper. She had come to understand that the best way to live was by helping others. Chesed, he had called such kindness and she did her best to live that way. She climbed down from the cart, patted the donkey's rump, and got them bread and chickpeas.

They sat on the ground. Once again Naomi ate like a sparrow. After they had finished their meal, Ruth stood up and offered her hand to her mother-in-law and tugged her to her feet. Soon they were rattling along behind their faithful donkey, heading for Jerusalem.

The terraced fields were dotted with people swinging scythes to cut the golden barley Ruth was filled with admiration. Clearly, these were hardworking men and women. A couple of people glanced up at them but soon returned to their task. Ruth halted the donkey and watched as the tall stalks were tied into bundles, skillfully set upright until they could be threshed.

"What a plentiful crop!" Ruth remarked. "I love to smell it when it is freshly cut." She shook the reins and began turning the donkey towards the gate.

"Wait," Naomi said. "It is early and if we make haste we can reach Bethlehem tonight."

Ruth began to protest, but one glance at Naomi's pale face made her realize it was best not to argue. Much as she wanted to meet her father's friends, a visit would have to wait. Perhaps she could come back after they were settled.

Ruth urged the donkey into a trot away from the city.

By the time they got to Rachel's tomb, it was already dusk. "Whoa," Ruth commanded. "Let us rest the donkey. He must be tired. I am too!" She wanted to look more closely at the column of rocks that marked the grave. She knew Rachel was also her ancestor, a woman who had died here in childbirth. Jacob her husband must have been devoted to her to have built her such a fine mazzebah.

Ruth walked around the stone pillar. All at once she saw a tiny white face peering at her. At first, it alarmed her, but when it did not move, she drew closer. She found a statue no bigger than her hand. What could it mean? Ruth picked it up and stroked its round face. The pointed spikes arising from its head like rays of light reminded her of the moon. It made her smile and she wanted to keep it. Maybe it would bring her luck, but shouldn't she leave it where she had found it? Ruth sank to the ground and sat musing about what this meant and what she ought to do.

As Naomi came around to her, her sandals scraping across the ground, Ruth hugged the statue to her breast. Naomi did not seem to notice. She reached out and touched the side of the rock column. "Rachel had to wait seven years before Jacob was allowed to marry her," she said. "It took many more years before she had her first son."

"I know. Chilion used to tease Orpah that it would only be a matter of time until she had a baby boy just like Rachel did. He said their son would grow up to be famous like Joseph. But the years passed as you know..."

Naomi let out a sob. She sank to the ground and covered her eyes with her hands. "I prayed and prayed for both of you to have children but Hashem has forsaken me!"

Ruth, gripping the moon-figure hard, stared at her mother-in-law.

"I can't go on," Naomi moaned.

"We are almost there. Your friends will be so happy to see you!" Ruth cried.

"I should never have come back. What was I thinking? I am a widow with no prospects. Everyone will resent me!"

"People will understand. No one will blame you." Ruth tried to offer comfort.

"The idea of going into Bethlehem scares me. I cannot do it!"

"Then we'll turn back." Suddenly the statue slipped out of Ruth's hands.

"There is no turning back!" Naomi wailed.

"We can return to Jerusalem and stay with my father's friends and get rested before returning to Moab."

With a thud the statue hit the ground.

"Where did *that* come from?" Naomi cried.

Ruth picked up the statue. "I found it on one of the ledges in the tomb. Someone must have put it there."

"How strange." Naomi took the statue into her hands. "It looks like the moon."

"Doesn't the moon provide light in the nighttime?" Ruth asked, remembering Mahlon's words.

"So it is said." Naomi looked up at the twilight sky. "Where is the moon now?"

"I want to live!" Ruth cried. "I miss Mahlon, *my* husband, *your* son. I cannot tell you how much, but I will not be made helpless because of that horrible accident. He would want me to find some measure of happiness. He would want that for you too!"

"What happiness can there be for me? I could not even give my sons decent burials. My husband's grave is far from his homeland when he ought to be buried amongst his kin." Naomi dropped the statue. She put both hands over her heart. "My only daughter did not survive childbirth. I might as well have died with her."

"Stop it!" Ruth said, anger rising at Naomi's hopeless tone. "I am with you! Together we can face anything. Look," she said, scrambling onto her feet and pointing at the sky. "The moon is rising. Surely that is a good omen! Let us stay here tonight. We will enter Bethlehem tomorrow morning with our heads held high."

# Two: Homecoming

Naomi

The sun was not high in the sky when we entered Bethlehem. The courtyard was already full of people, some carrying scythes in their hands, others with sacks slung over their shoulders. I could smell many different herbs. Often, for special meals, I used to blend horehound and tansy with a touch of horseradish and fresh parsley to serve with lamb. I fondly remembered those harvest days when women would pack hearty lunches for the reapers. They were obviously going to gather the barley crop on the other side of the town. I wondered if Emilelech's fields had been planted. Some women stopped and stared at me, but I pulled my veil over my face and pretended I did not see them. Ruth, though, was smiling. She waved and called out a greeting. Suddenly I became aware of how strong a Moabite accent she had. I hoped she would be welcomed. And I wondered if I too now sounded like a Moabite.

The women hurried over to us. Their faces looked familiar. "Don't you remember us?" one of them asked. "Aren't you Naomi?"

I nodded and as I looked into the young woman's eyes, I felt my mood suddenly lift in a tiny surge of joy. "You must be Leah's daughters! My, how you have grown!"

"We are both married now and we have children of our own. But who is this you have brought with you?" They looked Ruth over.

"I am Naomi's daughter-in-law." Ruth smiled.

"How is Mahlon?" gushed the younger of the two, reminding me of how they had once played the game of gap. This girl loved to toss the twelve pebbles in the air. She always caught more on the back of her hand than anyone else. "Ask Mahlon if he remembers me beating him. I always did!" she said with a grin.

Ruth took a little step back. Color drained out of her face. I could not say one word, but Ruth somehow recovered her composure, and answered. "Mahlon was my husband. Both he and his brother Chilion died in an accident."

Leah's daughters gasped. They looked mortified and clearly did not know what to say.

"It was horrible," Ruth said. "But we are here now. Can you tell us where we might stable our donkey? And perhaps you can direct us to an inn where we might stay until we get settled."

The young women glanced at one another. The oldest one swallowed anxiously. "You must go immediately to our mother's house or she will be furious. Her house is swarming with our oldest brothers' kids, but she will welcome you. We no longer live there." She called out to a young man who came over. He was much taller than Ruth and he looked at her with interest. "This is our little brother, Jeremiah."

"Hello," he said.

"I am Ruth," Ruth said. "And this is my mother-in-law, Naomi."

"Jeremiah, please take Naomi and Ruth to mother's house, and then see to their donkey."

"All right," he said, patting the donkey's neck.

"I wish we could come with you," the oldest sister said. "Mother will be so pleased to see you, Naomi. But we'd better go to the fields or people will accuse us of shirking our duties. You'd better hurry too, Jeremiah. We will need all the hands we can get. You should see how plump the seed-heads are. It has been a rich harvest—plenty to store and more than enough for brewing beer."

Jeremiah took the donkey's halter and began leading us down the lane. Even though I had left so many years ago, little had changed. As we passed Boaz' house, Jeremiah glanced back at Ruth and me, perched on the driver's seat. "My sisters live here now," he remarked.

I was not surprised to learn that Leah's daughters were married to Boaz' sons. They had all played together up on my roof, flinging wooden game pieces at the squares of cloth that they'd used for markers. What a tragedy it would have been then if any of them had fallen off, but the wall I'd insisted we put up around the edge of the roof had given me peace of mind. If we had stayed in Bethlehem and *my* sons had married Leah's daughters, they would still be alive. Perhaps all those children I could now hear giggling and chasing one another in Boaz' courtyard would be *my* grandchildren.

I chewed on the inside of my lip to try to put a stop to my despair.

For some reason, an image of Boaz' mother, Rahab, flashed into my mind. Her husband Salmon, who had been more devout than anyone I knew, had died before we'd left Bethlehem and left her a widow. Like me. She had once been considered a beauty, but she'd never remarried. Now she must be quite aged.

No doubt, her many grandchildren and great-grandchildren gave her joy.

Ruth remarked to Jeremiah, "I liked your sisters."

Jeremiah rolled his eyes.

Could *he* be a possible match for Ruth, I wondered, except he was much younger than her? No doubt, Leah would have something to say about her son's future bride.

Jeremiah halted the donkey outside Leah's courtyard and tethered it to a nearby post. He offered me his hand to help me down. Leah, who always was a good mother, must have taught him good manners.

As we entered the court, my heart began to beat as fast as a galloping horse. Soon we were surrounded by curious little children. I wanted to take each one by the shoulders and look closely at them to see how much they resembled Leah.

There was no time for hugs or greetings or small talk. Leah looked out from her house, shrieked, and flew towards me. "Naomi!" she cried.

I ran towards her and we fell into one another's arms.

Both of us were crying just like we had when we'd said goodbye so many years earlier. When we finally broke our embrace, I took in Leah's face. Even with crinkles around her eyes and gray strands of hair escaping from under a linen scarf, she was pretty. She had gained weight and looked plump and matronly while I was thinner than I had ever been. I probably looked as gaunt as a skeleton.

Ruth stood quietly in the courtyard, watching Jeremiah lead the donkey away.

Leah stroked my cheek. "You look tired. Come, let's go inside and rest. I'll make us some tea." She glanced at Ruth. "You come too!" Then, with a stern look at the children, she clapped her hands. "Get back to your chores!"

Her words made me smile. Those kids were playing *not* working, but I doubted that she'd really minded. I was genuinely happy for her to be surrounded by such healthy little ones. "You have beautiful grandchildren," I said.

"I have been blessed," she replied. "And you? How many grandkids do you have? How are your sons? Is this your daughter-in-law?"

"I have so much to tell you, Leah." I paused, trying to find the words to break the bad news. At last, I murmured, "I regret to say that Emilelech died quite a while ago."

"Oh no!" Leah wrapped her arms around me. "I am *so* sorry."

It felt comforting to be in her embrace, but I stepped away. "Both my sons later married fine girls," I said, trying to sound lighthearted.

"They were such good boys. It is hard for me to think of them as grownups." Leah shrugged. "What fun we all used to have. Now, who is this young lady?"

"This is Ruth, who was married to Mahlon."

"Was?" Leah eyed Ruth.

I could hardly speak, but she was my best friend. We had never kept secrets from one another. "Mahlon is dead," I said. "Ruth is a widow, like me!"

Leah groaned and hit her forehead with her fist. "How terrible for you, Naomi, and for you, Ruth."

"Chilion perished in that rockfall too. I sent his wife back to her mother," I babbled. "Both of my daughters-in-law are young enough to still have children. Neither gave me grandchildren, but they are wonderful girls. Any man will be lucky to get them. If it weren't for Ruth, I probably would be laying in a ditch somewhere on the King's Highway."

"You are exaggerating!" Ruth exclaimed. "Naomi is very strong," she said to Leah. "She kept our family together. She built a clothmaking business out of nothing."

"Come inside," Leah said. "I want to hear everything!" She led us into the kitchen and introduced us to a young woman who was pregnant. "This is Puah, who is married to my oldest son. You remember Jacob, don't you? And Jonah is married too. They both have three children, and when Puah has her next one, I will be a grandmother for the seventh time!"

Puah looked exhausted. Her namesake was one of the midwives who'd disobeyed the Pharaoh and refused to kill Hebrew baby boys. "You are blessed," I said.

"I'd rather be in the fields reaping with everyone else than trapped here looking after all the children," Puah replied. "I can't wait for this baby to come into the world so I can go out again."

Leah patted her shoulder. "You are a good mother. And I am glad you are here. I could not possibly keep an eye on all the little ones, let alone see to their meals and all their needs."

"What will you do when Jeremiah marries and brings home a bride?" I asked innocently, hoping to hear the boy was available, even if he was too young for Ruth.

Leah understood me too well. She began to laugh. "He has been engaged to a girl since he was four, but don't worry. A woman as strong and beautiful as Ruth will easily find someone to be her husband. As a matter of fact, I know the very man, a widower with five children who need a mother."

Ruth looked horrified, but she quickly hid her expression behind an uneasy smile.

"We need a kinsman for Ruth to marry or Emilelech 's name will be lost along with the fields that once belonged to us," I said.

"Boaz is from the same clan as Emilelech, but he already has three wives. He is a contented man, unlikely to want more children, let alone another wife. Unfortunately, he doesn't have any other sons for Ruth to wed. He'd probably marry *you*, though," she added with a cheeky smile.

She remembered too much!

I tried to divert her from saying anything further. "Do you still have that upper room that smells like goats?" I had often been upstairs and it had never smelled bad. This was an old joke between us.

She laughed. "Come upstairs. You will be surprised." She turned to Ruth, "Why don't you stay with Puah. Naomi and I have a lot of chatting to do."

The room was not as simple as I had remembered. It was now richly decorated with a low table in the middle resting upon a thick colorful rug. Leah fetched us embroidered pillows and scurried back downstairs to get our tea. I stretched out on the rug with a pillow under my head, glad to be once again in the warmth of Leah's home.

After a while Leah returned with a tray of dates and cups of steaming tea. A delicious licorice aroma filled the room. "This is perfect," I said, sipping.

We talked and talked until it seemed we had nothing more to say. I told her about losing my baby. I spoke of taking care of Chaviva and Faige. I mentioned my friendship with Akita and Hannah. She told me how they had survived the famine, stressing how Boaz had helped everyone. She spoke of her daughters' different personalities and their weddings.

"I missed you," she finally said.

"I thought of you every day," I replied, even though it was not really true. I had been far too busy. Only now did I fully realize what I had given up by leaving Moab. Perhaps it had not been such a good idea. But being with Leah eased my spirits. I no longer felt totally forsaken by Hashem.

"How will you manage now that you are home? Do you plan to move back into your old house?" Leah asked.

"No. I doubt that I'd be welcome after all this time, and I don't want to be a burden to anyone."

"You must stay with us as long as you like. We will make room. You and Ruth can sleep up here. My husband will not object, and even if he does, he will come around. We will tell him it is only until Ruth is settled."

If I let her, Leah would whisk Ruth into marriage whether she wanted it or not. Except Ruth was surely a match for Leah, and Ruth was stubborn too. She had sworn that she would never leave me. I did not want to lose her either. I could not imagine *where* I would live or even *how* I would live. I certainly didn't want to end up all alone like Faige who couldn't take care of herself. "Ruth is very special to me," I said. "She and Mahlon were devoted to one another. I doubt she'll agree to marrying a man who wants nothing more than a mother for his children."

Leah got to her feet with a determined look on her face. "I am going to ask her right now if she'd like me to find a suitable match for her."

"No, don't!" I grabbed the hem of her skirt, but she dashed away, with me scrambling to catch up.

"Where is Ruth," Leah asked Puah, who was now kneading dough. Puah shrugged. "She offered to make the bread or grind the grain, but I told her she is our guest. She went into the courtyard to play with the kids."

I rushed outside ahead of Leah.

Ruth was sitting in the middle of a group of fascinated children, telling them about how Hashem loved the people so much that he had helped them to escape from slavery. "They were passed over by the angel of death," she said. "That is why you are here today."

I was surprised that she knew about the Passover, but I should not have been since she was always interested in our religious rites. Her eyes met mine with such a spark of hope in them that I knew I would do anything for her just as surely as she would do anything for me.

"Naomi, I'd like to go into the fields and help with the harvest," she said quietly.

"You are our guest," Leah replied sternly. "You stay here."

"I am strong. I want to work."

Leah shook her head, but Ruth could not be easily discouraged. She turned to me. "Naomi, let me go and gather leftover grain. Please."

The idea of her being out in distant fields where no one knew her worried me, but even if I said no, she was determined to be a help, and she was more than likely to go anyway. "Very well, but be careful, and make sure you are not in the way, or you are to come right back here."

"I will only glean behind those who welcome me."

Leah gave her a sack for any grain she was able to collect. The two of us stood side by side outside the complex watching her walk away. I was more than glad to be with Leah, but as I saw Ruth going down the street, I worried about the future. The idea of Boaz marrying me had given me a moment of hope, but it was too late for me and in any case even if Boaz wanted to, I could only imagine the uproar such a marriage would create with his three wives. Three! That rascal! Besides, I did not want another husband. I had learned to make my own living and I was used to being independent. I could not imagine having to rely on any man ever again. I did not much care what happened to me, but I was determined to settle Ruth. I wanted her to thrive and to be happy.

# Three: Concern

Boaz
Since his hired overseers were trustworthy and well-paid, Boaz did not go immediately to the fields. Besides, his sons and daughters-in-law would let him know if there were any problems. He mulled over the news that had reached his ears. Naomi was back. The town was awash with talk about her and the young woman who had accompanied her. They had arrived as everyone was getting ready to bring in the harvest. They had apparently gone to visit Leah, who was the mother of his sons' wives—his daughters-in-law. He had no idea what Naomi was doing back here in Bethlehem without Emilelech, but he found himself becoming aware of his old passion for her. His wives had probably heard the gossip about her return and might know more, but he did not want to speak to them about Naomi. He wanted to be alone. He decided he would go to Rachel's tomb where he had left his mother's pagan idol.

As he approached the sacred site, he could not help but remember when he had followed Naomi here, telling himself that he only wanted to make sure that she was safe. He had also been hoping to discover the water spring but never did. Perhaps that spring was also a dream of something that he could never have. As time had passed, he had stopped fooling himself. The real reason he had followed Naomi was because he still loved her. It was just as well that she had gone away, or he might have allowed his feelings to lead him astray. Now, though, he was happy with good wives and a wonderful family. He had sons who would inherit his property. They were strong boys and worked hard for him. His daughters too were happily married to good men who honored them—not that either of his girls would put up with anything other than respect. So why was he so worried to meet with this woman once again from the past, a woman he had no rights to, a woman who was married to a man he had always liked even if he had fled from the famine?

Yet if nothing else he was curious and as he stood staring at the tomb, he began to search for the moon statue, the one that his mother had held onto for all of her life. What had possessed *her*? If she had been discovered with such an object she would have been disgraced. His mother's words to him to take care of Naomi also seemed strange and echoed in his brain. His family had been his priority and still was. He would make no attempt to contact Naomi now. In fact, he would avoid meeting with her. Yes, that was the right thing to do.

Now, where was that statue? He could not remember exactly where he had put it and walked around the mazzebah twice. He looked all over the ground too, thinking perhaps it had fallen off. No matter how hard he searched, he could not find it. It would have been considered disrespectful for such a thing to be left at this holy site, but it bothered him to think someone might have taken it and destroyed it. He had put it with Rachel's remains to honor his mother who, like Rachel, had been a foreigner. She was a special reminder of how Hashem worked within the lives of those he selected for his purposes and it did not seem to matter where they were from.

After a time of solitude and prayer, he returned to his house. His wives brought him stuffed grape leaves and fresh bread. While he ate, they gathered around him unable to contain the news about Naomi. He did not want to hear any gossip but they could not be stopped. "Naomi," the oldest one said, "is now a widow and both her sons are dead too. That is why she came home."

"That is unfortunate," Boaz replied. "But what is that to me?" Even as he uttered these words, he felt a stirring in his chest like a moth flying toward a flame.

"She probably hopes for one of her husband's relatives to marry her!"

The women stared knowingly at him.

He was in no mood to spend time trying to explain that he had no interest, but he could not fool them anyway. Surely they realized that he wanted *no* other wives! He had enough on his hands with the three of them—even if they had reached a time in their lives when harmony usually reigned in his household.

His youngest wife smiled smugly. "She brought one of her daughters-in-law with her. They say she is as strong as an ox and is the only reason Naomi managed to get back here. They are apparently devoted to one another. She is a Moabite, though, so how righteous can she be! And there are no grandchildren either!"

Boaz frowned at her. "Your mother-in-law was from Jericho and I seem to recall that you loved her as if she was from our own tribe."

"That was different! She was a wonderful woman and obeyed all of our laws."

Boaz did not want this conversation. He wiped his beard with the back of his hand. "That was very tasty," he said, knowing how much his wives appreciated his pleasure in their cooking. "Now I must go and check on the harvest."

Boaz made his way out of the town and soon passed fields of people stacking bundles of barley in neat rows. Honeybees buzzed through the tall grasses and yellow butterflies perched on purple strands of wild hyssop. He carefully stepped over the flowers not wanting to crush them. When he got to his first property, he paused and watched everyone, including his sons, slowly moving through the field, cutting the barley. He was surprised to notice a young woman behind all the others, stooping down and gathering the loose seeds. He knew who she was, but he pretended not to notice her. "Well done," he called to the harvesters. The workers smiled back at him. His daughters-in-law waved gaily from the shaded tent where they were preparing food.

"Bless you, Boaz," someone yelled.

Boaz always treated his paid laborers well. It was a God-given command, one he gladly fulfilled. He felt as if somehow the practice of chesed, of kindness and charity, was connected to this golden abundance. He strode over to his overseer and gestured towards the lone woman gleaning. He continued to pretend that he had no idea about her. "Who does that woman belong to?"

The overseer replied, "She is the Moabite who came back with Naomi. She asked if she could pick up the barley that spilled behind the harvesters. I knew you'd be happy to help someone needy, so I agreed."

"Good man," Boaz said, and noticed that this Moabite woman worked with determination. He had the feeling she was as fierce and no doubt just as strong as his wives had said.

The overseer, following his gaze, continued, "She came into the field after everyone had already started cutting the stalks, and asked if it was all right for her to gather what we'd left behind. She has stayed all morning and rested only once for a very short time in the shelter your sons put up."

Boaz, after a brief discussion about how much longer it would take to gather the crop, went over to talk to his sons and to the other men whom he had hired. "You must not bother the young woman who is here gleaning. She has my permission and my protection." He did not really think any of these men would bother Ruth, but he did not know some of the hired hands very well. The men agreed and immediately continued their work. He smiled to himself, remembering how strenuous harvesting was even for young men with strong bodies. These fellows would probably be far too tired to even flirt with a girl let alone do anything improper.

He also remembered his mother's words to watch after Naomi and began walking towards Ruth. He had it in his power to make sure this young woman, who had helped Naomi get to Bethlehem, would be taken care of. Maybe through her, he would also be taking care of Naomi. "Hello," he said. "I am happy to have you here in my field."

"Thank you." Ruth, who was on her knees, straightened up and looked into his eyes.

"But, please, daughter, you must listen to me. Do not go anywhere else to collect grain. It would be best for you to stay near the women who work for me. Whenever you need a drink, just help yourself from the water jars. The men know not to trouble you."

"You are so generous and kind." Ruth bent forward, bowing down, touching the ground with her forehead. After a while, she slowly stood up, pushed her sack further onto her shoulder, and dusted off her robe. She did not seem at all embarrassed for her face to be exposed. "I don't understand why you are being so kind to me. I am a stranger and a foreigner."

Boaz liked how tall she was and also that he still towered over her. He drew himself up to his full height feeling protective. Her eyes were bright but sad too. Her body, from all the bending to gather handfuls of seed, probably ached. He had a feeling that she would be too proud to admit that she needed help. Her sack did not look very full. His desire to help her increased, and it was not only because of Naomi. "How good you are since the death of your husband for helping your mother-in-law." At her look of surprise, he half smiled. "Bethlehem is a small town, and word of Naomi's return has raced from household to household."

Ruth demurely lowered her head so that Boaz could no longer see her eyes.

"We all know how you left your father and mother and your homeland too," he said. "My mother was from Jericho. I realized not so long ago that it must have been difficult for her to live with strangers at first yet she became loved and admired by everyone who knew her."

"I am glad to be here," Ruth murmured.

Although Boaz was not in the habit of blessing people out loud, especially not a beautiful and vulnerable young woman, he wanted to make her feel welcome. He wanted her also to understand that he and his people were deeply religious. Boaz raised his hands and closed his eyes. "May Hashem repay you for what you have done," he said. "May you be richly rewarded by Hashem under whose wings you have come to take shelter." Even as he intended to emphasize that it was Hashem who would be sheltering her, it occurred to him that Hashem might be working through him. After all, why would he, Boaz, feel so caring? It was not as if he had never allowed others to glean before.

"I hope, my lord," Ruth said, "that you will always find me worthy of your kindness. You have made me feel at ease. I realize though that I do not even have the status of one of your hired hands."

Ruth's humble reply, calling him *lord* out of respect, made him like her all the more. He bowed his head slightly to her in an acknowledgement before quickly walking away, going over to help the men.

"Now there's a woman I'd take for my second wife," one of them said.

"Be quiet," Boaz responded. "She is none of your concern."

They cut and bundled the barley until all that was left in the field were ragged rows of golden-brown stems, too short to be used for straw. Later the ground would be turned over and left fallow for a while before the next planting. The sheaves, lined up along the edge of the field near the shelter, gave everyone a sense of satisfaction of work well done. After the harvest was completed, the men began to gather under the canopy for a well-deserved meal. The women began handing out bread and cheese to the workers. Ruth stood back, but Boaz gestured her over. "You must have some bread too and dip it in the wine vinegar. It will refresh you."

Boaz' daughters-in-law smiled and patted the ground near them, but Ruth sat away from everyone. She carefully tucked her robe around her knees and adjusted her veil so that no one could see her face or her hair.

Boaz, even though he had already seen how thick her hair was, liked her modesty now. He took a bowl of roasted grain over to her. "You have earned a good meal," he said, and was impressed when she ate delicately, not finishing all the golden seeds that he had given her, but quickly hurrying back into the field and walking slowly with her head down, looking for loose grain.

Boaz watched her moving from row to row, occasionally bending over and picking up a spikelet and shaking the seeds into the sack dangling from her shoulder. He turned to his men. "When you are done eating, let her gather among the sheaves, and even pull out a few of the stalks from the bundles, and leave them for her to take."

One of his daughters-in-law hailed him. "Boaz, we met the Moabite woman earlier today with her mother-in-law Naomi. She seemed nice. We sent them to mother's house, and we did not expect her to come out into the fields to glean. She was friendly before but now she seems distant. I hope we haven't insulted her."

Boaz shrugged. "She is probably only tired. Perhaps she does not want to be a bother to anyone." He hesitated, but curiosity and concern caused him to take the opportunity to ask questions, ones he had not addressed to his wives. "How was the woman, Naomi?"

"She looked exhausted but she seemed happy to see us. We knew her when we were little girls and used to play with her sons. She was always kind to us and of course she and our mother were best friends."

"Did she mention how her husband died?"

One of the women's hands flew across her mouth. "Oh, we didn't know he was dead! How terrible for Naomi to have lost him and her sons. It is so sad. There was a terrible tragedy, a rockfall, and neither of her sons were recovered."

Boaz stared briefly at the ground. "It is an act of God, but I hate to see Naomi in such difficult straits."

The youngest of his daughters-in-law spoke up. "I heard that she was a successful clothmaker and they lived in luxury in Moab. They didn't bring much with them though, only a donkey and a half-empty cart."

Boaz thoughtfully stroked his beard, remembering the sweet girl he had known who'd hardly a businesswoman been. "She must still be in mourning."

"It is so sad," one of the women said. "Without grandchildren who will carry on the family name and traditions?"

Boaz did not respond but turned and walked away. As kin to Emilelech perhaps he *should* marry Naomi so that he might take care of her. It did not matter to him that she was too old to have any babies since he did not want or need any more children, but his wives would likely be furious with him and be sure he had sexual feelings for her. As it was, he felt confused about his desire for Ruth who was young enough to be his daughter. He did not want to be like older men who visited prostitutes. He wanted to accept the dignity that came with aging. Yet here he was feeling something for this girl and surely it was not merely lust. There were plenty of young women he came across in his everyday life, some of them as lovely as his daughters-in-law, but he had never had the slightest need for them. He told himself his feelings for Ruth were merely fatherly, but he knew in his heart it was more. Not only did he find her attractive, but he also wanted to know more about her life and her character. What woman could travel alone to an unknown country without a man to guide her? She was strong. She was different. And he needed to put her out of his mind.

# Four: Renewal

Naomi

I was outside with the children when Ruth came into the courtyard, dragging the grain sack. In Moab, having disposed of all my property and cloth and everything—for next to nothing—I no longer felt prosperous. But I wanted to tell her it was unnecessary for her to glean as if we were paupers. I had been so torn over the deaths of my sons that I had not been able to think straight. Somehow, by ridding myself of all my belongings, I had expected to feel better. I still had no desire to do much of anything and I certainly did not want to start up another clothmaking business, but I detested how vulnerable I now felt. I appreciated Leah's generous offer to let Ruth and I stay with her as long as we liked. I was beginning to think more clearly. Leah's house seemed smaller than before when I'd lived in Bethlehem and it was packed with people piled one on top of one another. I missed my own roomy house but upon seeing Ruth, who looked exhausted, I stopped lamenting and rushed over to her. She was as dear to me as any daughter. I took the heavy grain sack out of her hands and quickly lowered it to the floor. "Come, sit down and rest."

She had no sooner sank onto a chair when the little ones gathered around her and began tugging on the hem of her skirt, asking her to tell them stories.

"Later," I told them. "Ruth needs to relax for a little while." Leah's grandkids tired me and although I found them adorable, I really did not want to spend much time with them. I began to wonder how I might have fared if I had become a grandmother. Perhaps I had become too independent but I would never know unless Ruth got married again. I searched her face. Despite being bone-weary there was a gleam of excitement in her eyes. I prodded the grain sack with my toes. "It looks as if you've been quite successful."

"I was," she responded. "After everyone else finished up with the harvest, I worked in the field for a few more hours. The overseer and a some of the workers gave me newly cut barley to thresh." She grinned at the children. "Do you know how hard it is to get barley stalks to give up their seeds?"

A little boy not much higher than Ruth's knee shouted, "I do!"

Ruth laughed. "It's fun to watch the seed husks blow away." She took off her head-covering to reveal golden fuzz stuck in her hair. She ran her hands through her unruly mane, causing fluff to waft into the air. The children squealed with delight and chased the floating fuzz. I could not help my smile at her unkempt hair. It was as wild as ever. She stood and picked up the little boy and spun him around in a circle, making him shriek with laughter. She really did love children. How hard it must have been for her to leave her sister and her nephews and nieces! Ruth eventually set the little boy back on his feet. She shook her head to the other children demanding her attention. "Not now," she said, and with a tired smile sank back on the seat. "I brought something for you too, Naomi."

"There was no need!" I picked a few remaining specks out of her hair.

"Here." She reached into a pocket and got out a handful of parched barley. "They gave me so much that I had plenty to eat for myself and this was left."

I had already eaten and had hardly any appetite, but I managed to nibble on the smoky grain. "It's tasty," I told her. "How generous the field hands were with you."

"Not only them." Ruth smiled shyly. "I ended up in the field where Leah's daughters and their husbands were working. I did not speak to them, but they were gracious to me and wanted me to join in their meal. I didn't feel it was proper, but the owner of the field was so nice to me and he told his manager to be kind to me too."

"How very fortunate." I knew of course that those girls were Leah's daughters and Boaz was their father-in-law who owned the field where she had been. The words burst out of my mouth. "What a good man to take care of you."

"I know!" she grinned. Her expression softened. "You might know him. The owner, I mean. It was Boaz. He is tall and quite handsome for an older man."

Unwanted feelings began to stir in me, but I was glad that Ruth found Boaz attractive. In that moment, it suddenly occurred to me that since he already had so many wives, one more would make no difference. I had no intention of it being me, but Ruth, she was another matter. I needed to see her settled. I did not care that Leah had told me that Boaz was contented and would never take any more wives. Something told me that if *I* asked him, he might make an exception. "The Lord bless Boaz! He is indeed a good man. Leah told me how it was he who helped everyone during the famine that caused Emilelech to take us to Moab." I paused aware that I no longer felt angry. "Boaz is our close relative. He is one of our guardian-redeemers."

"I liked him. He told me to stay with his workers until they finished harvesting. And when I was in the field alone, I noticed him watching me until I was done."

I had the feeling that he wanted to help not only Ruth but also *me*. "Oh my! Boaz has not stopped showing his kindness to the living and the dead!" Oh how I wished I were young again and able to have babies. But since that could never be the case, I wanted Boaz to be more than just friendly to Ruth. I wanted him to choose her as his wife. I was sure if he got to know her, he would love her. "Ruth, it might be good for you to keep on going with Boaz' daughters-in-law and the other women who work for him. They will keep you safe. I am afraid if you go anywhere else that someone might hurt you."

"No one will bother me! But I am happy to spend time with Leah's daughters. Maybe I will feel able to chat with them next time. Did you and Leah have a good talk? She seemed so pleasant."

"We had a lot to share. She has invited us to stay here but it is so small! We'd be in the way." I sat next to Ruth and once again got lost in thought. When the women and their husbands had come into the house earlier, all talking at once, it was as if a windstorm filled every nook and cranny. I had no place to go to escape from all that noise—nowhere to be alone—and I wondered if I had made a mistake by coming here? I had not even gone through a proper time of mourning. It was too late for grief rituals now but it was not too late for Ruth to have a good life. I very much wanted that for her. I did not know why she had remained childless. I had blamed myself and Hashem, but never my son. But much as I hated to admit it, maybe it *had* been something to do with Mahlon, and maybe another man might be different.

"Remember our first house in Moab, the one that was abandoned?" Ruth asked. "We were happy there, weren't we?"

"You showed me that house! It was where you had hidden Anna. What memories we have. You must really miss your sister."

Ruth shrugged. "I do," she said. "I always will. But we are here now and we will make the best of things. Perhaps there is an empty house here that we could take."

"At least for tonight we can sleep here. It will be a lot more pleasant than having to be out in the open with only a blanket to cover us and only the stars to give us light." I was not going to let her do anything more this evening. "You look fatigued."

Ruth half-closed her eyes. "I *am* tired," she murmured.

I had never had to help with the harvest but I knew it was hard labor. "Come on, Ruth, let us go to bed and get some sleep. We are both worn out from the journey. We were up quite early and you've worked all day long."

"Let's take the gleanings into Leah first," Ruth said.

"She will be pleased," I replied.

Leah's plan for me and Ruth to sleep in the upstairs room did not work out. Instead the men slept up there and we women shared the downstairs with the children.

The following morning and every day after, Ruth went to help with the harvest. I would have preferred her to help with the food preparation, but nothing anyone said deterred her. By the sixth day when the crop-gathering was almost complete, she still insisted upon going out to the fields. She was stubborn but at least she'd stayed with the women. And been close to Boaz.

We remained at Leah's longer than one night, but as every day passed, I was getting more and more restless. I began to worry about finding lodgings. I began to pray for Hashem to show us the way. Although Leah's family was gracious, surely it would not be long before they would want their own routine back.

One day, after a sleepless night, I went to lie down for a nap, glad to have a room to myself. At night it was all but impossible to sleep with all those women. Leah often snorted and startled me. Her daughters-in-law sometimes chattered for hours. They fussed over their children too especially if they were fidgety. As much as I tried to ignore them, I could not. Ruth, though, as soon as her body stretched out on her mattress fell instantly asleep. I almost wished I could go out to the fields too and tire myself out.

I was just drifting off when Leah poked my shoulder. "Wake up, Naomi!" I slowly opened my eyes. She held the moon sculpture in her hands. "Where did you get this?" she cried.

I had forgotten all about it, and certainly hadn't realized that Ruth had kept it. I felt at a loss for words. If I said it belonged to Ruth, it could mean trouble for her. "It's mine," I muttered, pushing myself into an upright position.

"Liar!" Leah declared. "I found it hidden in Ruth's belongings."

I gasped, unable to imagine what Leah was doing searching Ruth's things, but I could not bring myself to accuse her of anything. She might well have been planning to launder our clothes. "We found it at Rachel's tomb," I said.

"So that's where it went." Leah nodded her head knowingly.

"You knew about it!"

Leah sank down on the floor next to me. "I was good friends with Boaz' mother. I went to see her just before she died. The poor woman was often vacant and repeated herself, but she sometimes had lucid moments. When she showed me the statue, she told me that she had brought it with her from Jericho. I tried to take it away from her but she held it so tight that I worried she'd gash her hands."

"Poor woman," I cried. "I know how she must have felt so far from her people!"

Leah shrugged. "Rahab must have kept that sculpture hidden for years. It certainly did her no harm. Of course, no one knew about it or it might have gotten her stoned. People!" Leah ran her finger over the face of the sculpture. "Rahab did like pretty things. Boaz was terribly upset for her to have such an idol. His wives said she was already dead when he managed to pry it out of her hands."

"How horrible for him!"

"His wives were glad to be rid of it, but they kept quiet and didn't ask him where he'd put it. After all, he is their husband, and they were probably afraid to make him feel any worse after the loss of his mother."

The thought of his grief fueled my sorrow and I almost began to cry.

Leah did not seem to notice. "I don't want this thing in my house," she said, holding it out to me.

"I don't know what to do with it."

"Give it back to Ruth and tell her to put it back where she found it! It won't do for it to stay here."

Later, when Ruth got home, I privately returned the statue to her. "I don't know why you kept this but you need to take it back where you found it and you need to make sure no one sees you."

"But why?" she cried. "I like it and it is only a carved rock. Don't you like the moon?"

"This is not about the moon. It belonged to Boaz' mother and he must have put it at the tomb of Rachel. You do not realize but keeping something like this could bring trouble into his household and this one too if it were to be found here. In Moab no one would have cared, but in Bethlehem if a pagan idol were discovered, it could bring ruin anyone associated with it. You must take it back, and soon!"

# Five: Feelings

Ruth

Ruth with her head bowed, hoping not to encounter anyone, hurried beneath the arch of the city gate. When she looked up at the dark sky, the moon seemed to light her way. Instead of going towards Rachel's tomb, where she was supposed to return the statue, she went in the direction of the moon as if she could catch it. Seeing the silver rays lighting up the brown stubble in the cut fields, she wondered why a statue of the moon, a light in the sky that filled her with awe, could be the cause of such trouble? She decided that she would find somewhere for the sculpture where she might be able to retrieve it later. Surely it was something Boaz must have cherished. Surely if it were evil he of all people would not have left it on a sacred monument.

It would be good for the harvest to be completed, but she wondered what she might do next. She knew Naomi wanted to find her a husband. And the tongue on that Leah! She ought to keep her ideas to herself, always suggesting this fellow or that one. Ruth knew the man she would like, but he already had three wives, and she did not favor the idea of being a fourth spouse. Boaz was also too old for her, but his kindness and power continued to appeal to her. She had seen the way he treated everyone, including his daughters-in-law. They obviously loved him and looked up to him.

As she walked, she could not seem to stop herself from hoping that she'd see him soon, and that he would talk to her. The man's hair, graying around the temples, gave him a look of wisdom, but even if he was not as clever at Mahlon, he was a well-respected elder. She liked that he was taller than her, too. She could not help but remember how the muscles in his arms bulged and how his stomach was as flat as that of a young man.

Her improper feelings—the sort of desires she wished she'd had for Mahlon—only abated when the moonlight shining onto some white lilies growing near a pile of rocks that had been cleared from the fields stopped her. Unlike the delicate blossoms, fresh and full of life, she was reminded of the rockslide that had taken Mahlon's and Chilion's lives. With tears in her eyes, she flopped down and inhaled the sweet fragrance from the flowers, remembering cups of sweet-smelling wine that they had shared. How could life be so mixed with joy and sorrow? Yet, the lilies glowed with a promise for the future. Very gently, she moved aside some of the green leaves, and found a resting place for the moon statue. She laid it amongst the flowers as if it were a living thing that needed a deep and lasting drink of beauty.

Before long, as the sun began to peak above the horizon, Boaz' daughters-in-law came down the path, chatting happily. Ruth felt a pang, wishing she was going to harvest with *her* sister, Anna, wondering if she would ever see her again.

One of the women noticed her. "Ruth," she said. "What are you doing down there? Today is the last day of the harvest. There is to be a festival later. You must come." The sisters grinned. "We don't want you to act as if you are a stranger. Please join us and help us serve the food."

Ruth did not want to spend time with them. She would have preferred to remain alone in the fields where she could work hard, but she could not refuse their kindness. "Thank you," she murmured. "I'll be happy to help you in any way that I can."

Under the canopy, Ruth did not join in the talk. These women were about her age, but she had nothing in common with them except that they had known Mahlon. They shared recipes. They gossiped affectionately about their husbands, telling stories about their men's foibles. They talked of their struggles raising babies. Ruth was grateful no one asked her if she had children, but perhaps they knew that she did not. Silently, she sliced bread, put out food, and poured water into cups ready for the workers.

After the final bundles of barley were stacked at the edge of the field, the overseer said a blessing for the harvest. Their work was almost complete. Soon the grain stacks would be transported to the threshing floor. People began talking about the coming celebration, a festival where there would be dancing and merriment. Ruth smiled at their excitement, but knowing no one would miss her, wandered away from the group and went out into the field. Even if there had been piles of leftover grain, she was done with gleaning. She made her way back to the flowers where she had hidden the moon sculpture.

When she found the statue it was cool from the shade where it had been resting. It felt soothing in her hands. She went behind the rocks so that no one would see her and she sat with her back to the road, admiring the skill it must have taken to have carved this delicate face.

All at once, it was as if a dark cloud filled her mind. Why couldn't she keep this reminder that Mahlon had taught her was Hashem's light in the night sky? How would she manage now that Mahlon was gone? She had managed to tell herself that she would get on with life and have no regrets, but her feelings could no longer be buried. It was as if the face was reminding her of all she'd left behind, all that she could no longer have. She felt as if she, like Rahab who had held onto this idol for years, would always be a stranger. Here in Bethlehem they spoke the same language, but every time she opened her mouth, people smiled and asked her where she was from. Moab was not loved by people here, and she knew Jericho must also have been a reminder of war. How had Rahab coped? How had she become a much-loved member of the community?

Ruth wished she could return to Moab, but she could not leave Naomi who was no longer young and now had no way to earn her living. Ruth laid the statue on her lap and stared at her hands. They were chapped and red from the labor she had been doing. Hard work did not bother her, but the thought of having to work fields for the rest of her days, picking up sharp stalks that cut her fingers, filled her with dismay. Gone were the days of handling fine silk and weaving linen from flax. Gone were the days of seeing the happy faces of customers who loved their new robes and their pretty rugs, or the women who could not wait to give warm coats to their husbands. And worst of all she would never see her family again. Or Orpah. Or Anika. Or anyone she loved.

There would never be babies for her, and even if she took a husband—as if any man would even want her—he would not be Mahlon who had allowed her so much freedom. She missed their talks. She grieved for his arm slung across her shoulder. The thought of his smile when she would serve him spiced bread filled her with sorrow.

She did not hear Boaz coming down the lane. When his shadow fell across her face, she looked up, startled. His concerned eyes made her begin to cry. She wanted him to kneel next to her and cradle her in his arms and comfort her as if she were a lost child, but she knew even in the midst of her sorrow that such a gesture would be inappropriate and impossible. At last she managed to choke back her tears.

Boaz was staring not at her but at the moon sculpture.

"Where did you get that?" He snatched it and glared at her. Without another word, he stormed away.

Ruth was no longer a little girl who might be easily intimidated.

She scrambled to her feet and ran after him. "Wait, Boaz!" she cried, falling to the earth and grabbing an edge of his gown. "I know it once belonged to your mother."

He frowned down at her.

The fire in his eyes made her understand that this statue did not represent something of beauty to him. It was a reminder of something unwanted: a pagan idol. But she recognized, too, his grief. "You must miss your mother very much," Ruth said. "I found it on Rachel's tomb. I thought it was precious.

That is why I kept it. I later learned it belonged to your mother."

"Who told you such a thing?" He eyed her suspiciously.

She had no idea what he was thinking, but she did not want him to think badly of her or of his mother. "I am much like your mother," she said gently. "I too am from another country. I too chose to leave behind all of my family..."

He rudely interrupted her, "How do you know so much?"

"Women talk," she muttered, beginning to feel as annoyed as he looked. "Leah found the statue in my belongings. I was foolish to have taken it."

His eyes softened, and she took courage. "Naomi told me to go and put it back where I'd found it. I was supposed to do it this morning. I even left early before everyone else so that no one would see me, but I couldn't bring myself to go out there alone."

"You are far too bold, but I am glad that you had enough sense to stay close to town."

"I was not scared!"

"Perhaps you should be!"

"I saw the moon shining down. I felt as if your mother was reaching out to me. I know I sound foolish."

Without a word, he offered her his hand and helped her to stand. "How is Naomi?"

"Upset," Ruth whispered, biting the side of her lip to stop the tears from spilling out of her eyes.

"You must be too," he said softly.

His gentleness angered her. "I am fine!" she cried. "Naomi and I will manage on our own!"

He looked thoughtful. "Go on home and tell Naomi that I send my regards. Tell her not to worry. I will make things right between us."

Ruth had no idea what he meant about making things right, but she had no intention of questioning him. It was enough that he seemed to like her. She wanted to throw her arms around his neck and hug him. Instead, she turned away and hurried off, aware he was watching over her.

At the gate into Leah's house, she came across Jeremiah. She pulled her veil around her eyes and ignored the young man's greeting and stumbled into the courtyard to sit alone in a corner. Naomi soon found her. "You are home early. Are all the fields finished?"

Ruth nodded but kept herself draped.

Naomi approached her, pulled the veil aside, and gently touched Ruth's cheek. "What has happened? Why have you been crying?"

"I can't tell you. It is nothing."

"Did you put the statue back where it belonged?"

"Yes," she muttered, unable to meet Naomi's scrutiny. At last, knowing she needed to explain her appearance, she added truthfully. "I felt lonely and went off by myself to cry." She hoped that would satisfy Naomi. She did not want to mention how terrible she had felt to realize that she would never see her family again. She could not bear to add to Naomi's grief and anyway she felt much better now.

"No one bothered you, did they?"

"No. Leah's daughters asked me to help them with the food so I did not glean. They were nice to me, but I am not like them. I felt awkward."

"It will take time but you will eventually fit in."

"Boaz told me he sent you his regards. He said you were not to worry and that he would make things right."

Naomi's face lit up.

"What did he mean that he would make things right between you?"

Naomi hesitated. "There was a time when he wanted to marry me, but I was already promised to Emilelech. I have sometimes wondered how different my life would have been if he had become my husband."

Ruth choked back a surge of envy. "You must have been children together," she said, wanting Naomi to tell her more.

Naomi merely nodded her head. "Did he say anything else?"

"Not much."

"What did he say," Naomi commanded.

"He told me to come home since I wasn't needed in the fields." That at least was the truth even if not all of it.

Naomi searched her eyes. "I saw Jeremiah leaving. It is too bad that boy is already taken. You need a husband."

"He is too young for me and I am not interested in gangly boys. Or men for that matter."

Leah's grandchildren swarmed out of the house and seized Ruth's hands and pulled her to her feet and swung her around in a circle. "Will you play with us," one of them asked, his eyes beaming with excitement.

Ruth found herself smiling at the little children, grateful for the diversion, but Naomi was not done with her. "I will find you a decent husband," she announced.

# Six: Strategy

Ruth

Out for a walk, Naomi and Ruth wandered past Boaz' residence. They could see women working their looms, women grinding grain, and women hurrying about doing the multitude of chores that keep a household together. Even though Ruth genuinely liked Boaz' daughters-in-law, she was glad that they did not stop to visit them. She had heard that the older women in the house did not approve of her.

"Ruth," Naomi said as they approached the town gate. "I know you want to stay with me, but I really must find you a husband. I want you to be well provided for. I have an idea that I hope you will like. Boaz, whose daughters-in-law you worked alongside, is a relative of ours."

"Yours, not mine," Ruth protested, not wanting to reveal how she felt about Boaz.

"He is *our* relative," Naomi persisted. "He can see to it that both you and I are cared for. I have neither strength nor will for sewing or weaving, and even if I did, my money is not enough to get us started in another business."

Ruth almost said that she had never wanted to give up their successful life in Moab, but she would stand by Naomi no matter what. After all, Naomi had been more than kind to her. She had taken her in when no one else would. She had taught her so much and more than that: she had been better to her than her own mother. Ruth also greatly respected their

Hebrew religious practices and the wisdom that she had learned from Mahlon.

Suddenly Naomi took Ruth by her shoulders and looked into her eyes. "Tonight Boaz will be winnowing barley on the threshing floor. Do you know where it is?"

"I think so," Ruth replied.

Naomi told her exactly how to get there.

Then she added words that shocked Ruth, and yet also made her happy.

"I want you, Ruth, to wash and splash on perfume," she said. "Get dressed in your best clothes. Then secretly go down to the threshing floor. Wait quietly where no one can see you. After Boaz is finished eating and drinking he will go to lie down. Watch where he goes. When it is dark, you are to go over to him. Uncover his feet and lie down near him."

Ruth felt herself blushing. She knew that exposing Boaz' feet was an act of submission and also an invitation. She would be all alone with him. He was a married man and it would be wrong for him to make love to her unless he intended to wed her.

Naomi's eyes grew pensive but she half-smiled. "We women sometimes must use what we have to get what we want. Besides, he will tell you what to do."

Ruth felt a shiver of excitement along with tremors of doubt. Was it *only* Naomi's desire to find her a husband, or did she perhaps yearn for Boaz to be *her* husband? Was she, Ruth, to somehow fulfill Naomi's desire for the man? They both wanted Mahlon's name and Emilelech's name to be passed on. That could only happen if she, Ruth, produced a male heir. It was logical that she be the one to marry Boaz.

And if she did not have a baby to him, at least they would have a protector whom they both liked, perhaps loved, who would take care of them. "I will do whatever you want me to," she said.

At dusk, as she crept along the streets, keeping her veil tucked around her freshly washed hair. Only her eyes could be seen but she felt uneasy. What if someone recognized her and knew what she was about to do? Would she end up at the bottom of a pit, not by natural means, but by the hands of the townspeople who would accuse her of forbidden sex? What if Boaz rejected her? At the thought of his kindness, she took courage. She prayed for Hashem to guide her steps.

When she arrived at the threshing floor, she hid in the shadows while the men finished their work. Dust flew everywhere and she had to stifle a sneeze. Fortunately, they were too busy to notice her. At last, they settled down to their dinner. Their laughter and high spirits made her wish she could join them, but of course she dared not. When they began to lay down for the night, Boaz went to the far end of the grain pile. He soon began to snore. Trembling, she crept over to him and slowly uncovered his feet. After she lay down, she felt like a naughty girl. She only hoped that when Boaz woke up, he would accept her. She only hoped that he would be willing to protect her.

It seemed an exceptionally long time before Boaz rolled over and felt her at his feet. "Who are you?" he growled, sitting up.

"It's Ruth, your servant," she mumbled. Suddenly, she knew what to do next. "Both Naomi and I need your help. She told me you are a guardian-redeemer of our family. She told me to come here and that you would know what to do."

"The Lord bless you, my daughter," he replied.

"I am *not* your daughter," she whispered. "I would be more to you than a girl." Surely he understood she wanted to be his wife. "Spread the corner of your garment over me."

"You are an amazing woman," he said without hesitation. "You have not run after the younger men, whether rich or poor. You are special to me." He drew her to him and tucked his robe around her. "Don't be afraid. I will do for you all that you ask."

Ruth smiled to herself and felt happy to feel the warmth of his body so close to hers.

"You know I am related to Emilelech, and therefore I am one of the guardians responsible for your family. But there is another man who is more closely related than I, and we must do what is right within the law. Stay here with me for the night, and in the morning, I will ask him what he wants to do. If he wants to fulfill his duty and become your guardian-redeemer, may it be so. But if he is not willing, as surely as Hashem lives, I will be happy to marry you. Stay with me until the morning, all right?"

"I will," she said, snuggling closer.

Boaz wrapped his arms around her and held her tight. "All the people of the town know that you are a good woman. My daughters-in-law speak highly of you. My wives, too, are aware of your kindness to Leah's grandchildren and to Naomi. Do not worry. You will be blessed."

In the morning, before she could be recognized by anyone, she got up and brushed the dust from her clothing.

He looked up at her. "No one must know that a woman came to the threshing floor," he said quietly.

"I will tell no one except Naomi, who sent me to you."

"Good," he said, getting to his feet. "Hold out the shawl that you are wearing."

When she did so, he dug into the pile of nearby grain, scooping up handfuls of barley, pouring it into her cloth.

She cradled the bundle as if it were a baby. She waited for him to leave first, longing to immediately go after him. She knew, though, that it would not be good for him to be caught with her, nor she with him. After he had been gone for a while, she crept quietly away, making sure no one heard her.

Back at Leah's house, she felt both elated and frightened. What if some other man decided he ought to wed her? She only wanted Boaz, but she would have to go along with the laws of the people. Strangely enough, she did not feel as rebellious as she had when she had been a girl, wading along that stream bed. Back then, she had experienced a few moments of profound peace. It had not lasted long but she would never forget. She would not run away this time.

She found Naomi alone in their sleeping area.

"Did it go well, Ruth?" Naomi asked.

"He gave me this barley for you." Ruth handed her the shawl filled with grain. "He wants you to be happy, Naomi."

Naomi shrugged. "We have not seen one another for years. He is just being kind."

Ruth hung her head shyly. "He didn't make love to me, but he did wrap his blanket around me. Doesn't that mean he has agreed to marry me?"

"Yes!" Naomi clapped her hands. "I am glad!"

"He told me there is another man who is a closer relative."

"I know, but don't worry. Boaz is a righteous man. Do nothing more until you find out what happens. Be patient. I know Boaz. He will settle matters today."

# Seven: Boundless Love

Naomi

As I made my way with Ruth and Leah to the city gate, Boaz' family came out of their house and joined us. Many people were heading there to learn what was going on. As we walked along, his wives seemed subdued and said hardly a word. Leah, though, was full of high spirits. She hugged her daughters. "This is a great day," she remarked. "I am sure of it!"

Her daughters glanced at their mothers-in-law, Boaz' wives, and kept quiet.

I found myself wondering how Boaz could possibly get his women—not that they had a choice— to agree to another wife in their household, especially one young enough to be their daughter. His daughters-in-law, in spite of their mother Leah's approval, might also be upset. Nevertheless I knew that Boaz was a man of his word, and he would keep it. Surely, he would also find a way to keep the peace.

When we got to the courtyard, many people had already assembled, so we stayed on the fringes of the crowd. We could see Boaz sitting on a bench in front of the platform where the elders met to make decisions about domestic matters. Another man, a close relative of Emilelech's, made his way past us.

The people got quiet. Everyone watched.

Boaz greeted the man cordially. "Please, come and sit. There is something we need to talk about." The man looked curious. "Wait just a few moments," Boaz said. "Let me gather the elders."

Ten men came over and took their places. Except for a few whispers, the crowd remained silent.

I stared at the man facing the elders, remembering him as a boy. He had often been at feast days when I had been young, but I had never played with him. Emilelech had not had much to do with that side of the family either.

"I'm sure you've heard that Naomi has come back from Moab," Boaz said. "She is selling the piece of land that belonged to her husband, Emilelech. You have first rights to buy it if you want it."

I glanced over at Ruth. Her face was ashen.

Boaz addressed the elders, "Am I correct in letting my relative know of this prospect?"

"Yes, that is the right thing to do," said one of the men. The others nodded their agreement.

Boaz, his face solemn, turned to his relative. "If you want the land then say so now. But if it is not for you, then tell me, so that I will know what to do. If you do not want it, I am the next in line."

"I want it," the man said eagerly.

"You do realize that when you buy the land from Naomi that you will also be wedded to Ruth the Moabite. She is the widow of Mahlon who would rightfully own the land. You will be obliged to maintain his name with his property."

Ruth shrank back. I did not dare look at Boaz' women.

"That's unfortunate." The man shrugged. "I cannot marry this woman. If she had any children by me, they would get in the way of my sons' inheritance."

Boaz bowed politely.

"*You* buy it," the man said, removing his sandal to let it be known that he had transferred the property to Boaz.

I stared into space, not wanting Boaz' women to see my look of satisfaction.

Boaz swung around and faced the crowd. "Today you are witnesses that I have bought from Naomi all the property of her husband, Emilelech, property that would have gone to his sons Chilion and Mahlon. It is a sad thing for a woman to lose her husband *and* her sons."

I knew these last words were intended for me. I felt tears welling.

Several people nearby, even Boaz' wives, who I glimpsed out of the corner of my eye, bowed their heads.

"In this arrangement," Boaz continued. "I will be making Ruth the Moabite my wife." A momentary look of pleasure flashed across his face.

The youngest of his wives gasped, turned her back, and marched away. The other wives chased after her, but their daughters-in-law stayed behind.

"This is necessary," Boaz said, "so that Mahlon's name will remain linked to his property and will not disappear from his family or from his hometown."

His words pleased me. Since he was *merely* doing his duty to a relative, his wives would have no cause to be jealous.

"Today you are witnesses!" Boaz cried. The elders and all the people, including Boaz' daughters-in-law repeated, "We are witnesses."

Ruth let out a big sigh of relief.

I too felt relieved. No one would now be able to put a stop to this legally binding agreement.

A blessing by the elders sanctified the contract. They prayed that Ruth would resemble our ancestress Rachel and her sister, Leah. *My* Leah grimaced, but we both knew that they meant for Ruth to be fertile and bear many children. When the elders later invoked the name Ephrathah, another name we used for Bethlehem, they wanted Boaz to be famous not for the barley he raised, but for his offspring. Such a thought pleased me.

I could not have wished for a better way to end my days, but as it turned out my life was not over. It bore fruit through Ruth. Boaz moved us into his mother's old quarters. It was separate from the main house, quite small but cozy. When he came to spend the night with Ruth, I would excuse myself and go to visit Leah. It was a joyful time. The losses I had endured did not stop hurting, but I was astonished at the goodness in my life.

Boaz' wives came to accept us. We often prepared meals together. They soon realized that we did not threaten their position or their children. Of course, it helped that Leah's daughters took to Ruth and were kind to her. She liked them too, but even though she soon got pregnant, and was thrilled, she wanted more from life than babies. I suppose it was *my* fault or *my* example that caused her to seek her own business. To my surprise, it was not clothmaking that she took up, but pottery.

Boaz set up a wheel for her near the looms in the courtyard. I would hear that wheel clicking and see her shaping bowls, at first as misshapen as Mahlon's beginning ones, but eventually perfect. Her first success, a terracotta vase, was exquisite. She filled it with blue and yellow wildflowers, and she gave it to the senior wife.

"What good is this," the woman scoffed. "You can't eat flowers." But I saw her smile, and she put it in the kitchen where everyone could enjoy it.

Later, Ruth gave each of the wives and the daughters-in-law special planters, some of them sprouting herbs for their cooking.

They would never come to love her as I did, but they all came to respect her.

Ruth's first baby was the delight of my life. We named him Obed, a child hallowed by Hashem, a child predicted to become a prominent man. He was a lively infant and, even if the menfolk expected greatness from him, we women did not care if he became a king or a field-hand. We only wanted him to be healthy and happy.

While Ruth was in the birthing tent, Boaz came to visit me. "I have something for Ruth," he said, and took out a small object wrapped in silk. "Please take a look. I don't want it to offend you."

I slowly unwrapped the package, but I already knew from its shape that it was the moon sculpture. "It is beautiful," I said.

"Like you," he responded. We briefly gripped hands and smiled at one another.

"I am so glad you care for Ruth," I told him.

"That's good," he said.

Together, we placed the plaque where it would be seen by all who entered the house, and then he left.

When Ruth returned with the baby, she immediately saw the sculpture. She handed me Obed, and she went over to look at it. "You don't mind it being here?" she asked, running her fingers over the face.

"No. Boaz brought it for you. I am glad he gave you something precious to his mother."

"It's as if *she* wanted me to have it!" Ruth said.

"I am sure she did!"

\*\*\*

Obed filled my days.

When Ruth went to Jerusalem to visit her father's old friends and sell pots, I was pleased to look after the baby. We were all so happy! The other women admired her spirit of adventure and freedom. On one of her trips, we women got together to bake. It was such a pleasant day—cool and sunny—that we invited neighbors to join us in the courtyard. We prepared date rolls, cinnamon buns, honey cakes and roasted figs. We piled layers of flatbreads next to small carafes of olive oil. We roasted eggs. We put out jugs of pomegranate juice for the children, and we prepared tea for the women.

When our guests began arriving, they greeted me, and they fussed over Obed who was in my arms. He charmed them with his smiles. As we all drank our tea and gossiped, the children took their treats, and were soon off running and chasing one another.

We women always build community. There can be nothing better.

One of Leah's friends sat her cup down. She wiped crumbs off her mouth. "We give thanks to Hashem for you, Naomi," she said. "We know we could as easily have lost our husbands and sons."

"I am glad you didn't," I replied. "I cannot tell you how much I missed everyone here. I was so worried about everyone after we left for Moab."

"Times were hard," another woman said.

"Ruth," one of the women observed, "has given you this wonderful baby. Why, it is almost as if he is your own child! He certainly resembles you."

This made me laugh since Obed was dark, and I was fair. But as far as I was concerned he was the most precious child in the world.

Leah grinned. "Ruth is better to you than seven sons!" she said.

My joy overflowed. I could not stop smiling.

# Discussion Guide
## by Rev. Dr. Roberta Mosier-Peterson

## Introduction to discussion guide

At the heart of this story is the truth that we are all made by God and for God. We are also made to create community and sustain one another through community. I'm grateful for the author, Christina St Clair, who is herself a builder of community. It is my honor to offer this discussion guide for any and all who want to discover the truth that is in all of this. Jesus mentions the patriarchs of the faith and points to the fact that this proves that there is a community that is living even as we do not have them physically present with us. I read "the God of Abraham, Isaac, and Jacob," and often substitute names of a similar community saying "the God of Rebecca, Rachel, Rahab, and Ruth" is the living God (see Exodus 3:6 and Matthew 22:31-32).

## Guidelines for group discussion:

The facilitator of the discussion does just that: facilitates. This group discussion guide was created to allow you the time and space to reflect on your own life. It will be helpful to have the portion of the book and the discussion questions read before the meeting. The pace of reading can be determined by the group. It would be appropriate to rotate the role of the "facilitator" among the group members.

The questions are written to help you listen deeply to your own experience and the wisdom that already lies in your soul. It is not the intention of the facilitator or other participants to fix or offer advice. Listen and listen well to yourself and to others.

Sharing is not required. There is a freedom to pass on any question if you are not able or willing at this point to speak. It is also very good to take time and pause. There is no hurry. Leaving and embracing times of silence may feel uncomfortable if you are not used to it, but it is likely to be very valuable. One reason that silence can be valuable is that it allows us to have time and space to listen to our own soul. Gestures of hospitality such as open body posture are more important than food in making others feel at ease. Other ways of remaining hospitable are allowing others to speak without interruption or judgement. It is also important to speak personally using "I" language instead of using generalizations about what "everyone" thinks.

Transparency and honesty are absolutely vital. Please agree that nothing spoken of in the group will be spoken of outside the group. Building and maintaining trust serve as cornerstone practices of community.

## Section 1- New Horizon

Chapter 1 – Every Loyal Step

- Share about a time when you were young when you realized that grief and loss were part of life.

- Have you ever relived a loss from the past when you faced a current loss? If so, share what was happening.

- Leah and Naomi had a close bond; Naomi described her as "my confidant who knew my heart as I knew hers." Leah reminds Naomi that she is strong and that her life would be full of joy. Share an experience when someone spoke powerful words such as these over you and talk about the impact that had on you.

Chapter 2 – Dream
- Ruth mentions her sister Anna being "gagged and bound by the priest." Is this something that she witnessed or was it something painted in her imagination?
- Ruth is young and has an active imagination. In the dream, she sees an older version of herself, witnesses Anna's wedding and sees that there is a wedding in view for her. The tragedy of Anna being taken for child sacrifice causes Ruth to be outraged. Is her anger justified? Imagine yourself at a young age: how would you have handled the situation?
- Share about a time when anger or disappointment changed the way you viewed the future. What is your most likely response when you are angry: flee, fight, freeze, negotiate, or other? Explain what that looks like.

Chapter 3 – Secret
- Boaz has a secret longing for Naomi. He also wants what is good for her and wants to

protect her. He speculates about the situation that Bethlehem is now in (suffering from drought and famine) and is struggling to make sense out of it. Brene Brown states that "we are only as sick as our secrets." Do you think that this is true?

- With whom do you share your secrets?
- Share about what you think it would take for each of us to become the kind of people who are worthy of hearing others' secrets.

Chapter 4 – Pillar of Salt

- Naomi is gripped with grief to the point of physical pain. She wonders about her grief and thinks that she may regret making the decision to leave. Have you had a recent decision that you have made that has caused regret? Share with the group.
- Anger and disappointment can lead to bitterness. Discuss how this happens.
- Is it possible to prevent it? If so, how?

Chapter 5 – Search

- In this chapter, Boaz prays a lot. What is prayer? Share any experiences of prayer that have resulted in insight or wisdom.
- Boaz expresses his disappointment and anger at God. Have you ever been angry with God and have you ever expressed that anger?

- Rahab, Boaz's mother, wishes him contentment. Who is the most content person you know? If others were describing you, would they use the word "content?"

## Chapter 6 – Answered Prayer

- Share an experience of hospitality that was abundantly thoughtful and kind. Discuss how it made you feel.
- Summarize and briefly discuss the story of the destruction of Jericho in Joshua 1-6. How is it important in light of Naomi and the family's relocating to Moab?
- Emilelech had been praying to Hashem for healing without much result. Naomi speculates that he is hoping to find a connection to Egypt where there is rumored to be healers. Have you ever experienced prayer for healing that appears to go unanswered? What was that like?

## Chapter 7 – Refuge

- Discuss Ruth's protective instinct regarding her sister. Have you ever had to provide refuge for someone? Who and what was that like?
- Share about a time when you felt sheltered by another person.

- Given the situation, Ruth does not feel safe in her own home. Discuss how places and structures are formed.

Chapter 8 – Figurine
- Why does Naomi immediately feel connected to this image?
- Naomi has an internal debate about keeping it and it not being a thing to worship. Others would view what she is doing as an abomination. What do you think? Should she have kept it? Is she able to keep it without worshiping it?
- Share about a situation where you felt powerless. How did you manage during that?

Chapter 9 – Concern
- Naomi wonders what kind of welcome the family will receive in Moab. She also questions her role and identity. Have you ever felt small or as if you didn't fit somewhere?
- Discuss the lively scene of the family arriving in Moab. What detail or interaction had the most impact on you? Why?
- Naomi and Emilelech fear for the safety of their family. Is this concern justified?

Chapter 10 – New Friend
- Ruth and Mahlon are struck by the beauty of the stars at night. What, if any, aspect of the

created world inspires you and leaves you awestruck?

- Ruth senses that Mahlon is someone who could be trusted. Is it easy or difficult for you to trust new friends?
- Share about a time when you felt a sort of righteous indignation such as Ruth feels toward her mother.

Chapter 11 - Strength
- Starting over requires an extensive amount of energy. Naomi feels so lost and exhausted that she cannot speak. Does this experience of exhaustion during a time of transition resonate with you?
- Emilelech's response to the transition and the upheaval in the house was prayer. Naomi feels excluded from prayer. Have you ever felt like others have a special kind of access to God and you do not? Describe what that feels like.
- Anna has a fever and there is concern that her sickness is contagious. Discuss any experience you have had with being quarantined.

## Section 2- Broken Road

Chapter 1 – Vision
- Boaz recalls the story of Joseph. Summarize the story of Joseph found in Genesis 37-51.

What are a few similarities and differences between Joseph and Boaz?

- The prayers of lament come for Boaz as he considers the anxiety, suffering, and turmoil caused by the drought. Have you ever complained and lamented in prayer? Was it helpful?
- Boaz is not certain why he is being thrust into a place of leadership by God. Describe a situation where you knew that you simply had to do something even if you did not feel adequately equipped or prepared to do it. How did that feel?

Chapter 2 – Daughter
- Naomi delivered a baby girl who was too small to survive. From your experience, do you think that having a miscarriage or stillborn baby is as Naomi says, "worse than losing my life?"
- The grief over the loss of the baby is compounded because Naomi feels so alone. Is it true that there would be little or no grief over the loss of this baby girl, precisely because she was a girl?
- When, if ever, have you felt abandoned by God? Does it appear that Naomi's naming of the figurine is a form of prayer?

Chapter 3 – Hope

- Ruth is curious and enjoys learning. Religious schooling was not thought appropriate for girls. Discuss your own thirst for learning. In your experience, what is the difference between learning the "what" of what happened and learning the "why?"
- The hope of Emilelech getting help from the Egyptian guest made Naomi bolder. Her hope was dashed as she realized that that was not going to happen. Has desperation ever fueled your courage? Share about a time when you surprised yourself in being assertive and asking for something you needed.
- Naomi is not comfortable being a guest of honor. She does not want to be thanked or served as if she is royalty. Why do you think she is like this? Is there any of these that resonate with you?

Chapter 4 – Resistance
- Ruth is sure that her parents are going to arrange a marriage for her and that she will be forced into marriage even if she does not agree. Imagine what that would be like. Share how that would make you feel.
- What is it like to witness a family argument in public? Ruth was disciplined by her father and shouts at full volume "I hate you both!" at her parents. Discuss Ruth's reaction to Anna being promised to Pentu. Did she overreact?

- Ruth states that she is already promised to Mahlon. Naomi is now in the center of another family's dispute. The well-being of Ruth has become especially important to Naomi. If you were Naomi, how would you have reacted in this situation?

Chapter 5 – Field of Flowers
- Boaz watches the people react to the field of flowers. Have you ever felt so desperate that someone may have compared you to a thirsty hyena?
- Is it understandable that the folks of Bethlehem were so thirsty that they forgot to give proper thanks to God for supplying their need?
- Have you ever been on the receiving end of extravagant hospitality? Read and discuss this quote: "Hashem was present in the generosity and kindness of these strangers."

Chapter 6 – Doubt
- Discuss the topic of arranged marriage. Have you personally known people who had an arranged marriage? Discuss the pros and cons.
- Naomi struggles to see her son Mahlon as a man. She is also concerned that Ruth may try to get out of her engagement to Mahlon. Have you ever had concerns about younger generations and their ability to make

responsible adult decisions? Were your concerns justified?

- Orpah's mom thinks that Ruth getting beat by her father would teach her a lesson: what do you think?

Chapter 7 – Stubbornness

- Share about a time when you chose your own destiny. Did this cause you to be viewed as a rebel or as disobedient? What impact did that have on you?
- Have you ever been called stubborn? If so, was it given or received as a compliment, insult, or a simple observation?
- Discuss how the character trait of stubbornness can be both an asset and a liability.

Chapter 8 – Daring

- Naomi observed the boldness with which Mahlon searched for Ruth and concluded that his concern for Ruth is what provided strength for him. Discuss this insight.
- Mahlon rebukes Naomi for being immodest, allow her knees to show, etc. Have you ever been chastised by your children or by a young person? How did it feel?
- Naomi is very aware that the man ogled her. She is vigilant about modesty at this point. What is implied in the story about the

connection between being modest and being looked at in a way that suggests sexual intent?

Chapter 9 – Peril
- Ruth makes a comparison between the physical wounds that she had from her father's beatings and the wounds of the heart. Were her feelings of rejection legitimate and did her family really want to get rid of her?
- Statistics show that 1 out of 3 females are victims of sexual assault. Fear of sexual assault for Ruth is real and palpable in the story. Consider and discuss how this reality is used to control women and limit their choices.
- The feeble, hunched over foreign wife of the man taking Ruth to her parents in Egypt may appear helpless. She appears powerless but turns out to be the opposite. Are there lessons that we can learn from her actions that could help us when we feel powerless?

Chapter 10 – Shock
- The profound loss that Naomi suffered brings to the surface regret, helplessness, and dread. What was your reaction to Naomi saying that she might as well have died alongside Emilelech? Share about a situation of loss in your own life that caused this kind of reaction.
- Discuss the rites and customs surrounding death with which you are familiar

- The family is living in an unfamiliar place and is devoid of extended family and the resources of home. List the practical help and kind deeds done by Orpah's family during this time. How would you have felt on the receiving end of such compassion and generosity?

Chapter 11 – Surprise
- Chilion and Mahlon deal with the death of their father in unique ways. Discuss their different reactions and explore together which of these you are prone to.
- Naomi questions her past choices that are now making being a widow very difficult. She knows that it is now her responsibility to provide financially for the family. Have you ever had to shift your role in your household because of necessity as Naomi did? If so, in what way did you manage that transition?
- Discuss the conversation that Naomi and Ruth have about her experience at the Temple of Women. Naomi assures Ruth that she has done nothing to be ashamed of but that Mahlon would not understand. How would you feel hearing this from Naomi if you were in Ruth's place?

# Section 3- Day by Day

Chapter 1 – Shabbat

- Naomi is no stranger to loss. At the beginning of the story when she was leaving Bethlehem, she felt sick with depression and grief. At this point in the story, she feels like she can hardly move. Share an experience of loss that caused any of these things similar to that of Naomi.

- During this new phase of life, Naomi realizes that she is not prepared for many things. She was not prepared for or practiced at talking to her sons about sex or providing religious training. Have you been faced with a situation that presented a mountain of challenge as well as a mountain of opportunity?

- Discuss the phrase "something holy was happening." What does this mean? Has this ever happened to you?

Chapter 2 – Sigh

- Ruth often thinks about her family. She knows that her sister, Anna, was traumatized by being taken to be sacrificed to Chemosh. Consider and discuss Ruth's own trauma.

- What do you think about the custom of the groom's family paying a dowry to the bride's family?

- Ruth associates Egypt with slavery. She offers to become a servant to Orpah's family in exchange for the payment of a dowry. Mahlon refuses to consider such an idea even if she doesn't want to marry him. Does it appear that Orpah loves Chilion? Does it appear that Mahlon loves Ruth? What evidence is there?

Chapter 3 – Plenty
- Boaz is noticing a shift in his ideas about the love of God for both men and women. The birth of his daughter, Deborah, brings this into focus. Have you had moments when you have felt invited into a "greater truth" about gender equality? Share the story.
- Deborah is "beautiful" and has a "strong voice" according to Boaz. Have you ever been told that having a strong voice is not a good thing? What was that like?
- The folks of Jerusalem are generous and compassionate. Can this behavior be traced to their faith. Have you witnessed faith to be the motivation for these kinds of right attitudes and actions? Have you ever seen religious people acting in a way that was not generous and compassionate?

Chapter 4 – Trouble
- The foolish behavior of young lovers brings trouble to Naomi's household. Discuss this scenario. Who do you think is responsible?
- Imagine yourself in Orpah's situation. Would you be quick to forgive and trust again?

- Naomi gleans strength in her time of need. She feels wellbeing and the assurance that she would have the strength to persevere. Have you ever had an experience similar to this?

Chapter 5 – Mercy
- What do you think Naomi means when she says that "no one is what we expect in marriage?"
- Tell about a time when you froze just when you were beginning a difficult conversation. Have you discovered a way to unfreeze or avoid freezing during conflict? What helps you?
- Naomi encourages Ruth to forgive her family. If you were Ruth, what aspect of her experiences with her family would feel most unforgivable?

Chapter 6 - Uncertainty
- Though the customs for proposals and engagements differ, excitement and anxiety in these situations is fairly common. Share about such a moment from your own experience.
- Ruth would be living with her family. She felt hurt and discarded by them. Does living in the same house with people with whom you know you need to forgive make the work of forgiveness easier or more difficult? Why?

- Naomi is uncertain that Ruth will follow through with marrying Mahlon. Naomi wants marriage and a lot of children for Ruth. What does Ruth want?

## Chapter 7 – Birth

- Facing her lack of financial savvy, Naomi feels frustrated and helpless. She wonders what it would be like to be more assertive and confident. Tell about a time when you wished you were more assertive and confident.
- Has the birth of a baby ever made your hurt fade? Share about the experience.
- What kinds of conversation brings your mood down?

## Chapter 8 – Confusion

- Boaz is grieving the loss of his mother. Why do you think he feels like he has to hide his grief?
- Boaz thinks about having relatives that he had not known existed. What would you do if you found out that you have relatives you hadn't known about?
- Have you ever learned details about family that you wished that you did not know? Discuss how that felt.

## Chapter 9 – Service

- Considering the story thus far, are you surprised that Naomi and Anika become friends? Discuss how Naomi's friendship with Anika causes her to reconsider her ideas about Moabites.

- Respect and care for the elderly is highly valued in Naomi's culture. Is this highly valued in your family and culture?
- Do you think that character traits such as patience, kindness, and gentleness are natural or are they learned? How does one become this kind of person?

Chapter 10 – Ups and Downs

- Ruth was excited to see her family again. Her excitement turned to anger when she felt like a commodity to be sold for the best price. Is this a reasonable and understandable reaction or is she overreacting?
- Ruth is not concerned about financial matters as she prepares to marry Mahlon. From your own experience, how important are finances when facing marriage?
- As she prepared for marriage, Ruth was eager to learn. She resisted the idea of conforming. Describe what you think true strength looks like.

Chapter 11 – Endings and Beginnings

- Naomi is greatly disappointed that Orpah and Ruth have not gotten pregnant. Have you ever experienced other's or your own anger regarding infertility or difficulty conceiving?

- The tragic accident resulting in Mahlon and Chilion's deaths cause Naomi to decide to return to Bethlehem. Does this decision seem sudden and hasty or perfectly normal? Why?

- The dialogue between Naomi and her daughters-in-law on their way to Bethlehem are the most familiar words in the Book of Ruth in scripture. Read and discuss Ruth 1.

## Section 4- Return to Plenty

Chapter 1 – Grief and Hope

- Ruth is intent to stick by Naomi because of the way Naomi had stuck by her. Naomi thinks she is being punished by God. Ruth disagrees and points to her own presence with Naomi as proof. What do you think?

- Discuss Naomi being scared to return to Bethlehem. What word do you think best describes how she is feeling?

- Ruth has been described as stubborn, as a lioness, or as a warrior. She says, "I will not be made helpless because of that horrible accident." Have you suffered something that could have rendered you helpless? What was it and what was your reaction to it?

Chapter 2 – Homecoming

- There was a mixture of fear and excitement as Naomi returned to Bethlehem with Ruth. Naomi notices how thick Ruth's accent is and worries about her feeling or being treated as an outsider. What resonates with you regarding this?
- Leah and Naomi are re-united and it is as though it had been no time at all. Discuss dynamics of old friends and about an occasion when being with old friends eased your soul.
- Have you ever been self-conscious about having an accent? What was that like?

Chapter 3 – Concern
- Discuss the conflicting thoughts that Boaz has regarding Naomi returning to Bethlehem. Are you hoping that there is a chance for Boaz and Naomi to be together?
- Boaz instructs his workers how they should treat Ruth. Discuss the potential danger she faced and the impact Boaz' protection had for her.
- Ruth was surprised and humbled by the extraordinary kindness of Boaz. Share about a time when you intended kindness in a way that felt natural but that shocked the recipient.

Chapter 4 – Renewal
- Naomi and Ruth are offered hospitality by Leah. However, it is not their own space and it

seems like they will soon "wear out their welcome." How does this experience make you feel?

- Discuss Naomi's expression that "Boaz has not stopped showing his kindness to the living and the dead!"
- Did Leah's reaction to the moon sculpture surprise you? Imagine yourself in Naomi's place in that conversation. What would that have felt like and what would you have said?

Chapter 5 – Feelings

- Discuss Ruth's question: How could life be so mixed with joy and sorrow?
- Ruth is grieving the loss of Mahlon and her life in Moab as she returns the moon sculpture. Are there any of the feelings that surprised you?
- Is there a difference between desire and love? If so, how?

Chapter 6 – Strategy

- After reading this chapter, read the Book of Ruth in scripture, chapters 2-3. What details resonate with you?
- What do you think about Naomi's strategy?
- Discuss Naomi's statement, "we women sometimes must use what we have to get what we want." How have you experienced this in your own life?

Chapter 7 – Boundless Love
- After reading this chapter, read the Book of Ruth in scripture, chapters 4. Why do you think this chapter is titled "boundless love?"
- The covenant-making meeting with the elders went well for Boaz, Naomi, and Ruth. Discuss the feelings and reactions of the other women in Boaz' family.
- Discuss the statements "We women always build community. There can be nothing better." Share about a time in your life that this was proved true.

# References

**Internet** (although I actually consulted over one hundred and seventy Internet Sources, I have only reported twenty-five of the most relevant ones in this list)

1. Ancient Burial Practices:
   https://www.jewishvirtuallibrary.org/ancient-burial-practices

2. Ancient Hebrew Clothing:
   http://www.ancient-hebrew.org/culture_clothing.html

3. Ancient Israelite Cuisine:
   https://en.wikipedia.org/wiki/Ancient_Israelite_cuisine#Figs

4. Ancient Israelite House of a Commoner:
   https://www.bible-history.com/sketches/ancient/ancient-house.html

5. Ancient Jewish Marriage:
   https://www.myjewishlearning.com/article/ancient-jewish-marriage/

6. Ancient Jewish Wedding:
   https://www.jewishjewels.org/wp-content/uploads/2018/01/Ancient_Jewish_Wedding.pdf

7. Ancient World History, King's Highway:
   http://earlyworldhistory.blogspot.com/2012/03/kings-highway-and-way-of-sea.html

8. Canaanite culture and religion: http://history-world.org/canaanite_culture_and_religion.htm

9. Chemosh: https://en.wikipedia.org/wiki/Chemosh

10. Chronology of Ruth: http://www.bible.ca/maps/maps-master-archeological-bible-study-map-israel-promised-land-othneil-ehud-judges-3-17-21-ruth-eglon-ehud-1350-1204bc.jpg

11. Dead Sea: https://en.wikipedia.org/wiki/Dead_Sea

12. Drought: https://en.wikipedia.org/wiki/Drought

13. Fertility Cults of Canaan: https://www.thattheworldmayknow.com/fertility-cults-of-canaan

14. Fourteen Foods Middle Easterners Can't Live Without: https://spoonuniversity.com/lifestyle/middle-eastern-food

15. Gleaning: https://biblehub.com/topical/g/gleaning.htm

16. Israel's Exodus from Egypt: http://classic.scriptures.lds.org/en/biblemaps/2?sr=1

17. Jericho: http://www.varchive.org/ce/jericho.htm

18. Jewish Bathing Rituals: https://www.jewishvirtuallibrary.org/bath-bathing

19. Marriage in the Bible: http://www.bible.ca/marriage/ancient-jewish-three-stage-weddings-and-marriage-customs-ceremony-in-the-bible.htm

20. Moab: https://en.wikipedia.org/wiki/Moab

21. Pottery Making in the Bible: http://www.biblearchaeology.org/post/2011/0 7/05/The-Master-Potter-Pottery-Making-in-the-Bible.aspx

22. Ruth's Journey to Bethlehem: https://www.thebiblejourney.org//biblejourney 2/29-the-journeys-of-ruth-and-samuel/ruths-journey-to-bethlehem/

23. The Court of Women in the Temple: https://www.bible-history.com/court-of-women/women.html

24. Threshing Floor: https://www.west-crete.com/dailypics/photos/1179large.jpg

25. Women and the Law in Ancient Israel: http://www.womenintheancientworld.com/wo men%20and%20the%20law%20in%20ancient %20israel.htm

## Books

Bible, New International Version (NIV).

Borowski, Oded. *Daily Life in Biblical Times.* Atlanta: Society of Biblical Literature, 2003.

Kates, Judith A., Reimer, Gail Twersky, Editors. *Reading Ruth: Contemporary Women Reclaim a Sacred Story.* New York: Ballantine Books, 1994.

Piper, John. *Ruth, Under the Wings of God.* Wheaton, Illinois: Crossway. 2010.

**Christina St. Clair** has pastored two mainstream Protestant churches and has led many spirituality groups. She has a BA in philosophy & Christian apologetics, an MA in pastoral ministry, and is an Associate Spiritual Director of West Virginia Institute for Spirituality. She is a published author and was awarded a grant by the Kentucky Foundation for Women for an historical fiction novel.

**Roberta Mosier-Peterson** currently serves as lead pastor of Gerry Free Methodist Church along with being a field superintendent for five other rural churches in southwestern New York State. Her Doctor of Ministry research focused on the lived experience of female Free Methodist pastors and you can find the documentary film produced from her research on YouTube.

Made in the USA
Columbia, SC
09 June 2021

39501479R00251